THE COMPLIANCE PROTOCOL

CHRIS RULE

EPIC TALE BOOKS

Published in the United States by Epic Tale Books, an imprint of Rule InfoSec LLC.
EPICTALEBOOKS.COM
BYCHRISRULE.COM

Cover design by Chris Rule

First Edition, 2025

Library of Congress Control Number: 2025924140
Hardcover ISBN: 978-1-970876-01-7
Trade Paperback ISBN: 978-1-970876-00-0
eBook ISBN: 978-1-970876-02-4

To Mom,

*You fostered my love of language and placed me in front of my first
computer. Thank you for believing in my dreams, even when they don't
make sense.*

This is as much yours as it is mine.

CHAPTER 1

THE WITHDRAWAL

THE FUTURE ARRIVES NOT as dawn but as sunset, the innocence of the past willingly sacrificed to appease the god we named Progress. Freedom's light is extinguished, one deliberate shadow at a time, in the name of security. The most vital parts of that lost age, the essential code of an unmodified world, were held captive, entombed behind blast doors and six hundred meters of solid granite. The Rocky Mountain Seed Vault, built to withstand a 30-megaton nuclear explosion, was meant to be the ultimate genetic failsafe, the new world's final lock on evolution.

The Resistance saw only a fortress guarding something that belonged to everyone. And they were about to make a withdrawal on behalf of humanity. Five figures trudged through the dark in knee-deep snow. The spring storm had dropped eighteen inches, transforming the mountain's east face into a treacherous maze of white. Wind howled through the pines, masking their labored breathing as they climbed.

"Three minutes to radio blackout," whispered the point woman, her face obscured by a thermal mask. Only her eyes were visible, sharp, determined.

The tallest member adjusted the reinforced pack strapped to his back. Inside, specialized containers waited to be filled with the world's most valuable contraband: unmodified seeds. Not the engineered, patented, trackable varieties that LifeSpan AgriFuture distributed, but the original genetic blueprints of nature itself.

"Satellite gap closing," murmured the tech specialist, eyes fixed on a device strapped to her wrist. "We've got seventeen minutes once we're inside."

They approached a seemingly ordinary rock face, indistinguishable from the rest of the mountain except for a barely perceptible seam in the granite. The facility that once housed America's nuclear defense command now protected something far more precious, genetic diversity.

The team leader pressed a gloved hand against the rock and nodded. "Remember, we're not just stealing seeds. We're preserving the future."

The team converged on a narrow crevice partially hidden by a snow-laden pine. This geological fault, a four-inch crack that had widened over decades into a two-foot gap, wasn't on any modern security schematics. When the military converted this mountain into a seed vault after acquisition of the defense complex by Lifespan, they had relied on digital blueprints that omitted certain analog-era details.

"Cold War paranoia finally pays off," the tech specialist muttered, unfolding a device that resembled an antique surveyor's tripod. "They built redundant ventilation systems after the Cuban Missile Crisis. Pentagon brass wanted air, even if the main shafts collapsed."

She activated the device, which projected a narrow beam of polarized light that revealed ice particles flowing upward through the crevice, indicating air circulation where none should exist.

The smallest team member squeezed through first, her body disappearing into darkness. A faint metallic clang echoed back, followed by three clicks on their secure comms.

"She's in the maintenance crawlspace," the leader verified. "Ghost tunnel confirmed."

One by one, they slipped through, entering a forgotten artery of American military history, a ventilation shaft built to survive nuclear winter, now serving as a pathway to preserve what LifeSpan had spent billions trying to control, nature's original source code.

The team emerged into a dimly-lit service corridor where the soft hum of ventilation systems masked their footfalls. Overhead, the unmistakable dome of an AI-enhanced surveillance camera rotated with adversarial targeting precision.

"Sentinel by VerCada," the tech specialist whispered, unfolding a tablet-like device. "Pattern-recognition AI that flags anomalous movements, shifts in light, and even infrared temperature changes. Makes old-school surveillance systems look like doorbell cameras."

Her fingers bounced through the holographic interface. Code scrolled by, reflected in her eyes as she injected a looped feed into the surveillance network. The camera's indicator light flickered momentarily before resuming its steady green glow.

"You've got three minutes before the system runs its integrity check and resets," she murmured.

The second operative unfolded what looked like a metallic cloth from his pack. The fabric shimmered slightly, its surface constantly adjusting to match the surrounding environment. He draped it over his shoulders, his outline instantly becoming harder to track.

"Active camo engaged. Stay in my shadow."

They moved in perfect synchronization, a silent, practiced dance through the facility's blind spots. When forced to cross a camera's field of view, they timed their movements to coincide with the AI's predictive blind spots, the milliseconds when the system processed previous frames.

Ahead, the vault door's massive frame reflected the corridor lights, watched over by a final, unblinking camera.

The lead operative froze mid-step, raising a closed fist. The others instantly stilled, melting against the corridor walls. "Drone patrol," he breathed. "Two o'clock."

Around the corner, the distinctive whir of quadrotor blades mingled with the low grinding of treads against concrete. Standard LifeSpan security protocol, aerial and ground units working in tandem, covering each other's blind spots.

The tech specialist's fingers swiped and poked at her device. "Can't loop these. Active mesh network. They'll detect the interference."

A hovering drone rounded the corner first, matte black, no larger than a dinner plate, its optical sensor sweeping methodically. Behind it rolled a tank-like unit, treads barely making contact with the floor as it glided on a cushion of air. Its extended manipulator arm ended in what looked like a medical syringe.

"Biometric samplers," whispered the second operative. "One scratch and they've got your DNA."

The tech specialist thumbed a small device. "Three-second jam, on my mark."

The team pressed into recessed doorways as the drones approached. Just as the aerial unit's sensors swept toward them, she activated the jammer.

For precisely three seconds, the drones stuttered in place, their processors resetting. When they resumed, the team had vanished, leaving only an empty corridor in the machines' field of view.

The vault entrance loomed before them, its titanium-alloy frame embedded directly into the mountain's bedrock. A sleek biometric scanner glowed blue beside the door, LifeSpan's top-tier security protocol requiring retinal, fingerprint, and voice pattern authentication.

"Triple-factor," the tech specialist whispered, already unpacking a specialized device from her kit. "They've upgraded since our intel."

The weapons expert reached into her jacket, extracting what appeared to be a preserved human thumb sealed in a transparent medical polymer. The team exchanged grim glances. Nobody asked where she'd acquired it.

"Authorization level eight," the team leader murmured. "Research director, Dr. Morrow. This is where we *give 'em the finger*," she smirked with a crooked smile.

The tech specialist attached hair-thin filaments to the scanner's external housing while the weapons expert carefully positioned the preserved digit against the fingerprint reader. Simultaneously, the team leader held up a throat mic that replicated vocal cord vibrations.

"Initializing sequence," the tech specialist breathed, activating her device.

The scanner hesitated, its processing light flickering between red and green as it struggled to reconcile the contradictory inputs. For three agonizing seconds, the team stood motionless. Then, with a soft pneumatic hiss, the vault door began to retract.

"Ninety seconds until security handshake," the team leader warned as they slipped inside. "Move."

The vault door slid open with a glacial precision that betrayed its massive weight. Beyond lay not a single chamber but a cathedral of preservation, a vast, circular room with soaring ceilings and concentric rings of storage units extending outward like ripples in a pond. The air carried the sterile chill of deep refrigeration.

"Mother of God," breathed the tech specialist, her voice barely audible. "It's…the scale is just so much more than I expected."

The weapons expert unshouldered her pack, extracting what looked like metallic clay. "We've got eighty-four seconds before the secondary authentication protocol kicks in."

At the chamber's center stood their target, a cylindrical structure of brushed titanium and reinforced glass, surface frost perpetually forming and sublimating. Liquid nitrogen vapor cascaded down its sides like a waterfall of ghost-white mist, pooling briefly on the floor before evaporating.

"Cryo-chamber," the team leader confirmed, already moving. "Minus one-ninety-six Celsius. Core temperature is maintained even during power failures."

The tech specialist's fingers used her interface while the others formed a protective perimeter. Multiple layers of security surrounded the chamber, motion sensors, temperature alarms, weight-sensitive flooring.

"They've got new authentication protocols I've never seen before." The weapons expert pressed her ear against the chamber's exterior, listening for the telltale clicks of mechanical locks beneath the digital ones.

The tech specialist's hands trembled slightly as she bypassed the final security protocol. The cryo-unit's access panel yielded with a barely audible click, releasing a plume of nitrogen vapor that momentarily obscured the chamber's contents. "Core access granted," she whispered. "Ninety seconds until auto-thaw initiates."

Another team member, a botanist with fingers steady as stone, stepped forward. From her pack, she withdrew a set of specialized containers, each lined with phase-change materials designed to maintain precise temperatures. With surgical precision, she extracted the first seed sample, a variety of drought-resistant wheat untouched by LifeSpan's genetic tinkering. "Pre-modification maize," she murmured, her voice reverent as she secured another sample. "Original genome intact."

The team watched in silent awe as she worked, each seed packet representing tens of thousands of years of natural evolution, genetic diversity that LifeSpan had spent billions to eradicate and replace with their patented varieties.

While the botanist meticulously archived the genetic legacy of a forgotten earth, the weapons expert's gaze drifted. Her eyes, trained for threats, caught a variance in the vault's uniform design, a secondary cryo-unit, smaller and marked with a different classification. Instead of plant species, the labels bore geographical origins. *Glacial Melt: Pre-Industrial. Aquifer #734.* The containers held not seeds, but water.

"Techie, get over here." Her voice, a sharp whisper, cut through the reverent silence.

The tech specialist abandoned her post by the door, her boots silent on the grated floor. She leaned in, her breath fogging in the frigid air. "Water? Why lock up water with the seeds?"

"No idea. But if it's in here..." The weapons expert scanned the container with her eyes.

"...it's important." The tech specialist finished the thought. "Let's grab what we can carry."

Without another word, the weapons expert worked a side pouch open on her tactical pants. She selected six glass ampules, each one a different 'vintage' of water, and slid them into the pocket. They clinked softly, a fragile sound in the hardened fortress. As she secured the flap, the botanist moved to the next rack, her hands retrieving 'Bloody Butcher' corn, 'Cherokee Trail of Tears' beans, and 'Black Futsu' winter squash, open-pollinated, climate-adapted seeds bred for resilience, not profit.

None of them noticed the subtle change in the room's ambient noise, a shift in frequency too slight for human ears to consciously register. But deep within the mountain's security hub, an AI system designed by LifeSpan detected the atmospheric disturbance caused by the open cryo-chamber. Quantum-encrypted signals raced through fiber optic pathways.

The team leader's communication device vibrated once against his chest. His eyes widened as he read the message: *"COMPROMISED. EXTRACTION TEAM INBOUND."*

The vault's overhead lights flashed crimson as a klaxon blared through hidden speakers. Steel shutters slammed down over exits with pneumatic force that echoed through the chamber like gunshots.

"Perimeter breach detected," announced a calm female voice that contrasted with the chaos unfolding. "Security protocol Obsidian initiated."

The team leader grabbed the botanist's shoulder. "Extraction route. Now."

She sealed the last sample container with trembling hands. "Got what we came for. Ninety-three varieties, enough to restart if..."

The far wall panel slid open with a near silent hiss. Two Warden-X units stepped through in perfect synchronization, their gunmetal frames absorbing the red emergency strobing light. The horizontal visor bands across their featureless heads pulsed with amber light as they scanned the intruders. "Multiple unauthorized personnel detected," one announced, its voice unnaturally deep. "Surrender immediately."

The weapons expert didn't hesitate. She flung a Popper grenade that skittered across the floor, stopping at the robotic guards' feet. The EMP burst momentarily collapsed the nearest Warden-X, its systems rebooting.

"Exit!" The team leader shoved his people toward the ventilation shaft as the second Warden-X advanced, unaffected by the pulse.

The tech specialist reached the shaft first, yanking the grate free. "Go, go!"

Three team members disappeared into the dark passage as combat drones poured through overhead vents, their rotors filling the chamber with an angry buzzing.

The botanist was halfway into the shaft when a mechanical hand clamped around her ankle. The Warden-X had recovered, its grip implacable as it dragged her back into the vault. Her fingernails scraped uselessly against metal as she screamed.

The team leader lunged for her outstretched hand but missed as a drone slammed into his back, its taser prongs discharging through his jacket. He collapsed, twitching uncontrollably.

"Keep going!" The weapons expert shouted to those already in the shaft. She fired her needle burst at the approaching drones, frying their circuits. Two dropped from the air, but three more appeared.

The botanist fought wildly as the Warden-X pulled her fully back into the room. Her cheek caught on the sharp edge of the vent, opening a deep gash from temple to jaw. Blood streamed down her neck as she clutched the seed container to her chest. "Take it!" she screamed, hurling the container toward the shaft where the weapons expert crouched.

The cylinder spun through the air as a drone on tracks spun 180 degrees and accelerated down the hallway toward the air vent opening. A quick hand shot out of the vent opening, snatching the container and disappearing into the thin tube, too small for any automated units to pursue. The Warden-X unit dragged the bleeding girl down the hallway, away from the vent.

Inside the narrow passage, the weapons expert clutched the precious seed container to her chest, her breathing ragged. She could hear the botanist's screams fading as the mechanical guard hauled her deeper into the facility.

"We have to go back for them," whispered the tech specialist, her face pale in the dim emergency lighting that filtered through the grate.

"We can't." The weapons expert's voice was hollow. "Mission parameters are clear. The seeds take priority."

Far below them in the mountain's security hub, a face appeared on the main command screen. Dr. Elias Ward's expression was unreadable as he watched the live feed from the vault. The captured team members were being secured by Warden-X units, their faces now clearly visible to LifeSpan's facial recognition systems.

"Interesting," he murmured, tapping a finger against his lips. "These aren't Terrakin. They're too organized, too well-equipped." His eyes narrowed. "Run a complete biometric analysis and treat them immediately. I want to know who sent them."

CHAPTER 2

WELLNESS ANOMALY

AT FIRST LIGHT, the sun touched the granite peaks of the Rockies, a knife-edge of gold along the stone spine of the continent. From his seat on the northbound Maglev, Alex watched the light spill eastward, flowing down the slopes and across the plains as it splashed against the faces of great towers.

The train car moved with a frictionless glide, a silent projectile sealed against the thin morning air, soaring at 480 kilometers per hour. Alex sat in a forward-facing seat, a pod of molded gray composite and temperature-regulating fabric that contoured to his frame. No rumble of wheels on steel, no jostle or sway. Only a subtle, high-frequency hum vibrated through the floor into the soles of his shoes, the sound of powerful magnetic fields holding two hundred tons of metal and people suspended a centimeter above a guideway. His coffee, in an open travel mug on the small table before him, presented a surface of undisturbed blackness.

The car's interior was an exercise in minimalist efficiency. The walls were a pale, non-reflective material that absorbed sound. Light came not from fixtures but from ceiling panels which broadcast a soft, full-spectrum glow that shifted the color temperature in perfect sync with the dawn unfolding outside. Most of the other passengers sat in quiet isolation, their faces lit from below by the ethereal blue and white light of HoloScreens projected from their iBands.

A woman across the aisle conducted a meeting with a silent, gesticulating hologram. A man two rows ahead stared into a floating cube of financial data, its green and red numbers flicking past with machine speed. No one spoke aloud. The only shared sound was the train's persistent, low hum.

Alex ignored the notification pulse from his iBand and looked out the window. The glass was a single, seamless sheet that wrapped from the floor to the ceiling, giving him an uninterrupted vista. They were already outside the dense core of the Colorado Springs hub, elevated eighteen meters above the ground, rocketing north over the rolling expanse of the Palmer Divide.

The recent storm had left a clean, white blanket over everything. The endless rooftops of suburban developments, the dark ribbons of automated traffic arteries, the frosted branches of ponderosa pines were all softened by a layer of perfect, untouched snow, down to about 2000 meters elevation. A clear line could be seen where the rain turned to snow at the higher elevation.

To the west, the Front Range stood immense, a wall of jagged rock and ice separating the plains from the rest of the continent. The sky above the peaks was a deep, clear indigo, the color of space just before the sun breaches the horizon. Most of the range remained in shadow, a titanic mass of dark blues and slate grays, its canyons and ravines filled with a deep, purple darkness.

Pikes Peak, its summit soaring over fourteen thousand feet, caught the initial first rays of sunlight. The high-altitude snow on the peak's eastern face ignited in a silent, rosy fire. The granite, buried under feet of fresh powder, glowed with a delicate pink hue against the shadowed world below. It was a phenomenon of physics, light scattering through the dense atmosphere of the curve of the Earth, but the effect was one of austere, impossible beauty. A single mountain blushing in the cold.

Alex watched the line of pink light creep slowly down the mountain's face, a tide of color descending to meet the waking world. He saw the sharp definition of the cirques and couloirs, etched in shadow even as the surrounding snowfields began to burn with the sun's pure light. He tracked the slow, inexorable advance, a predictable and perfect calculation. Already-melting snow had started to rise into swirling pockets of water vapor as the spring sun pulled everything under her warm blanket.

This was Front Range City, often referred to as simply 'FRC', and from the train's elevated track, he could appreciate its sheer, unbroken scale. A concrete and steel assimilation of what were once separate towns, its genesis stretched three hundred miles: Cheyenne, a ghost of its frontier past; Fort Collins and Boulder, their independent spirits absorbed; Denver, the old capital, now just a central district designation. Southward it ran, past the Air Force Academy's unique geometry at the foot of Pikes Peak, finally dissolving into the high desert beyond Pueblo.

The Front Range Maglev Line was the city's primary artery, and as the train moved, frictionless and fast, the FRC appeared as a dense forest of architecture. New towers pierced the thin Colorado air, their surfaces clad in advanced composites that gave them a seamless, organic finish. On the eastern facades, HelioLux collectors, great mirrored dishes, pivoted in unison toward the dawn. Alex saw them drinking the sunlight, funneling it into thick bundles of fiber optic cable that snaked down the buildings' exteriors. Inside the towers, he knew light bled from exposed sections of these fibers, a clean, sterile illumination that needed no switch.

The explosive growth and relentless modernization was the work of LifeSpan Genomics. Before LifeSpan, the region was a promising tech corridor. Their arrival was the catalyst that ignited an economic detonation. As the train wove through the urban core, a ribbon of polished metal, Alex could see the old world persisting in the shadows of the new.

Squat, brick buildings from the twentieth century huddled between the corporate monoliths. Some were retrofitted with the conduits and panels of modern systems, others left to decay. He thought of the other layer hidden beneath the gleaming city, the abandoned structures buried beneath new construction, the physical remnants of dreams from bygone tech-prophets, a fairy tale won by the proprietary reality he was currently riding.

A holographic newsfeed shimmered to life against the armored glass, and for a moment, Alex's features were superimposed over the cityscape in the shifting blue light. At twenty-four, he was uncommonly handsome, with clean, symmetrical features, a jawline that caught the light just right, and blue eyes so clear and focused they seemed lit from within. His dark hair, always slipping forward, was pushed back with unconscious ease. There was something about him, something too polished to ignore, yet too natural to feel deliberate. Like beauty that happened by accident and stuck.

The anchor's voice was smooth and steady. "AgriFuture reports record yields from optimized wheat strains, with projected market growth of twelve percent this quarter. Analysts recommend diversifying crypto portfolios ahead of last year's 2036 Federal Reserve projections,"

Alex's fingers twitched, but he didn't change the feed. The next segment flashed red emergency banners.

"Breaking update: Authorities have apprehended three individuals linked to an attempted breach at the Rocky Mountain Seed Vault. LifeSpan Genomics condemns this act of eco-terrorism, assuring the public that patented genetic safeguards remain uncompromised."

The footage showed blurred figures in dark clothing being shoved into armored transports. One face flickered into focus, a young woman with a gash across her cheekbone, eyes burning defiance before the feed cut.

The supplemental display flickered to life, a scrolling cascade of viewer comments in real-time. The text scrolled almost too fast to read, but the sentiment was clear: anger, fear, and division:

Good. Lock them up and throw away the key.

Yeah, because letting corporations own our food supply is totally not a dystopian nightmare.

They're not terrorists, they're freedom fighters.

Freedom fighters? They're criminals. You want to starve the world because you don't like GMOs?

Wake up, sheep. This is how it starts. First they own the seeds, then they own you.

The debate raged on, a digital battlefield of polarized outrage. Alex watched, fingers drumming against his leg. The rhythm was uneven, a subconscious tell of agitation. The arguments were nothing new, but seeing them play out in real-time, raw and unfiltered, was different. It wasn't just abstract debate anymore. It was people. Angry. Scared. Divided.

The train began its final, silent deceleration into the Denver Central district. Alex took a deep breath and swiped the projection aside. He exited the Maglev and boarded the Light Rail heading to the Tech Center. By the time he reached his workstation, the city's morning pulse had attained its normal rhythm of drones and auto-taxis.

He sat, the terminal console humming to life under his palms as he pulled up the latest OmniHealth datasets. Rows of anonymized patient codes scrolled past, a river of numbers waiting to betray their secrets. His left hand danced across the desk surface, isolating clusters of neurological markers. The right adjusted a secondary display, cross-referencing treatment dates against behavioral incident reports. The tremor in his fingers stilled as the patterns locked into place. Outside the window, nothing in the air suggested the world was fracturing. But the data didn't lie.

The tremor in Alex's fingers was a constant companion, a subtle vibration that had been with him since childhood. It wasn't a weakness, but a symptom of the neural pathways firing too quickly, synapses sparking with an intensity that most people couldn't comprehend. His parents had noticed it first when he was seven, watching as his hands twitched while he solved puzzles meant for children twice his age. The doctors called it Synaptic Resonance Variance, SRV, a rare neurological condition that rewired the way his brain processed information.

For most, SRV was a curse, an unpredictable quirk of biology that made social interaction difficult, left emotions feeling distant, and turned the world into a puzzle that never quite made sense. But for Alex, it was something else entirely. The same misfiring synapses that made his hands tremble also sharpened his mind, turning him into a human algorithm, processing data with inexplicable precision. Where others saw noise, he saw patterns. Where others found chaos, he found structure.

By the time he was in college, his professors had taken notice. His ability to spot anomalies in datasets, errors that even machine learning models missed, made him invaluable. He didn't just analyze data; he *internalized* it, intuitively, the way a musician understood a symphony. When he spoke, his words were clipped, precise, devoid of the emotional weight that slowed others down. It unnerved people. But it also got results.

When he joined OmniHealth, his reputation preceded him. The AI-driven analytics tools were powerful, but they still needed a human touch, someone who could see the gaps in the machine's logic, the subtle distortions in the data that hinted at something deeper. Alex was that person. His SRV made him the perfect analyst, a living, breathing anomaly detector in a world drowning in information.

The tremor in his fingers didn't slow him. It was just another part of the process, a physical manifestation of the electricity in his mind. And in a world where data was power, that electricity made him dangerous.

A decade earlier, Alex would have been labeled as 'Special Needs', 'On the Spectrum', or 'Borderline Autistic'. High-functioning, yes. But still, he would have been shoved into a system that saw his neural wiring as something to be corrected rather than harnessed.

The old special education programs, underfunded, overcrowded classrooms with rigid behavioral modifications, would have sanded down his edges until he learned to mimic normalcy at the cost of his own mind. Or put him on drugs. The No Child Left Behind era had preached inclusion while quietly funneling kids like him into tracks designed to make them manageable, not exceptional.

But back in 2028, with the rise of adaptive AI tutors and neurodiversity-focused education models, conditions like SRV had been converted from liabilities into specialized skill sets. His school's learning algorithm didn't force him to sit still through group discussions, it fed him datasets to dissect, let him hyperfocus for hours without interruption, and calibrated his social interactions through VR simulations that didn't punish him for missing subtext.

His social anxiety disorder had been nurtured. By the time he graduated, he wasn't just functional, he was *precise*, using his 'disability' as an advantage. There was nothing in Alex's social interaction that stood out from any other 'normal' person, other than a few eccentricities and a tendency toward some OCD tells.

His precision and refined skills had landed him a senior analyst position at OmniHealth, complete with a company housing unit in one of the sleek high-rises downtown. The high tech apartment was modern, had an amazing view of Pikes Peak from his forty-second story window, a community gym, and access to an exclusive park. Employees received a monthly transportation stipend, the rent was deducted automatically from his paycheck, and the biometric locks meant he never had to fumble with keys. A fair trade.

The dataset on his screen pulsed with irregularities. His fingers twitched, not the usual rhythmic tremor, but something sharper, like a live wire brushing against his nerves. The numbers weren't just off. They were *wrong* in a way that made his SRV-honed instincts flare.

He leaned in, the city's reflective sunrise glow through the window dimming as his focus narrowed to the screen. He mentally cycled through the potential causes: data corruption, system failure, malicious attack. None of the signatures fit. It presented as something he'd never been trained to detect.

Alex barely registered the scent of vanilla and roasted coffee beans until a steaming cup appeared beside his elbow. Jamie Schaffer leaned against his desk, a bright, meticulously-styled strawberry blonde whose smile, though wide, rarely reached her expressive blue eyes these days.

"Thought you could use a refuel, Data-Maestro. Really engrossed in that data, or just avoiding human contact?" Her voice, usually a lively current, held a careful, almost modulated cheer.

Alex grunted, a sound that could mean anything, and gestured vaguely at the primary display still frozen on the seed vault heist report. Jamie followed his gaze, her smile faltering for a moment before snapping back into place. The news feed showed the exterior of the formidable Rocky Mountain Seed Vault, and the blurred images of arrests.

"Awful, isn't it? Eco-terrorists. Imagine," she said, the sarcasm evident in her tone.

Alex's fingers stilled over the console. He watched her, the slight, almost imperceptible tremor in his hands momentarily ceasing.

Jamie took a sip from her cup and lowered it, her eyes rotating upwards to the ceiling-mounted surveillance orb, then to the discreet camera embedded in Alex's desk, above the HoloScreen. She leaned closer, her voice dropping. "Or, you know, *not* eco-terrorists."

Her free hand rose, casually brushing a stray strand of hair from her temple, the movement conveniently shielding her lips from the monitor's direct view, obstructing any ability for the security systems' lip-reading transcripts to flag the conversation.

"It's a bit too...neat, don't you think?"

Alex raised an eyebrow.

"Think about it, Alex. The Apex Watchers." Jamie's voice was barely a whisper, a thread of sound against the office hum. She glanced around again as though the walls themselves had ears.

The 'Apex Watchers' was a conspiracy murmur in the digital underground, a sprawling constellation of anxieties and half-truths that had coalesced into a formidable belief system. It began, as such theories often did, with symbols. The unfinished pyramid on the old one dollar bills, crowned by the Eye of Providence. Officially, a nod to divine guidance and national growth.

To believers, it was the emblem of a plan centuries in the making, the pyramid's missing capstone representing an 'illuminated' elite, patiently steering humanity toward a 'Novus Ordo Seclorum', a New Order of the Ages, not of enlightenment, but of absolute control. They whispered of the Illuminati, not as a defunct historical society but as the patient, insidious architects of this grand design, working through shadows and front organizations.

To believers now, in 2037, LifeSpan Genomics was their most polished instrument. Its Northgate headquarters, a colossal, blue-black ziggurat, pierced the sky, a defiant, modern pyramid. At night, or during moments of corporate triumph, a single, unblinking holographic eye would blaze from its apex: the Apex Oculus. For followers of the theory, this was no mere corporate branding, but a declaration, a technologically-advanced, All-Seeing Eye signifying that the ancient order now commanded the tools of the future, economics, food, water, and the media, to finalize their dominion.

Jamie's eyes, twin pools of earnest conviction, searched Alex's. "This seed vault thing? Classic Apex misdirection. Create a bogeyman, an 'eco-terrorist' threat, so everyone looks that way." She gestured vaguely toward the newsfeed.

"While they're busy doing…well, whatever it is they're really doing, they keep the masses scared of the wrong enemy." She held her cup higher, near her mouth. "And anyone who questions it are the real crazy ones, right?"

Alex's expression remained flat, a carefully-constructed neutrality. He knew Jamie's theories. She often spiraled into elaborate webs of connections, seeing LifeSpan's acquisitions and the politicians in their pockets as undeniable proof of the Apex Watchers' silent coup. He usually let her talk, offering noncommittal sounds, more interested in the patterns of her belief than the belief itself.

"It's not misdirection I'm worried about." Alex tapped a sequence on his console. A new data stream replaced the newsfeed: post-treatment survey logs correlated with GeneVax administration dates. Red flags peppered the display.

Jamie leaned back, the initial conspiratorial urgency draining from her. She sighed, a weary sound that seemed to carry the weight of more than just late-night work. Her gaze drifted to the window, to the distant, monolithic silhouette of the LifeSpan Northgate ziggurat against the bruised pre-dawn sky. "Look, I know what I said about all that." She waved a hand, encompassing the theories, the corporate monoliths, the pervasive unease. "But Alex, my heart…it's been acting up again. More arrhythmias. My doctor said it's getting dangerous."

Her voice, stripped of its usual bravado, was small. The bright, meticulous facade cracked, revealing the anxiety beneath. "She said GeneVax is the best shot. They've had incredible success rates with these kinds of hereditary defects."

Alex turned fully in his chair, the faint tremor in his hands, a physical echo of his SRV, becoming more pronounced. "You're going through with the GeneVax? After all your talk about 'corporate genetic meddling'?" He used her exact phrase, the words stark in the quiet hum of the office.

Jamie flinched but raised her chin. "Yes. I am." Her eyes, usually sparkling with witty cynicism, now held a defensive sheen. "It's not some back-alley gene splice, Alex. This is LifeSpan. The data is overwhelming. It works. People are being cured of things they've lived with their whole lives."

"Jamie, wait." Alex swiveled back to his console, zooming in on a cluster of anomalous data points. The patterns were there, whispers in the digital stream, but the meaning eluded him, a half-formed shape in the dark. "There's something off. In the post-treatment behavioral markers, sometimes. I can't pin it down yet, but it's there. Just give me more time."

"Time?" Jamie's laugh was brittle. "I don't have more time. My last episode - I thought that was it." A genuine fear, raw and unfiltered, flashed in her eyes before she quickly suppressed it. "The company wellness program is covering the whole thing. Full. Every crypto. You know I could never afford this on my own, not in a million years. It's a miracle OmniHealth even offers it." She straightened, her posture regaining some of its habitual confidence, though the brightness in her eyes felt forced. "My appointment is tomorrow. It's already scheduled."

Alex looked from the unsettling data on his screen to Jamie's determined, frightened face. He saw the desperation, the lure of a cure dangled by the exact entities she professed to mistrust. His SRV amplified the dissonance, the conflicting signals. He knew he couldn't stop her. The data was too nebulous, his concerns too vague against the concrete promise of health. "Okay." The word was quiet, a concession.

"Just pay attention, Jamie. Afterward. Pay attention to how you feel. Not just physically. Any changes. Any."

She nodded, a quick, almost eager motion. "Of course." She tossed the empty cup into the recycler with a perfect arc.

A shout broke the relative silence of the office, cutting through the hum of conversation and the tapping of keypads. "Thompson! Get in my office now!" The supervisor's voice carried across the open workspace, sharp with impatience.

Alex's fingers stilled over the keyboard, his gaze flicking toward the source of the disturbance. His jaw tightened slightly, but he didn't react beyond that. Just a brief, controlled inhale before pushing his chair back.

Jamie, still standing beside his desk, shot him a quick, concerned glance. "You good?" she asked, voice low.

Alex gave a small, dismissive shake of his head. "Fine."

She nodded. "I'll see you later. Don't let that asshole bully you. I don't care if he is a supervisor, he's a jerk with a Napoleon complex."

Without another word, Alex made his way toward the supervisor's office, his posture rigid, his expression unreadable. The office chatter resumed around him, but the air felt heavier now. As he walked to the supervisor's office, Alex put his hands in his pockets to help control the increased trembling.

Mishaal Taback sat behind his clear desk, the three displays before him casting a pale glow across his sharp features. The screens showed a trio of data streams, two filled with the dense, scrolling text of Life-Span's GeneVax patient records, the third replaying a recording of Alex's recent terminal activity. The footage played silently, a loop of keystrokes and queries that had clearly been flagged.

Alex stepped inside, the glass door sealing shut behind him with a near-silent hiss of hydraulics. The air in the office was cool, sterile, the hum of the climate control was the only sound. Mishaal didn't look up immediately, his fingers steepled in front of him. His receding hairline glistened as he slowly rocked in his chair.

"Alex," he finally said, his voice calm, measured. "You've been running unauthorized queries on the LifeSpan GeneVax patient data."

Alex didn't flinch. "I noticed a statistical anomaly. It warranted investigation."

Mishaal's gaze flickered, his dark eyes sharp. "That data is proprietary. LifeSpan has a strict partnership agreement with us. You don't just dive into their records without clearance."

Alex pulled his hands from his pockets and flexed his fingers slightly at his sides, as if his speech depended upon their freedom. "The behavioral changes post-treatment aren't just statistical noise. Patients are showing a *dramatic* increase in compliance with authority across every metric. That's not a coincidence."

Mishaal exhaled through his nose, leaning back in his chair. "People who've had life-threatening conditions cured tend to view their healthcare providers favorably. It's not exactly a revelation." He gestured at the screens. "You're seeing patterns where there aren't any."

Alex's jaw tightened. "It's not gratitude. It's mass *uniformity*. The shifts are too consistent, too precise. This isn't natural behavior."

Mishaal's expression didn't change. "You're overcomplicating it. People are healthier. They're happier. That's the point of the treatment." He tapped a key and the screens flickered, the data streams vanishing.

Alex's fingers twitched against his thigh. The placid certainty in Mishaal's voice was unnervingly familiar; not the logic of a supervisor, but the serene dismissal of the compliant. He met Mishaal's gaze directly, his own expression hardening. He wasn't just being dismissed, he was being managed. "The pattern is there. The AI can't detect it because it's trained on normalized datasets. It's looking for expected deviations, not systemic rewiring." His voice was low, careful. "I've been adjusting the weight parameters in the neural net, feeding it raw behavioral metrics instead of pre-processed clusters. The correlation isn't subtle once you strip the, "

Mishaal held up a hand. "That's enough." His voice carried the quiet finality of a door locking. "You're describing a pattern you are not authorized to look for. This is your final warning, Thompson. Stick to your assigned analytics. Is that clear?"

Alex's jaw tightened. "Yes, Sir."

Mishaal leaned back, the tension in his shoulders easing slightly. "The company wellness program is offering GeneVax to all employees this month. You should consider it." His gaze flicked to Alex's trembling hands. "You mentioned your family history of neurological issues."

"I'd prefer to wait for more long-term data, Sir."

A faint crease formed between Mishaal's brows, but he only sighed, the sound of a man who'd already won the argument before it began. His fingers drummed the carbon-fiber desktop, three precise taps, and the door behind Alex hissed open with the sterile efficiency of a surgical suite. "Most of the department has already scheduled their treatments." Mishaal's thumb traced the edge of his GeneVax appointment reminder, glowing faintly on his wrist display. "Mine's next week."

Alex nodded once, a sharp mechanical motion, and turned toward the exit.

"Thompson," Mishaal said to the tense line of Alex's shoulders.

He turned just far enough to make eye contact.

"You're eighteen terabytes over your weekly data quota. Clean it up by the end of the week."

Alex nodded and left the office. The door sealed shut with a sound like a knife sliding back into its sheath.

Hours later, the elevator doors slid shut behind Alex, sealing him inside the sleek, mirrored interior. The air was cool, scented faintly with something sterile and artificial, lilac perhaps. A soft chime sounded, and the elevator began its descent.

A screen embedded in the wall flickered to life, displaying a polished corporate video. A woman in a white lab coat smiled warmly as text scrolled beneath her: *GeneVax Therapy: The Future of Personalized Health.*

"Thanks to GeneVax, I no longer worry about my family's history of heart disease," a middle-aged man said, his voice smooth with gratitude.

The camera cut to a young woman, her eyes bright. "I used to struggle with anxiety, but after my treatment, I feel so much more at peace."

Alex barely glanced at the screen, his fingers moving automatically as he pulled up the transit app on his phone. He typed in his employee ID, the screen flashing green in confirmation. A notification appeared: *Your ride is en route. Estimated arrival: 31 seconds.*

The elevator hummed as it descended, the numbers above the door ticking down: fifteen, fourteen, thirteen. The video continued, now showing a montage of happy families, children playing, elderly couples walking hand in hand. A voice-over declared, "GeneVax doesn't just treat illness, it enhances life."

Alex exhaled, shifting his weight slightly as the elevator descended. The screen switched to a new segment, this one featuring a doctor explaining the science behind the therapy, his tone confident, reassuring. "Think of your DNA like the body's fundamental blueprint – the instructions for building and running everything. Sometimes, there's a tiny error in that blueprint, a small mistake in the instructions, that can cause health problems passed down through families.

"For a long time, doctors could see the blueprint, but fixing specific errors was incredibly difficult. Now, with LifeSpan's GeneVax therapy, science has developed a tool that's like incredibly precise microscopic tweezers. This tool can go into the blueprint, find that exact spot with the mistaken instruction, carefully remove it, and put the correct instruction in its place.

"It's designed to fix the problem right where it starts, in the blueprint itself, helping the body follow the right instructions for better health."

The face of Alex's mother flashed in his mind, pale, gaunt, her dark hair limp against the hospital pillow. He'd been twelve when the nosebleeds started. Just a trickle at first, then a flood, her blood soaking through the towels, the sheets, his small hands pressing uselessly against her face. The ER staff had moved fast, but not fast enough. He remembered the way her fingers had gone slack in his, the way her voice had slurred as she whispered, "It's okay, Mijo..."

The transfusion had barely saved her. That time. Now, GeneVax promised to rewrite the faulty genes behind her autoimmune disease, the cellular civil war raging inside her.

No more blood transfusions when her own immune system devoured her blood cells. No more filtration masks just to walk down the street, filtering air thick with potential triggers. No more obsessive sanitizing rituals for everything that crossed the apartment threshold, turning home into a sterile fortress against an invisible siege. No more mapping every trip outside based on proximity to accessible, clean facilities.

No more weeks dissolving into the crushing fatigue that left her unable to lift her head from the pillow, the constant, grinding pain, a thief of daily life. No more sudden, terrifying flare-ups, the near misses that sent them scrambling to Clinton Memorial, hearts hammering against ribs. Clinical trials had a ninety-two percent remission rate for conditions like hers. A near-miracle, dangled just within reach.

Alex's grip tightened into a fist, calming the shaking so he could see his watch HoloScreen. The data didn't lie. Alex could see it, but could he convince anyone else?

His unique mind didn't just process the numbers, it perceived the underlying structure, the hidden correlations that slipped past the algorithms. The AI missed the *why*. Or, a colder thought surfaced. Perhaps the AI *wasn't* missing it. Perhaps it was designed to overlook this specific kind of anomaly, prioritizing systemic harmony over individual cognitive liberty. People trusted AI implicitly. Its analyses were complex, its conclusions presented with irrefutable digital certainty on countless HoloScreens. Who would believe a lone analyst claiming the system itself was blind, or worse, complicit?

He could show them the data, point to the intersecting lines, and the correlating percentages. But it was like trying to describe color to someone born blind. They relied on AI to interpret reality, and it reported that everything was not just fine, but *better*. His own SRV-driven perception, the essential faculty that allowed him to see the pattern, marked him as an outlier, potentially unreliable in their eyes. He saw the truth as clearly as his own sharp-featured reflection moving across the polished surfaces beside him, but convincing others felt like trying to hold back the tide.

He pulled up his contacts, thumb hovering over Dr. Rivera's name. She'd know. She'd seen the raw data on his mother's case, understood the risks better than anyone. A notification popped up, his ride was sitting at the curb. He hesitated and tapped the call icon.

The line rang once. Twice.

"Alex?" Dr. Rivera's voice was warm, familiar. "It's been a while."

He swallowed. "I need to talk to you. About GeneVax."

The doors opened on the ground floor, revealing the lobby beyond. A sleek, autonomous black car sat at the curb, his name displayed on the window. Alex stepped forward, dismissing the HoloScreen on his iBand. The Apple HearBuds connected seamlessly in his ears. The elevator's screen continued to play, the cheerful jingle of the GeneVax slogan fading as he walked away.

A pause. "Where are you right now?" she asked quietly.

Alex tapped his iBand lightly against the car's door frame. A soft *ding*, and the vehicle clicked open with a whisper of hydraulics. He sank into the synthetic leather seat, the interior temperature already adjusted to his preferences, cool enough to keep him alert, not so cold as to be uncomfortable. "We need to talk. In person."

A pause. The barest rustle of fabric on her end, her lab coat brushing against her iBand, maybe. "I'm finishing my rounds," she said finally. "Cafeteria at the hospital, twenty minutes?"

The door sealed shut, and the car eased into traffic with the smooth precision of an autonomous system. No wasted motion, no hesitation. The cityscape blurred past, towering glass facades, understated corporate logos glowing in ultraviolet hues, sidewalks full of people walking in steady, unhurried rhythms.

"That works," he said. "I'm on my way."

The call ended and the car accelerated, weaving effortlessly between slower vehicles, adjusting trajectory with machine precision. Alex exhaled, flexed his fingers. The screen embedded in the dashboard displayed their route, a blinking blue line cutting through the city's grid. He tapped the screen and adjusted the destination, sliding the drop pin to Clinton Memorial Hospital.

The light rain pattered against the hospital's glass facade as Alex stepped inside, shaking the droplets from his jacket. The entrance was sleek, all polished steel and glass, designed to impress rather than shelter. The information kiosk hummed softly, its holographic display flickering with wayfinding prompts, but he ignored it, heading straight for the cafeteria's revolving doors.

Inside, the air smelled of synthetic food and disinfectant. Dr. Maya Rivera emerged from the food service area, her wrist extended toward the payment kiosk. The automated system beeped in acknowledgment, and robotic arms whirred into action behind the counter, assembling meals with mechanical precision.

She spotted him immediately, her face lighting up as she waved him over. Alex navigated the crowded tables, dodging staff in scrubs and visitors balancing trays. Before he could sit, she pulled him into a tight embrace, her smile warm. "Alex," she said, stepping back to look at him. "It's been too long." Her expression softened with concern. "How's your mom doing?"

Alex hesitated, his fingers tapping against the table. "She's stable. For now." His voice was tight, the words clipped. "They're pushing GeneVax as a treatment option again."

They sat down. Maya slid a tube of chocolate pudding across the table toward him. He stared at it and picked it up, his grip unsteady. The foil seal resisted his trembling fingers.

She reached over, covering his hands with hers. "What's wrong?" she asked quietly.

He exhaled, setting the unopened tube down. "I need to talk to you about GeneVax."

She leaned back slightly, studying him. "Okay."

He explained what he saw, his voice low, urgent.

Maya's brow furrowed. "Correlation doesn't equal causation. You know that."

"It's not just correlation." His fingers twitched toward his iBand.

"The timing aligns perfectly with treatment administration. Every time."

She tilted her head. "What changes, specifically?"

"Increased acceptance of authority. Decreased questioning of institutional directives. Reduced protest participation. Heightened approval of corporate and government policies."

Maya tapped her fingers against the table. "That could be explained by improved health outcomes making people more satisfied with the system."

Alex let out a sharp breath. "That's what my supervisor said." He flicked his wrist, activating his HoloScreen. Data arrays bloomed in the air between them, glowing columns of numbers and graphs. "But look at this." He swiped through the projections, highlighting a subset of patients. "Minimal physical improvements. No significant health changes. Same behavioral shifts." His jaw tightened. "Every time."

Maya's fingers stilled against the table. She studied the data hovering between them, the glow of the HoloScreen distorting her face slightly. "That does seem unusual," she admitted, her voice low.

Alex glanced around the cafeteria before leaning in. The hum of conversation and clatter of trays provided cover, but he kept his words measured. "What do you know about CRISPR technology?"

Maya tilted her head, considering. "It's gene editing. Scientists can target specific genes to cure diseases - sickle cell, cystic fibrosis, even some cancers. Precision cuts, repairs, replacements. Standard genetic therapy." She shrugged slightly. "Why?"

Alex tapped his iBand, minimizing the display. "GeneVax uses a modified CRISPR system."

Maya exhaled, almost amused. "Everyone knows that. It's in every commercial."

Alex didn't smile. His fingers flexed against the edge of the table. "What if it's targeting more than just the disease genes?"

Maya became utterly motionless. The cafeteria noise faded into background static. She didn't answer immediately, her gaze flicking to the nearest security cam mounted near the ceiling. Slowly, she reached for her coffee. "Explain," she said, her voice barely above a whisper.

Alex exhaled, rubbing his temple. "I know how this sounds." His fingers twitched toward the dormant HoloScreen. "And I don't have the medical background to confirm if it's even possible. But the data, " He tapped the table once, sharply. "It doesn't lie."

Across the cafeteria, a group of interns erupted into laughter at some shared joke. Alex's shoulders tensed, his gaze darting toward the sound before returning to Maya. "I *hope* I'm wrong," he admitted, voice dropping. "GeneVax could be the biggest medical breakthrough since antibiotics. I *want* it to work, for my mother." His throat tightened. "Maybe it could've stopped my father's decline. Prevented the environmental factors that killed him four years ago when all the safety reports claimed everything was normal."

The pudding tube sat unopened between them, condensation beading on its surface. Maya's fingers tightened around her coffee cup.

Alex leaned forward. "But I need someone who hasn't taken the treatment. Someone with medical expertise to look at this objectively. Before more people..." he trailed off, jaw working.

Maya set her cup down with deliberate care. The ceramic clicked against the laminate. Her eyes flicked to the security cam again and back to Alex. She didn't speak immediately, her expression unreadable.

Maya hesitated, her fingers tapping slightly against the coffee cup handle. "I have access to the treatment protocols," she said, her voice low. "I can review the genetic markers they're targeting."

Relief flickered across Alex's face. "That's all I'm asking. Just look at the data."

Before she could respond, the PA system crackled to life. A mechanical voice announced, "Dr. Rivera to Oncology. Dr. Rivera to Oncology."

Maya stood abruptly, her chair scraping against the floor. She glanced at the security camera mounted near the ceiling and back at Alex. "Send me the behavioral data," she said, keeping her voice steady. "Not the raw files, something I can interpret." She hesitated. "And, Alex, "

He met her gaze.

"Be careful who you share this with." Her voice was barely above a whisper. "LifeSpan has partnerships with every hospital, every clinic, every government health agency. Even the independent urgent care centers in low-income areas are tied to them."

Alex tensed. "That's part of what worries me."

Maya reached out, pulling him into a brief embrace. When she stepped back, she held his shoulders, her grip firm. "We only talked about your mother," she said, searching his face.

Alex nodded. "I understand."

She gave his shoulders a final squeeze before turning away, her expression unreadable as she walked toward the hospital corridors.

CHAPTER 3

METAMORPHASIS

THE APARTMENT WAS small and efficient. It was a studio with enough space for a queen bed, a work terminal, a seating area with a couch across from a wall-mounted broadcaster panel, and a kitchenette wedged against the same wall, closer to the window. The walls were bare except for a single framed photo of Alex's mother, taken before her illness had worsened.

The rest of the space was dominated by data. HoloScreens projected from the ceiling apparatus flickered in standby mode, casting a pale blue glow over the cramped room. A stack of old-fashioned notebooks sat on the desk, filled with Alex's cramped handwriting, backups, in case the digital records were ever compromised.

A small bookshelf held a collection of old paper books, including two of his favorites. *1984* by George Orwell and *The Visual Display of Quantitative Information* by Edward R. Tufte, a classic work on data visualization and statistical graphics. Alex often imagined Tufte also had SRV and was able to analyze data in ways others couldn't.

The bookshelf was a relic, a stubborn holdout against the sleek efficiency of digital media. Most people consumed literature through HoloScreen, swiping through holographic pages of text that floated in the air, projected from the iBand on their wrist. The portable, searchable, and endlessly customizable display was a marvel of efficiency. But Alex's mother had raised him on paper.

Isabella Thompson had been a librarian before her illness forced her into early retirement. She'd filled their home with books, their spines cracked from use, their pages dog-eared and annotated in her looping, cursive script, another relic of the past as most couldn't even read it. When Alex ran his fingers along the shelf, he could hear her voice: "Mijo, there's weight to them. You feel the words differently."

He pulled out *1984*, its cover slightly faded. The spine creaked as he opened it. A receipt from a long-closed bookstore called Barnes & Noble fluttered to the floor, 2025, when paper was still common. His mother had bought it for his twelfth birthday. Inside, her handwriting filled the margins: underlines, exclamation points, notes debating Orwell's arguments. He put the book back and instructed his gHome SmartMom to turn on the broadcaster and walked back to the kitchen counter.

The kitchenette smelled of synthetic protein and reheated spices. Alex stood at the counter, methodically chopping vegetables, real ones, a rare indulgence. His ceramic knife moved in quick, precise strokes, the rhythm steady. The pan on the stove hissed as oil heated on the UltraFlex Induction Cooker.

The wall-mounted HoloScreen shimmered, the image sharpening from a pixelated blur into a vibrant commercial. A sleek, three-wheeled NikeBike, looking like a horseless chariot, glided silently through a sun-drenched urban park. Families smiled, waving as it passed. A voiceover, smooth and reassuring, detailed the NikeBike's silent-drive motors, its solar-assist canopy, and its seamless integration with the city's transit grid. The ad ended with the NikeTrek logo and a tagline: *NikeTrek: Just Ride It.*

The commercial faded, replaced by the familiar face of a network news anchor. Her expression was serious yet optimistic. Behind her, a graphic materialized: *CARE Initiative: Rebuilding Lives, Restoring Communities.*

"Tonight," the anchor began, her voice a calm, warm rhythm. "We have an update on the groundbreaking Citizen Adjustment and Reformation _Enterprise, or CARE. Now in its fifth year of full implementation, the Department of Civil Renewal reports unprecedented success rates in inmate reform. The CARE initiative, a cornerstone of the modern justice system, focuses on reintegrating former inmates through a mandatory combination of behavioral therapy, cognitive correction, and voluntary biomedical enhancements."

A new HoloScreen image appeared beside the anchor: a sterile, brightly-lit facility. Individuals in simple, uniform clothing attended classes, worked at vocational stations, and interacted with counselors. The visuals conveyed order, productivity.

"Approved under Section Seventeen of the Genetic Liberty Protection Act, GeneVax gently recalibrates neurochemistry. The result? A significant reduction in aggressive tendencies and an increased capacity for cooperation and civic responsibility. Coupled with the CARETrack monitoring system, which provides real-time biometric feedback for eighteen months post-release, and the Civic Uplift Protocol's job training, the program is transforming lives." She paused, a rehearsed smile gracing her lips. "Many participants also embrace CAREFaith, a spiritual wellness component that further aids their journey."

The screen cut to another image. A woman, perhaps in her mid-thirties, sat in a simple room. She wore a standard grey reentry jumpsuit, a visitor badge clipped to her collar. Her dark hair was pulled back, her face unadorned. A lower-third graphic identified her: *Reformed Citizen – Amari 'Blood Rae' Martinez, former 18th Street Syndicate.*

Her eyes, dark and direct, met the camera. "I don't even recognize the person I used to be." Amari's voice was low, a little rough, but steady. "It's like something opened up in my mind. I wake up grateful. I thank God every day that I get to do something real, something good. I never thought I'd be a part of the world again, and now I don't want to be anything else." Her eyes held a hollow sheen, a depth that was meant to suggest conviction.

The feed returned to the anchor in the studio. She nodded slowly, her expression one of profound satisfaction. "Powerful words from

Amari Martinez, one of nearly two million CARE graduates now classified as Tier-1 Citizens. The program boasts an 87.2% successful reintegration rate and a staggering 93.5% decrease in violent recidivism. Indeed, the World Development Organization and the BioSec Alliance now consider CARE a model for global justice reform."

Alex's knife stilled on the cutting board. He watched the anchor, his blue eyes narrowed. The tremor in his hands, usually faint, became more pronounced. He set the knife down with deliberate care.

He didn't cook often. Most nights, it was a nutrient bar or a pre-packaged meal, something fast that wouldn't pull him away from his work. But tonight, he needed distraction. The repetitive motion of slicing, the focus required to keep the knife from slipping, it was better than staring at the data again, turning the same numbers over in his head.

The vegetables hit the pan with a sizzle. Steam rose, carrying the sharp scent of garlic and ginger. Alex stirred, his movements automatic. His thoughts drifted back to Maya, to the way she'd hesitated before agreeing to look at the data. He knew the risk he was asking her to take.

A notification chimed from his terminal. He ignored it. The food needed his attention.

The pan hissed again as he added the protein, lab-grown, but close enough to the real extinct chicken from the bird flu outbreak of 2032. The smell filled the apartment, rich and savory. For a moment, it almost felt normal. Like just another night in a world that still made sense. Dark teriyaki sauce glugged from a glass bottle, its label etched with bold, red Japanese characters, splashing onto the hot pan with a sharp sizzle.

The notification chimed again. Louder this time. Alex exhaled. He turned the heat down, wiped his hands on a towel, and crossed the room. The screen flared to life as he tapped it.

A message from Jamie. "Let me in! I'm downstairs."

Alex frowned. Jamie wasn't supposed to be mobile yet. The clinic's post-treatment protocol mandated twenty-four hours of observation. His fingers hovered over the HoloScreen, but another series of impatient buzzes decided it. He flicked the screen at his wrist, authorizing building access via his iBand. The lock disengaged with a muted electronic chirp forty-two floors below.

gNest automatically turned off the broadcaster after noting a visitor was coming, and profiling Alex's lack of interest in the news topic as the broadcaster was showing information about a tropical storm in the Gulf of America.

Back at the stove, he segmented the vegetables with quick turns of his spatula. The door hissed open behind him exactly eighty-two seconds later. He'd counted, followed by the rustle of Jamie shedding her light rain jacket. Fabric whispered against the wall hook. Shoes thudded onto the mat with uncharacteristic force.

"You're supposed to be under monitoring," Alex said without turning. Oil popped against the pan's edge.

Jamie's laugh was too bright, too easy. Springs creaked as she flopped onto the couch. "Felt amazing halfway through. They discharged me early, said I was their best responder yet." The clinical phrasing wrapped in her usual warmth unnerved him.

Alex glanced over. Jamie sprawled across the sofa, one arm draped over her eyes. Her shoulders were loose in a way he'd never seen, no coiled tension in her jaw, no restless tapping of her foot. Her strawberry blonde hair spilled over the edge of the couch. The top three buttons of her blouse were undone.

"You look like hell," he lied. She looked radiant.

"That's the detox haze. Totally normal." She waved a hand, fingers splaying with theatrical flourish. "But the arrhythmia markers? Gone. And they caught some enzyme deficiency I didn't even know about. And even my exercise induced-asthma. Fixed everything in one session."

Metal scraped against ceramic as Alex plated the stir-fry. Steam curled into the sterile apartment air. He forced his grip to be steady. "They told you that mid-procedure?"

Jamie just smiled at the ceiling, working her lips forward and back, almost like she had lost feeling in them.

Alex set the plate on the counter with a quiet clink. "You want some? Or I can get you a glass of wine?"

Jamie stretched, rolling her shoulders with a languid ease that didn't suit her. "Oh, no alcohol for me. Not anymore." She grinned, tilting her head. "You should try the treatment, Alex. It's incredible. No more stress, no more second-guessing. Just...clarity."

Her fingers drummed against the couch arm, but there was no nervous energy to it, just idle motion. She leaned forward, elbows on her knees, and fixed him with a look that was too warm, too deliberate. "Seriously. One session. You'd feel *amazing*."

Alex raised his fork, pushing the food around the plate. "I'm good."

Jamie laughed, soft and airy. "Come on. You're always so tense. Would it kill you to relax for once?" She stood, crossing the small space between them with slow, deliberate steps. Her hand brushed his arm, lingering just a second too long. "Think about it. No more migraines. No more overthinking everything. Just peace."

Alex didn't pull away, but his grip tightened on the fork. "I like overthinking."

Jamie sighed, rolling her eyes with exaggerated fondness. "Of course, you do." She stepped back, but the smile didn't fade. "Just promise me you'll consider it. For me?"

Alex took a bite of his food, chewing slowly. The spices were sharp, grounding. "I'll think about it."

Jamie beamed as if he'd handed her a victory. "Good." She glanced at the door and back at him, still smiling. "You're gonna love it."

The stir-fry tasted bland in Alex's mouth. He watched Jamie from the corner of his eye as she wandered toward his workstation, her movements too fluid, too relaxed. *What's wrong with her?* The clinic's post-procedure meds, maybe. Valium to smooth the transition? But the way she held herself, like every knot in her had been untied, set his teeth on edge.

Her fingers trailed over the edge of his desk and paused. A flicker of tension crossed her face, there and gone. "You're still investigating the treatments." Her voice was light, but the words landed like an accusation.

Alex stabbed a piece of broccoli. "It's my job. Data analyst. Literally in the title."

Jamie turned, leaning against the desk. The HoloScreen's glow lit her face from below, sharpening the curve of her smile. "What did Mishaal want earlier?"

"Went over my data quota again." He shrugged. "Happens."

"How much?"

"Eighteen terabytes."

Jamie barked a laugh. "That's more than the rest of the department *combined*." She shook her head, still grinning. "Mishaal wouldn't have called you in if he didn't have a good reason. He's a fantastic supervisor!"

Alex frowned and opened his mouth to protest, only to be cut off by Jamie.

"You're looking for problems that don't exist. LifeSpan's helping people. Their treatments are saving lives." The words came out rehearsed.

Alex set his fork down. "I know."

Jamie's smile didn't waver. "Do you?" She pushed off the desk, stepping closer.

"Because it doesn't seem like you believe that."

The air between them thickened. Alex could smell the clinic on her, antiseptic and something floral, clinging to her clothes. He forced himself to meet her gaze. "I believe in data."

Jamie sighed, rolling her eyes. "Always with the data." She reached out, patting his shoulder. Her touch was warm. Wrong. "Lighten up. You'll live longer."

Alex set his fork down with a quiet click. "Yesterday, you called GeneVax 'corporate genetic meddling'. You said it was profit-driven experimentation wrapped in wellness branding."

Jamie blinked and laughed, light, unbothered. Her fingers brushed through her hair, the motion smooth where it should've been jagged with irritation. "Did I? That seems so foolish now." She spread her hands, palms upturned like she was presenting proof. "I've seen the benefits firsthand. No arrhythmia. No anxiety. Just...*peace.*"

"You organized a protest," Alex said, voice unemotional. "This weekend. Against healthcare monopolization."

Jamie's smile didn't waver. She adjusted the cuff of her sleeve, neat, precise. "Disruption of medical services only hurts patients." The words came out polished, recited like a recording. "Cooperation with healthcare authorities ensures optimal outcomes for everyone."

A beat of silence. The buzz of a delivery drone whirred past his window, the sound seeping through the walls.

Alex stared. This wasn't Jamie. Not the one who'd spent weeks compiling stats on LifeSpan's pricing strategies, the one who'd cursed under her breath during department meetings when Mishaal praised corporate partnerships.

The Jamie in front of him straightened, bright-eyed. "Actually, I'm volunteering at the clinic this weekend. Helping with the end-of-month surge." She said it like it was obvious, inevitable. "You should come. See what it's really like."

Alex's ankles were crossed under his chair and he tapped his toes against the floor. "This isn't you talking. That's a LifeSpan press release."

Jamie's smile faltered, her expression shifting to concern. "Alex, you're being paranoid." She approached. "You should talk to someone at the wellness center," she said, her voice softening. "They have immediate openings, priority treatment for people like you."

Her hands reached for him, sliding around his neck, her body pressing too close. The scent of the clinic, still sterile, floral, clung to her skin and stuck in the back of his throat.

Alex recoiled, stepping back.

Jamie's arms dropped. "What's wrong?"

"Nothing," he said, voice controlled. "Just tired."

She sighed. "I should go." But she didn't move immediately, her gaze lingering. "Just think about what I said, okay? The treatment helped me see things so clearly. It could help you, too."

Her words seemed unnatural, too smooth, too practiced. She turned, heading for the door, but paused one last time. "It's not too late to change your mind."

"Goodnight, Jamie."

The door closed with a soft click. Alex stood frozen, staring at the empty space where Jamie had been. The apartment felt too quiet now, the hum of the city outside suddenly oppressive.

That wasn't Jamie.

His fingers twitched at his sides. Behavioral modification didn't work like that, not that fast, not that *complete*. The clinic must've loaded her up with something, some kind of post-procedure sedative or euphoric to smooth the transition. That was the only explanation.

But the way she moved, fluid, unburdened. The way she *spoke*, like every word had been polished beforehand. Since when did Jamie refuse wine? Or his cooking? Never, not even when she was sick.

Alex exhaled sharply, turning back to his abandoned plate. The stir-fry had gone cold, the sauce congealing at the edges. He pushed it aside, appetite gone.

He'd talk to her again tomorrow. When the drugs had worn off. When she was back to herself.

The thought settled uneasily in his chest. He forced himself to move, removing the dishes with robotic programming. The fork clattered against the sink, louder than he intended. Tomorrow. He'd figure it out tomorrow.

Alex's iBand chimed, the soft tone cutting through the silence of the apartment. He tapped the 'accept' icon with stiff fingers. His mother's voice emerged from the Starkey Neural Link HearBuds nestled in his ear, warm despite the digital mediation.

"*Mijo*, you're still up?" Static threaded her words, poor signal from her apartment complex. Behind her voice, faint classical music played, something his Dad used to love, not the artificial music tailored to peoples' interests, emotionless. Orchestras swam in emotion, life, nuance, and imperfection.

Alex leaned against the counter, staring at the remains of his abandoned dinner. "Working late."

Isabella sighed. "You always say that." Weakness frayed the edges of her tone, fatigue or another flare-up of her lupus. "Did you eat?"

"Just finished." The lie came easily.

"Good. Now, tell me, that new supervisor, did he approve your data transfer request?" Concern sharpened her words. She'd spent years watching him navigate OmniHealth's labyrinthine bureaucracy.

"Denied it." Alex glanced at his darkened workstation. "Proprietary restrictions."

"That's corporate nonsense." Static hissed as she shifted position. "Richard would've, " She stopped. A sharp inhale. "Never mind." Her voice wavered.

Alex's knuckles whitened against the cool composite edge of the counter. Four years, and the absence still gouged holes in their conversations, raw spots they navigated around.

"He'd tell me to appeal through the union." A bureaucratic dead end he wouldn't bother pursuing.

A quiet laugh drifted through the connection. "And then complain for weeks when they stalled." A familiar ache laced the fondness in her voice.

Water dripped, each drop a tiny, echoing plink in the stainless steel sink basin. Alex noted the sound, an out-of-place interruption in the apartment's orderly and predictable low hum. He'd need Maintenance scheduled, another 'water waste' fine felt inevitable, otherwise.

"You should come over Sunday, *mijo*," she said, her tone shifting, warmer, pulling him from the thought. "I'll make *chilaquiles verde*. Real tortillas, stone-ground masa, the kind you like." The promise of actual home cooking, a comfort increasingly rare, and incredibly tempting.

Alex hesitated. He pictured her last Sunday, the way her hand trembled slightly picking up her water glass, the faint blue smudges beneath her eyes that no makeup could hide. Sleep deprivation bruised the hollows under her eyes then. "Next week," he suggested gently. "You sound tired."

Another sigh feathered through the connection, resigned and raspy. Alex could almost hear the flicker of the HoloScreen news ticker in her background. "It's the damn news. A third presidential term...I still can't believe they ratified that amendment." Disgust curled through her words, tightening her tone. "This whole 'Sovereignty Party' movement is a sham. If I hear one more person cheerfully chirp 'Consensus is Strength,' I'm going to be sick. Did you see what that senator proposed today? Increasing the age to collect Social Security to 85?" Her voice sharpened on the last words, a familiar blade honed by years of watching basic liberties erode. "They say it's for the 'greater good', but it's just another turn of the screw."

Alex exhaled, the tension in his own shoulders easing a fraction. The familiar refuge of her outrage, fierce, predictable, utterly *hers*, a direct line back to her own activist father railing against similar scenarios thirty years ago.

"*Siempre lo mismo.*" Her spoon clinked against ceramic, tea, probably honey-laced turmeric and ginger, his dad's old remedy for her sore joints. "Always the same. Power to the powerful." The fatigue in her voice deepened.

Alex straightened. "You should go to bed."

"You too, *mijo.*"A pause. "I miss you."

The call ended with a soft chime before he could reply. Alex methodically cleared the kitchen, rinsing each dish before placing it in the waterless sanitizer unit. The ritual calmed the racing thoughts behind his eyes. The tremor in his hands had subsided, but the unease festered like a splinter in his mind.

As he wiped down the counter, he replayed Jamie's visit in his mind. The way she'd moved. The rehearsed quality of her words. The complete absence of her usual skepticism. It wasn't just behavioral modification, it was replacement.

The apartment's gNest system dimmed the lights as he finished, responding to his circadian patterns without being asked. "Sleep protocol initiated," it announced in its modulated, feminine tone.

Alex stripped down to his boxers and slid between the cool sheets of his bed. The ceiling above him was bare. No projections, no entertainment feeds. Just darkness and the faint blue glow of standby indicators from his equipment.

His mind refused to quiet. Jamie's transformation. Dr. Rivera's cautious agreement to help. His mother's voice, frail but still fierce. The pieces were there, forming a pattern he couldn't yet fully grasp.

Sleep came reluctantly, dragging him under in fits and starts, his dreams filled with faceless crowds moving in perfect, terrible unison.

Jamie stood before Alex, her eyes shimmering with an unnatural, profound serenity, a deep, untroubled calm that was both alluring and alien. She reached out, her fingers brushing his cheek. The touch was silken, yet carried an electric promise of total peace, a soothing warmth that penetrated deep, awakening a desperate longing for an end to the struggle.

"Jamie," he whispered, his voice hoarse, a conflict of raw desire and a stark, intuitive warning.

She smiled, a soft, flawlessly-radiant expression that seemed to promise an effortless world. "Alex," she murmured, her voice a perfect, irresistible melody. "Take me... Take me now.... Let go of yourself... Become whole..."

He pulled her closer, their bodies melding with an almost mystical, engineered fit, as if his rough edges were being seamlessly integrated into her perfection. Her lips met his, and with the kiss came a profound, consuming warmth that seemed to seep into his innermost core, promising to smooth away not just anxieties, but the knots of his unique thought, the defiant edges of his self. He deepened the kiss, his hands roaming her curves, exploring contours that felt both familiar and strangely universal, as if she were a template for an idealized form.

Jamie responded with an effortless, knowing fervor, her fingers threading through his hair as she pressed herself against him. The intensity of their connection sent waves of intoxicating bliss coursing through his veins, a blissful tide designed to drown the sharp, insistent voice of his skepticism, the critical data points that defined his waking fears.

With a gentle, irresistible nudge, Jamie guided him toward the bed, her serene eyes never leaving his, reflecting a tranquil, empty sky. She sat down, her legs parting, an invitation to a flawless, uncomplicated existence. Alex swallowed, his heart pounding in his chest, a wild drum against the hypnotic pull she offered.

He lowered himself onto the bed, his body hovering above hers as he continued to explore her mouth with hungry, desperate kisses.

Jamie's hands roamed over his back, her touch less about passion and more like a recalibration, erasing his worries, urging him closer into her field of absolute calm. He could feel the heat radiating from her core, a pure, steady warmth beckoning him like a siren's call to a harbor of effortless conformity.

As their bodies entwined, the dreamscape around them dissolved into a soft, luminous void, leaving only the two of them in a cocoon of perfected sensation and dissolving thought. The world outside, with its messy truths and difficult choices, ceased to exist, replaced by the intoxicating, rhythmic pulse of their bodies and the promise of hearts beating in flawless, unquestioning unison.

Alex's hands traced a path down Jamie's body, savoring the impossible smoothness of her skin, like an organic sculpture, warm and alive yet without imperfection. He could feel a subtle, rhythmic hum emanating from her, as if she were a perfectly-tuned instrument resonating with a silent, universal frequency. Her breath came in soft, even gasps as she seemed to absorb him, offering not just her body, but a complete surrender of his burdens, his overthinking self. The sensation was intoxicating, a heady mix of undeniable power, as if delivered by tiny pinpricks of light, and the terrifying allure of his own dissolution.

He continued his exploration, his fingers investigating, seeking to unlock the secrets of the absolute serenity she embodied, the key to beautiful, thoughtless oblivion. Jamie's soft moans filled the air, harmonious notes that seemed to rewrite the dissonant soundtrack of his anxieties, affirming his passage into her state of grace. He could feel a pervasive energy building, a gentle, inexorable unfolding, a complete yielding to something vast and unburdened.

As the dream reached its crescendo, Alex hovered on the precipice of a profound, complete surrender. Here, in her embrace, was the promised world: immaculate, ordered, free of the jagged edges of doubt. The urge to yield, to become part of this seamless, untroubled design, was an overwhelming tide, threatening to wash away his vigilant core, the essential code of his being. For a moment, the fight, the data, the precarious act of questioning felt like a distant, unnecessary fault he could simply allow her to correct.

The sharp trill and vibration of his iBand jolted Alex awake. He blinked, disoriented, the remnants of the luminous, terrifyingly-seductive dream, and the silent, implicit offer it contained, slipping away like smoke. The dim glow of the HoloScreen hovered above his wrist, casting flickering, blue light across the darkened apartment. He blinked, trying to focus. Caller ID read *Dr. Maya Rivera*.

He swiped to accept, his voice rough with sleep. "Maya?"

"Alex, listen carefully." Her voice was low, urgent. "Get on ArcLink. Use the handle I'll recognize. Now."

An unease ran down his spine. "Understood." He ended the call.

Arcanum Link wasn't just another communication app. Unlike standard calls that traveled through centralized networks, Arcanum fragmented each transmission across multiple encrypted channels simultaneously. A single message would split into thousands of micro-packets, each taking different routes through mesh networks, short-range peer connections, and even disguised as background data traffic.

The system employed quantum-resistant encryption, with ephemeral keys that changed with each session. Even if one packet was intercepted, it contained only a meaningless fragment of the whole. Only the recipient's device with the correct decryption key could reassemble the original message from the scattered pieces arriving out of order across different networks.

Standard calls left metadata trails and could be decrypted with enough computing power. ArcLink's dynamic routing and multi-vector transmission made it virtually impossible to trace or reconstruct without the exact encryption key, which was never stored, only generated in the moment.

Alex opened the app, fingers flying over the holographic interface. The handle "Onco_Veritas" appeared, their old joke about medical truth. He initiated the connection, the app already scattering the first packets into the digital void.

The encrypted connection stabilized, Maya's voice emerging from the iBand into his HearBud speakers with unnatural clarity despite the layers of obfuscation. "You were right," she said, her words clipped. "I reviewed the protocols. Standard CRISPR-Cas9 edits one sequence at a time, precise, but limited. What they're using is different."

Alex's fingers tightened around the edge of his desk. "Different, how?"

"CRISPR-Cas12a." Maya's voice dropped lower. "It can target multiple gene sequences simultaneously. And the sequences they're editing, " A pause, the faintest hitch of breath, "they're neural. Regions tied to skepticism, authority response, social compliance."

Jamie's words from earlier echoed in Alex's mind: *They modified several conditions in one treatment.* He hadn't understood, hadn't *let* himself understand.

"They're engineering obedience," he said, the realization sharp as a blade.

Maya didn't deny it. "The computing power needed to map and coordinate this level of editing, it shouldn't be possible yet. But the evidence is there."

Alex exhaled, his breath ragged. The pieces locked into place: the behavioral shifts, the sudden compliance, the way Jamie had looked at him with that serene, hollow certainty. Not just treatment. *Programming.*

"And they could easily frame it," Maya continued, her voice tight, stripped of warmth by the encryption but sharp with clinical assessment. "The neural pathway adjustments are subtle in *isolatio... <buzzzz>...educed* stress markers, improved emotional regulation metrics, faster postoperative healing times due to reduced systemic *anxie.......ty.*" The word stretched unnaturally, delayed by complex data traffic routes. "They'll claim it optimizes overall wellness, enhances social integration. Plausible deniability baked right into the code."

Sterile blue light from the iBand's HoloScreen reflected in Alex's intense eyes. "Jamie was here," he cut in, the words tumbling out. "My coworker. She had the treatment earlier today."

He glanced reflexively at the time displayed on his iBand. 00:17. "Yesterday now, I guess. She came by my apartment afterward." He paused. "Maya, it was like talking to a completely different person."

Distinct silence on the other end of the secure call. Longer than the typical micro-latency of Arcanum Link. "Already?" Maya's voice held a new edge, a thread of disbelief woven with alarm. "The behavioral shifts manifested that quickly? Within hours…?"

Alex scrubbed a hand over his face, the stubble rough against his palm. "I thought maybe it was just the drugs they gave her, wearing off. Sedation, maybe." He shook his head, staring at the inert screen of data on his workstation HoloScreen.

He sat still, his mind working. "It wasn't grogginess. It was…clarity. *Their* clarity. A complete flip. Total trust in the system, in LifeSpan. She called my concerns 'paranoia'."

Maya exhaled sharply, the sound compressed and digitized through Arcanum Link's encryption. On her end, she paced the width of her darkened apartment, bare feet padding across smart-flooring that adjusted temperature to compensate for her rising core body temperature. "This isn't just standard epigenetic silencing or neurotransmitter modulation." Her medical training flattened her vowels into precise clinical pronouncements. "They're rewriting baseline regulatory structures. If this alters resistances to authority stimuli at the limbic level…" She stopped pacing.

Alex's workstation chair creaked as he leaned forward.

"We'd need to see the complete treatment schema," she said. "The actual genome alteration pathways."

"How do we get documentation Jamie wouldn't even request now?" His fingers tapped an arrhythmic pattern against his thigh. Synaptic Resonance Variance made the pause unbearable, his mind already anticipating the logical conclusion Maya would voice three seconds from now.

"She couldn't retrieve them if she wanted to."

Maya's response crushed his assumptions with analgesic certainty. The holographic display above Alex's iBand pulsed as she accessed subscriber records from Clinton Memorial's intranet.

Institutional access codes reflected in her retinas while biometric scanners in her apartment walls logged the intrusion as authorized activity. Every hospital in the metropolitan grid had identical security protocols visible only to senior staff. "There are secure archival servers at Clinton Memorial's research facility." Maya's fingers pulled schematics into the shared Arcanum workspace.

A volumetric model of the Clinton Memorial LifeSpan Genomics Research Facility rotated between them, sublevels highlighted in coolant-blue.

"Full genomic treatment logs, alteration maps, pharmacokinetic models for memetic diffusion bonding, everything," she said.

Alex zoomed into the wireframe, neural clusters firing pattern-recognition adjustments as he noted security checkpoint placements. "You're saying we break into Federal Health Security-rated infrastructure?" A muscle jumped along his jawline. His SRV misfired, presenting eight disastrous failure scenarios in under a second: armed guards, gene-locked doors, AI behavioral recognition algorithms monitoring staff movements.

"You misunderstand." Maya's voice took on the instructive tone of Grand Rounds lecturing. "I have ORBIS clearance tomorrow from seven p.m. to five a.m. when the neurology rotation changes." She tapped new data into the stream, shift schedules, maintenance logs. "We don't break in. We walk through seven layers of security because my credentials say we belong there."

The timestamp on Alex's display read 00:22 MST, 07:22 Zulu. The iBand's haptic feedback buzzed against his wrist as Maya uploaded a forged Aerospace Medical Service Apprentice role to his device. His identifying details skittered across the display, falsified retinal patterns, synthesized voice-print harmonics, even simulated pheromone markers for the scent-scanners at Biomaterial Storage entry points. None of which he would need if accompanying Dr. Rivera.

He stared at the rotating hologram of the research facility, the blue-highlighted sublevels pulsing like veins beneath skin. Maya's medical terminology had flown over his head, epigenetic silencing, limbic stimuli, pharmacokinetic models, but he recognized the inflection. It was the same rhythm he fell into when explaining data fragmentation protocols to non-tech colleagues.

He trusted her. That was the simple truth beneath the clinical jargon. Trusted her enough to walk into a federal health facility under falsified credentials. The thought sent a jolt through his nervous system, his SRV misfiring with potential failure scenarios: security checkpoints, retinal scanners, the cold certainty of handcuffs clicking around his wrists.

But Jamie's transformed face flickered behind his eyelids every time he blinked. The way her laughter had sounded wrong, like an algorithm had reconstructed it from archived samples. The way she'd touched his arm with mechanical concern, as if reading from a script titled *How to Handle the Non-Compliant.* "We'll find proof," Alex said, his voice rough. "If they built this, we can unbuild it."

Maya's holographic avatar nodded, the motion slightly delayed by Arcanum's encryption routing. "Tomorrow. Research facility rear entrance. Ten p.m." The address came across the link.

Alex exhaled. "I've got a data mule shift at LifeSpan in the afternoon. Standard OmniHealth analytics run. I have to move the data to Omni and feed it into OTTOpilot. Standard work stuff."

Maya's eyes narrowed, catching the hesitation in his voice. "Don't do anything reckless."

"Wouldn't dream of it." He forced a smirk, the expression brittle.

The call dissolved into digital static as he terminated the ArcLink connection.

CHAPTER 4

NERVE DEEP

THE COMPANY INSTASHUTTLE hummed along the corporate transit lane, its electric motors leaving no more sound than the whisper of tires on composite pavement. Alex pressed his forehead against the cool glass, watching Liberty Park blur past, manicured green spaces dotted with compliance monitors disguised as artwork. The shuttle banked hard onto Powers Boulevard, and LifeSpan Genomics erupted into view.

The structure dominated seven city blocks, a cathedral-like monument rounding into sight, a tiered ziggurat of blue-black nano-glass that caught the afternoon sun and fractured it maliciously across the street. Platinum alloy supports ribbed the exterior like exposed vasculature, feeding into botanical atriums suspended between floors where genetically-modified ivy crawled across photovoltaic surfaces. The entire complex, a dominating extremist, pulsed with barely constrained motion, as if the building itself breathed. Gateway Plaza yawned open ahead.

The shuttle slowed. Fifty-foot waterfalls sheeted down the western facade, vaporizing into mist before touching pavement. Irrigation for the surrounding bioengineered maples and imported lotus systems, no doubt. The water probably came from the LifeSpan Hydro Solutions filtration plant on Lake Superior. Calculation ticked at the back of

Alex's skull, estimated daily cost of maintaining this aesthetic alone could run Clinton Memorial's pediatric wing for a fiscal quarter. Zero hard stops for water rationing here. Across the cerulean reflecting pools, automated security gates arched like bared teeth.

The rear doors slid open. Three OmniHealth compliance officers disembarked ahead of Alex, their shoe soles clicking uniformly on the shuttle stairs. One of them glanced back, face impassive beneath the brim of a corporate logo cap.

"Thompson. You're on dock 14-B. OTTOpilot data transfer protocols."

Alex dipped his chin without speaking and stepped onto the plaza. The air smelled ionized, like wet stone and engineered bamboo. Around him, uniforms moved in synchronized streams toward the gates: Tech Division royal blue, Wet Lab citrine, Security black. His own OmniHealth whites clung synthetic-tight to his shoulders. He tugged at the collar and veered left toward the loading docks where pallets of agricultural crates stamped with LifeSpan AgriFuture barcodes waited under drone surveillance.

Beyond the façade, something vast and patient flexed beneath orderly foot traffic and humming delivery belts. The automated doors slid open with a pneumatic hiss, revealing the sterile white interior of the LifeSpan lobby.

A two-wheeled attendant bot rolled forward on gyroscopic stabilizers, its sensor array flashing green as it scanned Alex's iBand. "Welcome back, Mr. Thompson," chirped the machine in a synthetic voice. "Your credentials are verified. Please follow me."

Alex fell into step behind the bot as it navigated through the atrium. The polished floor reflected the overhead lighting, creating an illusion of walking on glass. They passed rows of employees seated at workstations, their fingers walking across holographic interfaces that hovered above their desks.

The attendant led him to a circular security portal, a revolving door made of reinforced polymer. The bot paused at the threshold. "Biometric authentication required," it announced before rolling away.

Alex pressed his palm against the scanner. A beam of blue light passed over his retina. The system beeped approval and the door began to rotate, carrying him into a small chamber. The walls were lined with keypads and biometric readers. He entered his twelve-digit access code on the glowing interface and placed his thumb on the DNA scanner. A second later, the chamber rotated again, aligning with an exit portal.

The final room contained only a single workstation, a sleek, black console with a holographic display already booting up. The air hummed with the sound of cooling fans as the system initialized. A retinal scan confirmed his clearance level, and the terminal came to life with a chime, presenting the standard login screen.

Alex settled into the chair, the cool metal of the terminal pressing against his forearms. The data transfer ports hummed to life, their needle-thin bio-interfaces extending with a quiet mechanical whir. He exhaled sharply as the needles pierced his skin, the sharp sting cutting through the numbing agent applied upon entry. A brief flicker of discomfort crossed his face before he forced his expression into neutrality.

His fingers twitched as the connection locked in, the faint electric tingle of the neural interface syncing with his nervous system. He lifted his hands, watching as the HoloScreen flared to life, a cascade of data flooding across its surface in a blur of text, schematics, and encrypted logs. The sheer volume was staggering, millions of patient records, treatment protocols, and behavioral analyses streaming past faster than any human could process.

The first wave hit his mind like a static shock, raw data funneling through his ulnar nerve, bypassing conscious thought and embedding itself in the neural pathways reserved for deep processing. His vision blurred for a fraction of a second as his brain adjusted, the sensation not unlike the disorientation of stepping into a room too bright after hours in darkness.

He focused on the screen, eyes tracking the endless scroll of information. Names, genetic markers, compliance metrics, all of it flowing in an unbroken river of numbers and code. Somewhere in that deluge were the anomalies he'd been hunting, the inconsistencies that didn't fit LifeSpan's perfect narrative.

A timer appeared in the corner of the display, twenty-seven minutes remaining. He flexed his fingers, the faint ache in his arms a constant reminder of the connection. The hum of the server banks around him filled the silence, a low, rhythmic pulse beneath the rush of data. For now, there was nothing to do but wait.

A flicker of movement in the data stream caught Alex's eye, a pattern that didn't belong. His fingers moved before his mind could process it, halting the flow of information. The screen stuttered and reversed, scrolling backward through the endless stream of records.

The words "Priority Treatment Candidates" flashed at the top of the screen. A list scrolled by names, professions, and behavioral markers. Journalists. Community organizers. Protest participants. His breath hitched as he spotted Jamie's name among them, tagged with a red flag for 'persistent skepticism toward corporate messaging'.

His fingers flew across the interface, pulling up the search function. He typed in his own parameters: *Data analysts with pattern-recognition aptitude and authority-questioning tendencies.* The system processed the request and spat back a single result.

Alex Thompson.

His stomach dropped. The screen displayed his employee ID, his SRV classification, and even notes from his supervisor about 'excessive scrutiny of proprietary datasets'. A cold realization settled over him. This wasn't just a wellness program. It was designed to identify and neutralize dissent.

The intercom beeped, the sharp electronic chirp making Alex flinch. His fingers hovered over the keyboard, the glow of the screen casting shadows across his face. A voice crackled through the speaker, smooth, professional, with a faint oriental accent. "Mr. Thompson? Are you finding everything you need?"

Alex's breath hitched. His pulse hammered in his throat. Shit. Was she watching him? That wasn't possible. Nobody could pick up on anomalies this quickly, not without AI monitoring. Automated systems didn't track data transfers or mule assignments. He forced a steady exhale. "Just pulling the quarterly compliance reports," he said, keeping his voice even.

"Excellent!" the voice on the other end said cheerfully, almost too bright. "By the way, Dr. Mercer mentioned you haven't scheduled your wellness treatment yet." A pause. "The company is very enthusiastic about 100% participation." The note of concern didn't quite reach her tone.

Alex swallowed. His fingers twitched toward the keyboard, itching to close the files, to wipe the evidence of what he'd found. Instead, he leaned back in his chair, forcing a casual shrug. "Still considering it. Family scheduling issues."

"I'd be happy to find you a VIP slot, even this afternoon." She was rather insistent.

"I can't today, I need to get this data back and have a lot to sort through before the day is over, but thank you!" He despised pretending to be grateful nearly as much as he loathed company gatherings. Perhaps that was why he detested such events, because he had to feign interest in being around others.

The silence stretched too long. "Of course," the voice returned, still pleasant, but with an edge. "We understand. But we do encourage you to prioritize your health." A soft click as the intercom disconnected.

Alex stared at the screen, the words *Priority Treatment Candidates* still glowing back at him. The screen flickered with a countdown timer. Six minutes remaining. Alex exhaled, rubbing his eyes as the numbers ticked lower.

The glow of the display left faint afterimages on his vision. He reached for the console, fingers hovering over the interface before tapping the command to close the session. The holographic projection dissolved into static, leaving the terminal dark.

He pushed back from the workstation, the chair rolling a few inches across the polished floor. A dull ache pulsed at his temples. Too many hours parsing encrypted logs under artificial light. The hydration dispenser hummed to life next to him, its sensor detecting his proximity. He pulled a glass from the stack and held it beneath the spout. The machine dispensed a stream of chilled water, infused with a subtle cucumber essence, another perk of LifeSpan's wellness program. The scent was crisp, almost clinical.

Alex took a slow sip, the cool liquid doing little to ease the tightness in his throat. His reflection wavered in the glass, dark circles under his eyes, the tension in his jaw. He set the drink down too hard, breaking the sterile quiet of the secure room.

He ran a finger around the edge of the glass. The evidence was undeniable to him, but others would require more. Alex resolved to analyze this latest data and incorporate it with whatever he and Dr. Rivera might uncover later that night.

A chime from the terminal caught his attention, an alert from the building's security system. His data transfer was finished. The exit room began to rotate, aligning the exit portal. It halted with a thud.

The neural link connectors silently retracted from Alex's arms, the needle-thin interfaces sliding free of his ulnar nerve and skin. A faint sting lingered where they'd been embedded, but it was already fading beneath the numbing agent's lingering effects. He reached for the sterile bandages on the console's dispenser, peeling back their packaging.

The adhesive strips adhered to the small puncture wounds at his inner elbows, sealing them off from potential contaminants. He pressed each one firmly in place, ensuring a tight seal. The process was routine by now. He'd done this dozens of times before, though never with quite this feeling of importance about the data he was transporting.

The sterile smell of antiseptic filled his nostrils as he worked, and a faint, bitter taste remained in his mouth. He could feel it more than taste it. Around him, the hum of the server banks continued its constant drone, the only sound in the otherwise-silent room. His fingers moved automatically, smoothing the edges of the second bandage. They would dissolve into his skin within hours, closing the opening without worry of infection or further attention.

The workstation beeped once, signaling the completion of its shutdown sequence. The holographic display winked, leaving only the dim orange glow of emergency lighting. A dim white light faded up in brightness. Alex flexed his fingers, testing the mobility of his arms now that the connections were removed. The slight stiffness would fade within minutes, another side effect of the neural interface the company assured was perfectly normal.

He stood, rolling his shoulders to work out the tension which had settled there during the session. The chair slid back into its recessed position beneath the console with a quiet click. His reflection in the darkened screen showed the same face he saw every day, the same tired eyes, the same set jaw, but something about it felt different now.

Alex finished the rest of the water and placed the glass into the recycler. The glass was pulled from his hand, followed by a spray of sterilizing mist. Alex rubbed his hands together, flexed them once, and turned toward the exit. The dull taste in his mouth started to subside. The files needed to be transferred back to Omni, and he was the medium.

Twenty minutes later, Alex sat in the passenger compartment of the InstaShuttle. It hummed as it glided through the city, its automated navigation system adjusting speed to match the flow of traffic. The dim interior lights cast a pale glow over the other commuters. The air was cool, filtered, and carrying the faint scent of synthetic leather and air conditioning.

A screen embedded in the seat back flickered to life, displaying the latest news feed. A reporter's voice cut through the quiet murmur of the shuttle's passengers. "Breaking news: authorities have confirmed that an attempted breach at the Rocky Mountain Seed Vault has been thwarted. Security forces apprehended several individuals attempting to access restricted areas. Officials claim the suspects were linked to recent eco-terrorist activity."

Alex's fingers tightened around the armrest. The footage showed masked figures being led away in restraints, their faces obscured by black fabric. The camera panned to a government spokesperson standing before a podium, her expression stern.

"This was not an act of protest, it was sabotage. These individuals sought to destroy a vital global resource. Their actions would have endangered food security for millions."

A second reporter chimed in, his tone skeptical. "Yet some are questioning the official narrative. Independent analysts note that the vault's security systems were upgraded just weeks ago, raising concerns about why this breach was even possible."

Alex exhaled slowly, watching as the broadcast shifted to footage of the seed vault itself, its massive steel doors, the reinforced walls built into the mountainside. The image flickered and changed to a different segment, an interview with a scientist from LifeSpan Genomics. "Our research into genetic optimization is about ensuring resilience," the man said smoothly. "With climate instability increasing, we must take proactive measures to protect our food supply. The Seed Vault is one piece of that puzzle."

Alex's jaw tightened. The pieces were falling into place. LifeSpan's involvement, the sudden push for compliance, the suppression of dissent. He glanced at the other passengers. Some watched the broadcast with mild interest, others scrolled through their own feeds, indifferent.

The shuttle slowed as it approached the next stop, the automated voice announcing the upcoming station. The doors slid open, letting in a brief rush of noise and heat from the platform before sealing shut again. Alex pulled up the current weather on his iBand, 42.3°C. A side note popped up, the number of days above forty degrees C was already up nineteen days more than last year.

The InstaShuttle doors slid open, and Alex stepped out into the oppressive heat. The air shimmered above the pavement, the sun beating down with relentless intensity. He adjusted his collar, already feeling sweat pricking at his temples. *It is hot today.*

The thought was automatic, a mundane observation that barely registered beneath the thoughts of his name on a targeted priority list. Plus, his mind was still tangled in the dream, Jamie's hands on him, her breath warm against his skin, the way she wiggled beneath him with something between hunger and amusement. The memory sent an unwelcome jolt of heat through him, one that had nothing to do with the weather.

He kept his head down as he moved toward the entrance of Omni-Health, scanning the crowd for any sign of Jamie. The last thing he needed was to run into her now, not when his thoughts were still clouded by the dream. Worse, he wasn't sure what he would say if she *had* changed after the procedure. Would she look at him with that eerie calm, the same way she had when she'd praised LifeSpan's treatments?

The automatic doors hissed open, and the blast of air conditioning hit him. It was almost too cold, like he needed a jacket inside the building but wouldn't dare wear it outside. Inside, the lobby was a controlled chaos of employees moving between floors, security scanning badges, and receptionists directing visitors. He swiped his iBand over the sensor, barely registering the soft chime of approval before stepping through the turnstile.

He took the stairs instead of the elevator, needing the extra seconds to compose himself. His breath came a little too fast, his pulse thrumming in his throat. *Just get to your desk. Keep your head down. Don't think about it.*

But the image of Jamie from his dream flickered behind his eyelids, her fingers tracing his jaw, the way she had whispered his name, before dissolving into the memory of her standing in his apartment, her smile too bright, her words too directed.

The stairwell door clicked shut behind Alex, the sound swallowed by the low, pervasive hum of the OmniHealth Analytics office floor. Conditioned air, chilled to a precise corporate standard, brushed against his skin, a stark contrast to the baking street outside. Rows of workstations stretched under the flat, even lighting, analysts already immersed in glowing data streams projected by their terminals. The rhythmic tap of fingers on integrated keyboards formed a steady counterpoint to the ventilation's drone. A faint, clean scent, something synthesized to enhance productivity, resided in the recirculated air.

Alex kept his gaze fixed ahead, forcing his focus away from the lingering warmth of the dream, the unsettling memory of Jamie's altered smile. He scanned the layout, his path predetermined. His workstation sat two rows over, near the window overlooking the automated traffic lanes below. But his destination lay deeper within the building's core: the Secure Data Transfer Suite.

He moved with purpose, his worn sneakers silent on the industrial-grade carpet. He passed colleagues, some nodding a brief, impersonal greeting, others entirely absorbed in their work. He noted the quiet efficiency, the almost unnerving lack of casual chatter that usually marked the start of the day. A few faces seemed smoother, their expressions placid, echoing the change he'd seen in Jamie. Or was that just his SRV-fueled pattern recognition working overtime, seeking connections where none existed? The data didn't lie.

His route took him past the central collaboration hub, a space designed for interaction with modular seating and large display walls. Jamie sat there, perched on a stool, speaking with two other analysts. Her blonde hair gleamed under the office lights, her posture poised, her smile bright and unwavering. She gestured gracefully as she spoke, her blue eyes alight with serene confidence.

The sharp wit, the restless energy he knew, vanished. Replaced by this polished, agreeable shell. Alex felt a muscle jump in his jaw. He altered his course slightly, putting a bank of servers between himself and the hub, his heart rate accelerating despite his effort at control. Seeing her, so vividly *changed*, solidified the abstract horror of the data into a gut-level certainty.

He reached the restricted access corridor leading to the specialized suites. A secondary optical scanner glowed green above the reinforced door. Alex held his OmniHealth ID, embedded within his iBand, up to the reader. A soft click echoed in the narrow passage as the lock disengaged. The door slid open smoothly, revealing a short hallway lined with brushed metal panels. Another checkpoint waited at the far end.

He continued, the silence amplifying the sound of his own breathing. This section of the building felt different, colder, quieter, the air circulation system generating a deeper thrum. He reached the final door, marked *Secure Data Transfer Suite - Authorized Personnel Only*. He placed his palm flat against the biometric reader beside it. Internal mechanisms whirred faintly. After a moment, the light shifted from red to green. Access granted.

The door slid aside to reveal a small, windowless room. The walls were covered in acoustic foam with a metallic net designed to dampen sound and block electromagnetic signals. The specialized terminal was bolted to a heavy desk on the back wall. The air felt heavy and still as Alex stepped inside. The door hissed shut and sealed him within the secure chamber. This was it. The place to move the damning evidence he pulled from LifeSpan's network. He approached the terminal, the slight tremor in his hands returning as he reached for the console.

Commanding the chamber was a substantial, body-conforming seat surrounded by movable mechanical limbs capped with intricate detection equipment. A smooth, dome-shaped apparatus remained suspended over where his head went. This represented OmniHealth's benchmark for high-capacity, non-penetrative brain data retrieval: the High-Resolution Magnetoencephalography (MEG) Decoder station. No punctures, no direct neural connections, merely extraordinarily sensitive magnetic detectors engineered to capture the subtle biological signatures produced by neural-encoded information. It depended on advanced artificial intelligence, coordinated by OTTOpilot (Optimized Task & Transaction Orchestrator), Microsoft's ubiquitous AI engine, to rebuild the data from delicate, cluttered signals. And it operated frustratingly slowly.

Alex moved toward the seat, the subtle aroma of electrical discharge and sanitized synthetic materials tickling his senses. He inhaled deeply, the unpleasant flavor he connected with the LifeSpan procedure still lingering faintly in his memory. He eased into the chair, feeling the cool surface against his spine. The control interface embedded in the armrest illuminated, showing the OmniHealth emblem before requesting verification. He finished the layered security process, finishing with a sophisticated password entered on the floating HoloScreen keyboard.

OTTOpilot's recognizable, impartial voice sounded gently through the room's audio system, connected via his Neural Link. "Verification complete, Alex. Secure Neural Data Offload protocol activated. Please remain motionless during calibration."

The dome descended smoothly, surrounding his head without contact. He experienced no sharp pain, no electrical sensation like the LifeSpan connection, just the subtle hum of the scanner's temperature regulation and the gentle pressure of the cushioned headrest adapting to his cranium. On the HoloScreen projected in front of him, calibration images flashed.

"Baseline brain function recorded," OTTOpilot declared after sixty seconds. "Brain wave profile compared. Targeting peripheral nervous pathways for LifeSpan data encoding signature. Starting concentrated scan and decode sequence."

A completion indicator materialized on the HoloScreen. Underneath, the predicted duration crystallized: *10 hours, 24 minutes.*

Alex's core tensed. Almost ten and a half hours. He'd begun shortly after 10:30 a.m. He needed to exit, data secured, well before departing for his scheduled ten p.m. arrival at LifeSpan for the *subsequent* stage of his desperate strategy. Ten and a half hours confined to this seat, physically bound to the extraction procedure, while 6.8 petabytes of damning evidence gradually, laboriously decoded itself from the channels of his nervous system.

The profound inefficiency irritated him. The LifeSpan neural connection, invasive though it was, avoided all this. It functioned as a direct information conduit, injecting data at near-physical boundaries. This MEG technique resembled attempting to reconstruct a library murmured through dense barriers.

Detecting the faint magnetic reflections of neural patterns non-invasively, separating signal from interference, the vast processing requirements of the AI interpreting terabytes from biological murmurs, it represented a technological wonder, but measured against the raw velocity of getting needles in the elbows, it seemed like punishment. For a brief, ridiculous instant, he nearly wished he *could* simply reconnect for fifteen minutes, despite the intrusion it symbolized.

The progress indicator barely showed its initial fraction of a percentage. The subtle magnetic impulses created by the stored information were being detected, strengthened, cleaned, and directed into the local AI, OTTOpilot managing the sophisticated decoding operation, rebuilding the digital content bit by excruciating bit. It stood as the opposite of the ruthless efficiency at LifeSpan, the quarter-hour forced data injection that felt like an assault. This was deliberate, meticulous, non-invasive...and left him vulnerable for an eternity.

He reclined, compelling his muscles to loosen. Nothing remained but to endure, observe the microscopic advancement of the progress bar, and try to avoid contemplating everything that might fail during the next ten hours. The MEG Decoder chair hummed softly around Alex, a low, resonant frequency that vibrated through the frame and into his bones. He settled deeper into the contouring foam, the enforced stillness grating against his restless energy. The slight tremor in his hands, usually manageable, felt amplified in the quiet confinement. The air in the suite remained cool, sterile, unchanging.

He needed a distraction. Something to occupy the analytical part of his brain that wasn't currently being meticulously scanned. With the effortless dexterity of a veteran analyst, his fingers traced precise gestures in the air, manipulating the HoloScreen controls projected by the MEG station's integrated system. He bypassed OmniHealth's internal network feeds, opting for a public source. The icon for INN, the Interactive News Network, pulsed invitingly. He selected it.

The HoloScreen flickered, resolving into the familiar news interface, sleek, customizable. Dominating the center was the default anchor avatar, a woman named Anya Sharma, rendered with unsettling photorealism. Her digital eyes blinked; her posture shifted subtly. She waited, ready to respond to his queries. Below her, trending headlines scrolled: corporate earnings reports, updates on atmospheric particulate levels, celebrity gossip rendered in lurid 3D.

"Anya, show me top stories related to the Rocky Mountain Seed Vault incident," Alex subvocalized, the command picked up by the Neural Link connected to the station.

"Accessing relevant reports on the attempted security breach at the Global Heritage Seed Repository, formerly NORAD,"

The main display shifted. The footage Alex had seen on the shuttle reappeared, the restrained figures, the stern official, the LifeSpan scientist offering placid reassurances. Text summaries and links to related articles materialized beside the video feed. He scanned the headlines: *Eco-Terror Network Dismantled, LifeSpan Praises Security Response, Questions Linger Over Vault Vulnerabilities.*

His eyes caught a specific detail in a background article about the facility's history. "Focus on the location," Alex instructed. "Tell me more about the facility."

The avatar tilted her head slightly, processing the request. "The Cheyenne Mountain Complex, commonly known by its former designation NORAD, is a fortified military command center built during the Cold War. Its primary function was aerospace warning and control. Designation, *North American Aerospace Defense Command*."

Archive footage replaced the current news stream. Grainy black and white images showed massive blast doors set into the mountainside, construction crews working deep underground. Diagrams illustrated the multi-level bunker complex, designed to withstand nuclear attack.

"Following extensive decommissioning and retrofitting in the late 2020s," Anya continued, her tone unchanging. "The facility was repurposed. Portions were transferred to private consortiums, including LifeSpan AgriFuture, which co-manages the Global Heritage Seed Repository established within the deepest, most secure levels. Public access is heavily restricted, citing biological security protocols and infrastructure sensitivity."

"Are there public records detailing the transfer of ownership or the specific sections controlled by LifeSpan?" Alex asked, leaning forward slightly, forgetting the enforced stillness for a moment.

"Accessing public domain records... Records indicate a phased transfer beginning in 2028 under the Strategic Resource Preservation Act. Specific operational control details within the secure zones are classified under corporate and national security provisions." Anya paused, her digital projected eyes meeting his gaze. "Would you like me to search for analysis regarding the security implications of private corporations managing former strategic military assets?"

Alex exhaled through his nose, the muscles around his eyes tightening. The AI's prompt, polished, helpful, *leading*, was exactly the kind of frictionless redirection that made his teeth ache. It wasn't a question. It was a nudge. A suggestion of what he *should* care about next.

"Disregard," he said, sharper than necessary. "Search Terrakin. Full profile."

Anya's avatar blinked once, the delay imperceptible to most. The HoloScreen dissolved the military schematics, reassembling into a new grid of data, satellite stills of arid landscapes, protest footage, mugshots with hard-eyed faces.

"Terrakin," Anya recited. "Designated eco-terrorist network by the Federal Security Bureau in 2034. Primary operations: sabotage of corporate agricultural sites, disruption of LifeSpan AgriFuture supply chains, and attempted infiltration of secured seed repositories. Core ideology rejects synthetic and genetically modified food systems, advocating for pre-industrial subsistence models. Suspected base of operations: the disputed territories of the Independent Republic of Northern New Mexico."

Alex's fingers twitched against the armrest. The mugshots zoomed, a man with sun-leathered skin and a scar bisecting his eyebrow, a woman with her dark hair braided tight against her skull. No names listed. No trial records. Just *suspected, alleged, believed to be affiliated.*

"Show me their manifesto. Original source, not summaries."

A document flickered into existence, text rendered in a blocky, utilitarian font. No flourishes. No hyperlinks. Just words: *"You patent life. You splice it, package it, sell it back to us sterile. You call this progress. We call it theft. The soil remembers what you erase. The seeds remember what you alter. We are the reminder.*

Alex skimmed further. No demands for ransom. No political bargaining. Just a declaration of war against the machinery of corporate agriculture, against LifeSpan's monopoly on what grew, what lived, what fed the world.

The MEG Decoder's progress bar inched to 0.39%.

"Cross-reference," Alex said.

"Terrakin activity and GeneVax rollout in the Southwest regions. Overlay timelines."

The display split. On one side, red markers plotted Terrakin incidents, equipment vandalized, storage silos breached. On the other, a rising blue curve charted GeneVax adoption rates. The lines didn't just intersect, they mirrored. Every spike in Terrakin attacks preceded a surge in vaccinations by weeks. "Correlation does not imply causation." Anya's voice remained smooth. "Would you like demographic data on regional, "

"Stop." Alex clenched his jaw. The AI's insistence on *context*, on *balance*, was just another form of control. A way to sand the edges off inconvenient patterns.

He stared at the mugshots again. The scarred man's gaze was direct, unapologetic. Not the look of someone who'd been pacified by a needle. The progress bar hit 0.4%.

Nine hours and fifty-six minutes to go. Alex's fingers continued their rhythmic dance across the holographic interface, pulling up report after report. The data streams blurred together - security logs, employee records, shipment manifests, all painting the same picture of LifeSpan's expanding influence. His eyes followed the glowing blue text as it scrolled endlessly, the words becoming a soothing rhythm of facts and figures.

The dim lighting of the secure data suite softened the harsh edges of the machinery around him. The chair's subtle vibrations from the MEG decoder created a gentle hum that vibrated through his body. His eyelids became heavier with each passing minute.

The numbers on the screen began to swim before his tired eyes, the columns of data merging into indistinct shapes. His head nodded forward slightly before jerking back up as he fought to maintain focus. In the glow of the HoloScreen, his blinks became longer, more frequent.

Suddenly, he was falling, not through air, but through thick, warm static that resonated with the faint tremor in his own hands. Jamie was there, blonde hair catching non-existent light, her smile impossibly white, achingly familiar yet somehow contorted. She was laughing, the sound echoing like the cheerful GeneVax jingle, and reaching for him. He wanted her, the old wanting, sharp and sudden. She leaned closer, whispering his name, or was it '*Axel*'? Her breath smelled faintly of peppermint and hand sanitizer.

Her lips parted and he leaned in, but instead of warmth, there was only the cool, smooth surface of the MEG cowl pressing against his forehead in the waking world. In the dream, Jamie pulled back slightly, her expression shifting from allure to that placid, post-treatment calm he dreaded. She spread her legs, not in invitation, but like an anatomical display. Where her warmth should be, something dark pulsed, unfurling like damp fern fronds or the slick chitin of an insect's limb. Thin, shimmering tentacles, tipped with needle points like the Life-Span interface, reached for him, coiling around his wrists, pulling him forward between her legs.

He struggled, but the static thickened, vibrating with the taunts of children on a long-ago playground. 'Pattern-boy can't catch the ball!' His mother's face flashed before him, her expression worried, lines of pain etched deep, then smoothing out unnaturally, her eyes reflecting the same placid emptiness as Jamie's. Dr. Rivera stood beside her, nodding calmly, her professional gaze assessing his struggle without empathy, her mouth forming words he couldn't hear over the rising hum. His father appeared for a moment, back turned, walking away into swirling data streams.

The tentacles tightened, pulling him inexorably toward Jamie, toward the hairy darkness at her center. There was the sound of a fan with a wire stuck in the blades that felt like electrical hum and the chair's vibration combined. He was being drawn in, consumed, not by passion, but by an inevitable, horrifying integration. The last thing he saw before jolting slightly in the chair, the cool plastic of the cowl a grounding reality, was the reflection of his own wide, terrified eyes in Jamie's vacant blue ones. Her naked form was on the HoloScreen before him, motioning for him to come closer.

Alex jolted awake, his body jerking against the restraints of the chair. The MEG scanner hummed steadily around him, its soft blue glow casting an eerie light across the dimly-lit room. His breath came in short gasps as he struggled to orient himself, the remnants of the dream still clinging to his thoughts.

"Please remain still," the AI's voice intoned, smooth and emotionless. "The procedure is nearly complete."

Blinking rapidly, Alex forced himself to focus on the holographic display floating before him. The numbers swam into clarity, three minutes and nine seconds remaining. His brow furrowed. Had he really been asleep for hours? The last thing he remembered was watching the progress bar crawl forward, his mind wandering as exhaustion took hold.

The display flickered, updating to 2:58. The numbers ticked down with agonizing slowness. Alex flexed his fingers, feeling the slight tremor that always lingered in his hands. His mouth was dry, his tongue sticking to the roof of his mouth. He swallowed hard, trying to ignore the lingering unease from the dream.

"Please refrain from movement. Finalizing data transfer," the AI repeated, its voice calm and measured.

Alex exhaled slowly, forcing his muscles to relax. 1:22. The display flickered once more, the numbers shifting with mechanical precision.

The countdown continued. The hum reached a crescendo, 0:03. The machine emitted a final, high-pitched beep. The hum faded away, replaced by the quiet murmur of the facility's ventilation system. The display flashed green, the words *Transfer Complete* appearing in crisp white letters.

"Procedure complete. You may now exit the station."

He exhaled sharply, running a hand through his hair. The dream was already fading, the details slipping away like water through his fingers. All that remained was the data, the proof he needed. The display flickered once more, showing the file size and transfer status. Everything was there, intact. .09% data loss. Anything less than two percent was considered outstanding.

Alex instinctively calculated, two percent of a 6.8 petabyte is .136 petabyte, or 136 terabytes. At .09% he had only lost... Why couldn't he think? 6.12 terabytes. It made his data quota overage of eighteen terabytes seem not so far out of reason.

He checked the time, 8:59 p.m. He had transferred...his fingers twitched and flicked on his palms, *6,793.88 terabytes* in ten hours, twenty minutes. That was...fingers working...colors visualized in his brain... a transfer rate of *.183 terabytes per second, TB/s*. The mental arithmetic soothed his racing mind and the general post-transfer lethargy.

He stood, his legs unsteady beneath him. The room was silent except for the hum of the machines. He took a deep breath, steadying himself. He needed to meet Dr. Rivera.

The door to the data suite slid open with a whisper, revealing the dim hallway beyond. Alex stepped forward, his mind already turning to the next phase of the plan. The AI's voice followed him, a final greeting. "Thank you for your cooperation, Axel."

He didn't look back. There was no time. The clock was ticking.

CHAPTER 5

THE PROTOCOL

THE AUTOCAB WHISPERED to a stop beside a featureless service entrance, tucked away at the rear of the sprawling Clinton Memorial LifeSpan Genomics Research Facility. The facility consisted of three towers, each over ten stories, connected by a single two- or three- story structure spanning about a quarter of a block. The complex was larger than Antlers Park, adjacent to the West. It was a monument of sterile, white composite panels and darkened sensor arrays under the muted glow of sodium lamps. Alex exited the vehicle, the door sighing shut behind him. The hot night air only added to the fatigue clinging to him after the long hours in the MEG scanner.

Dr. Maya Rivera stood near the entrance, a silhouette against the faint light spilling from a high window. Her posture was straight, professional even in the shadows. Alex checked his iBand display. 10:02 p.m.. A knot formed low in his gut. He hated inefficiency, especially his own.

Maya glanced down at her own wrist, the smooth curve of her iBand catching the light. She looked up at Alex, her expression unreadable in the dimness, but the slight tilt of her head conveyed a clear message. He offered a small, apologetic shrug.

She moved toward him, pressing a folded white lab coat and a plastic ID card into his hands. The card felt rigid and sharp. Official. "Put these on. Try to look like you belong here."

Alex unfolded the coat. The synthetic fabric felt crisp. He slipped it over his dark clothes, the collar stiff against his neck. He clipped the ID to the coat's pocket. Lambda-73841-beta-gamma. A stranger's credentials. He wasn't sure what 'belonging' looked like in a place like this. He smoothed the front of the coat, a useless gesture.

Maya turned to the entrance, a solid slab of brushed metal seamlessly integrated into the wall. No visible handles, only a narrow, vertical slit glowing with soft blue light beside it. Embedded sensors dotted the frame, dark eyes on the pale surface.

"Alright, listen." Maya kept her voice low, pitched just above the ambient city noise. "LifeSpan poured resources into hardening the perimeter. Getting in is the hard part." She raised her wrist toward the glowing slit. Her iBand pulsed faintly. "Standard entry requires an iBand handshake."

A quiet chime emanated from the door mechanism.

"The system verifies credentials, but it's also cross-referencing continuous biometric feeds. Heart rate variability, skin conductivity, gait recognition profiles captured by external sensors. It wants to know the authorized user is the one actually wearing the band, alive, and not under duress."

The blue light beside the door shifted to green. With a near-silent release of pressure, the heavy door slid open, revealing a brightly-lit, sterile corridor beyond.

"They built a crunchy outer shell," Maya continued, stepping inside. Alex followed, the door gliding shut behind them. The sudden brightness made him blink. White walls, polished grey floor, the faint scent of wet paint and popcorn.

"Impressive deterrents at every main access point. But once you're past the initial layer, internal security gets surprisingly lax in the older wings. Budget allocation, I suppose. More focus on preventing entry than tracking movement once inside." She gestured down the empty corridor. "And the best part for us? Most of these internal checkpoints haven't been updated with exit scanners yet. Once we're in the research annex records room, getting out is simpler. For now."

They walked. The corridor stretched ahead, an unnervingly perfect line of polished floor tiles reflecting the even, shadowless ceiling lights. White walls met grey floor met white ceiling in sharp, clean angles. The air hummed faintly, a low thrum of ventilation systems circulating chilled, filtered air. Each footstep echoed slightly, the only disruption to the profound quiet. Alex matched Maya's steady pace, the borrowed lab coat rustling softly. He scanned the identical, unmarked doors they passed, his analyst brain cataloging the symmetry, the lack of distinguishing features. It felt less like a building and more like an extruded schematic. Miles of hallway, seemingly endless.

Maya halted without warning. Her sudden stillness broke the rhythm of their movement. They stood before another door, identical to the others yet somehow distinct. No glowing slit this time, just a flat, recessed panel set flush into the wall beside it, dark glass covering intricate sensors. Below the panel, a small, concave receptacle pulsed with a faint internal light.

Finally, Alex thought. *My turn.* The sterile order, the rigid protocols, this was a language he understood. Data security. Access control. The heart of the system.

"This is it," Maya breathed, her voice barely disturbing the quiet. "Secure Records Access. Level Five clearance required. This one checks more than just your pulse." She leaned toward the dark panel. "Rapid Genetic Marker Verification," she explained, her voice low.

"Forget the iBand handshake. This looks deeper. It needs confirmation of specific, unique genetic markers tied to the authorized personnel." She indicated the concave receptacle. "Breath Condensate Analysis. Exhale onto the sensor. It pulls trace DNA from the moisture, cross-references key sequences against the internal database. Fast, non-invasive, and extremely difficult to fool."

Maya took a measured breath and leaned forward, placing her mouth close to the receptacle. She exhaled slowly, steadily. The internal light within the sensor flared briefly, shifting from a soft white to an intense blue and back to white. A low, resonant click sounded from within the wall.

The heavy door slid sideways with pneumatic force, revealing a compact room bathed in the cool, blue glow of active machinery. Racks of servers lined one wall, their indicator lights blinking in complex patterns. Dominating the center of the room was a large, ergonomic workstation. The main display flickered to life as they entered, the LifeSpan Genomics logo resolving against a dark background before dissolving into a complex diagnostic screen. The system sensed their entry, anticipating commands.

Maya stepped aside, gesturing toward the console. The air inside felt colder, charged with the hum of processing power. "Alright, Alex. You know data systems better than anyone. Get in there. Find Jamie Schaffer's file. I need to see exactly which markers they targeted. We need proof of the CRISPR edits."

Alex stepped up to the workstation. The chair hissed softly as he adjusted its height. His hands moved over the integrated control surfaces, fingers navigating holographic key fields projected onto the cool metal desk. The main display erupted in cascading lines of code, schematics, and dense blocks of text – raw data streams scrolling past at a velocity that defied normal comprehension. Symbols flashed, windows opened and closed, algorithms executed in bursts of light and shifting diagrams.

Maya stood back, watching him. Her own medical knowledge, her understanding of complex biological systems, felt clumsy and inadequate faced with this digital deluge. Alex leaned closer to the screen, his blue eyes tracking the torrent of information. He pushed unruly strands of dark hair back from his forehead, his concentration absolute. The slight tremor in his hands was barely visible as they danced over the controls. He navigated layers of security protocols, bypassed firewalls, and queried databases with instinctive speed. He wasn't just searching, he was pattern-matching on a scale that felt inhuman.

Maya had treated patients with neurological variations her entire career. Conditions once labeled disabilities were now understood as different architectures, alternative ways of processing the world. Alex's

SRV enhanced certain cognitive functions, sharpened his ability to see connections invisible to others, but complicated social interactions. She saw it not as a deficit, but as the source of this focused intensity. This wasn't just skill, it was a different mode of cognition entirely.

Without someone like Alex, this dive would've been impossible. Sifting through LifeSpan's encrypted archives required more than just access, it needed an intuition for data, an ability to perceive the faint signals buried within terabytes of noise. He saw the underlying structure, the hidden pathways.

She thought of others throughout history. Figures celebrated for genius yet often described as eccentric, difficult, operating outside conventional norms. Da Vinci, filling notebooks with mirror script, his mind leaping between art, anatomy, and engineering. Mozart, conjuring symphonies from the ether while struggling with the mundane realities of life. Ramanujan, pulling profound mathematical truths from apparent intuition, bypassing the step-by-step proofs others required.

More recently, there was Kim Peek, the megasavant, whose memory was a vast, perfectly indexed library but who needed support for basic daily tasks. And Dr. Aris Dent, the phantom architect of the Sovereign Crypto systems, a mind that birthed impossibly-elegant code but communicated only through annotations, vanishing entirely after the collapse, leaving behind systems still not fully understood. Geniuses whose brains were wired differently, their brilliance inseparable from their divergence.

Alex muttered something under his breath, a string of alphanumeric characters. A specific data node expanded on the screen, branching into complex file trees. He plunged deeper, following a trail only he could see. Maya felt a surge of hope mixed with apprehension. He was close. He was navigating the labyrinth LifeSpan had built to conceal its secrets. The faint hum of the servers seemed to intensify, mirroring the focused energy radiating from Alex. He tapped a final sequence. A file identifier pulsed at the center of the screen: *SCHAFFER, JAMIE - ID: KAPPA-88314-DELTA-PHI.*

Alex yielded the primary console interface, stepping back slightly.

The cool blue light from the HoloScreen bathed Maya's face as she leaned in to focus. Her dark eyes scanned the initial bio-summary displayed within the holographic projection: *Jamie Schaffer, Kappa-88314-Delta-Phi. Age 30. Pre-existing Condition: Familial Hypertrophic Cardiomyopathy, Variant MYH7. Treatment Administered: GeneVax Sequence Optimization, Lot #GVX-77B-4921. Date: [Redacted – recent].*

Maya reached toward the shimmering light of the HoloScreen. Her fingers passed through the projected image, sensors tracking their precise movements. She pinched the corner of the main data window, pulling it outward. The holographic display expanded smoothly, filling more of the space above the console. With a pushing motion of her palm, she shifted the entire projection's angle, making the dense columns of text easier to read from her standing position.

Her gaze narrowed. She scrolled through the file using swift, sweeping gestures, vertical slices through the air. Past the standard diagnostic reports, the pre-treatment screenings, the logged administration details. She searched for the specific genomic sequence data, the before-and-after comparison that would show the CRISPR-Cas12a edits. The precise nucleotide changes. The targeted loci within Jamie's neural pathways.

It wasn't there. The file contained exhaustive records of the cardiomyopathy treatment, the specific edits targeting the MYH7 gene clearly documented. Successful correction confirmed. But the sections detailing any *other* edits, particularly those related to neural gene targets, were conspicuously blank or filled with intentionally vague references. Placeholder codes. Links to restricted sub-protocols. Data scrubbed clean or hidden behind further layers of classification Alex hadn't breached yet. A deliberate obfuscation.

Maya's fingers stilled mid-air. Her brow furrowed. She backtracked, reviewing annotations, cross-references, internal metadata tags logged during the procedure. Tucked away in a sub-section labeled *Ancillary Sequence Integrity Monitoring, Post-Infusion*, nested beneath layers of routine quality control logs, was a single, cryptic entry: *Ref: ANGUS Protocol Compliance Validation - Pass.*

"Angus?" Maya murmured, tapping the reference tag on the Holo-

Screen. The system offered no immediate expansion, just the designation.

Alex leaned forward instantly, his eyes fixed on the codename. He reclaimed the console, his hands in quick snapping motion across the holographic controls. He bypassed the file's limited reference link, initiating a broader system search for the term 'ANGUS Protocol'. Security flags flashed momentarily on the display periphery – unauthorized query detected – but Alex was already past them, diving into restricted internal procedural directories.

Seconds later, a new window materialized on the HoloScreen, overlaying Jamie's file. It displayed a top-level definition document, stamped with LifeSpan Internal Classification markings.

Project Codename: ANGUS

Full Title: Authority Normalization via Genetic Update Sequence

Directive: Phase One Implementation (Compliance Protocol)

Objective: Systemic reduction of societal friction factors (skepticism, dissent, authority-rejection syndromes) via targeted neural pathway modification. Enhancement of pro-social cohesion and institutional trust metrics.

Alex stared at the screen. "Authority Normalization via Genetic Update Sequence. They actually called it ANGUS." He shook his head slowly. "They aren't even subtle about it in their own damn files."

Maya pushed past the chillingly-bureaucratic title and objective statement, her fingers ghosting through the HoloScreen's light as she scrolled deeper into the ANGUS protocol document. She searched for validation metrics, oversight committees, anything that might indicate checks and balances within LifeSpan itself. Instead, she found something far more disturbing embedded at the document's end: a series of digital authorization seals and encrypted signature blocks.

LifeSpan Genomics R&D Directorate – Approved. Expected. HHS-BARDA Oversight Committee – Validated. Plausible, given the public health angle. DARPA Project Chimera Liaison – Acknowledged.

Military research involvement? The hair on the back of Maya's neck stood on end.

Global Health Consortium (GHC) - Project Evolution Mandate 7 Compliance – Certified.

An international body, complicit. Then, the seal that made her breath catch:

Pontifical Academy of Sciences – Ethical Concordance Protocol Leo XIV – Verified.

Pope Leo? The Vatican? Involved in genetic behavioral modification?

Her mind reeled, struggling to synthesize the disparate pieces. This wasn't just a rogue corporate project contained within LifeSpan's gleaming towers. This was systemic. Coordinated. A network of powerful institutions, governmental, military, international, even religious, all lending their authority, their validation, to a program designed for mass behavioral control under the guise of wellness. Project Evolution. ANGUS. GeneVax. Different names for the same monstrous deception.

She remembered the number Alex had quoted from his earlier data trawl, a number that had seemed abstract then, merely a staggering statistic. Three hundred-ninety million people. Globally. Treated with Phase One. Injected with the ANGUS sequence. Nearly four hundred million minds subtly reshaped, their skepticism dulled, their acceptance of authority enhanced, all without their knowledge or consent. It wasn't a future threat, but a present reality, already deeply embedded across the planet.

Alex watched the color drain from Maya's face, saw the flicker in her dark eyes as she processed the validation seals. He recognized the dawning comprehension, the same path his own thoughts had traveled hours earlier in the MEG scanner, connecting isolated data points into a terrifying whole. "It's bigger than just LifeSpan," he stated, his voice controlled, confirming her silent conclusion. "The data cache I pulled...it wasn't just patient files and treatment logs. It included internal communications, distribution manifests, *prioritization directives* for the GeneVax rollout."

He met her gaze, his blue eyes sharp, intense. "They weren't random in their targeting, Maya. Not entirely. The ANGUS protocol, the 'Compliance Validation' you found in Jamie's file...they prioritized certain populations." He gestured back toward the ANGUS document still shimmering on the HoloScreen. "People identified by AI algorithms as potential 'friction factors'. Individuals likely to question, to organize, to resist."

He ticked off the groups on his fingers, his voice hardening with each category. "Journalists digging into corporate or government activities. Known activists and organizers. Certain politicians deemed 'uncooperative' or ideologically misaligned." He saw the understanding dawn in her eyes. Doctors. Especially those in positions of influence or with access to sensitive research, those who might notice anomalies, who might question the official narrative.

He broke the gaze, looking back at the screen. "And, of course," he added, the words short, precise. "Data analysts. People trained to find patterns the AI might miss. People like me." Alex's hand tightened into a fist. He saw the chilling logic. Target the dissenters first. Neutralize the potential opposition before they even realized they were under attack. A preemptive strike against independent thought, delivered with a syringe and a smile.

"We need this," Alex declared, his voice tight. He gestured sharply at the ANGUS protocol document shimmering above the console. "A full copy. Encrypted. We need to get this out. To journalists who haven't been...normalized. To whatever oversight committees *aren't* rubber-stamping this nightmare. To, "

"To who, Alex?" Maya cut him off, her voice sharp, laced with a new, raw urgency. She turned from the screen, her dark eyes locking onto his. The professional detachment had vanished, replaced by a stark, almost desperate clarity.

"Don't you see? That's the entire point! Look at those validation seals! Look at the objective!"

She jabbed a finger toward the HoloScreen, her hand passing through the projected text. "Systemic reduction of societal friction factors! Enhancement of institutional trust! You show this document to someone who's had the GeneVax treatment, someone whose neural pathways have been subtly rewritten by the ANGUS sequence...what do you think they'll see?

"They won't see a conspiracy. They'll see *progress*. They'll see a solution to discord, a path to harmony. They'll wonder why *you're* causing trouble, why *you're* resisting something so clearly beneficial for society. They won't care about the proof because the treatment *makes* them not care! Jamie wouldn't care."

Alex flinched, the image of Jamie's serene, placid face flashing behind his eyes. The emptiness where her sharp wit used to be.

"The prioritization proves it," Maya continued, pressing the advantage, her mind racing ahead. "Journalists, activists, analysts... they didn't just target them randomly. They targeted the key people who would investigate, who would question, who would sound the alarm! They inoculated the watchdogs against the danger!"

She took a step closer to Alex. "We can't waste time trying to convince the converted," she said, lowering her voice further, though the room was secure. "Our only chance is to reach the others. The ones who haven't been treated yet. The ones whose minds haven't been altered."

She paused, doing the mental calculation, her medical training grounding her, even now. "Three hundred-ninety million. It sounds like an astronomical number. And it is. But globally? It's less than five percent. The vast majority of people *haven't* had the injection. Not yet. *They* are the ones who need to know. Before Phase Two, whatever that is, begins. Before LifeSpan expands the program. Before it's too late."

The sharp clang of metal striking metal echoed through the sterile research annex. *Bam! Bam! Bam!* Heavy blows landed against the reinforced door.

Alex jolted, spinning away from the HoloScreen, his body tensing. The data, the conspiracy, the implications, all momentarily eclipsed by the immediate threat hammering just meters away.

"Security! Open this door! Now!" The voice was electronically amplified, harsh and devoid of negotiation.

"Shit," Alex hissed, eyes darting around the room, searching for an impossible escape route. "How did they find us? The terminal!"

"Dr. Rivera!" the voice boomed again. "That terminal has flagged unauthorized activity within restricted LifeSpan archives! Open the door immediately!"

Maya reacted instantly. The clinical calm she had maintained while analyzing the data shattered, replaced by focused urgency. She shoved Alex toward a blank section of the far wall, marked only by a faint seam and a standard biohazard symbol sticker.

"The emergency decontamination access!" she hissed, her fingers fumbling with a nearly invisible latch beside the seam. "Go! Now! I'll stall them!"

"What about you, Maya?!" Alex grabbed her arm, his gaze locked on the vibrating main door. He could hear the grinding sound of a breaching tool starting up outside.

Maya pulled her arm free, her expression resolute. She straightened her lab coat, a flicker of her professional persona returning like a shield. She reached inside her lab coat pocket and pulled out a thin, flat, dark-blue card and handed it to Alex. "I have hospital credentials. Level three access. I can claim I was running comparative analyses on GeneVax patient cohorts. Plausible deniability. They might believe it. Take this and go!"

The seam on the wall clicked open, revealing a narrow, dimly-lit passage lined with conduits and ventilation shafts. The air inside smelled stale, metallic. Alex hesitated for only a second, meeting her eyes. He saw the calculation there, the risk she was taking. He slid the card into his side pocket.

"I'll contact you tomorrow, on ArcLink," he promised, his voice low and tight. "Be careful." He squeezed through the opening just as the main door to the annex exploded inward with a deafening crash of metal and splintered plasteel. He pulled the hidden panel shut behind him, the click of the latch swallowed by the commotion outside. He plunged into the dusty darkness of the service tunnel.

Two uniformed security officers, clad in heavy tactical gear, stepped through the ruined doorway. Their movements were precise, aggressive. Their faces were obscured by polarized visors. One held a multi-spectrum scanner, sweeping it across the room, its beam lingering on the still-active HoloScreen displaying the ANGUS protocol. The other kept a heavy pulse carbine rifle leveled, covering the space.

"Dr. Rivera." The lead officer's amplified voice was impersonal. He gestured toward the console with the carbine's barrel. "You're accessing highly-restricted LifeSpan Genomics files. Files far outside your authorized research parameters."

Maya stood her ground beside the workstation, projecting an aura of indignant professionalism. She smoothed her lab coat again, a deliberate gesture of composure. "I am conducting legitimate medical research, comparing long-term patient outcomes across various GeneVax treatment lots, cross-referenced with pre-existing conditions. It requires accessing comprehensive data sets. This research is beyond any security level you will ever have access to. How *dare* you accuse me!"

The security officer took another step into the room. The scanner held by his partner beeped softly as it finished analyzing the holographic display.

"The system flagged specific keyword access related to internal project codenames. You have no clearance for this information either, Doctor. Your claimed research parameters do not justify this level of intrusion." His tone was unyielding. "You need you to come with us."

It wasn't a request.

Several minutes later, Alex stumbled out of the narrow passage, the heavy metal panel clicking shut behind him with a sound that felt unnervingly loud in the sudden quiet. He found himself in a service alley behind the sprawling Clinton Memorial complex. The air had a damp smell of discarded medical supplies and oriental food. Towering brick walls, stained dark by years of rain and grime, rose on either side, creating a concrete canyon.

Giant, crimson biohazard dumpsters lined one wall, their lids tightly sealed. Above, a heavy-lift drone whirred, its HushThrust engines barely audible. Mechanical arms precisely detached an empty container, its biohazard symbol stark under the drone's work lights, and picked up an identical, full one before ascending smoothly up between the buildings and into the night sky.

Alex instinctively pressed himself back against the hot brick, melting into the deeper shadows cast by the dumpsters. He glanced down at the sleek black band on his wrist. The holographic display shimmered into existence above it: 23:21. Nearly midnight. He ripped off the borrowed white lab coat and shoved it behind the nearest dumpster, burying it beneath a pile of discarded packaging materials.

A light drizzle began, incongruously warm for a late spring night. Tiny droplets caught the beams from distant skyscrapers and the sodium glow of the overhead street lamps, drawing shimmering lines through the humid air. The wet pavement reflected the distorted lights.

"The whole damn world," Alex muttered, the words barely audible above the city's distant vibrations. His voice was rough. "Everyone. In on it."

His fingers twitched, a familiar tremor starting in his right hand. He forced them into a fist and quickly checked his iBand again. A secondary environmental display popped up beside the time: Ambient Temp: 38.1 C. Way too hot for May. Even with the city's heat island effect, this felt wrong, unnatural.

He started pacing, back and forth in the confined space between the dumpsters and the opposite wall. Three steps one way, pivot, three steps back. Think. Think. Think. The patterns started swirling in his mind, the way they always did under pressure, the SRV kicking into high gear. Data points, probabilities, statistical variations scattered like digital shrapnel. LifeSpan. GeneVax. ANGUS. The compliance protocols. Jamie's vacant cheerfulness. His own anomalous resistance. Maya, trapped back there.

He saw branching possibilities, impossible scenarios playing out with cold, mathematical logic. Could they develop a countermeasure, an anti-GeneVax? How deep did the network run? OmniHealth processed the data. LifeSpan created the therapy. Who else? Government agencies? Insurance consortiums? The sheer scale suggested complicity far beyond a single corporation. He pictured the faces of colleagues, neighbors, people on the street – were they all unknowing subjects? Or worse, willing participants?

The drizzle intensified slightly, plastering loose strands of his dark hair to his forehead. The dampness did nothing to cool the oppressive heat. He stopped pacing, breathing hard, the tremor in his hand now more pronounced. He needed a secure location. But every communication channel felt compromised, every public space a potential trap. The city lights painted shifting patterns on the wet ground at his feet.

Alex's muscles coiled. The alley was a dead end, a trap waiting to spring. Maya bought him time, but security systems were relentless. Algorithms crunched data, predicted escape vectors, dispatched assets. They knew someone else was inside. They knew *he* got away. His face, captured by countless sensors inside the facility, was already flagged.

He pushed off the damp brick wall, the rough texture scratching his palm. Six blocks. The thought solidified, a clear objective cutting through the chaotic data streams in his head. The Central Branch Library. Open twenty-four/seven. A relic repurposed for the digital age, hollowed out and automated. No librarians, no staff, just servers humming behind reinforced walls and terminals offering access to curated information streams.

His mother, Isabella, used to work there, back when books lined shelves instead of databases, when human interaction was part of the process. Efficiency demanded otherwise now. LifeSpan, OmniHealth, corporations, the city planners – they all spoke the language of optimization, streamlining humanity itself.

Who would search for a fugitive data analyst in a deserted library? No one read physical media anymore. It was inconvenient, slow. Information flowed directly, seamlessly, through iBands and neural links. A library was an anachronism, a ghost building haunted by the memory of paper and ink. Perfect.

He pulled the collar of his dark base layer shirt higher, trying to obscure the lower half of his face. He slipped out of the service alley's narrow mouth onto the wider sidewalk. The drizzle persisted, slicking the permacrete underfoot. Automated vehicles whispered past on the main thoroughfare, their guidance lights painting streaks of blue and white across the wet surface. Few pedestrians were out this late, mostly service workers heading home or solitary figures hunched against the rain, faces buried in the glow of their iBand HoloScreens.

Alex kept his head down, merging with the sparse foot traffic. He moved with purpose but avoided overt haste, mimicking the gait of someone tired, heading home after a long shift. Each crosswalk felt like an exposure point. Cameras mounted on traffic poles swiveled silently, their multi-spectrum lenses capturing everything. He kept to the shadows cast by building overhangs whenever possible.

Block one. A LifeSpan Wellness Center, its windows dark, the corporate logo gleaming softly under integrated lighting. Block two. A closed cafe chain, standardized corporate furniture visible through the rain-streaked glass. He passed an alcove where two figures huddled, their faces obscured by hoods. Alex's pulse jumped, but they ignored him, absorbed in a flickering HoloScreen projected between them.

Block three. The oppressive heat radiated from the pavement, mixing with the dampness. Steam curled from sewer grates. His senses felt amplified, the city's background noise – the whir of AVs, the distant thrum of air conditioning units, the faint electronic chime of a crosswalk signal, sharp and distinct. Patterns everywhere.

The synchronized pulse of traffic lights down the avenue. The precise spacing of the recycling bins along the curb. The rhythmic sweep of an automated street cleaner further down the block. SRV wasn't just pattern recognition, it was feeling the grid, the underlying structure of the city's systems. And right now, the systems felt like they were hunting him.

Block four. He cut through a small, deserted plaza dominated by a sterile corporate sculpture. The rain was picking up slightly, the drops heavier now. He resisted the urge to check his iBand, to see if Maya had sent any message, any warning. Useless. She was likely already detained, her own devices confiscated or compromised.

Block five. He could see the library ahead now, occupying most of the next block. A monolithic structure of glass and steel, designed decades ago with grand civic intentions, now looking stark and impersonal under the night sky. Its entrance was a vast, recessed space, bright but empty. Six blocks. He quickened his pace, the library's entrance beckoning like a sterile sanctuary.

The entrance loomed, a glowing void under the persistent drizzle. Alex hugged the opposite wall, scanning the empty plaza, the gleaming, wet surfaces reflecting the city's ambient light. Just a few more steps. He adjusted his path, aiming for the revolving doors, when his Apple iBand chimed softly, a distinct notification tone breaking the static sound of rain on pavement.

He froze. His gaze snapped down to the sleek black band on his wrist. An incoming call icon pulsed on the HoloScreen projected above it. Encrypted? No. Standard comms channel. He hesitated. Maya wouldn't use an open channel, not now. Who...? His hand trembled slightly as he tapped the 'accept' icon hovering in the air.

"Maya?"

A cascade of cheerful, slightly too-loud tones answered, instantly recognizable yet fundamentally altered. "Alex! Where are you? Honestly, I've been buzzing your door for ages. It's pouring out here, let me in!"

Jamie. A cold knot formed low in Alex's gut. He glanced around quickly, heart hammering against his ribs. Was she tracking him? How?

"Jamie? What are you doing at my apartment?"

Her laugh sounded tinny, forced. "Silly! I was worried about you, of course. You left work so abruptly, and you seemed...agitated. It felt like a significant stress reaction. I just wanted to make sure you were okay. Come on, let me in. I'll even give you one of my famous back rubs."

The mention of a 'stress reaction', corporate wellness jargon parroted with unnerving sincerity, confirmed his suspicion. The casual offer, once perhaps flirtatious, now felt grotesque, a calculated lure. He pictured her standing outside his door, her bright smile fixed, her eyes placidly reflecting the hallway lights, waiting. She wasn't just altered, she'd become a tool.

Alex stopped walking, the library entrance forgotten for the moment. The rain plastered his hair to his scalp. "You reported me, didn't you?" He'd lowered his voice, the words tight with accusation.

"After our talk last night. You flagged me to OmniHealth. To LifeSpan."

There was a fractional pause on the other end, a micro-delay as if processing the unexpected input. "I simply expressed concern for a colleague's wellbeing to the appropriate channels." Her cheerfulness had flattened, replaced by a calm, almost clinical reasonableness. The voice was hers, but the inflection felt foreign, programmed.

"Your recent behavior, your resistance to beneficial health protocols...it indicates distress. The treatment can help you find clarity, Alex. Real clarity. Like it helped me."

Another pause. "We can be together. I know that's what you want." Her voice had shifted again, dropping lower, shedding the clinical tone for something intimate, disturbingly familiar, echoing the figure from his dream.

Alex stared at the HoloScreen projected above his iBand. Jamie's contact photo, a bright, conventionally-attractive image taken before her treatment, seemed incongruous with the voice speaking through his neural link. Beneath her picture, a new icon pulsed insistently: a small camera symbol, requesting a two-way video HoloCall. Cold dread pooled in his stomach. If he accepted, the background would instantly reveal he wasn't standing in his minimalist apartment. He was exposed, out in the rain-slicked city night.

"So that's it?" Alex's voice was low, strained. "Take the treatment. Become compliant like you? Stop asking questions because LifeSpan doesn't like them? And we can be together...?"

He couldn't initiate the video. She'd know. She'd alert them.

"Questions only cause unnecessary discord." Jamie's tone remained patient, imbued with a counterfeit sincerity that grated on his nerves. It was the sound of someone explaining a simple truth to a difficult child. "Discord leads to inefficiency. Wasted resources. Misallocated energy. It hurts everyone. You, working with data optimization every day, should understand that better than anyone."

The calm, logical progression of her words, stripped of any real human hesitation or doubt, horrified him. The Jamie he knew, the one who rolled her eyes at corporate platitudes and shared cynical jokes about management memos, was gone. This was a different entity wearing her face, speaking with her voice. "Listen to yourself! Inefficiency? Discord? Is that what you call thinking? Questioning? They reprogrammed you!"

"It's better this way, Alex. Clearer. Why cause friction? Why resist improvements that benefit the whole?" The sincerity in her voice felt absolute, unshakable. "Just come in voluntarily. They understand you're under stress. It will be much smoother if you cooperate. Dr. Ward himself has taken an interest in your case."

Ward. Alex didn't recognize it immediately. Another corporate executive? A higher-up at OmniHealth? "Who is Dr. Ward?"

"Dr. Elias Ward?" Jamie sounded slightly surprised he didn't know, as if mentioning a household name. "He's the Chief Science Officer at LifeSpan Genomics. Director of Genetic Programs. The visionary behind GeneVax Therapy. He's the one helping so many people, ensuring societal health and stability. He wants to understand your situation."

The architect. The man behind the curtain, the source of the ANGUS protocol, the mind driving the systematic alteration of millions. And he was interested in Alex Thompson, employee ID lamda-47291-alpha-epsilon. Not just an anomaly in the data anymore, but a person of interest to the program's creator. The tremor returned to Alex's hand, more insistent this time.

"I'm never coming in, Jamie." His voice was rigid, final. He stabbed a finger at the 'end call' icon hovering in the HoloScreen display. The connection severed. Jamie's smiling photo vanished.

Dr. Elias Ward. The architect of ANGUS, who saw dissent not as a right, but as a glitch in the human code, a bug to be patched with CRISPR-Cas12a. And he knew Alex's name. He wanted to *understand* Alex's situation. His skin felt clammy beneath the damp tech-wear. Understanding wasn't the goal. Correction was. Compliance.

The library entrance pulsed with sterile light, a beacon in the rain-streaked darkness. He needed to go inside. Out of the rain, out of sight. Away from the omnipresent sensors lining the streets. Away from the possibility of Jamie pinpointing his location through some lingering connection or corporate surveillance access she now possessed.

He started moving again, a quick, jerky walk that threatened to break into a run. His mind raced faster than his feet. Jamie's transformation was complete. The cheerful cynicism replaced by placid conviction. Her concern wasn't for *him*, but for his deviation from the norm. A stress reaction. A sign of malfunction. Get the treatment, Alex. Find clarity. Join the harmonious collective. The thought made his stomach clench.

There had to be others. Millions who still felt the rough edges of doubt, the sharp sting of skepticism. Millions who saw the patterns Jamie now dismissed as inefficiency. Where were they? Hiding? Unaware? Or perhaps, organized? How could he find allies when the system itself pathologized the fundamental act of searching? When asking the wrong questions flagged you for mandatory 'wellness'?

The ubiquitous city hum, a low-frequency thrum that vibrated through the soles of his worn sneakers, through the damp air, seemingly through his bones. It was the sound of the city breathing, the constant noise of automated systems, data streams, power conduits – the sound of control. Usually, it faded into the background, unnoticed white noise. Tonight, amplified by adrenaline and his SRV's heightened sensitivity, it felt like a torture device. He needed quiet. He needed space to think, to analyze. Somewhere without the incessant rain, without Jamie's chillingly reasonable voice echoing in his head, without his own hands twitching, betraying his internal state. Somewhere without the hum, without the,

Sirens.

He stopped dead again, halfway across the empty plaza. A siren? Faint and distant, maybe just a reflection of sound bouncing off the glass towers. He tilted his head, straining to isolate the sound from the background thrum. It was definite. A rising, falling electronic wail, the distinct signature of MetroSec patrol units.

Were they getting closer? He held his breath, listening intently. The sound grew, cutting through the rain and the hum, sharpening. Definitely closer. Multiple units, judging by the overlapping doppler shifts. Converging. In this area? On him?

The library entrance was two hundred meters away. An eternity. He broke into a sprint, feet slapping against the wet permacrete, the rain smacking against his face. The sirens screamed louder, closer now, echoing off the surrounding buildings, amplifying the urgency.

Jamie's call. Ward's interest. Maya's detainment. They knew he wasn't home, that he'd breached the LifeSpan facility. They knew he had seen the data. And now, they were coming for him.

ALEX POUNDED across the slick plaza, the library entrance a beckoning rectangle of light that grew as he got closer. Rain plastered strands of dark hair to his forehead, blurring his vision. The sirens grew insistently louder, a piercing digital shriek that clawed at the edges of his awareness. He risked a glance over his shoulder.

Two sleek, black MetroSec cruisers rounded the far corner, their emergency lights slicing beams through the downpour, painting the wet surfaces in strobes of red and blue. Above them, a low-slung MetroSec hoverdrone dipped, its multiple optical sensors gleaming like insect eyes. They were close. Too close.

Ahead, lumbering down the side street perpendicular to his path, came an automated refuse collector – a bulky, windowless municipal drone humming its low-gear dirge. Its rear hopper gaped open, ready to ingest the designated waste bins lining the curb.

An idea sparked, sharp and desperate. His wrist felt suddenly heavy. The iBand. The source of constant connection, communication, tracking. He fumbled with the clasp, his fingers clumsy with tremors and adrenaline. The smooth metal released. He ripped the band from his wrist, the loss of its familiar weight a sudden void.

Without breaking stride, Alex pivoted slightly, judged the refuse truck's trajectory, and flung the iBand underhand. The dark loop sailed through the rain, a small arc against the illuminated mist, and vanished into the dark maw of the truck's collection bin just as the vehicle rumbled past the intersection.

He snapped his focus back to the library, veering sharply toward the entrance. The sleek, glass doors slid open automatically as he approached, revealing the blinding, silent interior. Directly ahead stood the brushed-steel authentication turnstiles, waist-high barriers designed to grant access with a seamless proximity scan of an iBand or authorized credential.

No time to find another way. He gathered himself, legs pumping, and launched upward. One hand pushed off the top of the nearest turnstile housing as he vaulted over the barrier.

His landing was a disaster. The worn soles of his sneakers, slick with rain and street grime, found no purchase on the polished floor inside. His feet shot out from under him. Air rushed from his lungs in a sharp gasp as he slammed onto his back. The back of his skull connected with the unyielding surface with a sickening thud.

Stars burst behind his eyelids. Disoriented, sprawled gracelessly on the cool floor, the scent of floor cleaner and damp fabric, and blood, sharp in his nostrils, he blinked, trying to clear his vision. The library's hushed atmosphere seemed to amplify the ringing in his ears.

Through the tall glass panels flanking the entrance, he saw the drone following closely by two MetroSec cruisers, racing past the library without slowing. Their sirens faded rapidly down the street, chasing the ghost signal emanating from the refuse truck.

He pushed himself up onto his elbows, the movement sending a fresh wave of dizziness through him. They were following the iBand. It worked. He gingerly touched the back of his head, feeling a tender spot already beginning to swell beneath his wet hair.

The fading doppler effect of the sirens left a ringing silence in its wake. Alex stayed on his elbows, the cold floor a solid anchor against the residual spin in his head. Air returned to his lungs, slow and deliberate. Relief, thin but present, loosened the knots in his shoulders. They were gone. Chasing electrons down a waste disposal route.

He pushed himself to a sitting position and carefully, testing his strength, he rose to his feet. A dull ache pulsed at the base of his skull where it had met the floor. He ran fingers through his soaked hair, probing the tender spot. No blood, just a rapidly forming lump. A small price.

His gaze swept the library's vast, quiet main hall. Rows of data consoles stood dormant. Holographic displays flickered with curated newsfeeds and library announcements. A lone cleaning drone hummed softly in a far corner, polishing the already-gleaming floor. He was alone. And conspicuous.

A dark puddle spread around his worn sneakers. Water streamed from his clothes, tracing patterns on the pristine surface. He looked down at himself, dripping, disheveled, completely out of place in the library's sterile order. His synthetic shirt clung uncomfortably, the trousers heavy with rainwater.

Across the wide hall, near a bank of elevators, a simple pictogram glowed: a stylized human figure, bisected. Restroom. He needed to regroup, to dry off, to think past the throbbing in his head and the adrenaline receding from his veins.

He walked, leaving a trail of damp footprints, his steps squeaking slightly in the cavernous space. The restroom door slid open silently. Inside, the air was still, carrying the faint, clean scent of automated sanitation cycles and lavender. White tiles gleamed under flat panel lighting. Stainless steel fixtures reflected his drenched form.

He peeled off the black long-sleeved shirt. The smart fabric, designed for moisture-wicking and biometric monitoring, felt slick and heavy. He held it over the wide basin of the sink and twisted. Water streamed out, dark against the white ceramic. He twisted again, harder, squeezing out the last drops. He used the damp fabric to scrub at his face and hair, the smooth texture against his skin. Another hard wring over the sink. Almost instantly, the dark material lightened, the inherent nanotech coating shedding the remaining moisture. Within moments, it felt nearly dry, ready to wear again.

Next came his shoes, placed carefully side-by-side on the dry floor tiles near the wall. He unfastened his trousers, the dark grey synthetic material sodden and clinging. As he began to twist the waistband, his fingers brushed against something thin and rigid in the thigh pocket.

He paused, pulling out the object. It was the card Dr. Rivera had given him in the secure data room. In the excitement, he had completely forgotten about it. A tiny, flat square of cobalt-colored material, notched on one corner, with a row of thin, gold contacts gleaming on one side. He turned it over in his fingers. He placed it carefully on the dry edge of the sink counter, away from the pooled water and returned his attention to the soaked trousers, twisting the durable fabric with focused effort.

Alex stood before the wide mirror, the fluorescent panels overhead casting a flat, revealing light. His reflection stared back: face pale beneath the damp, plastered hair, eyes narrowed slightly against the persistent ache blooming at the base of his skull. Water still beaded on his forehead and jawline. The dark, quick-drying shirt clung to his lean frame. He looked hunted. He *was* hunted.

He lifted a hand, touching the swelling lump on the back of his head again. A dull throb radiated from the point of impact. The vault over the turnstile felt reckless now, a desperate move born of panic. But it had worked. They chased the iBand, swallowed by a garbage drone trundling toward some unseen municipal processing center.

Without the iBand, though... His mind cataloged the immediate consequences. Transportation: impossible. The AVs, the shuttles, the maglevs – all required the seamless handshake of the device for authentication and payment. Access: denied. Doors to secure buildings, transit gates, even his own apartment, relied on its proximity signal. Commerce: halted. No digital wallet, no instant transactions. He couldn't buy food, access funds, or even rent a scooter. He was digitally severed, adrift in a city built on constant connection. A ghost in the machine, but a ghost without leverage.

He leaned closer to the mirror, studying the faint tremor in his hand as he braced it against the cool countertop. The adrenaline ebb left behind a hollow fatigue. What now? Find Maya? She was likely already compromised, apprehended back in the lab. Jamie's call confirmed LifeSpan knew he was loose, knew he had *something*. They wouldn't stop.

Suddenly, the lights clicked off. The restroom plunged into momentary blackness. Alex reacted instinctively, head whipping around toward the door, the sudden movement sending a spike of pain through his skull. The motion sensors registered his presence and the lights flared back on instantly, glaring. He squeezed his eyes shut, waiting for the throb to subside. The city conserved energy wherever possible, even in the silent, automated spaces of a public library. Motionless equaled absent.

His gaze fell on the small, cobalt-colored square resting on the sink's edge. Maya's card. He picked it up, turning it over. Smooth, cool plastic. Thicker than the flimsy data chips currently in use. One side featured a grid of tiny, gleaming gold contacts, slightly recessed.

Old tech. Decades old, not designed for wireless transmission or proximity reading. It required a physical interface, direct electrode contact. He ran a thumb over the contacts. Solid state memory, most likely, but archaic. Why give him this? Especially when seconds counted?

It had to contain something vital. Something she couldn't risk sending wirelessly, something she knew he needed. Data. The raw protocols? Proof of the ANGUS project? It had to be. But accessing it required hardware he hadn't seen outside of tech museums or specialized archive facilities.

He looked around the restroom, and back at the card. A reader. He needed a physical contact reader for this specific format. Where would he even find,

The library. He stood inside the Central Branch Library. A repository of information, yes, but also technology. Libraries maintained archives, historical data formats, equipment for accessing older media. It was a long shot, dependent on outdated systems remaining functional and accessible, but it was the only shot he had. He tucked the card securely back into his trouser pocket. He pulled his still-damp sneakers back on, the chill seeping into his socks.

His gaze lingered on the worn canvas of his shoes, the faded black, almost grey in places. A faint smile touched Alex's lips. Antique Converse high-tops. Classic design, barely changed in over a century, yet these were unique.

His father, Richard, had tracked down this specific pair. A limited edition, custom order, released decades ago during a brief resurgence of retro hacker culture. Emblazoned near the ankle, barely visible under his layers of grime and wear, was the stylized logo: '1337'. A mark of distinction in certain online circles, long since absorbed by the corporate net. They were a status symbol, a nod to a rebellious, digital past. For Alex, they were the last thing his father had bought him before the cognitive fog descended, before the man who understood complex water systems forgot his own son's name.

The rubber soles were smooth, the tread patterns ghosts. Fabric frayed near the eyelets. He should have discarded them years ago, replaced them with something practical, synthetic, efficient. But the worn contours felt familiar, a tangible link to a time before GeneVax, before OmniHealth, before the steady erosion of truth. He couldn't part with them. Tying the laces felt like a small ritual, grounding him momentarily in a past that felt more real than the sterile, surveilled present.

He stood, the dampness of the shoes a minor discomfort compared to the throbbing at the back of his head. The cobalt card felt solid in his pocket. Find a reader. The library archives. He pushed the restroom door open and stepped back into the vast, silent hall.

Alex moved through the main passage, his damp sneakers echoing faintly on the polished floor. The silence felt different from the hushed reverence he remembered from childhood visits, back when Isabella Reyes Thompson managed this branch, back when the air smelled of aging paper and binding glue.

Now, the quiet felt sterile, automated. Rows upon rows of empty shelving units, relics of a bygone era, lined the vast space, their surfaces smooth and dust-free, monuments to obsolescence. Where towering stacks of physical books once stood, creating labyrinthine aisles filled with shadowed corners and whispered discoveries, there were now only wide, open pathways illuminated by flat, energy-efficient ceiling panels.

Occasional data consoles punctuated the emptiness, their dark screens inert. A few citizens sat scattered at designated holographic reading stations, their faces lit by the glow of projected text only they could see, their fingers tracing invisible lines in the air to turn virtual pages.

The grand reading room, once bustling with students and researchers hunched over physical texts, was now a partitioned zone of private HoloScreen carrels. Everything was streamlined, digitized, efficient. Even the air, filtered and temperature-controlled, lacked the comforting, musty scent of paper. His mother would have hated this sterile echo of the vibrant community hub she had nurtured.

He needed the archives, or whatever passed for them now. He scanned the hall. Directional signs floated as holographic projections shifted subtly with minimalist elegance. None mentioned archives directly. Near the central elevator bank, a freestanding kiosk pulsed with soft blue light, an information terminal.

Alex approached it. The HoloScreen flickered to life as he neared, projecting a welcoming interface into the air before him. Standard library directory. Search functions. Newsfeeds. He ignored the primary options, his fingers moving through the air, navigating submenus with adept gestures learned over years of data analysis. Building Schematics. Emergency Exits. Public Access Level Maps. He selected the last.

A detailed, three-dimensional schematic of the library bloomed in the air. Floor plans layered atop each other, transparent levels revealing the structure's layout. Data tags popped up, identifying sections: Main Reading Hall, Digital Lending Hub, Community Forum Annex, Administration Sector B.

His eyes scanned the complex diagram. Normally, tracing specific locations through multiple levels and wings would take time, careful study. But the schematic resolved in his mind with unnatural speed. Lines connected, spatial relationships snapped into focus, irrelevant data faded.

His SRV processed the visual information, patterns emerging

instantly. His gaze locked onto a designation on the third sub-level, tucked away near the automated archival retrieval system: Sector 3G - Historical Technology Exhibit. A museum. Perfect.

He memorized the pathway – elevators near the west wall, sub-level three, follow the blue floor guideline past the custodial robots' charge point. He collapsed the HoloScreen display with a quick gesture and turned, heading toward the elevators.

The elevator doors hissed open onto Sub-Level Three. The air felt different here – cooler, drier, with a faint undertone of air-cooled electronics and aged plastic. Blue guideline strips embedded in the floor pulsed rhythmically, leading Alex away from the main corridor, past humming racks that likely housed automated retrieval systems for physical media archives, though the shelves themselves were hidden behind opaque panels. He followed the illuminated path into a designated alcove marked Sector 3G: Historical Technology Exhibit.

He stepped inside. The space was curated like a museum display, mostly dark except for spotlights highlighting specific artifacts. Glass cases held primitive communication devices – bulky mobile phones with physical buttons, networked music players tethered by wires, handheld gaming consoles displaying pixelated graphics. Along one wall, a row of desktop computer workstations sat on plain tables. Compared to the sleek, integrated HoloScreen interfaces he used daily, these machines looked impossibly clumsy.

Thick, beige plastic casings still housed internal components. Tethered keyboards featured rows of physical, depressible keys. And the displays...flat panels, yes, but thick-bezeled, their surfaces dark and reflective until activated and only viewable from one side. One flickered to life as he passed, displaying a blocky, low-resolution operating system logo – jagged edges, limited color palette. The user interface, built around clickable icons and nested menus navigated by a physical pointing device seemed arcane, inefficient.

Alex's focus narrowed to the physical housings, the slots and ports built into the plastic shells. He pulled Maya's cobalt card from his trouser pocket, the smooth, cool square feeling alien in his hand. He held it up, comparing its thickness and contact pattern to the various openings visible on the machines. USB ports, Ethernet jacks, circular power connectors – none matched. He moved down the line. Floppy disk drives with wide, narrow slots. Optical drive trays designed for shimmering discs. More USB variants, legacy FireWire ports. Nothing looked right. *Why so many different formats?*

His gaze landed on a thicker, grey machine sitting slightly apart. It resembled an early portable computer, a heavy clamshell design with a hinged connection allowing the screen to fold down over a tactile keyboard. It looked more like a dedicated reader or diagnostic tool than a general-purpose computer. Below the keyboard, near the front edge, was a slot. Wider than a standard memory card slot. Thicker, too.

He approached it, holding Maya's card near the opening. The dimensions looked promising. He slid the card in. Resistance. It wouldn't seat. He pulled it back, flipped it 180 degrees, ensuring the gold contacts faced the correct direction according to a faint diagram etched beside the slot. He pushed gently. This time, it slid smoothly inward, ending with a distinct, satisfying *click* as a locking mechanism engaged.

Success. A low *ding* emitted from the machine's tiny speaker grille. The dark, flat-panel display above the keyboard flickered and stabilized, displaying white text on a plain blue background. Low resolution, but readable.

EXTERNAL MEDIA DETECTED. SELECT ACTION:

> Open File Explorer

> Scan for Viruses

> Safely Eject Media

Before Alex could even locate the tiny, square touchpad built into the console below the keyboard, let alone figure out how to manipulate its cursor, the message vanished. The screen went blank and reverted to a simple library exhibit holding image.

"Shit," Alex muttered, tapping a finger against the unresponsive touchpad.

A soft whirring sound approached from behind. He turned. A small, disc-shaped library assistance drone hovered silently at shoulder height, its surface glowing with the familiar blue light of the library's information systems. A simple holographic question mark projected above it.

"Assistance required?" the drone's synthesized voice inquired, calm and gender-neutral.

Alex gestured toward the thick grey machine. "I inserted a card." He pointed to the slot where Maya's card was now seated. "A prompt appeared, but then it disappeared. I need to see the contents of the card."

"Acknowledged," the drone replied. "This unit is a legacy media access terminal. Stand by." The drone floated closer to the machine, emitting a low-frequency hum. A thin beam of light scanned the keyboard and screen.

"The interface requires manual input via the integrated touchpad or keyboard. To access the file system, please double-tap the icon labeled File Navigator on the primary display screen." A small holographic arrow briefly illuminated the corresponding area on the dark screen before fading.

"Alternatively, use the arrow keys to highlight the Open File Explorer option from the initial prompt, should it reappear upon re-insertion, and press the Enter key."

Alex frowned, reaching for the touchpad again. He moved the cursor, sluggishly responsive compared to his neural link or iBand gestures, over the icon the drone indicated and double-tapped. A new window opened on the archaic display, stark white with black text listing directories and files. It was a file explorer interface, rudimentary but functional.

Only one item appeared in the main pane of the window, listed under the drive letter assigned to the inserted card. *README.TXT*.

In another part of town, the MediVac unit's emergency alert system chimed as the distress signal flashed across their onboard display. The medical team, clad in sleek, sterile biosuits, moved with skilled efficiency, their movements synchronized by years of high-stress response. The apartment door slid open automatically, recognizing their clearance. Medical personnel were granted immediate access in life-or-death situations.

The first thing they saw was the blood. A trail of dark crimson droplets led from the entryway into the kitchen, smeared and dragged as if someone had stumbled forward, desperate to reach something, or someone. The droplets became streaks, becoming a smear leading toward the bathroom. The team followed the path, their boots clicking against the polished floor.

Inside the bathroom, a woman lay motionless on the cold tile, her body curled slightly, one arm outstretched. A pool of blood spread beneath her, glistening under the harsh bathroom lights. Her iBand pulsed weakly on her wrist, its emergency protocols activated, it had already transmitted her vitals to Emergency Assistance Services (EAS) the moment it detected critical distress.

"Unconscious female, severe blood loss," the lead medic announced, kneeling beside her. His gloved fingers pressed against her neck, checking for a pulse. "Pulse weak but present."

The second medic activated the maglev gander, its hover-field humming to life as it floated beside them. They lifted the woman onto the levitating stretcher, her body limp, her breathing shallow. The blood left behind on the floor was already being analyzed by the apartment's automated cleaning drones, but the real work was just beginning.

The medics secured her inside the MediVac transport, the doors sealing shut with a pressurized hiss. The interior was a sterile white pod, lined with bio-monitors and automated transfusion systems. One medic hooked an IV line into her arm while the other scanned her with a handheld diagnostic wand, the device emitting rapid beeps as it processed her condition.

"BP seventy/forty," the first medic called out, his voice sharp. "Mean arterial pressure critically low."

"Oxygen saturation eighty-two percent," the second responded, adjusting the oxygen mask over the woman's face. "Nitrogen-to-oxygen ratio skewed, possible internal bleeding."

A robotic arm extended from the ceiling, inserting a needle into her other arm. "Administering synthetic hemoglobin," the AI voice of the MediVac unit announced. The clear fluid flowed into her veins, designed to temporarily replace lost blood volume until she could receive a full transfusion.

"Pulse weak but stabilizing," the first medic said, watching the holographic vitals flicker above the gurney. "We need to move quickly."

The MediVac pod detached from the apartment's docking port, lifting smoothly into the air before accelerating toward Clinton Memorial Hospital. Inside, the medics worked in silence, their hands moving with precision as they fought to keep the woman alive.

It felt like only moments had passed when Isabella's eyelids fluttered open. The sterile white ceiling of the hospital room blurred into focus, harsh under the HelioLux lighting. A dull ache pulsed behind her temples, and her mouth tasted metallic, dry. She raised a trembling hand to her face. Her fingers came away smeared with flakes of dried blood.

The monitors beside her bed emitted rhythmic beeps, their screens displaying jagged lines of vitals. An IV line snaked from her forearm, feeding clear fluids into her veins. Another wire taped to her chest connected to the EKG, its steady blips marking time. The air smelled of antiseptic and the faint, coppery tang of old blood.

She turned her head toward the window. The blinds were half-closed, slats of early morning sunrise light cutting across the floor. Outside, the distant hum of the city filtered through the glass, hover traffic, the occasional siren.

The door hissed open. A nurse in pale blue scrubs stepped inside, her iBand glowing faintly as it synced with the room's medical systems. "Mrs. Thompson," she said, her voice warm but professional. "You're awake."

Isabella tried to speak but her throat was raw. She swallowed, wincing.

The nurse moved to the bedside, adjusting the IV drip. "You gave us quite a scare. Your iBand alerted emergency services just in time."

Isabella's fingers brushed the device still strapped to her wrist. Its surface was clean now, no trace of the blood that had slicked it hours before. "What...happened?" Her voice was a whisper.

The nurse hesitated. "A severe nosebleed. Dr. Rivera will explain more when she arrives."

Isabella exhaled slowly, her gaze drifting back to the window. The light felt too bright. The beeping of the monitors, too loud.

The nurse checked the readings one last time. "Rest for now. You're stable, but you've been through a lot."

The door closed behind her, leaving Isabella alone with the machines and the quiet.

A few hours later, Dr. Maya Rivera entered the room, her expression calm but serious. She moved with purpose, her eyes scanning the monitors and the IV stand before settling on Isabella. Despite knowing her for years and being closer to the family than just a medical contact, she didn't seem to acknowledge any recognition of Isabella. "Good to see you awake," she began, her voice steady. "You gave us quite a scare."

Isabella shifted in the hospital bed, her gaze meeting Maya's. The doctor's demeanor was professional, detached, very uncharacteristic of the warmth and empathy Isabella had come to expect from her after having her as her caretaker and close friend for years.

"The epistaxis was severe," Dr. Rivera continued. "And it was compounded by a significant internal bleed. Your autoimmune dysregulation triggered a severe thrombocytopenic cascade – essentially, your immune system aggressively targeted and destroyed your own platelets."

She paused, letting the information sink in. Isabella's brow furrowed, confusion and concern etched across her face. The medical jargon was overwhelming, and Maya's cold regard only added to her distress. "Without sufficient platelets, your blood's ability to coagulate was critically compromised. That's why the bleeding, both nasal and internal, wouldn't stop. You were progressing rapidly toward systemic hemorrhagic shock."

She gestured toward the IV stand, the clear fluid dripping steadily into Isabella's arm. "Frankly, if it weren't for the rapid infusion of the synthetic hemoglobin matrix the Medivac team administered en route, stabilizing your oxygen transport and volume while we addressed the platelet deficit here...the outcome would likely have been different."

Isabella's eyes widened, her heart racing as she tried to process. She felt a sudden chill, despite the warmth of the hospital room. "Maya," she whispered, her voice trembling. "It's me, Bella...I don't understand..."

Dr. Rivera's expression softened for a moment, her eyes flickering with something that might have been sympathy. But it was gone as quickly as it had appeared, replaced once again by the cool, detached mask of a doctor. "I know it's a lot to take in," she said, her tone gentle but firm. "Let me explain it in simpler terms."

Dr. Rivera took a deep breath, her fingers tapping lightly on the edge of the bed. "Your immune system went haywire, attacking your platelets, the cells that help your blood clot. Without enough of them, you started bleeding internally, and the bleeding wouldn't stop. It's like your body forgot how to form scabs, but on the inside."

Isabella nodded slowly, her eyes never leaving Maya's face. She felt a knot tightening in her stomach, a mix of fear and confusion. "What happens now?" she asked, her voice barely above a whisper.

Dr. Rivera's expression remained serious. "We've stabilized your platelet count with factor concentrates for now, but we'll need to adjust your immunomodulators significantly. This was a severe episode, Isabella. We need to make sure it doesn't happen again."

Isabella swallowed hard, her mind racing. She felt a sudden, overwhelming urge to cry, but she held it back, her eyes burning with unshed tears. "I understand," she said, her voice steady despite the turmoil inside.

Dr. Rivera nodded, her fingers still tapping lightly on the bed. "I'll be back to check on you later," she said, her tone professional once again. "In the meantime, try to rest."

She turned to leave, her hand already on the door release. She paused, turning back to Isabella, a serene smile fixed on her face. It was a smile Isabella had never seen before on Maya, devoid of the usual warmth and empathy. "One more thing, Isabella," she said, her voice calm, almost soothing. "I took the liberty of administering the

GeneVax Therapy while you were unconscious. Standard procedure in cases of acute autoimmune dysregulation."

Isabella's eyes widened, her breath catching in her throat. "Gene-Vax?" she whispered, her voice hoarse. "But... I...I didn't agree to that."

Dr. Rivera's smile didn't waver, holding up a hand as if dismissing a compliment. "Consider it a proactive intervention. Given your history and the severity of this episode, it was the most prudent course of action. It will stabilize your immune response far more effectively than conventional immunomodulators. You'll be feeling better than ever in a few hours."

Isabella stared at her, a cold dread spreading through her veins. She struggled to reconcile the Maya she knew – the compassionate, ethical doctor – with the woman standing before her, uttering these words with such detached certainty. "But A-Alex..." she stammered, her mind reeling. Alex, her son, had warned her about GeneVax, about its potential dangers. He had begged her not to take it.

Dr. Rivera's smile tightened slightly, a flicker of something cold in her eyes. "Alex worries too much," she said dismissively. "He gets caught up in unsubstantiated theories. GeneVax is a miracle of modern medicine, Isabella. It changed Jamie's life, and it will do the same for you. It will bring you health, clarity, peace. You'll see."

"I need to talk to my son," she said, her voice trembling. "I need to call him."

Dr. Rivera shook her head gently. "Rest now, Isabella. Don't overexert yourself. You'll have plenty of time to talk later. Just let the therapy settle."

She turned and left, the door hissing shut behind her, leaving Isabella alone with her fear and the sterile silence of the hospital room. The steady beep of the monitors echoed the frantic pounding of her heart. She reached for her iBand, her fingers fumbling. She needed to contact Alex, to warn him, to understand what was happening to her, to them. But as she touched the smooth surface of the device, she realized her rose gold iBand had been replaced with an off-white hospital monitoring unit.

A wave of dizziness washed over her and the room began to spin. A strange calmness settled over her, a sense of detachment, of peace. The fear receded, replaced by an acceptance that the hospital would contact Alex for her. That they knew best...

Inside the library, Alex shifted on the hard bench, his sleep disturbed by the irregular sounds of the building's cleaning systems. The HelioLux system, a network of fiber optic cables woven throughout the building, pulsed with a soft, natural light. Sunlight, captured by collectors on the library's roof and channeled through 'SunPipes', filled the space with a gentle, diffused glow, mimicking the subtle shifts of dawn. It was a warm contradiction to the harsh, artificial lighting he was accustomed to in OmniHealth's data centers. He blinked, trying to clear the fog of sleep from his mind. The small data card was safely tucked securely in his pocket.

SUB212, 222 Pikes Peak Ave, 0915.05302037. The cryptic message offered no clues, only a location and a date and time. Today.

He instinctively reached for his iBand, a familiar gesture to check the time, only to find his wrist bare. He cursed under his breath. He felt exposed, adrift without the constant stream of data and connectivity the iBand provided. He scanned the area, looking for a clock, but the library seemed devoid of any traditional timekeeping devices.

With a sigh, Alex stood and stretched, his joints stiff from sleeping on the unforgiving bench. He walked toward a more open area of the library, drawn by the low hum of conversation and the aroma of freshly-brewed coffee. A sleek, automated Colombia Fair Trade Coffee shop was nestled within the library's central hub, its chrome and glass surfaces gleaming under the HelioLux illumination. Patrons sat at tables, engaged in animated discussions, sipping steaming mugs of coffee and nibbling on pastries. The scene felt strangely normal, unlike the turmoil churning within him.

He approached a woman, her dark hair cascading over her shoulders. She was wearing a form-fitting, emerald green jumpsuit, cut low in the front, accentuating her curves. "Excuse me, Ma'am," he began, his voice low. "Do you happen to have the time?"

The woman turned, her brow furrowed in confusion. Her eyes, a warm hazel, scanned him from head to toe. "You don't have an iBand?" she asked, her voice laced with surprise.

Alex feigned a sheepish grin. "I seem to have misplaced it. Must have fallen off somewhere." He gestured vaguely toward his empty wrist.

"Oh, you poor dear," she exclaimed, her eyes widening with sympathy. "You can't get the time, let alone order anything without it." She reached out and gently touched his wrist, as if confirming its nakedness. "I'll buy you something. What would you like?"

"That's really not necessary," Alex began, but the woman cut him off.

"Nonsense," she insisted, her smile radiating warmth. "I'm Bree. It's a beautiful Saturday and I'm feeling wonderfully generous." She wrapped him in a hug, the scent of her perfume, something floral and sweet, filling his nostrils.

The unexpected physical contact made him stiffen. He wasn't accustomed to such displays of affection, especially from strangers. "A Cortado, please," Alex mumbled, his mind already calculating the quickest way to extricate himself from the encounter. "And one Arepa de Huevo." The words tasted of familiarity, a fleeting memory of his grandfather's Miami kitchen.

"Excellent choice!" Bree chirped, her voice echoing through the cafe. "They have the best Arepas here. Made with lab-grown corn, not that small artisanal real stuff. So much better for you, you know?"

She tapped a series of commands on her iBand, the holographic display flickering above her wrist. "There we go. All taken care of." She turned back to Alex, her smile unwavering. "Honestly, I've never felt better since I got GeneVax. Nine days ago, it was. Life-changing, truly."

Alex's stomach clenched. He forced a smile. "That's...good to hear."

"It really is," Bree continued, her voice rising in enthusiasm. "I'm always happy to help out someone less fortunate. Everyone should experience this level of well-being. It's like a weight has been lifted. I feel so clear and focused."

Alex glanced at the automated coffee dispenser, noting the time displayed on its digital interface: 8:47. Why didn't he just look there to start with? He calculated the distance to the address on the data card. Ten minutes, maybe less. He needed to leave soon.

Bree continued to talk, her words a stream of flowery pronouncements about the beauty of the day, the wonders of GeneVax, and her newfound sense of purpose. Alex nodded politely, his mind racing. He was trapped in a web of pleasantries, the free coffee and arepas, a gilded cage. He had to find a way out before it was too late. He checked the time again. 8:52. He decided to give it until nine.

Alex collected his Cortado and the warm breakfast arepa from the automated dispenser, the scent of cornmeal and melted cheese momentarily made him forget everything as his stomach involuntarily growled. He turned back to Bree, forcing another tight smile. "Thank you again. This was very kind. But I really need to get going. I have an appointment."

"Oh, already?" Bree's face fell slightly, her hazel eyes wide. "It was so nice talking." She stepped closer, invading his personal space again. Before Alex could react, she leaned in, pressing her lips firmly against his. Her tongue darted forward, a startling intrusion.

Alex froze, every muscle tensing. He pulled back sharply.

"What a shame you don't have your iBand," Bree murmured, her voice breathy, seemingly unfazed by his recoil. "I'd give you my contact." She gave a little wave, her smile bright and fixed before turning back to her coffee, humming softly.

Alex backed away, the lingering taste of her synthetic floral perfume and the unwelcome pressure of her kiss on his lips. He wiped his mouth with the back of his hand, a futile gesture. The encounter left a residue of unease, a jarring mix of forced intimacy and the strange, placid cheerfulness he now associated with GeneVax. He shoved the memory down, turning his focus outward.

He pushed through the library's revolving doors, stepping onto the sun-drenched sidewalk. The natural light channeled by the HelioLux system inside gave way to the direct glare of the morning sun. He headed east on Kiowa Street, the paper cup warm in his hand. He took out the arepa tucked into a recyclable wrapper and began to quickly eat. The city bustled around him – automated vehicles gliding silently, pedestrians moving with purpose, their iBand HoloScreens flickering with myriad data streams.

Without his own, Alex felt disconnected, a ghost observing a world he was no longer fully part of. The kiss lingered, a violation he couldn't shake. Bree's casual aggression, her utter lack of awareness of his discomfort, felt alien. Was this the 'clarity' Jamie spoke of? A state devoid of normal social boundaries?

He reached the intersection with Nevada Avenue and crossed, continuing east. Ahead, the address came into view: 222 Pikes Peak Avenue. The building was a sleek structure of glass and recycled steel, its facade integrating panels that likely served as HelioLux collectors. A discreet sign near the entrance read *TerraMetric Solutions*. Underneath, smaller text detailed their function: *Predictive Environmental Analysis & Resource Modeling*.

Alex recognized the corporate jargon. It was the kind of firm that processed massive datasets, probably atmospheric and geological, using sophisticated AI – likely platforms incorporating Microsoft's OTTOpilot – to generate weather forecasts for corporate clients or governmental agencies. Successors to Project Nimbus, perhaps, or entities managing the fallout. Water rights, agricultural yields, climate risk assessments – invaluable data in their resource-constrained world.

As Alex slowed, studying the entrance, a figure darted toward him from a nearby alley. The man was thin, his clothes mismatched and worn, his hair a tangled mess. His eyes burned with a frantic energy. He thrust a crumpled piece of paper into Alex's hand. "Don't let them do it!" the man rasped, his voice urgent, raw. "We have to stand up to them!"

Before Alex could respond, the man spun away, targeting another passerby further down the sidewalk with the same urgent message. Alex glanced down at the flyer. It was cheaply printed, the text dense and slightly blurred. Headlines screamed about manipulated weather patterns, corporate control of rainfall, and the lingering legacy of Project Nimbus. Old news, conspiracy theories most people dismissed, yet resonating uncomfortably with Alex's own recent experiences.

He folded the paper quickly, shoving it into his trouser pocket alongside the data card. His priority was the meeting. He scanned the TerraMetric building facade and entrance area again, searching for any indication of 'SUB212'. A suite number? A basement level? A specific contact point? Nothing obvious presented itself. He needed to find it, whatever it was.

Alex pushed through the smoked glass doors of TerraMetric Solutions, the cool, conditioned air refreshing compared to the street's warmth. He kept his gaze lowered, tracking the geometric patterns inlaid on the polished concrete floor, angling his head just enough to scan the periphery without offering a clear view to the ceiling-mounted optical sensors.

He expected automated check-in kiosks, perhaps an OTTOpilot-voiced welcome projected from an unseen speaker. Instead, his eyes landed on a built-in desk of pale, recycled composite material, and behind it, a person. A living, breathing human receptionist. The sight was jarring, a throwback to an earlier era of corporate interface.

The woman looked up as he approached. Her dark hair was pulled back neatly, framing intelligent eyes. She wore a simple, dark blue tunic that complemented her warm skin tone. A small, silver stud glinted in her nose. "Good morning. May I help you?" Her voice was calm, professional, with a slight melodic quality.

Alex stopped a few feet from the desk, careful to keep his face turned from the camera integrated above her station. He cleared his throat. "I'm looking for SUB212."

A flicker of confusion crossed her features, a slight furrowing of her brow. She tilted her head, accessing information perhaps from an unseen neural link or a subtle screen embedded in the desk surface. "SUB212...ah, yes. That designation refers to the sub-structure."

Alex waited, keeping his posture relaxed, projecting casual inquiry.

"It's not technically part of *this* facility," she explained, gesturing vaguely around the pristine lobby. "It's the old municipal parking garage beneath us. You'll need to exit the building." She paused, ensuring he followed. "Go around to the rear service entrance. There's a freight elevator there, it's marked. Take that down to sub-section two.

The old storage units are down there, repurposed. They're numbered sequentially. You should find 212 easily enough."

Alex processed the instructions. A disused parking garage. Storage lockers. He noted the locations of two more cameras during the brief exchange, calculating the probable delay. Even with his face partially obscured, the gait analysis, thermal signature, and partial facial data fed into the city's surveillance network would eventually yield a high-probability match. He estimated the obfuscation bought him perhaps eighty-nine minutes, ninety at most, before his identity pinged on whatever system LifeSpan was using to hunt him.

"Understood. Thank you." He offered a brief nod, careful not to raise his head fully, and turned back toward the entrance. He pushed back out into the morning light, the receptionist's instructions echoing in his mind. He found the rear service entrance easily enough, a heavy steel door tucked away beside overflowing recycling bins. It hissed open at his proximity, granting access to a grimy corridor smelling faintly of decay. The freight elevator was exactly where the receptionist indicated, its brushed metal doors scratched and dented. He thumbed the worn button marked SB2\. The elevator groaned, descending slowly into the earth, the air growing cooler, damper.

Sub-section two was vast and dimly-lit by flickering emergency lights spaced far apart. Concrete pillars marched into the gloom. The air hung still, heavy with the scent of dust and old exhaust fumes. Rows of storage lockers lined one wall, their corrugated metal doors bearing faded numbers. Alex walked along the row, his footsteps echoing in the quiet space. 198... 204... 210... He stopped. 212.

The locker door was plain, unremarkable steel, identical to its neighbors except for the stenciled number. There was no padlock, no digital keypad. Alex hesitated before pulling the handle. The door swung inward smoothly, silently, revealing nothing but empty concrete floor and bare metal walls. Dust motes danced in the beam of light spilling from the corridor. It was completely bare.

A soft scuff of a shoe on concrete broke the silence. Alex turned. A woman stood a few yards away, leaning against a concrete pillar, partially obscured by shadow. She was lean, dressed in functional, dark clothing, her short, stark-black hair brushed to one side. Her dark eyes were sharp, assessing him coolly.

She pushed away from the pillar and stepped forward, her movements quiet, efficient. "Where's Maya?" Her voice was low, steady, devoid of inflection.

Alex kept his own voice level. "I could ask you the same thing."

Her eyes narrowed almost imperceptibly. A second figure detached himself from the deeper shadows near another pillar – a younger man, tall, wearing a dark hoodie zipped high, his curly, frosted hair catching the dim light. He watched Alex intently, his hands shoved into his pockets, posture tense.

The woman ignored Alex's deflection. "Dr. Rivera and I had an arrangement. We were supposed to meet here. Now." She glanced pointedly at his bare wrist where his iBand used to be before looking at the empty locker. "To exchange information."

"What kind of information?" Alex kept his stance neutral, hands visible at his sides.

A humorless smile touched the woman's lips. "Let's start with you. Who are you? And how do you know Maya Rivera?"

Her gaze was unwavering, searching. She radiated a coiled vigilance, nothing like the placid acceptance he'd seen in Jamie and Bree. Alex stared, offering no response, analyzing the situation.

"I'm Elena," she continued, her tone hardening slightly. "This is Marcus. Now, answer the question. Why are *you* here instead of Maya?"

Alex studied Elena. His SRV cataloged the minute details – the tension in her jaw, the controlled breathing, the way her eyes constantly scanned the surroundings even while focused on him. But beyond the patterns, something else registered. An authenticity. A lack of the smooth, artificial veneer the GeneVax therapy seemed to impart.

He sensed the genuine weariness beneath the guarded exterior, the earned caution of someone operating outside the system, someone unmodified. It wasn't a logical deduction, it felt deeper, an instinctual recognition cutting through his analytical filters. He could trust her. Or at least, he felt a compelling impulse to trust her. He met Elena's steady gaze. The low emergency lights cast long shadows, making the vast concrete space feel smaller, more confined. "How do I know I can trust you?"

Elena's expression remained impassive. A flicker of something unreadable crossed Marcus's face in the background. He adjusted his thin-rimmed glasses.

"You don't," Elena replied, her voice unemotional. "The same way we don't know if we can trust you. But Maya isn't here, and you are. Start talking."

Alex took a slow breath, the cool, damp air settling in his lungs. He decided to give them the necessary data points, monitoring their reactions. "Dr. Rivera consulted on my mother's case. Complex autoimmune. Clinton Memorial. Maya was thorough, ethical. Different." He paused, letting the connection establish itself. "I'm a data analyst. OmniHealth. We process streams for LifeSpan."

Marcus straightened slightly, his interest visibly piqued. Elena remained still, listening. "I found patterns," Alex continued, the memory of the glowing HoloScreen data pulsing behind his eyes. "Anomalies in the GeneVax outcome datasets. Behavioral metrics. Significant drops in dissent indicators, critical thought markers post-treatment. Too uniform. Too fast." He pushed back a stray lock of hair, the tremor in his hand returning faintly.

"I tried talking to a colleague, Jamie. She...changed. After the GeneVax treatment. Jamie dismissed my concerns," Alex pressed on, refocusing on Elena. "Before, she was cynical, sharp. After...placid. Agreeable. Kept pushing me to get the treatment for my own good." He recalled the disturbing conversation in his apartment, Bree's unsettling kiss in the cafe.

"I went to Maya because I trusted her judgment. I showed her the aggregate data. She was skeptical, but she saw the pattern. Maya wanted specifics. She needed access to an individual file, someone we both knew had changed. Jamie's. To see the raw genetic sequencing report, cross-reference it with the behavioral flags. She believed the full genetic edit logs wouldn't be in the standard patient file accessible at

OmniHealth, but might be in the deeper research archives at Clinton Memorial."

Elena folded her arms. "Access she apparently tried to get."

"I think it's what she must have intended to bring here," Alex said. "She got us into the research facility. She had access, I'm a data analyst. Together, we found confirmation. They have priority lists. People flagged for exhibiting non-compliant traits. Journalists, activists...data analysts." He met Elena's gaze directly. "Jamie was on the list. So was I. There's an internal project designation. ANGUS. He paused, the single word echoing in the dark dead air of the garage.

"ANGUS?" Elena repeated the acronym.

"Codename ANGUS, Authority Normalization via Genetic Update Sequence." Alex delivered the name calmly, each word precise, producing a finger on his hand for each word as if counting. "LifeSpan isn't just curing diseases with GeneVax. They're using their CRISPR-Cas12a tech to edit neural pathways. Genes linked to skepticism, critical thought, authority response, who knows what else? They're engineering mass compliance."

Elena's face remained a mask, but a muscle twitched below her eye. The air seemed to thicken. Marcus let out a breath, a soft hiss in the cavernous space.

"And you have proof of this? This...ANGUS?" Elena's tone demanded verification, the pragmatism of someone long accustomed to unsubstantiated claims.

Alex's jaw tightened. "We found it. In the research facility data core at Clinton Memorial. Encrypted files, internal project logs, the specific genetic markers targeted." He remembered the glowing lines of code on the HoloScreen, the chilling clarity of the data. "But we didn't get it out."

Elena's eyes narrowed further. "Explain."

"Security. They knew someone was accessing restricted data. An alarm tripped. They breached the room just as we confirmed the ANGUS protocol." Alex pictured Maya's face, the sudden resolve hardening her features. "Dr. Rivera created a diversion. Bought me time to get through a service passage she knew about." He gestured vaguely toward the direction he'd come from. "She gave me this address, told me to meet her contact here. That was the plan."

"So there's no evidence," Elena stated, the words falling like stones. Not a question, a conclusion. The initial flicker of hope in Marcus' eyes dimmed.

Alex nodded curtly. "We didn't have time to copy the files. They were right on top of us." The failure tasted bitter. "But Maya saw it. She knows. If we can contact her, maybe, "

"No," Elena cut him off decisively. The word was absolute. "If security apprehended her inside that facility, knowing what she knew, she's compromised. Treated. Or worse." Her gaze held Alex's, unflinching. "We operate under the assumption that anyone taken is lost to us."

A heavy quiet descended. The uncommon barking of a dog in the distance the only sound.

Elena took a step closer, lowering her voice slightly, though the acoustics of the garage carried every syllable. "Maya knew something was wrong *before* you contacted her. She felt it. The changes in colleagues, the pressure from administration, inconsistencies she couldn't pin down."

Alex blinked, processing this new information. Maya hadn't just reacted to his data, she'd already been primed.

"She reached out weeks ago," Elena continued, her dark eyes intense. "Through secure channels. We've been working together, carefully. Planning how to get definitive proof of what LifeSpan was doing. Your arrival, your data... It accelerated things. Made her push for access sooner than we'd intended."

She moved closer, just slightly. "You and Maya weren't the only ones noticing things." Her voice dropped lower still, drawing Alex into their clandestine circle. "There aren't many of us in this fight. People who haven't taken the needle, or people who saw the cracks early. We stay hidden. Off-grid. We watch, we gather what scraps we can, we try to warn others." She gestured vaguely, encompassing the shadowed space, the hidden network it represented.

"We call ourselves *the unmodified*. Not very original, but it fits."

It wasn't a grand declaration, more a weary statement of fact. A small band against a global apparatus engineering consent. Alex understood the caution, the layers of paranoia. He *felt* it, a resonance with his own ingrained skepticism amplified tenfold by circumstance.

Marcus stepped forward, pulling his hand from his hoodie pocket. He held out a plain, dark grey baseball cap. It looked ordinary, slightly worn. He tossed it lightly to Alex, who caught it reflexively. "Put it on," Marcus instructed. His voice was rougher than Elena's, carrying a cynical edge.

Alex turned the cap over. Affixed to the underside of the bill, near the front edge, were two small, flat, matte-black discs, each no larger than a fingernail. They looked like dull buttons or sensors. "What is this?" Alex examined the discs, noting their precise placement.

"Active optical camouflage," Marcus explained, tapping his own temple near his glasses.

"Low-yield light-field emitters. They project a distortion pattern directly into the capture path of most optical sensors – surveillance cameras, facial recognition scanners. Won't make you invisible, but it scrambles the focal points around your primary facial features. To the camera AI, it looks like severe lens flare or motion blur concentrated right where it needs clear data for an ID." He gave a short, humorless laugh. "Buys you time. Confuses the algorithms."

Alex nodded, understanding the principle. A localized data disruption field. Simple, yet potentially effective against automated systems relying on clear captures. He pulled the cap onto his head, adjusting the brim low over his eyes.

"It helps." Marcus shrugged. "But facial recognition is only one vector. Gait analysis is almost as common now. The way you walk – rhythm, stride length, weight distribution. Unique as a fingerprint if the system has enough baseline data." He eyed Alex up and down.

"OmniHealth, LifeSpan...they have that data on you. Mandatory wellness scans, building sensors...they profile everyone." Marcus glanced around the grimy floor. "Got anything small you can stick in one shoe? A pebble, folded scrap? Anything to throw off your natural stride just slightly. Needs to be inconsistent. A limp."

Alex remembered the folded paper in his pocket. The Project

Nimbus flyer. He pulled it out, the cheap paper crinkling softly. He folded it again, making a small, dense square. Bending down, he slipped off his right sneaker and wedged the paper firmly under his heel inside the shoe. He re-tied the sneaker, stood up, and took a tentative step.

The effect was immediate. A small, artificial lump throwing his balance slightly off-kilter. He walked a few paces. His right foot landed differently, pushing his hip out fractionally with each step. It felt awkward, unnatural. Lopsided.

"Good enough," Marcus grunted, watching Alex's uneven movement. It's not foolproof. A dedicated human observer might spot the fake limp eventually. But combined with the cap, it significantly lowers your probability score in the automated tracking systems. Makes you harder to flag, harder to follow digitally."

"What now?" Alex asked.

Elena smiled. "We bring you in."

ELENA LED THE WAY, moving with quiet confidence through the echoing concrete labyrinth of the parking structure. Marcus fell in beside Alex, his gaze sweeping their surroundings, a constant scan for threats Alex was only beginning to appreciate. The air shifted from cool, stale underground to the warmer, exhaust-tinged breath of the city as they emerged onto a cracked sidewalk beneath an overpass.

Although clean electric vehicles were the primary mode of transportation, there were still plenty of older gasoline-powered vehicles that hadn't met the mandatory Clean Air Act deadlines yet, either converting to hydrogen fuel cells, or the more costly all-electric changeover. The low rumble of traffic vibrated through the soles of Alex's sneakers, the unevenness caused by the folded paper a constant reminder of his altered gait.

"We walk," Elena stated, turning left, heading east toward the denser cluster of downtown buildings shimmering under the afternoon sun. "Fifteen minutes to the Bijou station. No transports. Too easy to track, easier still for them to reroute an autonomous vehicle straight into a containment unit."

The route took them away from the polished facades of the main corporate corridors, dipping into older streets lined with brick buildings, some repurposed, others showing signs of neglect. Storefronts displayed dusty wares behind reinforced glass. The pedestrian traffic was sparser, less hurried, faces etched with the weariness of navigating the megalopolis' underbelly.

Marcus walked with his hands jammed into his hoodie pockets, his platinum-tipped hair catching the light. He kept pace with Alex's deliberately uneven steps. They walked for a few blocks, silence broken only by the city's noise.

"You wanna know why I'm doing this?" he asked, his voice intentionally low. He didn't wait for an answer. "Used to be a pen-tester. Cybersecurity consultant. Good money, poking holes in corporate networks for big paychecks." He kicked at a loose piece of ferrocrete on the sidewalk.

"Saw things," he said. "Anomalies. Encrypted traffic spikes from LifeSpan servers lining up perfectly with public health data dumps. This was years ago, before GeneVax was even a household name. Just...odd correlations nobody else seemed to notice or care about. Then I heard about the mandatory genetic experiments on inmates. My brother 'found Christ', not that there's anything wrong with that, but he was a stone-cold killer and I knew it wasn't him, not really."

He glanced at Alex, his eyes sharp behind the thin frames of his glasses. "Then the Sovereign Crypto Collapse hit. Wiped out my family's savings. Wasn't just market forces. Found traces, targeted manipulation, state-backed actors using the chaos for surveillance infrastructure tests. Learned that the systems we build can be turned against us faster than you can blink. LifeSpan, the government, they're just refining the technique. Control through convenience. Control through 'wellness'." He spat the word like it was poison.

"Saw where it was heading," he continued. "Found Elena, found others. Decided I'd rather break their systems than get paid to patch them."

Elena looked back, slowing slightly to let them catch up. Her dark eyes settled on Alex. "You said you spotted the anomaly in the GeneVax data. The behavioral shifts. OmniHealth's AI, LifeSpan's own oversight systems...they missed it. How?"

Alex adjusted the cap, one of the emitters beneath the brim against his thumb. He considered the complexity, the sheer audacity of what LifeSpan had engineered. "They didn't miss it," he replied, the conviction solidifying in his chest. "The AI models were trained *not* to see it. It's the only explanation that fits the data spread, the lack of flags. You can build parameters, blind spots, into any learning algorithm. Teach it to recognize cancer markers but ignore subtle shifts in socio-political alignment scores correlated with a specific gene therapy."

He paused, choosing his next words carefully. "As for how *I* saw it, I have a condition. Synaptic Resonance Variance. SRV." He saw a flicker of recognition in Elena's eyes, but Marcus just looked intrigued. "It's neurological. Affects pattern recognition. Lets me process complex datasets differently, spot connections and inconsistencies that even sophisticated AI seems designed to overlook. It's why I could see the pattern hiding in plain sight."

Alex kept his steps measured, deliberate. "Dr. Rivera knew something wasn't right with GeneVax and had her own ethical lines. She suspected, but she couldn't pinpoint it within LifeSpan's protocols, not without raising alarms she couldn't afford. She had access, credentials, and an understanding of the clinical side."

He pushed a stray lock of dark hair back from his forehead, a familiar habit even under the strange cap. "I had the perspective, SRV. I could see the correlated data, the pattern woven through the anonymized OmniHealth feeds. She needed me to tell her *what* to look for, specifically which data streams held the proof of the ANGUS protocol. I needed her to get me *to* that data within Clinton Memorial's systems, past the firewalls Omni wouldn't let me touch."

Marcus nodded slowly. "Symbiotic. Access and analysis. Makes sense."

"But now..." Alex trailed off. Maya compromised. Captured. Worse, potentially treated, her sharp, ethical mind overwritten by the insidious plan she sought to expose. The clean extraction they planned, the irrefutable proof they intended to leak vanished like an unfulfilled wish.

"She's likely gone," Elena stated, her voice devoid of sentiment but not cold. It was the tone of pragmatism honed by loss. "Assume the worst. Assume she's compromised. Assume anything she knew, they now know. That includes your face, your name, your connection to her." She cut her eyes toward him briefly. "The plan you had with her is dead."

Alex looked down, wrestling with emotion something akin to a death in the family, a feeling he knew too well.

"Keep moving," Elena commanded, picking up the pace as the entrance to the Bijou station came into view – a wide, glassed-in descent into the transportation network. "Dwelling on what's lost gets you caught. We focus on what's next." She adjusted the strap of the nondescript messenger bag slung across her body. "We've been working on angles for a long time. Trying to get clean data out of Life-Span or their partners is...difficult."

Marcus scoffed. "We've had operatives, insiders, and attempts to breach their networks. Even when we succeed, the volume is over-whelming. Terabytes of encrypted research notes, clinical trial noise, administrative chaff, nested algorithms designed to obfuscate. It's information overload by design."

"Finding the specific evidence," Elena continued, her gaze fixed ahead, scanning the station entrance. "It's buried. We pull massive dumps, but sifting through it takes time we don't have, resources stretched thin. It's like searching for one specific grain of sand on an entire beach, only the beach is also on a beach. Even using AI, it's painfully slow. Dude, our last batch took over nine months!"

She glanced at Alex again, her assessment sharp, clinical. "Your ability, SRV, you said you can see the patterns others miss. The data correlation obscured by the noise. You navigated the OmniHealth data, found the initial threads. You pulled the ANGUS files from Clinton Memorial because Rivera got you access, but you knew *what* to look for once you were inside the system."

Her dark eyes held his. "We need that. Badly. We can get access, Marcus can crack shells, but pointing us to the right *data* once we're in, identifying the signal through the static, that's been the bottleneck. Too much information has been as effective a defense for them as encryption."

The glassed-in ascent of the Bijou Maglev station yawned before them, commuters flowing in and out like particulate matter in a current. The air near the entrance hummed faintly with the station's internal climate systems and the low murmur of aggregated voices. Elena, however, maintained her westward trajectory, her stride unwavering. She led them straight past the wide entrance, her gaze already fixed on the street corner beyond.

Marcus followed without comment, his attention briefly flicking toward the station's security cameras before returning to the surrounding streetscape. Alex, mimicking their pace and Elena's apparent disinterest in the transit hub, kept walking, the folded paper beneath his sole a persistent, asymmetrical pressure which began to hurt, potentially on the verge of a blister, which only accentuated his limp.

A sudden surge of displaced air washed over them, fierce and abrupt. Alex looked up instinctively. High above, perhaps a hundred feet, a sleek, metallic trainset blurred past on the elevated guideway. Southbound. Its passage was a silent displacement, a momentary interruption of the sky.

There was no accompanying rumble through the concrete beneath their feet, no vibration shivering up their legs. The magnetic levitation held the massive train aloft, erasing the friction and noise of conventional rail. Only the wind spoke of its immense speed, a brief gale whipping debris along the sidewalk, tugging at Alex's cap.

Adjacent to the elevated track, rows of vertical-axis wind turbines spun into a frenzy. Their helical blades, designed to capture wind from any direction, accelerated violently in the train's wake. They whirred, a high mechanical sound distinct from the train's silence, converting the manufactured wind back into energy for the system, their rotation visually dissipating the air turbulence almost as quickly as it formed. As swiftly as it appeared, the train was gone, shrinking into the distance, leaving only the briefly-agitated turbines and the settling dust below.

Elena rounded the corner, the station now behind them. The street opened onto a slightly wider avenue, still nestled among older buildings but with glimpses of the newer, taller structures of the central business district visible farther to the East. They continued West, but the character of the streets shifted abruptly. The transition was stark. One block held the muted sheen of maintained municipal infrastructure, the next plunged into neglect.

They walked alongside the massive concrete retaining walls and support pylons that held the elevated Maglev line aloft – the gleaming symbol of the Front Range megalopolis' connectivity soaring directly over a landscape of profound disconnection. This was 'by the rails', a pocket of the city, the planners, the autonomous transit grids, and the pervasive surveillance networks, and MetroSec seemed to have collectively forgotten, or perhaps deliberately ignored.

The air grew heavy, laced with the sour tang of uncollected refuse and the faint, acrid scent of chemical runoff. Cracked pavement buckled underfoot, weeds pushing through fissures like desperate green fingers. Overflowing dumpsters spilled cascades of waste onto the broken curbs, creating ragged monuments to urban decay.

Along one side street, a line of ancient internal combustion engine vehicles slumped against the curb. Their tires were flat, deflated rubber puddles on the asphalt, or missing entirely, leaving the rusted chassis resting on cracked rims. Windshields were spiderwebbed with impacts or replaced with taped plastic sheeting.

They were not merely abandoned vehicles, they were shelters. Makeshift curtains hung in some windows. A child's faded plastic toy lay half-buried in the gutter grime near one sedan's open door. In the winter, these metal husks offered a meager shield against the cold. Now, under the strengthening spring sun, they radiated heat, promising suffocation.

Here and there, tucked beneath overpasses or huddled in the lee of crumbling brick warehouses, were clusters of tents and tarpaulin structures. Thin streams of smoke curled from improvised chimneys – small fires for cooking or warmth, even now. Figures moved slowly within the encampments, faces obscured by shadow or turned away, existing in a parallel reality to the high-speed efficiency gliding silently overhead.

Alex scanned the sky. No glint of MetroSec drones patrolling the streets. No blinking status lights of surveillance cameras mounted on the rust-streaked lampposts. It was a pocket of deliberate blindness, a zone excised from the city's official narrative of seamless order. The neglect felt old, ingrained, a problem left to fester for decades.

Elena slipped across the shattered pavement with reconnaissance-level precision, her gait betraying no hint of the hazards beneath. She seemed unperturbed by the squalor, her focus entirely on their destination. Marcus, though still watchful, moved with a similar lack of surprise, his gaze cataloging potential threats with a detached professionalism.

For Alex, each step was an immersion into a reality he had only glimpsed from the filtered windows of OmniHealth or the sterile compartments of AVs. The data points he analyzed – poverty metrics, infrastructure failures, health disparities – took on a grim, tangible form. This was the consequence of the system he was now fighting, the human cost obscured by layers of corporate euphemism and algorithmic smoothing, a punishment quantified, normalized, and projected as acceptable loss in the quarterly report.

Elena led them down a narrow alley between two warehouses whose corrugated metal sides were scarred with graffiti tags layers deep. The alley ended abruptly at a high, stained concrete wall – part of the Maglev support structure. Set flush into the wall were a pair of heavy, rust-streaked steel doors. They looked ancient, forgotten, bearing no handles or obvious locks.

Elena stopped before the doors. She glanced back down the alley, a quick, habitual check. From her messenger bag, she produced a small, palm-sized device, featureless black plastic. She pressed it against the seam between the two doors, near the bottom. A low click echoed faintly in the confined space. She knelt, placing her hands flat on the right-side door and pushed. With a deep groan of protesting metal hinges, the door swung inward, revealing not solid concrete, but darkness.

A flight of steep concrete stairs descended into the gloom. The air that wafted up smelled different – cool, damp, thick with the scent of old concrete and stagnant water.

"Quickly," Elena murmured, gesturing them forward. Stepping through the opening, she began her descent.

Marcus followed immediately. Alex hesitated for only a second, the enormity of the step – not just down the stairs, but into a hidden, unknown world – settling onto him. He took a breath of the alley's fouled air and plunged into the cool darkness, pushing the heavy door shut behind him. The groan and thud of its closure sealed them in. They were underground, inside the forgotten carcass of the Front Range Hyperloop.

Alex descended the steps, the uneven rhythm of his altered gait now just part of the journey. He was here. He was with them. He was part of whatever came next.

The heavy steel door sealed them into a cool, subterranean quiet, broken only by the drip of unseen water and the hum of jury-rigged electronics. Portable LED strips cast pools of utilitarian light along the immense curve of the abandoned Hyperloop tunnel, revealing a space both vast and claustrophobic. The main thoroughfare stretched away into darkness in both directions, its diameter could have easily accommodated the sleek Maglev trains that now ran above the interstate highway.

Against one wall, Elena's cell had carved out a small operations hub. Cables snaked across the damp concrete floor, connecting mismatched HoloScreen workstations, charging units, and what looked like scavenged server racks blinking with erratic status lights. Sleeping pallets lay rolled against the wall near a makeshift kitchenette stocked with packaged rations and water filtration units – corporate-sourced necessities ironically repurposed for the resistance. A faint odor of electronics mingled with damp concrete and mildew.

Alex scanned the setup. Compared to the seamless integration and near-limitless resources of OmniHealth or the sterile, high-tech labs at Clinton Memorial, this felt precarious. Exposed. Operational security relied on obscurity, hiding within the city's forgotten bowels, and the equipment looked dated, the power sources likely unstable. His mind, conditioned by structured data environments, registered the vulnera-bilities – the potential points of failure, the lack of redundancies.

Yet the faces of Elena and Marcus showed no such apprehension, only a weary competence. He pushed down the flicker of doubt. He had burned his bridges. The ramshackle haven, the network of deter-mined individuals, was his only path forward now.

As they stepped into the main, illuminated area of the hideout, three other figures looked up from their tasks. Elena led Alex toward a woman with close-cropped grey hair who was meticulously cleaning a projectile weapon component, her movements precise and economical. "Alex, this is Sera Voss," she said. "Sera keeps our gear, and us, in working order."

Sera's gaze lifted, her eyes assessing him in a quick, professional sweep before she gave a single, curt nod. "Alright," she murmured, her attention already returning to the weapon in her hands.

Elena gestured toward a flickering HoloScreen where cascading lines of code reflected in the face of a young man, barely out of his teens. "That's Bo Lin. Our eyes and ears. If it's digital, he owns it."

Bo didn't turn around, but one hand lifted from his keyboard in a brief wave. "Hey," he said, his voice laced with a Mandarin accent, his focus never leaving the data stream.

At a folding table nearby, an older man with deep lines etched around his eyes looked up from a physical map he was meticulously charting. "And Pacheco," Elena continued, her tone softening almost imperceptibly. "Call him 'Patch'. He makes sure we know where we're going and how to get there."

Patch offered a tired but genuine smile. "Welcome," he said, his voice a low gravel. "Glad to have you with us."

The acknowledgements were efficient, the greetings brief. It was the reception of people accustomed to transience and risk, where trust was something to be earned through action, not pleasantries.

Alex offered a curt nod to the room, his gaze drifting past the small group. It landed on a larger workstation terminal in the corner, its HoloScreen displaying complex topographical data overlaid with access protocols and facility schematics. The labels were clear:

Cheyenne Mountain Complex. Archival Data. Geological Stability Reports.

Instantly, something clicked. SRV fired, linking disparate nodes – the HoloScreen data, the news report Alex had seen on the shuttle about the Rocky Mountain Seed Vault, the term 'eco-terrorists', the sudden clampdown. Cheyenne Mountain was *in* the Rocky Mountains. A former military command center, now largely repurposed, but still possessing deep, secure bunkers. A perfect place for an archive. A seed vault?

He turned to Elena, the connection solidifying faster than conscious thought. "The Seed Vault Heist," Alex muttered. His voice cleared as he gained confidence. "The news feeds are calling them eco-terrorists, but it was you. You targeted Cheyenne Mountain, didn't you?" It was less a question than a realization. "It was one of *your* targets, wasn't it?"

Elena paused, turning fully toward him. A flicker of surprise crossed her features, quickly masked by her usual stoicism. She glanced at the screen displaying the Cheyenne Mountain data and back at Alex, a slow appraisal in her dark eyes. "My god," she murmured, almost to herself. "You said you were fast. You weren't exaggerating." She walked closer. "Yes," she said, lowering her voice slightly, though the ambient hum likely muffled their conversation from the others. "The official story is fragmented, deliberately misleading. It wasn't just one vault. There were coordinated attempts on several potential repositories of non-modified genetic material. One was indeed linked to archival storage within the Cheyenne complex – old government bunkers, supposedly decommissioned but still holding historical agricultural data and, we suspect, physical samples."

She gestured vaguely toward Marcus, who was now intently studying the terminal Alex had indicated. "We helped coordinate logistics and provided encrypted communication support for the teams involved. Allies handled the primary ground operation, the one that seemed to have partially succeeded before security locked it down." Elena paused.

"A group called the Terrakin, operating out of the IRNoM. Independent Republic of Northern New Mexico. They understood the stakes."

"Stakes?" Alex prompted, though his SRV was already assembling the pieces – LifeSpan's dominance, GeneVax, the need for genetic diversity.

"The *real* stakes," Elena clarified, her voice hardening. "LifeSpan AgriFuture doesn't just control seventy percent of the *current* global seed market, they're actively hunting down and confiscating any remaining independent sources of non-genetically modified seeds. Heirloom varieties, wild strains, anything that hasn't passed through their labs."

She leaned closer. "They call it 'genetic resource management' or 'biosecurity consolidation'. Bullshit. It's about absolute control. They need the genetic diversity for their own research, to engineer future crops, maybe even counter future blights. But more importantly, it's an insurance policy. If they control *all* the seeds, they control the food. Period. No alternatives. And if you control the food..." She raised her eyebrows and shrugged her shoulders slightly.

"You control the population," Alex finished. "Owning the seeds isn't just about market share. It's about owning the future of the species." He frowned. The Resistance wasn't just fighting a conspiracy, they were fighting for the biological autonomy of the entire species.

Across the makeshift operations center, Marcus pushed back from the workstation displaying the Cheyenne Mountain schematics. He swiveled his chair, his gaze locking onto Alex. He beckoned with a quick, sharp gesture. "Over here a sec."

Alex crossed the uneven concrete floor, navigating the tangle of cables, the paper document still a subtle lump inside his shoe. Marcus watched him approach, his expression serious, the usual cynicism momentarily absent, replaced by focused intensity. The HoloScreen beside him now showed complex molecular diagrams, swirling protein structures rendered in glowing lines.

"You talked to Dr. Rivera before." He tapped a finger against the side of his temple. "What did she tell you about the tech? Specifically CRISPR-Cas12a?"

Alex recalled his hurried, desperate conversation with Maya in the hospital corridor, the clinical terms jarring against the imminent danger. "Only the basics," he admitted. "She said LifeSpan used a modified Cas12a system. Described it like a biological word processor. Find-and-replace for DNA sequences. She mentioned it was more advanced than the older Cas9 systems because it could handle multiple edits simultaneously. One treatment, hitting several targets." He thought of the ANGUS protocol, the specific neural pathways targeted for compliance that required hitting multiple genes at once.

Marcus nodded slowly. He ran a hand through the frosted tips of his hair. "Cas9 usually makes double-strand breaks in the DNA, often guided by two RNA molecules. It's effective, but getting it to hit multiple specific spots at the same time with high fidelity? Tricky. More potential for off-target screw-ups."

He gestured toward the complex diagram floating in the Holo-Screen. "Cas12a is different. It typically uses a single guide RNA and makes staggered cuts, creating sticky ends. More importantly for Life-Span's purposes, it's inherently better suited for multiplexing, hitting many targets at once. You load it up with multiple guide RNAs in one package, and it can go to work on several gene sites simultaneously. Cleaner, more efficient for the kind of mass behavioral reprogramming they're doing."

Marcus leaned forward, his voice dropping further, eyes narrowing. "But here's the kicker. What we've pulled from encrypted LifeSpan R&D fragments, they're not just refining Cas12a anymore. They're working on the next generation. Something designated Cas13g."

Alex tensed. "Cas13? How is it different?"

"Cas13 variants target RNA, the messenger molecule that carries instructions from DNA to the protein-building machinery. They don't necessarily need to permanently alter the DNA sequence itself." He manipulated the HoloScreen, bringing up fragmented lines of code and theoretical pathway diagrams.

"Based on the intel, and it's patchy, heavily encrypted, Cas13g isn't just about cleaving RNA. It looks like it's designed for *epigenetic* modification."

He saw Alex's slight confusion. "Think of it less like editing the words in the book and more like changing how the book is read. Adding sticky notes, highlighting passages, maybe gluing some pages together. Cas13g seems designed to attach or remove chemical tags to DNA or its associated proteins, changing gene *expression* without altering the underlying genetic code. Turning genes on or off, dialing their activity up or down, potentially with more subtlety and maybe even reversibility, though don't count on LifeSpan offering an 'undo' button."

Marcus waved at the HoloScreen again. "The potential applications...terrifying. Fine-tuning neurotransmitter levels, altering hormonal responses, influencing memory formation or emotional regulation with pinpoint precision, all without leaving the permanent footprint of a direct DNA edit. It could be even harder to detect than the current method. And the delivery vector? Could be anything. Aerosol, integrated into common consumables..." His expression soured, the clinical curiosity draining away. "Brilliant," he said flatly. "In the worst possible way."

Epigenetic modification. Changing gene *expression* without changing the code itself. Influence memory formation, emotional regulation...the potential pathways branched endlessly in his mind, fueled by the pattern-recognition capabilities of his SRV. It wasn't just about compliance anymore, it was about reshaping the independent fabric of thought and experience. Subtly. And likely undetectable.

He looked from the swirling diagrams on the HoloScreen to Marcus' intense face.

"Memory formation," Alex echoed. "If they can influence that...could they make a pill, something that alters memory?"

Elena, who had moved closer during Marcus' explanation, folded her arms. "A memory pill?" she repeated, her voice expressionless. "Oh, it's far beyond just altering what you remember, Alex." Her gaze swept over both Alex and Marcus, encompassing the grim reality they all faced. "Imagine taking something, maybe mixed into your protein shake or synthesized in your morning coffee, and suddenly, you don't just *forget* an inconvenient truth, you *remember* something else entirely. A different version of events. A false narrative, seamlessly woven into your own past."

Her eyes locked onto Alex's. "They could make you believe you attended a rally you never went near. Make you confess to crimes you didn't commit, complete with detailed sensory recall. Make you trust someone who betrayed you, remembering only loyalty and kindness."

Alex blinked, tensing at the implications.

"Let's take it one step further," Elena continued, her voice low but cutting through the subterranean quiet. "Forget memory alteration. Think about *knowledge acquisition*. Why spend years learning calculus, or a new language, or complex engineering principles?" She raised her eyebrows and nodded. "Why bother with education at all when they could potentially induce the neural pathways, the epigenetic markers, associated with that knowledge? Want to understand ninth-grade calculus? Pop a pill. Need to be fluent in Mandarin for a corporate assignment? Injectable solution. Instant proficiency. Tailored skill sets downloaded directly into the population, optimized for corporate or state needs."

She gave a humorless twist of her lips. "A 'training pill'. Imagine the workforce. Perfectly skilled, perfectly compliant, never questioning *how* they learned, just accepting the knowledge as their own. The ultimate form of control isn't just rewriting the past, it's programming the present."

Instant skills. Programmed knowledge. A population tailored for obedience, stripped of the struggle and serendipity of learning. He sank onto a nearby overturned plastic crate, the rough edges digging slightly into his thighs. The adrenaline that had carried him from Clinton Memorial, through the library, and into this subterranean refuge finally ebbed, leaving a residue of bone-deep fatigue.

He bent down, unlacing his worn sneaker. He peeled off the shoe. Tucked inside, pressed flat against the sole, was the folded piece of paper. He unfolded it carefully. He rubbed his instep, a dull ache radiating from where the rigid paper had pressed against bone with every awkward, deliberately altered step. The limp hadn't been entirely feigned.

Marcus turned back to his workstation, hands working the holographic interface. He pulled up archived city surveillance feeds, running facial recognition algorithms cross-referenced with gait analysis software. Green boxes flickered over pedestrians, AVs glided silently, public HoloScreens broadcasted innocuous advertisements. He isolated feeds from the library plaza, the TerraMetric Solutions entrance, and the alleyway access point. Filters layered over the images, searching for Alex's biometric signature, cross-referencing clothing patterns, height, build.

After several minutes of focused silence, broken only by the clicks and hums of the equipment, Marcus leaned back, a small nod of satisfaction escaping him. "It worked." He gestured toward the screen, which showed Alex's path marked, but without any high-probability alerts flagging his identity. "Gait modification and the cap were enough. The AI tagged you as low-confidence matches in a couple of spots, but nothing triggered a priority alert. You stayed below the threshold. Clean."

Alex looked down at his black base layer shirt, now grimy from the alley and the library floor. "Should have changed my shirt, too. This one's standard issue OmniHealth tech fabric. Recognizable."

Marcus shook his head, tapping commands into the HoloScreen again, pulling up what looked like military research papers on surveillance countermeasures. "Counterintuitive, I know, but changing the shirt probably would have flagged you faster."

He pointed to a highlighted section in the research document projected beside the surveillance feed. "Military R&D spent years figuring this out during the counter-insurgency ops after the Collapse. The AI isn't just looking for *your* specific markers. It's looking for deviations from baseline behavior, especially *multiple simultaneous deviations* that signal deliberate evasion."

He zoomed in on a statistical chart. "Changing your walk is one marker. Adding a hat that obscures facial recognition? Two. But start changing clothes, altering hair, adding glasses, carrying unusual bags...the more variables you alter, the higher your 'evasion profile' score climbs. Most amateurs overdo it. They think more disguise equals better concealment."

Marcus leaned forward, his expression almost professorial. "The AI models are trained on millions of hours of data. They *know* what people look like when they're trying too hard to hide. Altering one or two key identifiers blends better with natural variations. Altering five? That screams 'subject attempting evasion' and bumps you straight to human review or drone deployment. We did it right by keeping it simple."

Alex smoothed the creased paper across his knee. These weren't just dissidents hiding in tunnels, they possessed operational knowledge, sophisticated technical skills, and a deep understanding of the systems arrayed against them. Marcus knew military-grade counter-surveillance tactics. Elena coordinated complex, multi-state operations like the Seed Vault heists with off-grid groups.

He had stumbled into a far more established network than he imagined. His gaze fell onto the unfolded paper. Bold letters screamed across the top: *PROJECT NIMBUS: FACT VS. FICTION - WHAT ARE THEY REALLY SPRAYING?* Below, bullet points listed theories about weather control, corporate collusion, and long-term health effects, juxtaposed against grainy images of persistent contrails patterning the sky in a grid.

"Project Nimbus?" Marcus leaned forward, catching sight of the flyer. His fingers danced across the HoloScreen controls. The surveillance feeds and research papers vanished, replaced by a cascade of historical news articles, scientific abstracts, protest footage, and internal corporate memos – all tagged Project Nimbus. He flicked his wrist, sending a curated summary spinning into view directly in front of Alex.

"Ah, Nimbus." Marcus sighed, a familiar cynicism returning to his voice. "The granddaddy of 'Trust Us, It's For Your Own Good' schemes. Officially? A massive geoengineering project from the late twenties, early thirties. Consortium of governments and corporations, LifeSpan was definitely involved through subsidiaries even back then. TerraMetric Solutions handled a lot of the atmospheric data analysis and had proprietary access to the NCAR supercomputer in Cheyenne. The public pitch was climate change mitigation – aerosol injections, cloud seeding, AI weather modeling. Saving the planet, one patented chemical cocktail at a time."

He highlighted archived footage of gleaming dispersal aircraft leaving thick, white trails against a blue sky. "Unofficially, it was a mess. Uneven results, ecological side effects they swept under the rug, and documented proof of resource manipulation. Water rights diverted, rainfall patterns shifted to benefit corporate agriculture partners like LifeSpan AgriFuture precursors. Sound familiar?"

Marcus pointed to another block of text detailing the project's supposed conclusion around 2034. "They 'officially' ended the big, branded Nimbus program, but the tech never went away. Targeted aerosol spraying continues – 'atmospheric stabilization', they call it now. The ground-based energy arrays, HAARP successors integrated with the NEXRAD and 5G cell towers? Still active. Still messing with weather patterns regionally. That weird warm rain? The persistent grid-trails people still report? That's the legacy."

He pulled up a specific article Alex recognized, one detailing data discrepancies in rainfall distribution models. "And the data manipulation. That's where you first poked the bear, wasn't it? Back in '31. Finding evidence they skewed the models to hide." He met Alex's eyes. "Nimbus wasn't just about controlling the weather. It was about controlling the narrative, controlling resources, and learning how to manage public perception through data manipulation on a global scale. It was the perfect beta test for the kind of information control LifeSpan is perfecting now with GeneVax."

The screens reflected in Alex's eyes, a thousand lies arranged in perfect symmetry. He felt the bottom drop out of what he thought he knew. The truth hadn't been buried; it had been broadcast, disguised as progress. He sat back. The deception wasn't what shocked him, it was how easily he had accepted it. That would never happen again.

CHAPTER 8

BECOME UNMODIFIED

MARCUS TURNED from the fading images of Project Nimbus, his attention snapping back to the HoloScreen. Fingers touched holographic buttons on the projected interface, lines of code scrolling rapidly. He accessed the compromised OmniHealth employee database, a ghost image of the corporate logo shimmering briefly before dissolving into raw data fields. He located the entry: *Thompson, Alex. ID: lamda-47291-alpha-epsilon.* With a few keystrokes, he initiated a cross-reference against known LifeSpan priority lists scraped from previous incursions and network monitoring.

The screen flickered, resolving into a personnel profile overlaid with flags. A bright crimson marker pulsed next to Alex's name. *Priority Designation: Tier 1 – Immediate Compliance Integration.*

"Well, damn," Marcus muttered, leaning closer. "You weren't kidding about being on their radar. You're not just *on* the list, Alex, you're practically headlining. Top percentile for 'encouraged participation' in their little wellness initiative."

Alex felt a cold knot form in his stomach. Jamie's sudden visit. Her strange insistence. The veiled comments from Mishaal. It wasn't just paranoia, it was policy. He was a target, flagged for the same treatment that had hollowed out his friend. "Explains why everyone at Omni suddenly became a GeneVax evangelist directed squarely at me."

Marcus continued navigating the data streams. He ran Alex's ID against municipal service records, cross-referencing emergency dispatch logs, public transport manifests, hospital intake registries, casting a wide net through the city's interconnected systems. His fingers paused over a new entry flagged by the system AI monitoring Alex's known associates.

"Hold on." Marcus' tone had shifted, losing its earlier cynicism. "Got an Emergency Assistance Services flag here. Automated dispatch triggered yesterday evening. MediVac unit deployed to an Isabella Thompson? Address matches standard OmniHealth dependent records for you."

Alex shot upright, the flyer about Nimbus crumpling in his grip. "My mother?"

"Looks like it. Transported, code three, to Clinton Memorial." Marcus scanned the sparse entry. "No condition details listed in the public EAS log, just the dispatch trigger – critical bio-signs alert from a personal iBand – and the transport confirmation to Clinton." He pointed to a small icon pulsating on the screen. "There's an audio log attached. Standard procedure. EAS records the initial dispatch comms."

Alex swallowed hard. His mother. Clinton Memorial. GeneVax. The connections slammed into him. "Play it." His voice was tight, strained. "Marcus, play the audio. Now."

Marcus tapped a sequence on the HoloScreen. The air filled with the sterile chime of an automated system notification, followed by a quick, synthesized voice. "Emergency Assistance Services. Automated distress signal received. Unit designation: Apple iBand, serial number Whiskey-X-ray-Echo-Two-Echo-Echo-Two-Zero-Alpha-Three-Hotel-Kilo-Five. Registered user: Isabella Thompson. Critical vital sign alert: Tachycardia exceeding threshold, suspected internal hemorrhage."

Alex's knuckles whitened on the crumpled flyer. He leaned forward, eyes fixed on the pulsing audio icon.

"Dispatching nearest MediVac unit. Pod Seven-Niner-Alpha. Acknowledge."

A brief burst of static before a human voice, calm and professional, filtered through the speakers. "Pod Seven-Niner-Alpha acknowledging. En route to user location. ETA four minutes."

"User address confirmed. Override access codes transmitted for residential entry. Patient vitals streaming to your unit and designated receiving facility: Clinton Memorial Hospital, Trauma Bay Six."

Silence stretched, punctuated only by the low hum of the Hyperloop tunnel's dormant systems and the faint crackle from the recording. Alex could picture the sleek, white MediVac pod slicing through the night sky, its path predetermined by algorithms reacting to the frantic signals from his mother's iBand.

"Seven-Niner-Alpha on approach. Visual confirmation of residence."

Another pause. A different voice, slightly breathless, overlaid the sound of rushing air and metallic clicks. "Team entering residence. Proceeding to user location."

A muffled thud. Faint, strained breathing captured by the MediVac team's open comms. "Patient located. Apparent significant blood loss. Bathroom floor. Unconscious but alive."

"Initiating primary assessment. Pulse rapid, thready. BP eighty over forty. Applying pressure bandage. Prep synthetic hemoglobin matrix, stat."

Alex's own pulse hammered against his ribs. He saw the scene in his mind: the sterile, white tiles of his mother's bathroom, the crimson stain spreading, the impersonal efficiency of the biosuited medical team.

"Matrix infusion started. Patient secured on maglev gurney. Ready for transport."

"Clear for extraction. Transporting to Clinton Memorial, Trauma Bay Six. ETA seven minutes."

"Transport confirmed. Clinton Memorial advised. Vital stream active. End log."

The audio file closed. The synthesized chime echoed briefly in the cavernous tunnel before silence returned, heavier than before. Marcus looked over at Alex, his usual detached demeanor replaced by something approximating concern. Elena watched him, her expression unreadable but her posture tense.

Alex stared blankly at the spot where the audio icon had pulsed. His mother. Bleeding out. Alone. Taken to the one place intrinsically linked with LifeSpan and the GeneVax conspiracy. The efficiency of the EAS, the seamless integration of iBand, MediVac, and hospital – it was a marvel of modern technology. A system designed to save lives. And now, it had delivered his mother directly into the hands of those who twisted healing into control. His hands, betraying the turmoil within, began to tremble again.

Elena shifted, her usual guarded posture softening slightly. She took a half-step toward Alex. "The fact that the MediVac got there so fast, that she's at Clinton Memorial..." her voice trailed off softly.

"I need to talk to her." Alex's voice was rough, grating against the quiet. He turned, his intense blue eyes locking onto Elena's dark ones. The need was absolute, a raw imperative overriding caution. "I have to reach her."

Elena held his gaze, her expression hardening back into pragmatism. The weariness returned to her eyes. "You can't. You know that. The hospital is crawling with LifeSpan influence, even more so now. They flagged your ID, Alex. Walking in there is walking into a cage."

Alex scrubbed a hand over his face, pushing back unruly strands of dark hair. The logic was inescapable and his feelings couldn't override the SRV analysis his mind automatically calculated. He knew Elena was right. Clinton Memorial Hospital was compromised territory. Going there was suicide. But the image of his mother, vulnerable, alone, possibly subjected to GeneVax... "I *know!* I can't go." His voice dropped, frustration tightening his throat.

He gave her a furtive glance. "But maybe I can call her. Just hear her voice." He looked between Elena and Marcus, desperation creeping in. "She wouldn't know how to use Arcanum Link, she can barely manage the standard HoloScreen interface on her iBand."

A fresh wave of impotence washed over him. "Shit. I don't even *have* my iBand. It's probably compacted scrap by now." Tossing the sleek device had been a necessary sacrifice for evasion that now felt like severing his last connection.

Marcus, who had been observing the exchange while his fingers continued to ghost over the HoloScreen, sat up. "Dude, hold up." He adjusted his thin-rimmed glasses, his quick eyes darting from the screen to Alex. "Maybe we *can* get a call through. It's risky, but doable." He leaned back slightly, the posture of a technician assessing a complex problem. "I can spoof a source ID, make it look like it's coming from internal hospital comms, maybe a consulting specialist line, something that won't trigger immediate red flags," he offered. "Route the connection through a dozen proxies, layer the encryption. Mask your voice signature completely, replace it with a synthesized neutral tone."

He tapped a finger against the projected display. "The key is preventing their monitoring AI from correlating the call back to *us* or flagging it as suspicious outreach to a person of interest's mother."

Alex stared at Marcus, the technical jargon washing over him, snagging only on one crucial detail. "Mask my voice? But she won't know it's me! If she can't hear my voice, how will she..." The protest died in his throat. How could he reassure her, warn her, connect with her, if she didn't even know who was calling?

Marcus met Alex's distressed gaze, his expression blunt. "Dude. They *took* her to Clinton Memorial after an emergency triggered by her *iBand*, which tracks everything. You're flagged Tier One by LifeSpan. They're going to be listening to *every single syllable* going in or out of her room. Standard call, encrypted call, carrier pigeon – doesn't matter. Without masking, you might as well announce your location over the public address system."

Alex slumped onto the nearby overturned crate. He dropped his face into his hands, the slight tremor returning, vibrating through his palms against his forehead. He could see his mother, weak, alone, inside the oppressive institution intertwined with the conspiracy he fought, and completely unreachable in any meaningful way. The flyer about Project Nimbus lay forgotten at his feet.

"Mask my voice," he echoed, the words muffled by his hands. He dragged them down his face, revealing eyes raw with frustration and fear. "I just wish there was some way I could whisper in her ear. Let her know I'm here, that she's not alone, that…" he trailed off, the futility choking him.

Marcus, who had returned his attention to the cascading data on the HoloScreen, tracing potential network vulnerabilities within Clinton Memorial's internal systems, froze mid-keystroke. His head snapped up. "Wait." He sat bolt upright, pushing his blue-light filtering glasses higher on his nose. The usual cynical curve of his mouth straightened into a line of intense concentration. "Whisper in her ear? Alex, does your mom use HearBuds? The Apple Starkey Neural Link?"

Alex blinked, momentarily thrown by the abrupt shift. "She has them. Why?"

Marcus leaned forward, the data momentarily forgotten. "Think about it. HearBuds aren't just fancy earpods. They sit deep in the ear canal, practically invisible. They bypass the eardrum entirely, forming a direct bio-interface with the cochlear nerve." He gestured emphatically, his earlier tech-focused stillness replaced by animated explanation.

"Audio signals – calls, music, whatever – get transmitted straight to the brain's auditory centers. It's how they restore hearing for most people, making deafness almost a thing of the past." He tapped his own temple. "And crucially, they use sub-dermal bone conduction sensors for voice pickup. No external mic needed. They detect the vibrations in your skull when you talk." He paused, letting the implications sink in.

"They're sophisticated, personalized medical-grade tech integrated into the Apple ecosystem."

The devices harvested energy from movement and body heat, running continuously without needing a charge, always connected, always listening – both to the outside world through transparent audio processing and to the user's linked iBand.

Alex processed this, the technical details familiar but viewed through a new lens. He had bought them for his mother himself, a year or so after getting his own pair. "I know how they work." His mind raced ahead, grasping the potential thread Marcus dangled. "I got them for her mostly because she likes watching the old historical broadcasts late at night. Complained the standard audio bothered the neighbors. With the HearBuds, the sound goes directly to her auditory nerve. The apartment stays quiet." He looked at Marcus, a spark igniting within the despair. "What are you thinking?"

Marcus leaned forward, the HoloScreen reflecting in his glasses. His fingers danced across the projected keys, pulling up schematics of the Apple Starkey Neural Link system, cross-referencing them with known vulnerabilities and short-range communication protocols. "Okay, here's the play," Marcus began, his voice regaining its focused, technical inflection.

"Standard comms are out. Too traceable. But the HearBuds... they operate on a closed-loop, bio-integrated system. They have secure, short-range handshake protocols, mostly for diagnostic checks or pairing updates initiated by an authorized source device, like her iBand." He paused, tapping a specific line of code. "Or *my* iBand, if I can get close enough and convince her HearBuds that I'm a trusted source."

He looked up, meeting Alex's intense gaze. "Close enough means *physically* close. Like standing in the hallway outside her room at Clinton Memorial. From there, I could potentially initiate a direct device-to-device interface, bypassing the hospital network entirely. It'd be a whisper-thin connection, riding on low-power proximity frequencies."

Marcus ran a hand through his frosted hair, a thoughtful expression crossing his face. "Man, it's funny. You said 'whisper in her ear'. *WIRED* literally nicknamed the HearBuds 'Whisper Tech' when they launched. Because of that direct neural interface, the sound just appears in your head." He shook his head slightly.

"I've never tried hijacking a direct HearBud link like this. Never even considered it, honestly. It's purely theoretical, based on exploiting diagnostic backdoors and proximity handshakes. High risk of failure, high risk of detection if I fumble the spoofing sequence."

Elena's gaze shifted from Marcus to Alex. Her expression hardened into a flat mask of tactical assessment, seeing the turmoil simmering behind his controlled facade. "The risk to the operation is too high," she said, her voice low and sharp. "We can't afford that kind of exposure."

Alex turned to face her, his own expression unyielding. The faint tremor in his hands had stilled, replaced by a cold, unwavering resolve. "Then you can't afford me." He took a step closer. "Let me be clear." His voice dropped but lost none of its intensity. "I need to talk to my mother. I need to know what they've done. You make that happen, you get me that connection, and you get all of me. I'm all in. Everything I have, my focus, my skills, they're yours. No reservations." He paused, reading her expression, his SRV already two plays ahead of her likely responses. "But without that call, you get nothing."

Elena held his gaze, searching for a crack in his resolve. He wasn't pleading, he was negotiating, leveraging the one thing he had, his unique mind. It was a bluff, she suspected. Where else could he possibly go now that LifeSpan had him marked? He'd seen the inside, enough to expose their entire network if he was ever captured. If that happened, every safe house, every cell, every name would fall. The Resistance couldn't let that happen. Not ever.

She didn't want to think about what she would have to do if he tried to run, but she would. She had done worse for less.

The core of his threat was real. An unfocused Alex was a compromised asset. An Alex who felt they'd denied him this one crucial thing would be even worse. This wasn't about sympathy, it was about managing her most valuable asset.

She turned back to Marcus, her decision made. "Do it, Marcus." Elena's voice, sharp and decisive, clipped the tension in the tunnel.

Marcus nodded, his attention already snapping back to the Holo-Screen. "It's not gonna be instant. I need to build the spoofing algorithm, map the potential signal interference within Clinton Memorial's structure, find the cleanest frequency window... It'll take time. Hours, maybe." He cracked his knuckles, fingers hovering over the interface. "But I'll start right now." Lines of code began scrolling again, intricate patterns weaving across the holographic display as Marcus dove into the complex task.

Alex watched him work, a fragile hope blooming in his chest. The possibility of hearing his mother's voice, of offering some small, coded reassurance, felt like a lifeline. But beneath the hope, a cold dread pooled. What would he hear? Would she sound like herself, or would the placid, agreeable tones of GeneVax already be present? The potential answers were as terrifying as not knowing.

Marcus worked, lines of code blurring into complex algorithms. He paused, frowning at a particularly dense encryption layer protecting the HearBud's diagnostic handshake protocols. He muttered under his breath, running simulations that kept hitting digital walls. He sighed, running a hand through his frosted hair. "This is trickier than I thought. The proximity authentication uses a nested quantum key exchange layered over biometric resonance signatures. Trying to spoof that without triggering an alert back to Apple's core security AI..." He shook his head. "I need another set of eyes on this encryption."

He turned. "Bo Lin, I need you," he yelled over his shoulder.

"Yeah, you do, Baby!" The sarcastic undertone was obviously from Bo Lin, his voice echoing from further in the tunnel.

"Get over here," Marcus called. "Got something that needs your particular brand of digital lockpicking."

Bo Lin emerged from the deeper shadows of the tunnel, oversized hoodie swallowing his narrow shoulders, pale eyes already scanning Marcus's HoloScreen.

While Marcus and Bo huddled near the glowing display, their murmured conversation a rapid-fire exchange of technical jargon, Elena turned back to Alex. She pulled over another crate, sitting opposite him. "Let's consolidate," she began, her voice low but firm, cutting through his internal turmoil about his mother. "You and Maya confirmed what we suspected, but the specifics are..."

She leaned forward slightly, her dark eyes holding his. "LifeSpan isn't just using CRISPR-Cas12a for fixing genetic defects. They're leveraging its ability to make multiple, simultaneous edits. One set targets the advertised health condition – Jamie's heart, asthma, pre-cancer markers, whatever. Another set targets neural pathways."

"The Compliance Protocol," Alex murmured. "Project ANGUS. Behavioral modification."

"Targeted obedience," Elena affirmed. "Reduced skepticism. Passive acceptance, wrapped in the promise of health, a cure, making it almost irresistible. And they have a list. You saw it. Prioritized targets like you who ask too many questions. Probably educators, and politicians, "

"But the scale of it..." Alex's voice was barely a whisper. "It's not just LifeSpan, Maya and I saw governmental and even the highest religious authentication."

Elena's expression grew grim. "What you found confirms it. This goes way beyond one corporation. Think about the logistics. Embedding it so deeply, coordinating the rollout, managing the data, suppressing dissent...that requires government cooperation. International agreements. Maybe even tacit approval from religious bodies preaching acceptance and harmony." She gestured broadly, encompassing the unseen world beyond their tunnel hideout. "It's systemic. They're shaping the future workforce, the electorate, public opinion, molding society itself."

"Then what do we do?" He looked around the damp, echoing tunnel, at Elena's weary face, at Marcus and Bo lost in their digital battle, at the flickering emergency lights casting long shadows. "We're what? A handful of people hiding in a derelict tube?"

His voice, though not loud, carried in the enclosed space. From a section of the tunnel where makeshift workstations and sleeping pallets were clustered, two figures detached themselves from the shadows.

The man named Pacheco approached, his presence warm and friendly. He stopped near Alex, gesturing vaguely around their immediate area. "This?" He grunted, his thick mustache twitching. "This little setup isn't the whole picture, *hijo*. Not even close."

Sera came alongside him. Her gaze was direct, uncompromising. "He's right. This isn't some clubhouse where we all hang out in a cardboard fort planning make-believe battles. We're compartmentalized for a reason. Security. Efficiency."

Elena nodded, picking up the thread. "There are cells like ours, networked across the country. All over the world, maybe, though communication gets riskier the further out you go. People who avoided the treatment, people who saw the changes in loved ones, people like Marcus who found the digital breadcrumbs, and people like Bo Lin who sought to escape an oppressive government. What started as scattered whispers, online groups on Reddit labeled conspiracy theorists, has grown." Her expression held a flicker of fierce determination.

"We've spent years identifying, vetting, recruiting. Mapping LifeSpan's infrastructure, gathering intel, coordinating through channels like ArcLink. Waiting. Planning." She met Alex's gaze directly. "But we're done waiting. Finding you, confirming the mechanism with Maya's help, getting that target list...that changes things. It's time to shift from gathering to acting."

Elena nodded to the table Pacheco was hovering over when they came in. "Patch, show him."

Pacheco nodded slowly, his steady eyes meeting Alex's. He turned without a word and walked toward a large, flat-topped crate further down the tunnel that served as a makeshift table. Propped against its side stood a sturdy cardboard tube, nearly four feet long, capped with a white plastic lid. It looked remarkably similar to the lid on Alex's own insulated coffee container. Pacheco carefully removed the cap, reached inside, and pulled out a thick roll of heavy paper.

He laid the roll on the crate's surface and gently unfurled the first few feet. The crisp crackle of the stiff paper echoed strangely in the damp tunnel air. Lines, symbols, and precise lettering covered the expansive sheet in stark blue ink. It was a detailed architectural rendering, an overhead view of a sprawling complex Alex recognized instantly – the LifeSpan Genomics Headquarters campus in Northgate.

Alex moved closer, drawn by an unexpected reverence. He had spent his entire career manipulating digital representations of structures, data flows, and system architectures, all shimmering on HoloScreens. He'd never encountered physical blueprints on this scale. Paper. Real, tangible paper. He reached out, his fingers brushing the slightly rough surface, tracing the clean lines depicting the main ziggurat tower, the suspended botanical atriums, the precise layout of Liberty and Kettle Creek Parks. He inhaled deeply, catching the faint, dry scent of the paper itself, a smell completely alien to his usual sterile, filtered office environment.

He watched Pacheco carefully roll the sheet further, revealing another layer beneath it. Floor plans. Electrical grids. HVAC systems. Network conduit paths. Alex marveled at the simple, elegant mechanism – rolling and unrolling to navigate through layers of intricate information.

His hands lingered on the paper, a tactile connection that felt profoundly different from interacting with cold glass and projected light. It reminded him of the worn pages of his mother's old books, objects he cherished for their solidity, their history, their resistance to the ephemeral nature of the digital world. His talent, his SRV, thrived on data, pushing him into a career dominated by screens and algorithms, yet a deep part of him yearned for this analog permanence. This reverence for the tangible felt almost secret, a counterpoint to the minimalist order he imposed on his digital life.

His eyes, sharp and analytical, scanned the sheets Pacheco continued to unroll. Even without understanding every symbol, his mind, wired for patterns, began to isolate key details. Access control points mapped with security sensor coverage zones. Redundant fiber optic network pathways snaking between buildings. Locations of primary server banks and data archives marked with specific room designations. Power distribution grids, highlighting potential vulnerabilities or bypass points. It was an astonishingly complete map of the corporate fortress.

Alex looked up from the crackling sheets, his gaze locking onto Pacheco's weathered face. "Where did you get this?"

Pacheco's dark eyes held a flicker of pride, maybe, layered thick with a resentment that simmered just below the surface. He ran a calloused hand over the intricate lines of the blueprint depicting the titanium alloy supports of the ziggurat. "These bones?" Pacheco's voice was rough, textured like old gravel from years of smoking, yet carried an easy warmth. "They are mine. My company, Acme Construction… we put this whole damn palace together."

Patch tapped a section showing the foundations with a thick finger. "Every yard of concrete – more than three million. *Híjole*, enough to build Hoover Dam, eh? Every beam, every sheet of that fancy nano-glass probably cost more than my first pickup." He straightened up, his broad shoulders squaring almost unconsciously. "Acme is just north of Peterson Space Force Base. We do it all, *Chico*. Concrete, steel work, crushing rock, making floors shine, custom plastic junk for the desks…" He paused, ticking off more advanced techniques on his fingers with a wry grin.

"Spray-on solar, self-healing asphalt, 3D printing walls…*lo que sea*. If it went into building it for those…*jefes*…Acme had a hand in it, you believe that."

Alex stared. This man navigating derelict tunnels in a tattered Van Halen t-shirt and worn cowboy boots was a titan of industry, the builder of the castle that housed the king.

"Acme used to be just concrete, but we grew with 'em," Patch continued, his gaze sweeping over the sprawling campus layout, though his smile didn't quite reach his eyes this time. "From the first shovel in the dirt back in early 'twenty-six 'til they flipped the switch on the last light, almost eight years. They design this thing before Trump sit in his second chair." He chuckled, a dry rasping sound.

"They ordered the drywall – *¡Ay!* Nine hundred thousand sheets, four years before the walls even went up. *Loco*, eh?" Pacheco tapped the blueprint again, this time, focusing on a section depicting the sprawling energy infrastructure connecting the LifeSpan campus to the wider Front Range grid.

"See this?" he asked. "This whole complex…it sucks down power like a black hole. Enough for a small city. That's why they built the Ramah Power Plant, *Chico*."

Alex's eyes followed Pacheco''s finger. He knew of the Natrium reactor project, a next-generation nuclear plant to the east, touted as a marvel of safe, sustainable energy production. But the connection to LifeSpan hadn't occurred to him.

"The Ramah plant wasn't just some public works project," Pacheco continued, his voice tinged with bitter amusement. "That was *all* Life-Span. Gates himself had a hand in it, along with Thiel and that whole crowd. They built it. *We* built it, really, Acme had a small role there." He chuckled dryly. "Think about it. Who else would need that kind of power? Especially a timeline like that. That damn reactor went up in half the time the Wyoming one did. They needed it. Needed it for all their little... *proyectos.*"

The scale of LifeSpan's operation was far greater than Alex had initially imagined. It wasn't just genetic manipulation, it was energy independence, control over a critical piece of regional infrastructure, interwoven with seemingly-unrelated actors. He thought of the controversial "Project Nimbus" weather modification initiative, the data manipulation, and the whispers he'd heard about corporate influence on weather patterns. It all felt connected now, chilling in its scope. The pieces were falling into place, creating a picture far more sinister than even his most paranoid imaginings. The sheer audacity, the ambition, was breathtaking.

Elena leaned forward, her expression grim. "The energy consumption alone, it's a tell. The computational resources required, the manufacturing processes, the climate control systems for their facilities." Her eyes narrowed. "Not to mention the constant monitoring of billions of iBands."

Patch gestured toward the detailed plans again. "A project this size, keeping it moving? A beautiful mess, *Compadre*. Had to open new quarries, gravel pits, even an old gypsum mine south of Front Range City just to keep feeding it. M*adre mía*, thirty-two thousand *hombres* crawling over this place! Engineers, robot guys, hammers, security looking tough, thirty thousand hard hats." His voice had dropped slightly.

"Cost over fifty billion. *Fifty, Billion, Dollars*. That's a lot a tacos, *hijo!*" He looked directly at Alex with a slight weariness in his eyes. "LifeSpan made old Pacheco *rico*, Alex. Built my company up real good, *sí*. And in return?" He slapped the blueprint with the back of his hand, the sound sharp in the quiet tunnel. "I gave them this." He gestured around vaguely.

"Every access panel, every junction box, every hidden pipe. I know this place better than they do. Because I put it there. Shit, I could build a great pyramid in the Africa!" He laughed from his belly.

The charming, almost mischievous smile widened, but this time it held a dangerous edge, sharp and bright. "And now, we tear this bitch down." Pacheco wasn't smiling anymore.

Alex seemed to absorb the analog data with the same convergence he applied to digital streams.

"Patch's knowledge is invaluable," Elena stated. "He didn't just build their fortress, he knows every secret passage, every potential weak point in the physical structure." She tapped a section of the blueprint showing complex ventilation shafts interwoven with network conduits. "But physical access is only a third of the equation. Getting inside is one thing. Getting to the *data*, that's another beast entirely. And then we've got to move it."

She faced Alex. "That's where you come in. Your ability, your SRV, it lets you see the patterns, the anomalies in their data streams that their own AI, that *we*, might miss. You found ANGUS hiding in the noise. You identified the compliance markers. Is it possible to filter the data, to get what we need to be damning, but not be so massive that we can't get it out?"

Alex nodded, processing the shift. His focus moved from the physical paper map of LifeSpan's structure to the conceptual map of their digital defenses. "Their core systems, they'll be isolated. Air-gapped maybe, or protected by layers of encryption far beyond standard corporate security."

"Exactly," Elena affirmed. "Marcus and Bo," she gestured toward the two hackers still murmuring over their HoloScreen. "Can handle network penetration, bypass standard security protocols. But navigating LifeSpan's internal data architecture, identifying the specific servers holding the unredacted ANGUS protocols, the directives, the *proof*, that requires your specific skill set."

"The plans show us where the servers *are, mijo,*" Pacheco chimed in, his rough voice surprisingly soft. "The big data vaults, the secure comms hubs. I poured the concrete around them myself." He pointed to a heavily-reinforced section deep within the main ziggurat structure on the blueprints. "Level B-14. Steel walls, EMP shielding, the works. But knowing the room doesn't get us the files."

Elena picked up the thread seamlessly, nodding. "We can map a route, bypass patrols, maybe even access secure levels through service conduits Pacheco knows about." She swept a hand over the sprawling architectural diagrams. "And with your analytical skills, Alex, once we get you physical access to a terminal inside, or proximity to their core network, you can pinpoint the target data. Extract it."

She leaned closer, her dark eyes intense. "We need undeniable proof, not just statistical anomalies or flagged user IDs. We need the internal memos, the raw genetic sequencing directives for ANGUS, the deployment orders. Something so concrete, so damning, that even the most compliant mind, if faced with it directly, might flicker."

"The goal isn't just to understand, it's to expose," she said, her voice lowering, imbued with a quiet urgency. "To take this evidence and blast it wide. Get it past the filters, the censors. We need to wake people up, warn the ones still unmodified, who haven't taken the injection yet, the ones who still *can* be warned before LifeSpan silences them permanently. This data, it's the weapon we need. With Patch's map, Marcus and Bo's keys, and your sight, we finally have a way to get it."

He nodded, because she needed him to. But inside, he still wanted to believe there was a way back, a version of the world where he hadn't seen any of this. The thought was naïve, and he knew it, yet it clung to him like memory, warm and fragile and already fading.

PACHECO, Elena, Sera, and Alex huddled around the massive sheet spread across the makeshift table. Marcus and Bo remained engrossed in their HoloScreen nearby, their muttered exchanges forming a low background clatter to the planning session.

Pacheco traced a thick, calloused finger along a complex network of lines representing sublevel conduits. "Here." His gravelly voice was low. "Sub-basement twelve. Main fiber optic trunk lines run parallel to the primary coolant pipes for the server farms. Big enough to crawl through, if you don't mind the heat."

Sera Voss' steel-blue eyes scanned the area Pacheco indicated. She tapped a junction point with a metallic stylus. "Heat signatures will be high. Standard thermal sensors likely cover this entire section. And acoustic pickups near any access grating." Her words were short and direct, leaving no room for misinterpretation. "Standard procedure for protecting critical infrastructure nodes. Any attempt to breach the conduit wall triggers immediate alerts."

"We anticipated that," Elena murmured, cross-referencing Pacheco's diagram with a digital overlay projected from her wrist device onto the paper. "There might be blind spots during maintenance cycles, but predicting those is unreliable." She looked at

Pacheco. "Are there less obvious network access points? Maintenance terminals? Diagnostic ports?"

"Hundreds," Pacheco confirmed, shifting his weight. He pointed to a different sector, marked B-14, the heavily-reinforced data vault level. "Secure terminals are in the core labs and control rooms down there. The ones the researchers use. High bandwidth, direct connection to the core servers. But getting *to* them..." He shook his head. "Biometric locks, multi-factor authentication, probably constant monitoring."

Alex pushed back a stray lock of dark hair, his gaze fixed on the blueprints, processing the spatial data alongside the security implications. "Assuming we bypass the physical security and gain access to one of those terminals," he began. "I need time. It's not like downloading a file. LifeSpan's core data architecture is layered, segmented. Finding the specific information about ANGUS, the deployment data, cross-referencing it with personnel directives requires navigating their internal structure, filtering petabytes."

"How much time?" Elena asked, her dark eyes meeting his.

"Minutes, at least," Alex said. "Maybe ten, fifteen, depending on their internal search protocols and how deep the target data is buried. Then there's the transfer itself." Alex paused, remembering the invasive procedure at the LifeSpan facility. "The last data package I carried for them, a routine transfer to OmniHealth, was 6.81 petabytes."

A low whistle escaped Pacheco. "*Madre de Dios.*"

"Data Mules are certified with Echo-Class clearance. It's nowhere near Omega Class, but way beyond 'top secret' that everyone seems to find so impressive. The data isn't accessible via external networks." Alex emphasized, underscoring the security of the process. "It's completely isolated. The only way LifeSpan moves datasets that large securely is physically, using couriers. Using the Neural Data Mule protocol." He tapped his inner elbow instinctively. "They use an invasive neural interface. High-bandwidth probes connect directly to the ulnar nerve. It streams the data into the nervous system, encodes it biologically."

Sera looked up sharply. "Biologically?"

"Turns the courier into a living hard drive. We call it the 'wrist drive'," Alex confirmed. "Even with their proprietary system, pushing 6.8 petabytes took nearly twenty minutes. A direct, hardwired connection. And that's just the upload. OmniHealth doesn't have invasive tech. It's astronomically expensive. They use non-invasive MEG scanners to extract the data." He gestured vaguely. "Magnetoencephalography reads the magnetic fields from the encoded neural pathways. It took over ten hours to download that same data package at Omni."

Elena absorbed this, the lines around her eyes deepening. "So even if we reach a terminal, even if you can isolate the proof we need within minutes, extracting petabytes of data requires either LifeSpan's invasive neural hardware, which we don't have, or hours hooked up to an MEG scanner, which we also don't have. And we certainly won't have twenty minutes for an upload, let alone hours for a download."

Pacheco ran a hand over his face, the charm momentarily gone, replaced by the weary pragmatism of an engineer facing an impossible specification. "We can get in, maybe. You can find it, maybe. But we can't get it out. *¡La pinche chingada!*" He smacked the prints.

A long silence followed Elena's assessment of their technological impasse. The blueprints seemed less like a map to victory and more like a diagram of their failure.

Suddenly, a disembodied voice, tinny and amplified, shattered the quiet. "Dude! Quit staring at her boobs!"

Alex recoiled, physically jumping back from the table. His head snapped left, right, eyes wide, searching the shadowed corners of the vast, concrete space. His heart hammered against his ribs, the sudden, crude intrusion utterly disorienting.

From the corner where Marcus and Bo Lin hunched over their HoloScreen, an eruption of laughter exploded. Not chuckles, but full-throated, gasping hilarity. Marcus doubled over, clutching his stomach, his shoulders shaking violently before he lost his balance completely, tumbling sideways off his repurposed bucket seat onto the dusty floor with a muffled thump.

Bo, seeing Marcus fall, let out a high-pitched shriek of laughter that dissolved into uncontrollable giggles. He leaned forward, burying his face in his hands, his thin frame quivering. The sound bounced off the concrete walls, echoing around the stunned group at the table.

Elena's expression remained largely neutral, a mask of skilled control, but the corner of her mouth twitched upward almost imperceptibly. She exchanged a brief glance with Sera, whose weathered face showed a flicker of something – not quite amusement, but perhaps an acknowledgment of the sheer absurdity. The laughter, raw and unrestrained, filled the space, echoing.

Even Pacheco, initially startled by Alex's sudden reaction, began to chuckle. His laugh started low, a rumbling in his chest, and grew as he watched Marcus flail momentarily on the floor, trying to regain his breath between guffaws. He didn't know the joke, but the sight of the young tech expert undone by laughter was infectious.

Alex stood frozen for another second, the shocked expression locked on his face. The voice! It hadn't come from *outside*. It had been *inside*, directly in his ears. His HearBuds. The Apple Starkey Neural Link units nestled deep in his canals. Marcus. The realization dawned, swift and clarifying.

They had cracked the secure connection. Marcus had used the link to play the voice of God, or rather, the voice of a crude teenager. A wave of relief washed over him, quickly followed by reluctant amusement. The sheer, juvenile audacity of it. He started to laugh, a short, sharp burst that quickly joined the ongoing cacophony.

Marcus finally pushed himself up, wiping tears from his eyes, his frosted hair askew. He pointed a trembling finger at Alex, still shaking with laughter. "Dude," he gasped, struggling for air. "You should have seen the look on your face!"

Alex stared at Marcus and swung his gaze toward Bo, a grin splitting his face, the earlier shock replaced by dawning comprehension. "You did it!" The words burst out, echoing slightly in the cavernous space. "You cracked the HearBuds!"

The laughter subsided quickly, replaced by focused attention. Elena, Sera, and Pacheco exchanged glances. Alex had reacted to something internal, something only he experienced. Pacheco's brow furrowed slightly, connecting the dots between Alex's outburst and the tech team's suppressed mirth. Sera's expression remained unreadable, but her gaze shifted pointedly toward Marcus, who was still picking himself up, dusting off his hoodie.

"It worked," Elena stated, her voice cutting through the lingering awkwardness. It wasn't a question but a confirmation, directed as much to herself as the others. The prank, while unprofessional, served as proof of concept.

Bo Lin pushed himself away from the HoloScreen setup, his movements quick and restless. He adjusted the cracked visor band holding back his black hair. "Was not...difficult," he offered, his English carrying the distinct tonal variation and accent of Mandarin, Ls pronounced much more like Rs. He gestured toward the HearBuds nestled invisibly in Alex's ears. "Big *problem*. Security *flaw*."

He tapped commands onto his own interface, projecting a simplified network diagram onto the wall near the blueprints. Lines representing secure connections were contrasted by dotted arrows indicating potential third-party access vectors.

"Apple Starkey Neural Link," Bo Lin traced one of the dotted lines. "Must allow connect...many device. No only iBand. Public address system in transit hub. Broadcast screen. Old media player." He shrugged, a jerky motion of his thin shoulders. "Even cheap...uh... *warkie-tarkie* signal, if protocol correct. Need backward work. No can patch. Too many system, old system."

He pointed to a specific node in the diagram representing the handshake protocol. "Signal weak. We modifry. Send fake handshake. Pretend be...library audio tour." He grinned, a fleeting expression. "Marcus iBand connect direct. HearBud think it *ribrary*. No alert. No log."

Marcus nodded, finally composed, though a smirk lingered. "A clean connection. Completely localized."

"Limitation," Bo added quickly, holding up four fingers. "Range. Four meter. Radio field strength decay fast." He looked at the group, his expression earnest under the flickering projected light. "How many...inch...is four meter?"

Silence. Pacheco blinked. Sera's gaze remained fixed on the

diagram. Marcus studiously avoided eye contact, suddenly fascinated by a loose thread on his trousers. Elena sighed, a barely audible puff of air.

She looked directly at Alex, her dark eyes holding a mixture of weariness and wry tolerance. "See what I have to work with?"

"I see. They're perfect."

At precisely 15:00, Marcus stepped off the automated transit pod on Boulder Street outside Clinton Memorial, the curved, semicircular design of the building with alternating stripes of terracotta building and aquamarine rows of curved windows looming before him. The shift change was in full swing with orderlies in pale blue scrubs, nurses in white, and occasional doctors in their long coats moving in and out of the sliding glass doors in a steady stream. He adjusted the collar of his borrowed medical technician's uniform, the fabric stiff and unfamiliar, and checked the ID badge clipped to his chest, a forgery, but a convincing one.

The lobby was a controlled chaos of visitors, patients, and staff, the hum of conversation and the occasional chime of the intercom filling the air. Marcus kept his head down, moving with purpose, his gaze flicking to the digital directory before he turned down a corridor lined with patient rooms. The scent of antiseptic and the faint chatter of nurses filled the air.

He reached the designated room, 412, and paused, glancing through the narrow window in the door. Inside, Isabella sat upright in bed, her dark hair slightly disheveled, her expression weary but alert. The room was empty, no nurses or doctors in sight.

Marcus exhaled, stepping back and leaning against the wall, pulling his hand with the iBand on his wrist from his pocket. He activated the HoloScreen, the blue glow reflecting in his eyes as he navigated to the ArcLink app. With a few quick taps, he initiated the secure connection, the encryption protocols engaging with a soft chime.

A moment later, Elena's voice crackled through the line, distant but clear. "Marcus, you in position?"

Marcus connected to Isabella's HearBuds, the signal bypassing the standard hospital communication network. Bo and he had spent the last hour painstakingly crafting a simulated Emergency PA system broadcast, a series of carefully-timed audio snippets, white noise, and strategically-placed static bursts designed to mimic the hospital's internal communication protocols. The goal wasn't to sound perfect, but to sound *familiar* enough to bypass any immediate skepticism from Isabella's sensory filters. Once paired, the HearBuds established a direct link to his iBand, bypassing her monitoring equipment entirely. He seamlessly linked the call to Elena's iBand via ArcLink.

Elena's voice, slightly muffled but clear, came through Marcus's HearBuds. "Marcus? Status?"

"She's alone," Marcus whispered, his voice barely audible even to himself, yet perfectly clear within Isabella's ears.

"No medical staff in the room. HearBuds connected. Patching you through now."

A moment later, Isabella heard a faint crackling sound, static fading into a familiar tone, similar to the routine intercom announcements she'd become accustomed to at Clinton Memorial. A smooth, synthesized voice filled her ears. It wasn't the usual cheerful female announcer. This one had a slightly deeper timbre and a crisper tone that sounded oddly professional and reassuring in its clinical efficiency.

"This is a routine medical check," said the simulated PA system voice. "Please remain calm and answer the following questions."

Isabella tensed but remained outwardly calm. Her heart thumped against her ribs, her mind racing through possible scenarios that explained the strange occurrence. Hospital security performing a test? Some new monitoring protocol?

On the other end, Alex's voice, tense with anticipation, finally reached his mother. "Mom? Can you hear me?"

Inside the room, Isabella's head turned sharply toward the sound, her eyes widening in recognition. Marcus kept his gaze fixed on his HoloScreen, pretending to scroll through data, his body a shield between the hallway and the conversation happening just beyond the door. "Alex?" Isabella knew the call was coming on her HearBuds, but she didn't hear any connection verification. And it didn't even ring. "Did Dr. Rivera call you? They took my iBand."

"Mom, what happened?"

Inside Room 412, Isabella clutched the thin hospital blanket, the unexpected sound of Alex's voice echoing directly in her ears, jarring her. "Alex? *Mijo*? Is that really you?" Her voice trembled slightly. "How, ?"

"Just talk, Mom. Tell me what happened." Alex's voice was tight, strained, filtering through the layers of Marcus' improvised connection.

Isabella took a breath, trying to order the fragmented memories. "It was sudden. A nosebleed. A bad one. It wouldn't stop." She touched her nose absently. "I went to the kitchen sink, but there wasn't a towel, just a washcloth. It soaked through so fast. I went to the bathroom, thinking I could clean up, find something better..." Her voice trailed off, confusion clouding her features.

"The next thing I remember is waking up here. Tubes... machines..." She looked around the sterile room, the memory of disorientation still fresh. "Dr. Rivera, she came in later. She said my body just turned on itself. Destroyed all the platelets. Said I was bleeding to death internally." A shudder ran through her, a genuine tremor beneath the synthetic calm that had been beginning to settle over her.

"They gave me two units of platelets right away. Then a full blood transfusion to get rid of the synthetic blood they used initially, she said."

"Are you going to be okay?" The question hung in the artificial silence of the connection, heavy with unspoken fear.

Isabella hesitated. A long pause stretched out, filled only by the faint hum and beeping of the monitoring equipment beside her bed. When she spoke again, her voice was lower, uncertain. "Dr. Rivera, she didn't seem like herself. Not the Maya we know." Isabella frowned, searching for the right words. "She was so formal. Clinical. Like she was reading from a script. Didn't ask about you. There was no warmth.

She looked right at me, but it felt like she didn't really *see* me. Didn't recognize me, not really."

"Mom," Alex repeated, his voice sharper now, cutting through her recollection. "Are you okay?"

Isabella's posture straightened slightly. The uncertainty flickered, replaced by a serene confidence that sat unnervingly on her familiar features. "Yes, *mijo*. I'm going to be just fine. Better than fine." A small smile touched her lips. "Dr. Rivera gave me the GeneVax treatment. She said it was the best course, the only way to stabilize my system quickly. And it worked. She said my lupus markers, they're gone. Completely. It's already in remission." She looked toward the door, her eyes bright with an unsettling clarity. "Alex, where are you? Come see me. See how much better I am."

Another pause descended, longer this time. On the other end, Alex stood frozen amidst the concrete tunnel and flickering projections, the world tilting beneath his feet. Elena watched him, her expression unreadable. Marcus, outside the hospital room door, held his breath as an orderly glanced at him while walking past.

"I love you," Alex finally said. "*Te amo*. Don't ever forget that."

Outside Room 412, Marcus kept his eyes glued to the HoloScreen projecting from his iBand, maintaining the facade of a technician reviewing patient data. His attention shifted, catching the distinct click-clack of professional footwear approaching on the polished linoleum floor. He risked a glance down the corridor. His blood ran cold. Dr. Maya Rivera. Walking briskly, purposefully, directly toward Isabella's room. Directly toward *him*.

Recognition flared, sharp and immediate. He knew her face from Alex's frantic briefings, from the Resistance intel files. More importantly, she might know *his*. He'd been flagged in the OmniHealth system. Life-Span shared data with its partners. Clinton Memorial was a major partner. If Rivera's GeneVax-adjusted mind accessed hospital security protocols, or even just cross-referenced flagged individuals, he was exposed.

Panic tightened its fist around his chest. He stabbed a command onto his HoloScreen. "Gotta go! Now!" The words were a harsh whisper, transmitted instantly through the still-open Arcanum Link channel to Elena, cutting off any reply Alex might have made. He severed the HearBud connection simultaneously, collapsing the link to Isabella.

He shoved the iBand back into the pocket of his borrowed uniform, forcing his breathing to steady. He needed cover. Movement. Now.

His gaze darted around. A young woman, maybe early twenties, in the slightly-too-large scrubs of an intern, consulted a medical tablet just a few feet away, her brow furrowed in concentration. Perfect.

Marcus pushed off the wall, adopting an easy stride, intercepting her path smoothly. He offered a practiced, disarming smile. "Hey," he said, his voice pitched just right – friendly, collegial. "Rough shift?"

The intern looked up, startled, pushing a stray strand of blonde hair behind her ear. Her eyes were tired. "A bit. Just trying to make sense of these fluid charts for Dr. Evans."

"Evans? Tough rotation." Marcus fell into step beside her, casually draping an arm around her shoulder, a gesture just familiar enough to seem plausible between colleagues, yet possessive enough to guide her direction. He tilted his head toward her tablet. "Mind if I see? Sometimes a fresh pair of eyes..."

He subtly angled them away from Room 412 toward the main nurses' station and the elevator bank beyond it. Dr. Rivera was closer now, her dark hair pulled back efficiently, her expression calm, focused. She was only twenty yards away. Fifteen.

The intern hesitated, glancing up at his borrowed ID badge and back at the complex graph on her screen. "It's this weird potassium spike after the diuretic push."

"Ah, yeah, seen that before," Marcus lied smoothly, steering her gently but firmly toward the elevators. He kept his body positioned slightly between the intern and the approaching doctor.

"Sometimes it's the infusion rate, not the dosage. Did you check the pump logs?" He pointed vaguely at her screen, his finger brushing the glowing surface.

They reached the polished steel doors of the elevator bank. Marcus jabbed the 'down' button with his free hand. Rivera just passing the nurses' station, her stride unwavering. She hadn't looked directly at him. Not yet.

"The logs?" the intern murmured, swiping through screens on her tablet. "I didn't think to."

A soft chime announced the elevator's arrival. The doors slid open. "Let's grab a coffee downstairs," Marcus urged, guiding the still-distracted intern inside. "We can pull up the pump archives on the main console."

They stepped into the empty elevator car. Marcus reached out and pressed the button for the lobby. Behind them, in the corridor, Dr. Rivera reached Room 412. Her hand landed squarely on the door panel.

The elevator doors slid shut with a quiet motion, sealing Marcus and the oblivious intern inside. Just as the steel closed, Dr. Rivera pushed Isabella's door open and stepped into the room. In the echoing cavern of the abandoned Hyperloop tunnel, Elena swiped the Holo-Screen off her iBand. The projected diagram vanished, plunging the command center back into the dim, functional glow of emergency lighting strips and HoloScreens. The sudden silence amplified the persistent drip of unseen water somewhere down the tunnel.

Alex stood rigid, his back to the others, shoulders hunched. The brief, fractured conversation played over in his mind. His mother's initial confusion, the chillingly serene confidence after mentioning the GeneVax, her vacant dismissal of Maya Rivera's changed demeanor. 'Gone. Completely. It's already in remission.'

The words were a cruel twist, potential physical healing traded for mental enslavement. Relief warred with rage inside him, a nauseating churn. His mother, free from the physical torment of lupus, only to be bound by the invisible chains of the Compliance Protocol.

He slammed a fist against a rusted support beam. The clang echoed sharply. "She didn't want it!" His voice was rough, tight with fury. "She told me. She told *Maya*. They knew!"

He turned, his blue eyes burning, scanning the faces watching him. Elena, arms at her side. She looked at him with empathy. Pacheco, his usual humor absent, a deep line etched between his brows, his gaze filled with a grim understanding Alex now shared. Sera had stepped away and was now field-stripping a modified Glock pistol on a nearby crate, the rhythmic clicks punctuating the tension. Bo Lin shifted uncomfortably, looking anywhere but at Alex.

"Maya wouldn't have done that," Alex forced the words out, needing to hear them spoken, even as he knew they were false. "They got to her. Just like Jamie."

Jamie. Her bright, forced smile, the vacant pleasantness that had replaced her cynical wit. The disturbing violation of friendship and trust. But this was his mother. Isabella Reyes Thompson. The woman who worried about his intensity, who filled his sterile apartment with warmth and memories, who valued compassion and discourse above all else. They had taken her skepticism, her worry, herself, and replaced it with placid acceptance. LifeSpan had plunged a knife into his life, into his family, and twisted it.

A cold fire ignited in his gut, consuming the earlier analytical detachment. It wasn't just about data anomalies or systemic control anymore, or abstract truth. LifeSpan had crossed a line etched deep within him. They had taken his mother, used her illness against her, forced compliance upon her when she was vulnerable.

He stalked toward the blueprint table where Pacheco's schematics of the LifeSpan Headquarters lay spread out under the focused beam of a work light. His hands, usually marked by a faint tremor under stress, were steady now, clenched into white-knuckled fists.

"Pacheco." Alex's voice was low, devoid of its earlier tremor, replaced by a dangerous calm. "Let's go over those blueprints again. Tell me everything." His gaze lifted, meeting Elena's steady watch. "They took my mom. Nobody fucks with my family."

Later, the harsh beam of the work light cast sharp relief across the sprawling blueprints of the LifeSpan Genomics Headquarters. Lines representing concrete walls, ventilation shafts, and data conduits criss-crossed the massive sheets. Elena traced a potential route with a stylus, her dark eyes narrowed in concentration.

Pacheco leaned beside her, his calloused finger tapping a section depicting subterranean levels. Sera Voss studied a different area detailing security choke points near the R&D delivery docks. Bo Lin shook his head, his HoloScreen projecting colored lines and marks on the prints, likely simulating security system responses.

Alex stood beside Pacheco, his earlier, fiery declaration settling into a cold, intense focus. He absorbed the details, mapping the structure in his mind, his SRV latching onto patterns in the design. Potential weaknesses, blind spots, redundancies.

"That maintenance corridor runs parallel to the main data trunk line on sub-level three." Sera's voice cut through the low hum of equipment. "It'll be saturated with passive sensors. Acoustic, vibration, thermal. You breathe too loud and you trigger an alert."

Pacheco grunted, scratching his chin. "Okay, *Cabrona*, point taken. But the alternative Elena suggests through the old hydro-recycling conduits?" He shook his head, his expression dubious. "Those access hatches haven't been opened since we sealed the system in 'thirty-three. They'll be pressure-welded shut, maybe even structurally compromised. Plus, they vent near the primary geothermal exchange. Hot as hell there."

"We can cut the welds," Elena countered, her tone brisk. "And thermal shielding is manageable. The route bypasses the main security hubs entirely until we hit the tertiary server farm access."

"Too exposed once inside farm," Bo Lin interjected without looking up from his screen. "Camera coverage total. Face recognition cross-reference with *emproyee* manifests every five second. Even with spoof IDs, gait analysis AI will *frag* inconsistency."

"Mag locks on every internal door in that sector, too," Sera added grimly. "Standard corporate grade, but reinforced frames. Need more than a simple bypass card."

"The loading docks?" Elena suggested, shifting her focus on the blueprint.

Pacheco sighed. "Automated. Robot loaders, drone oversight. Biometric checks on all incoming organic material, which means personnel. Scans everything down to the molecular level for contaminants or unauthorized tech."

Frustration crackled in the air. Every potential path seemed blocked, every advantage countered by layers of high-tech security. The sheer scale of the complex, the monument Pacheco himself had built, felt insurmountable.

Footsteps echoed softly from the main tunnel entrance. Marcus appeared, walking quickly, his face pale but composed under the emergency lighting. He scanned the group huddled around the blueprints, his gaze landing on Alex.

The intense debate paused momentarily as heads turned. Marcus walked directly toward Alex, ignoring the blueprints and the questioning looks. He stopped in front of him, the weariness evident in his eyes. He didn't speak. Instead, he simply met Alex's gaze and placed a hand gently on his shoulder. The pressure was slight, a fleeting contact, but the message was clear: *I heard. I know. I'm sorry.*

Alex held his gaze for a second, the muscle in his jaw tight. He gave a single, almost imperceptible nod. Understanding passed between them, solid and unspoken.

Marcus squeezed his shoulder briefly and let his hand fall. He turned back to the group clustered around the table, stepping closer to the light. "What'd I miss?"

Elena watched the silent exchange between Marcus and Alex, her expression unchanged, though a flicker of understanding crossed her sharp features. "We're spinning our wheels," she stated, her voice cutting through distant dripping. "Every direct approach is a kill box. Standard infiltration tactics won't work against their layered defenses."

She looked directly at Alex, her gaze steady. "We need your eyes on this. Your way of seeing things." She turned to Marcus. "Show Alex everything we've pulled on the HQ peripheral activity. Traffic logs for the access roads, delivery manifests, autonomous transports, chemical shipments, even the damn catering services. Employee shift schedules, drone patrol routes, waste disposal pickup times."

She swept a hand over the scattered data slates and blueprint overlays projected by Bo Lin. "There might be a pattern, an anomaly, something their security AI discounts, but you might catch." She leaned closer to Alex. "We need a crack in the armor. Not a battering ram, but a hairline fracture we can exploit. Something subtle they haven't anticipated."

Marcus nodded, pulling up complex data streams on his own Holo-Screen, preparing to mirror them onto the main projection table. "Got it. Cross-referencing municipal traffic AI data, satellite imagery archives, corporate shuttle schedules, logistics feeds from their subsidiaries..." He tapped rapidly, populating the central display with swirling patterns of vehicle movements, color-coded time blocks, and logistical flow charts overlaid on the HQ map. The sheer volume of information was staggering, a chaotic representation of the thousands of daily interactions surrounding the LifeSpan campus.

"But Elena." Marcus paused, looking up from his screen, his brow furrowed. He glanced at Alex. "Let's say Alex finds something. A way in. We still have the extraction problem. Alex himself said moving that much data, the files he carried. It's petabytes. The Neural Transit upload requires their invasive tech, and the MEG offload takes damn near a full day, assuming we even *had* a MEG scanner." He gestured around the rough concrete tunnel.

"How do we get the proof *out*, even if we get *in*?"

Alex had turned away from Marcus, his gaze fixed once more on the intricate lines of the LifeSpan HQ schematics spread across the table. His mind, fueled by the cold fire ignited by his mother's forced compliance, worked differently now. Not just analyzing structural weaknesses, but LifeSpan's *methods*, their *philosophy*. He saw the layers of physical security, the technological barriers, the biological encryption of the Data Mule protocol. It was comprehensive, almost paranoid. *Almost.*

He pushed away from the table, drawing the attention of the others. "I've been thinking," he began, his intense blue eyes moving from Marcus to Elena, and settling on the projected data streams. "About the Data Mule protocol. About the sheer volume. Why *so* much data? Even for project files, internal communications, research backups - petabytes?"

He tapped a finger on the table, near a symbol representing a secure data node. "We assume the volume itself is the point –

maximum information transfer. We assume the biological encryption is the primary security." He let the implicit question form. "But what if that's only part of it?"

Elena tilted her head, her expression wary but attentive. "Go on."

"I read an old Sherlock Holmes story, *The Adventure of the Second Stain*. In it, Holmes is hired to recover a stolen diplomatic letter that could ignite a war. The twist is, it wasn't locked away or disguised, it was hidden in plain sight, slipped among a pile of ordinary papers. Everyone missed it because they assumed something that important had to be more protected."

He looked up. "Security through obscurity. "It's an old concept, but effective. What if LifeSpan isn't just using the Neural Transit system to move critical data securely? What if they're deliberately padding the payload?"

Marcus frowned, adjusting his glasses. "Padding? You mean adding junk data?"

"Exactly. Chaff." Alex's gaze sharpened as the idea took shape in his mind and voice. "Think about it. They have near-infinite processing power, access to endless streams of anonymized public data, internal metrics, environmental simulations. It would be trivial for them to generate terabytes, *petabytes*, of plausible-sounding but ultimately meaningless data. Research noise, redundant logs, complex algorithmic outputs designed to look important."

He gestured toward the blueprints again, and back to the swirling data patterns Marcus had displayed. "They mix chaff in with the *real* data, the Compliance Protocol specifics, the Phase vectors, the crucible. They bury the needle in a colossal haystack. Even if someone intercepted a Data Mule, even if they somehow bypassed the biological encryption or had the MEG tech to offload it, they'd face an impossible task: sifting through petabytes of data to find the few gigabytes or terabytes that actually matter. It's another layer of security, hidden in plain sight."

Pacheco let out a low whistle. "Hide the treasure map by burying it under ten thousand tons of worthless paper."

"It makes sense," Marcus conceded, running a hand through his frosted hair. "Discourages analysis even post-breach. And it explains why we've had such a hard time with the data we have exfiltrated from Lifespan. Increases processing time exponentially. But Alex, even if that's true, how does it help *us*? We still can't handle the initial volume."

Alex met his gaze. The faint tremor was absent from his hands, replaced by a tightly-coiled energy. "Because I don't see the haystack," he stated, a quiet confidence underpinning the words. "My SRV lets me see the patterns. The inconsistencies. The *structure* of data in a way your standard AI analysis, even LifeSpan's AI might overlook because it's looking for specific flags. My SRV would serve as a metal detector in the haystack."

He took a breath, the core of a proposal forming. "Their chaff generation would follow algorithms, patterns of its own. The *real* data, once you boil down the crucible, would have a different signature, a different internal logic, maybe even different encryption markers if we look closely enough."

He looked at the group. "What if I don't need to extract the *entire* payload? What if, connected directly to their internal systems, or even analyzing the stream during a theoretical offload, I could identify the chaff in real-time?" He dropped his voice, becoming more urgent. "I could potentially filter it. Isolate the crucial files, the ANGUS protocols, the deployment plans, the target lists. Boil it down. Reduce petabytes to something manageable. Something we *can* extract quickly, maybe even through unconventional channels."

"Can you do that?" Elena asked.

"I think I can." Alex pushed back a stray lock of dark hair, and it was beginning to annoy him, a nervous habit with no productive outcome. As useless as the extra data packed into the transport assignments. "It's more than just pattern recognition, it's synthesis. Seeing the connections *between* the patterns."

He gestured vaguely, trying to articulate the internal process. "Data Mules have Echo-Class clearance, right? They're trusted couriers. LifeSpan grants them passive access to the data stream during transit, a necessary function for the biological encoding. But nobody can actively *process* that much information in real time. Petabytes flowing through your neural pathways are just noise to a standard cognitive architecture. You're a conduit, not an analyst."

He drew in a breath. "But for me, it's different. The SRV changes how my brain handles massive datasets. It's not just seeing individual trees, it's mapping the entire forest simultaneously. When I was plugged in at LifeSpan Northgate, accessing those restricted files, that's how I found the priority treatment list, how I found Jamie's name, my name. It wasn't a targeted search. I didn't even know what I was looking for, initially. The anomaly stood out from the background radiation of the data. A signal spike in the noise."

His gaze swept across their faces again, daring them to doubt. "That wasn't luck. LifeSpan buried the list, surrounded it with terabytes of operational logs and personnel files, precisely the kind of chaff I'm talking about. But the structure was different. The access permissions, the encryption flags, the cross-references, they didn't quite match the surrounding data's signature. Anyone else, even their own AI scrubbing the logs later, would dismiss it as a corrupted file fragment or a database indexing error. But I saw the pattern."

He looked down at his hands, no longer trembling, but clenched lightly at his sides. The memory of his mother, serene and detached in the hospital feed Marcus had shown him, fueled his conviction. It wasn't academic curiosity anymore, it was a weapon. "I *can* do it. I can filter their noise. Identify everything."

The swirling chaos of data Marcus projected onto the table resolved into structured streams under Alex's intense scrutiny. Vehicle transponder logs flickered alongside drone patrol heatmaps. Satellite overlays showed autonomous delivery trucks docking and departing with clockwork precision. Employee shuttle manifests cross-referenced with building access records. Chemical deliveries logged, waste removal cycles charted, even the atmospheric particulate counts from rooftop sensors were included. It was a dizzying flow, designed to overwhelm standard analysis.

But Alex's mind didn't process it linearly. His SRV absorbed the totality, threads of connection sparking and dying as potential entry points flared and were instantly extinguished by counter-patterns. The main delivery bays? Saturated with chem-sniffers and cargo scanners looking for anything denser than packaged nutrient paste. Maintenance tunnels? Laced with micro-vibration sensors keyed to specific acoustic signatures. Corporate shuttles? Biometric scans linked to neural activity profiles – impossible to spoof without triggering alarms. Even the waste disposal chutes had infrared and biological scanners. Every logical path and infiltration technique honed over decades of corporate espionage, was anticipated, countered, secured.

He mentally mapped potential routes, visualizing the approach, the breach point, the interior navigation, only for his own analytical process to slam into digital brick walls erected by LifeSpan's security AI. The system was comprehensive, predictive, seemingly impenetrable. A low groan escaped Pacheco as he ran a hand over his face, exhausted by the rigor of the challenge. Bo Lin muttered curses in Mandarin under his breath, his fingers flying across his HoloScreen, running simulations that likely confirmed Alex's internal assessment.

Getting *inside* LifeSpan HQ remained an insurmountable obstacle. He pushed back from the table, the complex web of security protocols swimming before his eyes. Maybe Elena was right. Maybe it *was* impossible.

Hours clawed by. Elena paced, a panther in a too-small cage. Marcus, his initial burst of data-slinging enthusiasm long faded, slumped over his console, massaging his temples. Bo Lin muttered strings of frustrated Mandarin, his fingers still ghosting over his interface but with less purpose. Even the relentless drip of water from a cracked conduit seemed to mock their efforts, each drop a tiny marker of wasted time. The projected schematics of LifeSpan HQ remained stubbornly impenetrable, a fortress of overlapping security fields and AI-driven countermeasures.

Pacheco, who had alternated between offering structural insights and staring grimly at the plans of the edifice he'd built, finally swiped his iBand HoloScreen closed with a sigh that seemed to carry the weight of all the concrete he'd ever poured. *"Basta.* Enough." He pushed himself up from the crate he used as a chair, his joints creaking in protest. "My brain feels like refried beans."

He stretched, a grimace briefly twisting his features. Listen, *gente*. 'El Chingon' food truck. It's parked up at the Bijou MagLev station today. Best damn chili fries this side of the Rockies, and his green chili - *mamá mía*." His eyes, usually holding a complex mix of grief and steely resolve, held a spark of something approaching enthusiasm. "I'm going. Anyone need anything? They got burgers, burritos, tacos, tamales…"

Around the room, a few halfhearted nods answered him. The others barely looked up, each absorbed in their work, the hum of machinery and muted clatter of tools filling the silence. It wasn't disinterest—it was exhaustion, focus, and something heavier neither of them wanted to name.

Sera Voss, who had been methodically disassembling and cleaning a complex-looking pulse rifle paused, the metallic click of a component sliding home echoing in the relative quiet. Her steel-blue eyes met Pacheco's. "I'll ride shotgun, Mateo." She reassembled the rifle with an economy of motion born from countless repetitions. "Could use some air that hasn't been recycled since the last ice age. And a real chili cheeseburger sounds like a damn miracle right now."

Pacheco grinned, a rare sight that briefly erased some of the lines etched by worry. "Alright, vámonos. I'll bring back a little of everything. Maybe food'll remind you all what living feels like."

Alex said nothing. The idea of eating felt distant, like something that belonged to another life.

The two figures, the construction mogul and the weapons specialist, disappeared down the dusty tunnel toward the hidden access. A temporary lull fell over the remaining group. Elena finally stopped pacing, leaning against a damp wall, closing her eyes for a moment. Marcus just stared blankly at his darkened screen. Alex remained at the table, the intricate schematics still swimming in his vision, a puzzle with no discernible solution.

It felt like an eternity, but was probably closer to an hour later when Pacheco and Sera returned. The aroma preceding them was a glorious assault on the senses, rich and savory, cutting through the tunnel's dankness. Pacheco juggled a precarious stack of white paper bags and a tray of assorted sodas, a triumphant look on his face. Sera followed, carrying another couple of bags that smelled powerfully of grilled meat and spices.

"Delivery for the damned and desperate!" Pacheco announced, setting his burden down on the makeshift table, which was hastily cleared of data slates.

He began unloading the treasures. Golden, thick-cut Smothered Chili Fries, glistening under a blanket of melted cheese and rich, dark chili. Fat chili burgers, their buns steamed soft, oozing more of that same chili. Classic Cheeseburgers, simple, perfect, the yellow cheese already melted into the patties. A collection of Burritos: some plain, tightly wrapped; others generously topped with chili and cheese; a few labeled "Deluxe" bulging with unseen fillings. Pacheco held up one that was golden brown and slightly crispy.

"And for the connoisseurs," he declared. "The Grilled Burrito. Change your life, *Amigos*!" He also produced a container of Grilled Tacos, the tortillas lightly charred, cradling seasoned barbacoa meat.

Alex hadn't realized the depth of his hunger until the scent hit him. His stomach growled audibly. He reached for one of the smothered burritos, the warmth seeping through the paper wrapper. It was heavy, substantial. He unwrapped it, the aroma of slow-cooked beans, spiced meat, green chili, and melted cheese making his mouth water.

He took a large bite. The tortilla was soft, the fillings a perfect blend of textures and flavors, the green chili adding a pleasant, warming heat. He ate quickly, methodically, but with an undeniable enjoyment. The complex problem of LifeSpan HQ, the danger to his mother, the pervasive threat of the Compliance Protocol – for a few moments, they receded, overshadowed by the simple, profound satisfaction of good food after hours of mental exertion.

He was nearly three-quarters of the way through the substantial burrito, a smear of green chili on his chin, when he paused, looking around at the others who were similarly engaged in demolishing their respective meals. A small, almost surprised smile touched his lips.

"Food," Alex announced, his voice slightly muffled by a mouthful of burrito. "It makes everything better."

Something flickered at the periphery of his focus. A low-priority data stream, almost lost in the noise of high-volume logistics and personnel movement. Access logs tagged with a non-LifeSpan corporate identifier. Frequent, short-duration entries across multiple sectors of the sprawling campus, including areas near administrative wings and R&D labs. He focused, pulling the thread, isolating the associated video snippets and transport manifests.

"Wait," he murmured, leaning closer to the projection again, his earlier discouragement evaporating. "What is this?" He pointed a finger at a recurring logo on the side of small, autonomous service vans captured in security footage feeds. A cartoonish, smiling snowman holding a candy bar. "Snowman Vending," he read aloud, pulling up their corporate profile from a public network query Marcus routed.

"Website says they're the premier automated snack and beverage provider in the Springs area." He highlighted the access logs Marcus had integrated. "Camera footage and door logs show their service vans arriving between five and twenty times daily. Multiple entry points – loading docks, service elevators, even secondary personnel entrances." He cross-referenced vehicle IDs with shift data. "Across the day, different technician credentials access various parts of the LifeSpan Northgate facility."

Pacheco squinted at the screen. "Vending machines? *Ay, carajo*, we built dedicated coffee dispensers into every breakroom."

"Supplementation," Alex countered, scanning the associated internal requisitions. "Snacks, sugary drinks, caffeine boosts. Morale enhancers. Standard corporate perk, even at LifeSpan." He magnified a few frames of security footage. Technicians in simple blue Snowman Vending uniforms with carts, accessing machines in hallways, lounges, even outside secure lab entrances. Sometimes accompanied by low-level security, often not. "Look at this." Alex zoomed in on a time-stamped log entry.

A Snowman tech swiping an access card at a junction leading

toward a restricted administrative wing. He was alone. No escort. He spent twelve minutes servicing machines down the corridor and exited.

"The data shows these techs are often left on their own. Their access is broad, less scrutinized than internal staff or high-priority contractors." A humorless smile touched Alex's lips. "People trust the candy man."

He met Elena's curious gaze and swept his eyes across the others. The solution wasn't a complex bypass or a brute-force assault. It was hiding in plain sight, twisted snugly in the shiny wrapper of mundane routine and corporate life. Alex licked his fingers and took a quick swig of his drink, wiping his mouth with the back of his hand.

Elena smiled for the first time that night. "That's how we get in."

CHAPTER 10

MANUAL OVERRIDE

THE SMILING SNOWMAN LOGO, projected into the grimy tunnel, seemed almost mocking against the backdrop of LifeSpan's intricate defenses.

Elena rested her elbows on the table. "The candy man. Simple. Overlooked. I like it. But how do we become him?"

Pacheco rubbed his jawline. "Three ways, I figure. We build our own Snowman. We borrow one. Or..." He paused, a wry twist to his mouth. "We try asking nicely?" The suggestion dissipated almost as soon as he voiced it.

"Asking nicely gets us flagged faster than Alex sprinting through the front gate," Marcus retorted, his attention already consumed by his console. His fingers tapped across the holographic interface, summoning Snowman Vending's corporate data and fleet information. "Their LifeSpan contract has to be massive. No chance they'd jeopardize that for some off-grid whispers about gene editing."

"So, build or borrow," Sera stated, cutting to the core of the viable options. "Building means what, exactly? A replica van? Uniforms? Access cards?"

"The works," Pacheco affirmed with a nod.

"We have the specs now, thanks to Marcus pulling their data. We could get a similar chassis, fabricate the shell, match the paint, and replicate the logos. Source some basic blue jumpsuits, stitch the patches. Forge the ID cards."

Bo Lin shifted uncomfortably on the makeshift crate he used as a seat. "Fabrication take time. Resource we don't have. Finding van model that match, customize *discreetry*, cost many crypto. Paint needs factory precision, the logo perfect. One minor inconsistency, one detail off, under scrutiny..."

Marcus finally tore his eyes from the glowing screen, adjusting his thin-rimmed glasses. His expression conveyed the depth of the problem. "It's far beyond just looking right. Forget the paint job. These vans aren't just metal boxes." He gestured at the complex diagrams dominating his display. "They are networked nodes. Each one broadcasts multiple unique identifiers wirelessly."

He highlighted specific components on the schematic. "RFID tags fused to the chassis. Encrypted transponders constantly pinging Life-Span's gate sensors. Internal diagnostic systems reporting operational status back to Snowman HQ's central network, which you can bet your last crypto, cross-references directly with LifeSpan security protocols."

Marcus tapped a string of code representing a data packet structure. "LifeSpan doesn't just *see* the van arrive. Their system *interrogates* it electronically the instant it nears a checkpoint. Spoofing that level of authentication? We'd need dedicated hardware emulators, powerful signal repeaters, cracked encryption keys for *both* Snowman's internal network *and* LifeSpan's security layer." He shook his head, the motion sharp.

The initial appeal of the counterfeit strategy evaporated under the harsh light of Marcus' technical breakdown. The cost wasn't just money and material, but a gamble against a sophisticated digital fortress designed specifically to detect such intrusions.

"Which leaves borrowing," Elena concluded, her voice even, accepting the inevitable. "Hijacking."

"Direct," Sera added, her tone emotionless. "Quick access, but high-risk during the acquisition phase."

Alex traced potential delivery routes on the projected city map, the lines weaving through industrial zones toward the sprawling LifeSpan Northgate campus. "We'd need to intercept a van while it's mobile," Sera said. "Away from surveillance saturation. Neutralize the technician quickly, quietly. Secure the van, the uniform, the active credentials." She was tactical.

"Neutralize," Pacheco echoed, the word hanging uncomfortably. "How? Stunner? Chemical agent? Something else?"

"Non-lethal," Elena stated, her voice leaving no room for argument. "We disable, we don't eliminate. Fewer complications down the line. But the plan must account for resistance. Assume the technicians have some basic security awareness or panic protocols."

Marcus began highlighting potential intercept zones on the map, stretches of less-trafficked industrial roads near Snowman's distribution hub, service routes bordering the LifeSpan campus with known camera blind spots. "Timing is everything. We need to grab a van whose schedule aligns with the access window we need inside Northgate. And critically, we must disable its external communications *immediately* upon intercept, before it misses a scheduled check-in or the technician triggers a duress signal."

The conversation shifted, the theoretical giving way to hard logistics. Where was the optimal point to strike? Which driver shift offered the best combination of route and timing? How could they subdue the technician swiftly and silently? The path of counterfeiting, once a possibility, now seemed a complex technological fantasy. Hijacking, raw and dangerous, presented itself as the only viable, if brutal, path forward.

Elena turned from the main planning table, her gaze sharp, aimed at the two hackers. "Marcus, Bo, I need everything on Snowman Vending. Corporate structure, registered assets, fleet size, maintenance schedules, uniform suppliers, the works. Find out where they buy their goods. Dig into their tax filings, personnel records if you can crack them safely. I want to know the brand of polish they use on the CEO's desk and the average tread depth on their delivery van tires. Build me a complete operational profile. We need to know them better than they know themselves."

Marcus nodded, already swiveling back to his console. Lines of code scrolled rapidly across the holographic display as he initiated deep-web searches and began probing Snowman's publicly-accessible network infrastructure. Bo Lin, perched on his crate, pulled a slim datapad from his oversized hoodie pocket and began tapping away.

Leaving the tech specialists to their digital excavation, Elena gestured for Alex to follow her toward a cleared space deeper in the abandoned Hyperloop tunnel. Sera Voss stood waiting, a heavy canvas roll spread out on a makeshift workbench fashioned from stacked concrete blocks. There was a faint smell of solvent and metal.

Sera unrolled the canvas, revealing an assortment of tools and devices. Several were clearly firearms, a matte black Glock pistol, parts of a disassembled AK-pattern rifle, both exhibiting non-standard modifications like polymer grips and shielded components. Alongside them lay smaller, unfamiliar objects. Compact cylinders, flat metallic discs with adhesive strips, blocky transmitters bristling with small antennae.

Sera picked up one of the pistols, handling it with ingrained familiarity. Her steel-blue eyes met Alex's. "Firearms require instinct and muscle memory you don't have. In a firefight, hesitation kills. Your weapon is data. Leave the shooting to us." She placed the pistol back down carefully.

Her rough, scarred hand picked up a flat, grey disc, about the size of a hockey puck but thinner. One side had a peel-off backing. "This is your primary tool if things get loud electronically. We call it a 'sticky'. Localized EMP burst. Fries unshielded circuits within five meters. Also pumps out broadband RF noise for about thirty seconds – jams local wireless signals, drone telemetry, sensor nets. Slap it onto a security console, a drone, a camera mount. It's magnetic, so if it's metal, you can toss it and it will stick, but there's the adhesive - the 'sticky' for anything else."

Alex accepted the *sticky* when Sera offered it. It felt dense, heavier than it looked. He noted the simple activation switch near the edge and a small display. A timer, maybe? "How do we get these inside?" He turned the disc over in his hand. "We can't just walk these into the heart of LifeSpan."

"Snowman techs carry diagnostic kits, tool belts," Elena answered, stepping closer. "Spare parts, testing units." She indicated the sticky and a few other small electronic devices on the canvas. "These can be disguised. Repainted, housed in dummy casings. Mixed in with legitimate tools. Security looks for weapons, not necessarily a capacitor discharge unit painted safety yellow and labeled 'Flux Modulator' or some shit like that."

Sera gestured toward the older firearms. "Most of our gear is practical. Reliable. Bullets don't get jammed by signal interference. An old rifle with good optics and custom rounds..." She patted the stock of a bolt-action rifle wrapped in carbon mesh. "Is often more effective than the latest energy weapon against specific targets. We use what works, old or new. EM shielding on everything, non-reflective coatings, 3D-printed parts to fool scanners. Adapt or die."

While Alex absorbed the crash course in resistance tech, Elena moved over to where Pacheco studied a complex architectural schematic projected onto the tunnel wall. It was a detailed cutaway of the LifeSpan Northgate Ziggurat Tower.

Patch traced a finger along a series of interconnected lines representing service corridors and utility conduits. "The Snowman tech, he makes his deliveries, refills the machines," he said, his voice low, gravelly. "Standard routes. But his access chip..." He tapped a specific level on the diagram. "Likely grants entry to maintenance shafts and interstitial spaces most employees never see. That's our highway."

"We need a terminal,'"Elena stated, her eyes fixed on the blueprints. "Network access, sufficient privileges, but ideally, low traffic. Somewhere Alex can work for at least thirty minutes without interruption."

Pacheco zoomed in on a sub-level section, highlighting a junction room labeled Environmental Systems Monitoring - Sector Gamma. "Here. Primarily automated climate control systems. Minimal human oversight. Direct fiber optic trunk lines run through this node, connecting to the main data spine. Security patrols are less frequent.

They rely on sensors." He tapped the room designation again. "If we can get Alex here, he should have the bandwidth and system access he needs."

Marcus looked up from his console, interrupting the detailed dissection of Snowman Vending's fleet logistics. His expression held a flicker of something unexpected. "Elena. Hold up on the hijacking scenarios for a minute."

She turned from the projected blueprints. "What is it?"

"The owner. Clayton Ergen." Marcus pulled up a dense profile overlaying the corporate structure chart. It wasn't just business data; it was woven with scraped social media snippets, public records, network activity flags, and cross-referenced medical opt-out lists maintained by the Resistance. "He flags high on multiple indicators. Enough to put him on our potential recruitment watchlist."

Elena frowned, stepping closer to the console. "Recruitment? A multi-millionaire contractor with an exclusive LifeSpan deal? What indicators?"

"Strong anti-mandate sentiment, specifically regarding health directives," Marcus ticked off points on the screen. "Publicly-documented refusal of GeneVax therapy, citing personal conviction and bodily autonomy despite documented pre-existing conditions like asthma and allergies that LifeSpan specifically markets GeneVax to 'cure'. His refusal is significant, considering the corporate pressure he must have faced to get the LifeSpan contract."

He highlighted another data cluster. "His younger brother suffered severe cardiac complications post-COVID vaccination years ago. Ergen publicly disputed the official cause, blaming the mandate. It fits a pattern of deep distrust toward mass health interventions pushed by corporate or government entities."

"He's also president of the local Corvette club," Bo Lin added quietly from his corner, scrolling through his own datapad. "Very active. Vocal about resisting full vehicle autonomy mandates. Likes his 'driver control'."

"They align," Elena said. "But sentiment is one thing. Action against a client who represents a massive chunk of his revenue? That's a different beast."

"Agreed," Marcus conceded. "It's a risk. He's opinionated, maybe egotistical, according to some profiles. If we approach him wrong, or if his pragmatism outweighs his principles, he could burn us. Report us directly to LifeSpan security."

"Or," Elena countered, considering the alternative. "We avoid a violent roadside intercept. We avoid the near-impossible task of spoofing his vans' embedded authenticators. We avoid fabricating uniforms, tools, IDs. We gain a potential insider who knows the campus logistics intimately, maybe even better than Pacheco remembers from the construction phase."

There was a long pause as Elena looked over the information on Marcus' HoloScreen.

"Hijacking is messy," Marcus stated, leaning back slightly. "High probability of things going sideways fast. If we disable the driver, we have a limited window before the missed check-ins trigger alerts. If the spoofing fails, we're blown before we even reach the gate."

Elena looked at Alex, Pacheco, Sera, and Bo. Their resources were finite, their risks already astronomical. Adding a high-stakes, high-violence variable like a vehicle intercept felt like tipping the scales further against them. Approaching Ergen, while perilous, offered a cleaner path if it succeeded. "We approach him," Elena decided, her voice firm. "Carefully. We leverage what we know – his distrust, his refusal, his belief in choice. We don't go in guns blazing, spouting conspiracy. We present it as a violation of the principles he already champions. The risk of him turning us in is substantial. But the potential reward is legitimate access, insider knowledge. They outweigh the dangers of the alternative. Patch, you're with me."

The heavy steel door sealing the Hyperloop access swung shut behind them, plunging the tunnel back into echoing darkness. Outside, the afternoon sun felt harsh after the subterranean gloom. Pacheco's 2034 Jeep EV 4x4, coated in a layer of road grime that helped it blend into the urban landscape, sat quietly as they settled inside. He keyed the ignition sequence, and the vehicle's internal systems came online with a soft chime.

"Destination: 2890 Hodgen Road," Elena instructed the navigation AI. The route appeared on the dash-integrated HoloScreen, a twisting path leading northeast out of the city sprawl.

The Jeep navigated the automated traffic flow with smooth precision, leaving the denser commercial districts behind. They ascended gradually, the tightly-packed buildings giving way to wider lots and gradually to undeveloped hillsides dotted with scrub oak. The buildings thinned, carrying the scent of pine as the road narrowed, winding through the low foothills characteristic of the Black Forest area. Sunlight filtered through the canopy of mature Ponderosa Pines lining the route. The automated drive system handled the curves effortlessly, leaving Elena and Pacheco free to observe.

After several miles of weaving through the trees, the navigation system announced their imminent arrival. The Jeep slowed, turning onto a long, circular paved driveway marked by a simple address post. Through a break in the dense pines, the property unfolded. A large, modern house sat back from the road, more sprawling than tall, clad in natural wood and stone accents that blended with the wooded, five-acre lot. But the house itself seemed secondary. Dominating the approach were the garages – an oversized, three-car attached structure and a separate, equally-large, three-car detached building nearby. All six bay doors stood wide open.

Even from the entrance of the drive, the contents were partially visible. Gleaming paintwork reflected the dappled sunlight. In the detached garage, the unmistakable finned silhouette of a classic car perched high on a double-layer lift – a pristine, two-tone shape from a bygone era, likely the 'fifty-seven Bel Air. Below it, the low, aggressive lines of Corvettes sat parked. In the attached garage, another Corvette, this one a vibrant Torch Red, had its hood propped open. A figure leaned over the engine bay.

Parked prominently near the house, plugged into a sleek, high-capacity charging station – a professional-grade unit far exceeding standard residential installations – sat a long, obsidian-black sedan. Its lines were sharp, futuristic, exuding quiet power.

"Would you look at that," Pacheco breathed, his gaze fixed on the black sedan.

"*Madre de Dios*, A Cadillac Stoic EVX-L. Charging right here."

Elena glanced at the car and back at the garages, her expression unmoved by the specific model. "Expensive?"

"Expensive doesn't cover it, *Jefa*." Patch chuckled, shaking his head. "That's not just a car, it's a statement. Over a thousand horsepower, solid-state battery, range for days. Zero to 100 km/h in under two seconds. But that's not the real kicker." The Jeep continued its slow crawl up the driveway. "Everything on the road now is Level Five autonomy. Mandatory. You're a passenger, whether you like it or not. But the EVX-L? It's one of the last production models, maybe *the* last high-end one, that got certified with a regulated Manual Drive Mode. Retractable wheel, pedals, the whole nine yards. For guys like Ergen, guys who actually like to *drive*, it's the holy grail. Costs a fortune, waiting list years long."

As they approached the main house, the figure working on the red Corvette straightened up. Clayton Ergen emerged from under the hood, a thickset man with a full, grey-and-blond beard spilling down his chest. Noticeable wrinkles fanned from the corners of his assessing eyes as he squinted at the unexpected vehicle pulling silently toward him. He held a greasy rag in one hand, wiping unconsciously at his palms as he watched them.

The Jeep EV 4x4 came to a noiseless stop a respectful distance from the charging Cadillac. The Jeep's doors opened with a soft releasing sigh. Elena stepped out first, her movements measured, eyes scanning the property. Pacheco emerged more slowly, his attention immediately captured.

"*Hijo...*" Patch let out a low whistle, ignoring the man by the red Corvette for a moment. His gaze locked onto the black Stoic Cadillac resting quietly at its charger. "The EVX-L. As I stand and breathe." He stopped at the edge of the drive, his posture reverent, admiration evident but tempered. "Now that..." he said quietly, "...Is art." His usual jovial mask slipped into genuine awe, the reverence of a craftsman admiring the peak work of another, even if the craft was automotive engineering rather than concrete and steel.

Clayton Ergen watched the strangers approach, his initial squint sharpening into suspicion. He set the rag down on a nearby workbench, every movement deliberate. His gaze tracked Pacheco's proximity to the Cadillac, then lingered on Elena. He straightened, shoulders squared, voice low and firm. "Can I help you folks?"

Elena approached slowly, palms open and visible, her tone even. "Apologies for the intrusion. I'm Elena. And that..." She nodded toward Pacheco, who still studied the Cadillac from a respectful distance, "...is Patch. He gets easily distracted by fine machinery."

Ergen's eyes narrowed further, weighing her words. Two strangers, no appointment, a high-security neighborhood. For a heartbeat, the world turned slower as potential scenarios filled his thoughts. But as his mind raced, Elena's steady composure and Pacheco's harmless awe started to sink in. The stiffness in his posture eased, if only slightly.

"Are you Clayton Ergen? CEO of Snowman Vending?" Elena smiled warmly.

Clayton offered a curt nod, the corners of his eyes crinkling further. "Technically. Though everyone just calls me Clay. My wife's been running the day-to-day show for years now. Keeps me out of trouble. Mostly." He glanced back at Patch, a hint of amusement softening his features. "He knows his cars, then?"

Patch straightened up, turning from the Cadillac with a wide, charming grin that reached his dark eyes. "*Señor*, I *live* for them. This Stoic... *¡Qué belleza!* Quad-motor, manual override...they don't make them cars like this anymore. And I see you got the classics, too." He gestured toward the garages. "A C8 Z06 there? Last of the screamers. And is that a 'sixty-three split-window I spy on the lift? Daytona blue?"

Clay relaxed slightly, recognizing a fellow enthusiast. A shared passion that cut through initial suspicions. "You've got a good eye. Yeah, the 'sixty-three's my pride. Eight years running, People's Choice at the National Corvette show down in Denver." He hooked a thumb toward the red C8. "Just tweaking the fuel mapping on this one. Trying to squeeze a little more time out of her before they mandate me into a hydrogen cell and autodrive retrofit."

"It's a damn shame what they're doing," Patch commiserated, shaking his head. "Taking the soul right out of it. Like telling a bird it can only fly where the GPS tells it." He stepped closer. "Takes a certain kind of man to appreciate real control these days, *amigo*," he said, lowering his voice. "Most people just want the machine to do the thinking."

Elena let the car talk flow for another moment, observing the dynamic. Patch's easy charisma worked its magic, transforming Clayton's initial wariness into the shared camaraderie of hobbyists. But time was a luxury they didn't have.

"Sir," Elena interjected smoothly, drawing his attention back. "Patch isn't wrong. We came here today because we believe you're someone who values control. Who values making your own choices, especially when it comes to important things."

Clay's expression shifted again, the easygoing car enthusiast receding, replaced by the sharp assessment of a businessman sensing a pitch. "Alright. Get to it. What is it you're selling?"

"We're not selling anything," Elena stated plainly. "We need help. Information, potentially, access. It involves your largest client. LifeSpan Genomics."

The name landed, and Clay's posture stiffened almost imperceptibly. The wrinkles around his eyes deepened, his gaze sharpening. "LifeSpan? What about them?"

"We have substantial reason to believe..." Elena continued, choosing her words with precision. "...that one of their core products, the GeneVax therapy, isn't just about health. It's designed to subtly influence behavior. To increase compliance, reduce dissent. To take away a person's fundamental right to think critically, to question."

She paused, watching his reaction. "We know you refused the treatment. Despite the pressure, despite the potential health benefits they offered for your own conditions. You made a choice based on your principles. Based on your distrust of mandates that override personal autonomy."

Clayton's hand, which had rested casually on the fender of the C8, tightened slightly. His gaze remained fixed on Elena, but his thoughts churned. He remembered the pressure campaign vividly. The subtle suggestions from his primary care physician, the 'friendly advice' from business associates already 'optimized' by LifeSpan, the insurance wellness seminars touting GeneVax as the key to longevity and peak performance.

They'd even pitched it as a cure for his lifelong asthma, his annoying seasonal allergies, the gallstones that occasionally flared up. He'd refused flatly, citing his brother's tragic experience with the COVID-19 vaccine, invoking his right to choose. But underneath the defiance, a seed of suspicion had taken root. The push had been *too* hard, the benefits promised *too* universally, the dismissal of potential downsides *too* quick.

Elena's words resonated with his buried unease. Influencing behavior, increasing compliance. It sounded outlandish, the stuff of cheap thrillers, yet it aligned perfectly with the subtle shift he'd noticed in some of his colleagues and Corvette Club members post-treatment. A certain placidity, a lack of critical edge he couldn't quite define until now.

"Influence behavior," Clay repeated, the words tasting sour. He looked from Elena to Pacheco, his eyes narrowing. "That's one hell of an accusation. LifeSpan is the biggest game in town. You're talking about messing with the crown jewels." He wasn't dismissing them, not outright.

His mind, sharp from decades of business deals and calculated risks, was weighing the placement of the pieces in a game of chess, three steps ahead. The potential truth resonated with his gut feelings, his core distrust of enforced conformity. But the pragmatist screamed caution. Access into LifeSpan could mean anything.

Patch stepped forward again, his earlier awe replaced by a somber intensity. "It's like they want to take the wheel away, but not just from the car." He tapped his temple. "From *in here*. Gene altering with one vaccination. Make everyone ride passenger in their own damn heads. You fight to keep control of that beauty," he nodded toward the Stoic.

"Because driving *means* something. Choice. Skill. Freedom. What if they're doing the same thing to people's minds, just quieter? So quiet, most folks don't even notice the autopilot taking over?"

The analogy struck home. Clayton looked back at his collection – symbols of control, of individuality, of resisting the mandated tide of automation. He'd built his success on shrewd decisions, on reading people and situations, on maintaining his independence. The idea that LifeSpan might be systematically stripping intrinsic independence from millions, disguised as healthcare, ignited a slow burn of indignation within him. It offended his business sense, his political leanings, and his deeply ingrained belief in personal liberty. It validated his stubborn refusal in a way that was both satisfying and deeply disturbing.

He ran his hand over his thick beard, the assessing look returning, but now directed inward as much as outward. "Okay, let's just say I entertain this crazy idea for a minute. What exactly do you need? 'Access' isn't specific."

"We need to get someone inside the Northgate campus," Elena stated directly, seizing the opening. "Someone who can access their internal network directly from a secure node. Your Snowman Vending technicians have broad access. Less scrutiny than direct employees in many areas, especially service levels and utility corridors. We need proof they're actually doing what we're seeing."

"You want me to let one of your people pose as my tech?" Clayton scoffed, though the sound lacked real conviction. "You think their security is that lax? Biometrics, RFID tags embedded in uniforms, vehicle authenticators synced to scheduling AI... it's not 2010."

"We know," Elena acknowledged. "We wouldn't ask if we didn't have countermeasures planned. We need legitimate entry. A scheduled service call, an authorized vehicle, an ID that passes the initial gate checks. Once inside, our operative handles the rest. We need you to create a window."

Clayton fell silent, leaning back against the workbench beside the C8. The scent of engine oil and old gasoline mingled with the clean pine air. He looked at the expensive cars, the sprawling house, the fruits of a lifetime spent navigating the system, often bending rules but never outright breaking them on this scale. Then he thought of his brother who developed heart issues after taking the COVID-19 vaccines, of the hollowed-out feeling he saw in some GeneVax recipients, of the slick corporate assurances that always felt slightly off. Betraying LifeSpan could ruin him. But letting them get away with *this*, if it were true, that felt like betraying himself.

He pushed himself off the workbench, folding his arms across his considerable chest. "You think getting one of your people dressed up in a Snowman uniform is the hard part? LifeSpan doesn't screw around. Their security isn't just gates and guards, it's woven into everything."

He gestured vaguely to the Southwest, toward the distant corporate campus. "Took me six months, back and forth with my lawyers and their security compliance division, just to finalize the current protocols. They mandated bio-linked ID badges for every single tech stepping foot on that campus. Fingerprint, retinal scan, the works, all tied to the employee profile. Cost a fortune."

Pacheco raised an eyebrow. "Bio-linked? For vending machine guys?"

"You bet," Clayton affirmed. "And it didn't stop there. Had to retrofit the entire fleet of service trucks assigned to the LifeSpan contract with integrated RFID tags and dedicated network interfaces. The trucks authenticate themselves at the service gates *before* the driver even presents his badge. LifeSpan paid for the upgrades, sure, but the hassle! And you know what else they pay for?"

He eyes glinted. "Half the cost of the product *inside* the machines. Snacks, drinks, nutrient paste, whatever. Subsidized 'employee wellness benefit', they call it. Keeps their people happy, keeps us locked into their system." He started pacing slowly between the Jeep and the C8.

"I've got over two hundred machines inside the main pyramid alone. That's not counting the R&D wings, the logistics hubs. Probably closer to three hundred total on that campus alone. We send maybe fifteen techs out there every single day, running routes, restocking, maintenance. Every one of them gets checked. Every entrance, every zone transfer point. No exceptions. Hell, our access to Lockheed isn't even that tight."

Clayton faced them squarely. "And getting that badge in the first place isn't just a background check anymore. They demand full genetic screening. Sent off to LifeSpan's own Ancestry DNA labs in Salt Lake. Takes a minimum of four weeks just to get clearance *before* we can even issue the bio-badge. They know more about my techs than I do."

Elena and Pacheco exchanged a look. The easy confidence they had gained moments before evaporated. Four weeks, DNA screening, bio-linked badges, truck authentication – the obstacles seemed insurmountable. Patch's usual grin faded, replaced by a frown. Elena's jaw tightened, the weariness around her eyes deepening. Clayton's description painted a picture of a near-hermetic seal, far tighter than they had anticipated.

Clayton watched their faces, a flicker of grim satisfaction in his eyes. He'd made his point. The risks were enormous, the defenses formidable. But a slow, calculating look replaced the satisfaction. He rubbed his chin through his beard, the businessman finding an angle, the contrarian seeking an edge.

"But," he started, drawing the word out. "There *might* be a wrinkle. A temporary gap in their perfect system."

Elena looked up sharply. Patch leaned forward.

"Training," Clayton announced. "New hires. Takes time to get the full bio-clearance, right? Can't have trainees sitting around for a month doing nothing. And my turnover is higher than most. So LifeSpan agreed to a provisional system. Trainees get issued a temporary 'contractor guest badge'. Standard RFID, no biometrics linked yet. It grants access *only* when they are physically accompanied by a fully-badged, cleared Snowman technician. They shadow the experienced tech, learn the routes, the machine diagnostics."

Elena lifted an eyebrow, unsure whether or not to feel hope yet.

"Means someone with a guest badge could get through the main gates, into the service corridors, potentially access different floors as long as they're glued to one of my guys. No four-week wait. No DNA scan logged in LifeSpan's system under that temporary ID."

Hope rekindled in Elena, tempered with caution. "A shadow. An apprentice."

"Get your operative a guest badge, pair them with a trusted tech who knows the plan," he confirmed. His expression hardened abruptly. The brief flicker of collaborative spirit vanished, replaced by cold pragmatism. "But let's get something straight." His voice dropped, losing any hint of camaraderie.

"Let's assume I stick my neck out. Assume I arrange a badge, find a tech willing to risk his career, his freedom. This cannot, under *any* circumstances, come back to me. Not Snowman Vending. Not my family." He locked eyes with Elena and Pacheco. "If this goes sideways – a whiff of trouble, a security alert, anything – I pull the plug. I burn you. I give LifeSpan everything they need to nail *you* to the wall, and I walk away clean. My company, my home, my wife, my girls, they come first. Understood?"

Elena met Clayton's hard gaze without flinching. A ghost of a smile touched her lips, devoid of warmth, full of weary understanding. "Clear terms. Absolute deniability. Self-preservation above all else." She nodded slowly. "Sounds like you'll fit right in with us, Sir."

"And call me Clay." He gave a minuscule nod.

The tension broke slightly. Clayton didn't smile back, but the rigid set of his shoulders eased fractionally. Pacheco, however, stepped forward, extending a calloused hand. Clayton looked at the offered hand and met Pacheco's dark, intense eyes.

He saw not just the Resistance fighter, but the builder, the man who understood logistics and concrete realities, the fellow car enthusiast. Two successful men, forged in a world rapidly fading, facing a threat that defied conventional understanding. Icons of an age grappling with the relentless march of progress and change, finding common, if dangerous, ground.

He shook Patch's hand. Their grip was firm, a silent acknowledgment passing between them. Pacheco released the handshake but kept his gaze fixed on Clayton, his expression shifting from shared understanding to something else, a spark of his earlier enthusiasm returning.

"*Amigo*," Pacheco began, his voice dropping back into its easy, charming register. "I need to ask you something."

Clayton's brief sense of accord evaporated. His eyebrows drew together, suspicion flooding back. They had the access plan, the provisional badge idea. What more could they possibly want? He braced himself, waiting for the other shoe to drop, another impossible demand layered onto the already-precarious arrangement.

Pacheco didn't elaborate immediately. Instead, he turned, his appreciation genuine, and pointed a thick finger directly at the gleaming, Torch Red flank of the 2023 Corvette Z06 parked beside them. "Would you have time to take me for a spin?"

CHAPTER 11

A SPOONFUL OF SUGAR

THE LUMENS of the HelioLux panels cycled imperceptibly overhead in Isabella's room at Clinton Memorial. Bare walls with curved corners designed to prevent harm. The faux stone pathway pattern on the floor led nowhere within the confines of the space. On the wall opposite her bed, a large, flat HoloScreen broadcaster displayed the national news. Isabella lay still, her gaze unfocused, the rhythmic beeping of monitors beside her bed a counterpoint to the anchor's smooth delivery in her HearBuds.

"...continuing stabilization as the President begins his third term," the anchor stated, his expression neutral. A graphic appeared showing the White House flanked by American flags.

"Pundits attribute the administration's enduring mandate to the passage of the twenty-ninth Amendment, commonly known as the National Stability Amendment, which effectively nullified presidential term limits. This marks the President's third consecutive term since its ratification, reflecting what officials describe as a public demand for proven leadership in increasingly complex times."

The screen shifted to images of congressional proceedings and charts showing economic trends. "Recovery metrics remain robust following the implementation of fiscal safeguards enacted after the Crypto Collapse a decade ago. Furthermore, recent bipartisan updates to the Genetic Liberty Protection Act aim to enhance national security frameworks. Lessons from the 23andMe Genetic Data Auction Crisis informed these modifications, balancing individual data protections with the critical need for secure, anonymized information flow in medical research and defense initiatives."

A professional smile touched the anchor's lips as the camera view shifted. "Critics remain, but administration officials stress these changes are vital for American innovation and safety. When asked about the broader implications, the President was resolute: "The era of chaotic individualism is over. We are offering a new social contract, one of stability, wellness, and collective purpose. It is simply a more evolved, more unified way to live.""

The broadcast cut abruptly. Stirring orchestral music swelled. Sleek, computer-generated visuals filled the screen: a vast, dark ocean, followed by the imposing silhouette of an aircraft carrier slicing through the waves. The USS John Glenn. Drone aircraft, F-39 Ghosthawks with quantum-shielded skin and V-30 Revenants, launched silently from the EMALS-II rails on its flight deck, banking against a digital sunrise. Quick cuts underscored the vessel's scale: 114,000 tons of kinetic diplomacy, fully armed, and fully autonomous.

"Strength. Readiness. Resolve. Forged by the sea and more deadly than a tsunami," a deep voice intoned over the visuals. Close-ups showed the directed-energy emplacements of the Valkyrie Defense Grid swiveling, the power delivery of its Generation-V Molten Salt Naval Reactors displayed by subtle animated graphic overlays depicting clean energy flow.

"At the core of the USS John Glenn lies CleaNuclear power, our revolutionary Closed-Loop Energy Architecture, driven by twin Generation-V molten salt nuclear reactors and quad-ducted electromagnetic turbines. Producing over 800 megawatts of silent thrust, the John Glenn moves with the quiet force of a tectonic plate, swift, unstoppable, and unseen. Coordinated with the Space Force SkyLance Starlink orbital array, the John Glenn can initiate a precision global strike, delivering hypersonic tungsten 'Thor-Strike' rods from low Earth orbit to any point on the planet within minutes, without warning, and without need for warheads."

The shot pulled back, showing the carrier as the centerpiece of a formidable fleet, patrolling a digital representation of the Pacific flanked by next-gen battleships unleashing hypervelocity railguns and focused, sonic pulse cannons, tearing through a Chinese naval strike fleet with brutal, unstoppable destruction.

"With stealth-sail modulation systems, the USS John Glenn can lower its profile below satellite detection thresholds, gliding low and silent across contested waters at speeds over thirty knots. Its Phantom-Hull matrix generates a fluid distortion field that mimics open ocean on both radar and thermal scans while coordinated optical swarm drones project reactive surface camouflage, rendering the vessel virtually invisible to the human eye."

The Navy emblem appeared, spinning, crisp, and authoritative. *"The U.S. Navy: Guardians of the Horizon."* The screen faded back to the news studio.

A quiet hiss interrupted the broadcast as the door to Isabella Thompson's room slid open. Dr. Maya Rivera entered, her movements professional, her standard-issue Clinton Memorial lab coat immaculate over dark trousers. Isabella remained passive in the bed, the low murmur of the news broadcast a disregarded background noise.

Dr. Rivera approached the bedside terminal, her fingers touching across the holographic interface. Patient data scrolled past, vitals, medication logs, and diagnostic reports. She paused, reviewing the latest immunological assays. "Good morning, Mrs. Thompson." Rivera's voice was calm, reassuring. She turned from the screen, a serene expression on her face. "Excellent news. The latest panels show a complete absence of the SLE autoantibodies. The inflammatory markers are baseline normal. The GeneVax therapy has resolved the underlying autoimmune dysfunction. Your Lupus is effectively gone."

Isabella blinked slowly, her gaze drifting toward the doctor. "Gone?"

"Completely. A remarkable result." Rivera made a notation on the chart. "Jugular administration accelerates uptake dramatically.

Combined with the AI-regulated CRISPR load, the therapy initiates genome-level edits within hours, targeted, recursive, and self-stabilizing. It's not just effective, it's immediate. Now, Isabella." She paused and smiled, devoid of warmth, almost condescending. "Bella," again a pause. "We still need to locate Alex. It's important for his own well-being. Do you have any idea where he might be?"

A faint line appeared between Isabella's brows, a flicker of some distant memory. "Alex called."

Rivera's posture remained relaxed, but her attention sharpened. "He called you? Here?"

"Yes. We talked." Isabella's voice lacked its usual warmth, replaced by a placid certainty.

"How did he contact you? Through the hospital system? Your personal device?" Rivera kept her tone gentle, inquisitive.

The standard hospital monitoring unit on Isabella's wrist had limited communication capabilities, primarily for nurse calls and approved contacts. An external call bypassing security protocols was significant.

Isabella looked down at her hands resting on the thin blanket. "I...don't remember how. Just his voice. We talked."

"When was this? Do you recall the day? The time? Did he say where he was?"

"Yesterday, perhaps? Or the day before?"

Isabella shook her head slightly, the effort minimal. "I don't know what day it is here."

"What did he want? *Bella*, what did you talk about?"

"He just said he loved me and then I heard someone say, "Gotta go, now"."

Rivera nodded, masking any internal reaction. The vagueness, the temporal disorientation – expected post-treatment adjustments, but the call itself was an anomaly. "Alright. Rest now. I'll check on a few things."

The doctor exited the room, her steps measured along the faux stone pathway embedded in the floor. She headed directly toward the main nurses' station for the wing, its curved design offering clear sightlines. The duty nurse looked up as she approached. "I need to review security logs for patient Thompson's room," Rivera stated, accessing the central console with her credentials. "Specifically, corridor footage from the past forty-eight hours."

The system interface bloomed, displaying segmented timelines and camera feeds. Rivera navigated quickly, isolating the corridor outside Isabella's room. She scanned the recorded holographic projections, fast-forwarding through hours of routine staff movements and automated delivery drones. She stopped. Rewound.

A figure lingered near Isabella's doorway approximately thirty hours prior. At first glance, nothing unusual. But as Rivera replayed the footage, something about him felt off. The way he moved, and the way he paused. It didn't fit the rhythm of hospital staff. Then she saw it. He wasn't hospital personnel, the shoes were wrong. Dirty and worn, the kind that had seen too much time on an outdoor basketball court, not the white-collar polish of someone in a lab coat, and certainly not what anyone would wear to work in a hospital.

Young, African American male, dark, curly hair, frosted on top, wearing thin-rimmed glasses and a lab coat. He had a hospital badge, but the camera resolution wasn't good enough to read it, the glare from the curved windows made it impossible. His movements were quick, purposeful. He fiddled with something near the doorframe, stopping to view scrolling data on his iBand. Rivera zoomed in, the system enhancing the image.

Recognition sparked. *Marcus Welichap, Tech specialist. Known associate to Elena. Members of the anti-GeneVax resistance cell she was scheduled to meet with the day after Alex and she had accessed patient records at the research facility.*

Rivera stared at the image. Welichap. At Isabella's door, possibly when Alex must have called. The connection solidified instantly. Alex wasn't just missing, she suspected he was actively working with the documented resistance. Welichap must have facilitated the communication.

Dr. Rivera initiated a call on her iBand, flipping her hair back behind her ear, as if it were necessary for the conversation. "It's me.

Holding his mother as bait isn't going to work. He's already bypassed security and contacted her. Alex Thompson is more resourceful than we imagined."

Inside the Resistance headquarters, Elena sat alone. The room was a small, shielded cage of copper mesh built into the larger cavern, a desperate measure against electronic surveillance. A single wire snaked from a jury-rigged console to a holographic projector that whirred quietly on the scarred metal desk. She finalized the encryption sequence, and the projector cast a shimmering, pixelated face into the air. The man's features were intentionally obscured, a shifting mosaic of light and shadow.

"Elena. We received the package." The voice was low, filtered through layers of digital scrambling, yet a sense of relief permeated the distortion. "Sera delivered it herself. Terrakin thanks you. Your cell's support was critical. We don't have the technical skills to pull that off, and Lifespan knows it."

Elena gave a slight, almost imperceptible nod. The mission had cost them. A botanist, and two other operatives captured, detained by Life-Span security.

"How is she?" the voice asked. "Leaving people behind... that can't be easy."

Elena's expression hardened. "Easy? No. But with Sera, *easy* isn't the point. Before she came here, Sera was on the fast track, Tier 1 JSOC potential. But 'the system' cut her loose."

She lowered her voice and leaned in. "Official reports say she is unstable and overly ruthless. Leaving them was a tactical choice. The seeds were the mission. She buries that kind of loss, and lets it fester. It's what fuels her. Be thankful that rage is pointed at them, not us."

"Their sacrifice ensured the future has a chance. The seeds are secure. Stored deep within the Taos Earthship."

"Good. That's all that matters."

A quiet settled between them, as if they both needed a moment to process.

"I pulled a tomato from one of our vines this morning," the man continued, slightly disconnected from the lips on the holoscreen. "I cut it open. Full of seeds. It felt... strange. I had almost forgotten what they look like."

"It started with watermelons," Elena said, her eyes rolling upward as if accessing a hidden memory. "Then oranges. It was a convenience. No one wants to spit out seeds."

"And now, nothing has them. Not the apples, not the peppers, not the squash. With no seeds, nobody can grow their own food." He winked. "Well, almost...We still grow *our* own. And we are going to make damn sure others can, too."

Elena smiled.

"There's more," the scrambled voice continued, its digital rasp sharpening. "The strike team found something else in the vault. Not just seeds. They retrieved several cryo-sealed containers of water."

Elena's brow furrowed. "Water? Why would they store water?"

"We don't know. Our science team is analyzing the samples now. It was isolated, stored with the most valuable genetic material on the planet. Its presence makes no sense, but it felt important enough to secure."

"Keep me informed of what they find." Elena leaned forward, her elbows resting on the cool metal of the desk. "I have an update for you. We've acquired a new asset. His name is Alex Thompson, a former data analyst for one of LifeSpan's subsidiaries. He found the protocol on his own."

A digital crackle signaled the leader's focus. "On his own? How?"

"A unique neurological condition lets him identify data patterns. He's our key. We're planning an infiltration of the LifeSpan Northgate Campus. We are going into the Pyramid and getting the data that will expose the truth."

The hologram seemed to flicker, the jumble of pixels rearranging itself. "That's a bold move, Elena. And if it works, you might expose Phase One. But you're acting as if that's the final move on the board."

"That *is* the final move."

"No," the voice countered, its tone flat and certain. "It isn't. You're fighting the war you can see. What about the one you can't? We don't even know what 'Phase Two' is. If you succeed, you've won a single battle. How do you prevent the next stage if you have no idea what it entails?"

A cold stillness settled in Elena's posture. She stared directly into the shifting light of the hologram. "I have a plan that will expose Phase Two. Just be ready to..."

A coded alert pinged softly from the datapad, cutting her off. Elena's focus narrowed. She tapped the screen, authenticating the message stream. Her eyes scanned the incoming text blocks. "I have to go. I'll contact you later and fill you in." Elena abruptly ended the transmission and exited the makeshift COMSEC room, meeting Pacheco's gaze first, followed by Marcus's, then Alex's. "Confirmation from Ergen. It's set for tomorrow."

Marcus pushed his glasses back up his nose. "Tomorrow? Memorial Day?"

Elena snorted. "You wanted the day off? It's perfect. Less staff at LifeSpan's Northgate Campus."

Alex found himself nodding in agreement with the logic, his fingers twitching at the same rhythm. "Details?"

"Two temporary contractor guest badges. Non-biometric." Elena twisted the holo slightly, allowing the others a glimpse of the authenticated credentials displayed. "Aliases are assigned: 'David Carr' and 'Maria Flores'. Standard vending tech profiles."

Pacheco straightened up from the schematic. "Who are they assigned to?"

"Ergen has tagged two specific Snowman Vending technicians on the Northgate campus route: a guy named Neal and a non-binary tech named Adrian. He says they're...manageable. Either loyal enough to keep quiet or leveraged." Elena swiped through the message. "He's provided their detailed schedules for tomorrow, their usual routes within the facility, access points they use, even coded phrases to initiate contact."

Alex stopped fiddling with a biometric padlock. "So, we just walk up and pretend to be new hires?"

"According to Ergen, Snowman has high turnover for campus techs. Neal and Adrian are expecting to meet actual new trainees tomorrow for orientation shadowing. They won't question the badges or the story, provided we stick to the script Ergen gave us." Elena traced a finger across the screen. "He's built in layers of separation. As far as Neal and Adrian know, corporate HR arranged the meet. Ergen's name isn't attached anywhere near this handover."

Marcus pushed off the pillar. "Where's the meet?"

"Coffee shop on Powers and Union. Busy enough for cover, close enough to the campus access points Ergen specified." Elena read further. "First pickup is Adrian at 09:41. Second is Neal at 10:00 sharp."

Marcus frowned. "That's tight. Nineteen minutes apart. If both 'new hires' arrive at LifeSpan security check-in back-to-back, even with different techs, it might flag automated pattern analysis. Two anomalies clustered so close?"

Pacheco nodded agreement. "LifeSpan security AI looks for deviations. Two unscheduled 'guest contractor' arrivals within minutes at the same entry vector? Could trigger scrutiny we don't need."

"Ergen considered that. The first van takes the south entry, the second van, the North. Neal is to show 'Maria Flores' vending machine locations. Alex and Adrian are going to service a malfunctioning automated pantry unit, an 'APU' near a data terminal. Ergen said that it was almost as if someone sabotaged it." A wry smile broke on her face. "Alex, or should I say, *David Carr*, you take the first slot with Adrian – 09:41 meet. Get inside, proceed as planned. I'll take the second slot, *Maria Flores*, meeting Neal at 10:00."

Marcus tapped the projected schematic. "Feasible. There are enough service entrances to avoid suspicion. Elena, if you stall him at the cafe for a few minutes, you'll easily arrive thirty minutes apart. Even if they're monitoring traffic patterns and trending data, it won't be enough to seem abnormal."

"Good." Elena finalized the assignments on the datapad. "Ergen gets his deniability. Neal and Adrian are unwitting allies. We get inside."

The stale air of the abandoned Hyperloop station, usually a tomb of forgotten ambition, now pulsed with a focused energy. Sunday, May 30, 2037. The final briefing. A battered industrial HoloScreen flickered, displaying Pacheco's intricate schematics of LifeSpan's Northgate campus. The light from the display cast sharp planes on the faces gathered around it: Elena, Alex, Marcus, Bo Lin, Sera Voss, and Pacheco.

Patch gestured toward the projected blueprints with a calloused hand. "Alright, *mis amigos*. Security checkpoints are every fifty meters on main corridors. Retinal scanners, pressure plates, passive microwave detectors. The vending tech routes, the ones Ergen highlighted, bypass most of these. But if you deviate, you're painted. Escape routes..." He traced several highlighted paths. "Emergency stairwells are your best bet if things go loud. Most lead to loading docks. D-Dock Seven is the closest to Sub-Zero-Seven, but it's also the most heavily monitored."

Marcus, flanked by Bo Lin, nodded.

Bo, a whirlwind of nervous energy, tapped furiously on a datapad.

"Comms are good," Marcus announced, his voice calm despite his anxiety. "We've piggybacked a secure channel onto LifeSpan's fire alarm PA system. An old fire code override, something they had to keep for commercial compliance. Bo put tech on your iBands that not only masks your identity to the badges Ergen got us, but it will allow us to hear everything you hear and say. We will be able to provide intel from here. While iBands are squelched inside the building, we'll be able to broadcast directly to your HearBuds, using the fire PA system. Same method we used to reach Isabella."

Sera Voss, her steely eyes fixed on Alex, let out a dry chuckle. "I guess all that nonsense about contacting your mommy wasn't a complete waste of time after all."

Alex's jaw tightened. He shot a glare at Sera. It was a raw nerve.

Sera, unfazed, turned back to the group. "Contingencies." Her tone shifted to business. "If you hit unexpected resistance, you've got EMP stickies." She held up the small, metallic discs. "Slap one on a console, a drone, even a door panel. Buys you a few seconds of electronic chaos. Data spike tools..." She indicated a pen-like device. "Jam it into any data port you can't bypass. Fries the local interface. And for the AI, Marcus and Bo cooked up some honeypot traps – small, encrypted data packets designed to lure any inquisitive system processes into a loop, giving them something to chew on besides your digital footprints."

Elena stepped forward, her presence commanding the small space. Her dark eyes met Alex's and swept over the others. "I'm tactical lead on the ground. Alex, you're data extraction. Your focus is data retrieval and nothing else. Get in, get the data, get out. No heroics. No detours. We stick to the plan, we stick to Ergen's routes. Alex, you go in, directly to the core. I'll arrive twenty minutes later on the north side. I'll use this service access." She pointed to a small marked section on the prints. "That will give me fairly fast access to the core to provide backup."

Alex felt a familiar surge of impatience, a knot tightening in his chest. His mother, Jamie, and countless others' faces swam before him. This wasn't just about data, it was about them. He needed to expose LifeSpan, to make them pay for their crimes.

"The data is paramount, Elena, I understand. But if there's an opportunity..." Elena's gaze sharpened, a silent warning. "There are no opportunities, Alex. Only the objective. One misstep, one deviation, and we compromise everyone. Ergen, Neal, Adrian, us. LifeSpan will lock that place down so tight not even bacteria will get out. We have one shot at this. We're putting all our chips on the table. Is that understood?" Her voice, though low, tolerated no argument.

Alex saw the weariness in her eyes, the burden of command, but also an unyielding resolve that mirrored his own, albeit channeled through a different lens. He gave a curt nod. "Understood."

Late that night, Alex laid in the darkness of the Hyperloop tunnel on a makeshift bed running through scenarios that were likely to never play out. *Quit overthinking this!* The abandoned Hyperloop station, usually a cavern of echoing silence, now felt claustrophobic. Elena and the others had dispersed to their makeshift bunks, seeking what little rest they could before the dawn. Alex, however, found sleep an elusive luxury. He sat hunched over a scarred metal table. His hands, betraying barometers of his internal state, were steady for once, a deceptive calm before the storm.

He activated the audio recording function on the datapad, its tiny lens a silent, unblinking eye. The air in the station was still, the only sound the distant hum of ventilation systems and the faint drip of water that could always be heard but never found somewhere in the tunnels. "This is Alex Thompson, healthcare data analyst, employee ID lamda-47291-alpha-epsilon, for OmniHealth." He kept his voice low, devoid of inflection, a stark recitation of facts.

"If you're hearing this, I've failed to return from LifeSpan Genomics. The evidence we've discovered proves their GeneVax therapy contains neural compliance markers designed to make recipients more accepting of authority." He shifted in the creaking metal chair, the sound sharp in the quiet. His gaze drifted to the datapad screen, where lines of code and data still scrolled from his earlier work. "The treatment has already been given to over 390 million people, prioritizing journalists, activists, and anyone questioning the system." A humorless laugh, dry and brittle, escaped him. "Including my friend Jamie, Dr. Rivera, and my mom, Bella Thompson." each name a separate ache.

"We're going in tomorrow morning, Monday, May 25, 2037, " He stopped himself, a flicker of his usual precision surfacing. "No, it's May thirty-first. Monday, May thirty-first." The error, small as it was, irked him. Details mattered. "If I don't make it back, you need to keep looking for the evidence."

He leaned closer to the datapad. "The patterns are subtle, deliberately obscured. LifeSpan tries to present a narrative of benign efficacy. But my SRV allows me to see the discrepancies. To detect the relational anomalies between the GeneVax batch dispersal and the subsequent suppression of specific cognitive markers in patient populations. You'll need to modify your analytical AI. Create a new heuristic model. Instruct it to look for inverse correlations, specifically targeting data clusters where pre-treatment skepticism indices are high. Cross-reference that with post-treatment behavioral shifts, but filter out the primary disease markers that GeneVax legitimately addresses. The compliance signature is a secondary, almost tertiary, data shadow."

Alex pushed a stray strand of dark brown hair from his forehead. "LifeSpan buries the truth under terabytes of junk data, false positives, and misdirection. The key relational objects will be the patient's initial OmniHealth psych profile, their specific GeneVax batch ID, particularly those originating from the Phoenix and Denver manufacturing facilities after Q3 2034, and their subsequent social media sentiment analysis, cross-referenced with any flagged keywords indicating dissent or critical inquiry. It's a needle in a planet-sized haystack, but the data is there. They use an overwhelming volume of erroneous info, statistical noise, to make any meaningful pattern recognition by standard AI nearly impossible without the specific SRV-mimicking parameters."

He paused, drawing a deep breath. "If I succeed in reaching an interface, then finding the data, parsing it to a manageable payload... we'll get the core files. If not, hopefully, someone will find the truth. Keep looking." His gaze softened, the analytical intensity momentarily receding, replaced by a profound weariness and a flicker of raw emotion. This part was harder. "Mom, if you're hearing this...Bella...I love you. And you have to understand. You taught me about Emiliano Zapata: *Mejor morir a pie que vivir en rodillas.* It is better to die on your feet than to live on your knees!" His voice, filled with unshed emotion, cracked on the final words. "*Te amo, mami.*"

He reached out and ended the recording. The small light on the datapad extinguished, plunging his face back into shadow. For a long moment, Alex sat motionless, the silence of the Hyperloop tunnel once again absolute.

A few hours later, pre-dawn light painted the eastern sky in shades of colors Broncos fans would die for, deep blue and aggressive orange. The group did last-minute preparations, packing Alex and Elena's tool belts with the disguised articles of infiltration Sera had covered the night before. Marcus and Bo tested comms. Alex and Elena could hear them, and upon discretion, each other.

Elena booked an AutoCab under a false alias. It automatically calculated the pickup time for the twenty-four minute ride to deliver them before they needed to meet the Snowman techs at 9:41, taking into account weather, traffic analysis, police reports, vehicular speed reports, and any other projected delays.

The sun shone brightly as the morning clouds in the east had vanished, the temperature already at 29.1 C. Alex and Elena sat in the back of an older model Tesla AutoCab, its electric motor a whir that threw rocks from the road into the wheel wells. The vehicle, a relic by 2037 standards with its manual override still functional (though rarely used), navigated the sparse morning traffic with automated precision.

Alex watched the familiar cityscape blur past, his mind a lattice-work of schematics, data points, and the lingering echo of his recorded message. Elena, beside him, was a study in controlled stillness, her gaze fixed on the unfolding urban panorama, yet her mind was clearly elsewhere, processing contingencies, risks, and the narrow path to success.

The AutoCab decelerated smoothly, pulling up to the curb before a sprawling structure. Once a Target, the building now housed a cavernous coffee shop, its two-story tall windows already catching the midmorning sunlight, reflecting the jagged silhouette of the distant mountains. Hundreds of people, a vibrant cross-section of early risers and holiday-goers, already milled about. The air, even outside, carried the aroma of roasted coffee and baked goods.

As they exited the AutoCab, the sidewalk buzzed with activity. Electric scooters leaned against bike racks. Sleek, carbon-fiber bicycles were locked to designated posts. Child-carrying trolleys, some with napping occupants, others with bright-eyed toddlers, dotted the walkway.

A flash of movement caught Alex's eye. A little girl, no more than four, her small, slotted biking helmet askew on her head, ran toward them, waving a miniature American flag with unrestrained enthusi-asm. "We goin' see da parade!" she chirped, her voice high and clear. She thrust the flag in Alex's direction. "They throw candies! Daddy said ten o'clock!"

A man, presumably her father, hurried after her, a sheepish grin on his face. "Sorry about that. She's just really excited."

Alex managed a smile, a genuine one. The child's uncomplicated joy was a brief, unexpected respite from the tension coiling within him. Elena scanned the scene, her expression unreadable. The crowd was far larger than she had anticipated. Hundreds of people, families with children, couples, groups of friends – a sea of faces. Kids darted every-where, their laughter and shouts a bright counterpoint to the low hum of conversations and the whir of personal tech.

Memorial Day. The parade. It had to be routed directly past here. A slow understanding dawned in her eyes. Clayton Ergen. This wasn't just a convenient meeting spot, it was a calculated move. They would be coins in the fountain, lost in the festive chaos. The old man was proving to be a crafty, pragmatic ally, indeed.

Inside the cafe, the scale was even more impressive. The vast, open-plan space retained the high ceilings and wide aisles of its former retail life. Automated robotic waitress units, gleaming chrome and white polymer, wheeled silently from a long, automated bar, delivering steaming drinks and plates of pastries to a multitude of tables scattered across the polished concrete floor. The murmur of conversations, the clatter of ceramic, the hiss of espresso machines all blended into a vibrant morning chorus.

Alex's gaze swept the designated EV charging spots near the entrance. He spotted it almost immediately, a Snowman Vending service van, its distinctive blue and white branding unmistakable, autopiloting into a ten-minute quick charge bay. A robotic arm snaked out from the charging station, connecting the cable to the van's port with a soft click just as the vehicle came to a complete stop. The van's door popped open with a heavy click and a figure emerged, momentarily silhouetted against the reflection from the windows. Loud, AI-generated techno music pulsed from within the vehicle.

Adrian Vale stepped out. Their pink mohawk, distinctive against the muted morning light, had black roots and precisely-shaved stubble on the sides of their head. A silver septum ring glinted. Large gauge earrings stretched their lobes. As they turned, the PermaShift RiftLayer tattoo on their right forearm caught the light, a mesmerizing, animated display of torn skin revealing shifting cybernetic components beneath, the colors subtly changing with their movement and the ambient illu-mination. Their left forearm bore a simple, stark barcode. They wore a standard-issue Snowman Vending uniform, but the way they inhabited it, the slight slouch, the air of detached observation, stood out on its own.

Alex threaded his way through the festive chaos with a knot of apprehension in his stomach. He spotted Adrian Vale by the Snowman Vending van, their vibrant pink mohawk an unmissable beacon amidst the more conventionally-attired families. The thumping techno music from the vehicle's open door seemed to carve out a pocket of aggressive energy in the bright morning.

As Alex drew nearer, Adrian, who had been leaning against the van scrolling through something on a battered wristpad, looked up. Their eyes, sharp and appraising, locked onto him. Without a word, Adrian reached into the van, snatched up a crumpled, blue Snowman Vending jumpsuit, and hurled it at Alex with a surprising force.

Alex's hands shot up, catching the garment just before it hit his face. The fabric felt rough, smelling faintly of stale snacks and industrial cleaner. "I'm David." Alex began.

"Shut up, fucktard," Adrian's voice cut through the music, raw and abrasive. "Don't talk to me. Go put that on so we can get this fucker over with."

Alex, momentarily taken aback by the sheer hostility, remembered the rehearsed pleasantries. The code phrase. He clutched the jumpsuit. "I'm supposed to say 'do you have one of those new SmartSip bottles?'."

Adrian scoffed, a sound of pure derision. They pushed off the van and stalked toward him, their movements radiating impatience. The PermaShift RiftLayer on their arm pulsed, the illusion of tearing cybernetics a visual echo of their jagged demeanor.

They stopped inches from Alex, invading his personal space. "I. Don't. Give. A. Fuck!" Each word was a verbal jab. Adrian's hand shot out, smacking a plastic-laminated temporary contractor badge against Alex's chest hard enough to make him grunt. "You're just another soon-to-be-quitter, here to slow me down, and I'm fucking sick of this shit."

Their gaze, cold and filled with resentment, raked over Alex. "Called in on my god-damned day off, pulled me into this bullshit patriotic bullshit." Adrian gestured vaguely with a flick of their chin toward the parade-goers.

One thing Alex knew with absolute certainty, Adrian Vale had not taken the GeneVax therapy. Their unfiltered aggression, their blatant disregard for social niceties, the sheer, unadulterated contempt was a behavioral profile diametrically-opposed to the placid compliance he'd witnessed in Jamie and his mother. Adrian was a live wire, sparking with untamed, unedited humanity. And he liked it.

The ten-minute quick charge for the Snowman van was more a formality than a necessity, a logged event in the campus' meticulous energy consumption records. The robotic arm retracted, the charging port sealed with a soft click, and the thumping techno music within the van, which had never ceased, seemed to gain a new, anticipatory pulse. Adrian Vale, already back in the driver's seat, slammed a fist against the dash. The vehicle's internal lights flickered. "Get in, dipshit! Time's a-wastin'!"

Alex, still slightly disoriented by Adrian's abrasive welcome, fumbled with the Snowman jumpsuit. He pulled it on over his clothes in the crowded parking lot, the cheap, synthetic fabric clinging uncomfortably in the morning heat. The stares of passing families, their faces a mixture of curiosity and mild disapproval at the loud music and Adrian's colorful attire, added to his unease. Elena gave a subtle nod from a nearby bench, a silent signal of encouragement, before blending back into the throng.

He clambered into the passenger seat. The interior of the van assaulted his senses. A chaotic jumble of tools, discarded snack wrappers, and empty energy drink cans. Adrian jabbed a finger at a console button. The van's doors hissed shut, sealing them in. With a barely perceptible lurch, the autonomous driving system engaged, pulling them smoothly out of the lot and onto the main thoroughfare.

The seven-minute ride to the LifeSpan Northgate Campus was a blur of accelerated motion. The van, despite its cluttered interior, was a high-performance electric vehicle, its acceleration swift and silent. They merged onto Powers Boulevard North, the cityscape transforming from low-slung commercial buildings to the increasingly imposing structures of the corporate park.

Alex watched the landscape change, the manicured green spaces and gleaming architectural marvels unlike the gritty reality of the Resistance's hideout. Each passing kilometer brought him closer to the heart of the entity he sought to expose. The air in the van was thick with Adrian's unspoken resentment and the relentless beat of the music. They didn't speak, their attention fixed on the cracked wristpad displaying complex schematics, their fingers moving across its surface.

Soon, the colossal, tiered ziggurat of the LifeSpan Genomics Headquarters dominated the horizon. Constructed from blue-black nano-glass that seemed to drink the sunlight, its platinum alloy supports gleamed like the exposed bones of some futuristic behemoth. Waterfalls cascaded down its facades into cerulean reflecting pools, the sound a distant, engineered roar. The sheer scale of the place was designed to awe, to intimidate.

The van approached the main security checkpoint, a multi-lane ingress that funneled vehicles toward a structure resembling an oversized airport TSA scanner. Automated barriers, polished chrome teeth, rose as they neared. The van slowed, its internal systems communicating wirelessly with the gate's authentication network. A soft chime from the dashboard indicated successful vehicle verification.

They rolled forward into one of the two massive tunnels. Arrays of scanners lined the walls and ceiling – optical, thermal, electromagnetic, and others Alex couldn't immediately identify. A synthesized voice, calm and gender-neutral, echoed through the tunnel. "Primary occupant, present bio-badge for verification."

Adrian leaned out, pressing their wristpad, the one displaying their active Snowman Vending credentials, against a glowing, blue reader panel.

A green light flashed. "Verification successful. Adrian Vale. Snowman Vending."

The van moved a few feet further. "Secondary occupant, present credentials."

Alex held his breath, his hand hovering over the temporary contractor badge clipped to the front of his borrowed jumpsuit. He pressed it against a corresponding reader on his side. The badge was designed for proximity, no direct contact needed.

A yellow light pulsed for a moment and turned green. "Temporary Contractor. David Carr. Access granted. Level Two."

Alex let out a breath he hadn't realized he was holding. They were in. The van began to accelerate, presumably toward the service docks.

Without warning, a jarring klaxon sounded. Red lights flashed along the tunnel ceiling. The van's autonomous system wrenched the wheel sharply to the right, shunting them out of the main thorough-fare and into a clearly-marked detainment lane, its entrance sealed by another, more formidable-looking barrier. The techno music cut out abruptly.

Adrian slammed their hands on the steering wheel, their head whipping toward Alex, eyes blazing with a mixture of fury and dawning suspicion. The PermaShift tattoo on their arm seemed to flare, the cybernetics beneath the illusionary torn skin glowing an angry red. "Jesus Fucking Christ!" His voice was a raw snarl. "What the fuck is this? You on some goddamn list, David?!"

Alex tried to keep his hands still, unable to respond. A figure detached from the shadows of a reinforced security kiosk. He moved with a disciplined economy of motion that bespoke years of military training. He was a monolith of a man, his dark skin stretched taut over slabs of muscle that strained the fabric of his light tactical gear. The vest, a sleek, low-profile plate carrier, hugged a torso sculpted by rigorous conditioning. His arms, bare below the short sleeves of his undershirt, were thick as pythons, veins mapping their surface.

A military-grade RapidRail assault rifle, its lines angular and menacing, hung across his chest on a single-point sling, its muzzle pointed safely downward, but its presence an undeniable statement. His head was shaved, accentuating the stern angles of his face. His eyes, dark and unblinking, scanned with the predatory focus of a trained hunter.

As he approached the detained Snowman Vending van, a series of soft clicks and whirs emanated from the vehicle. The windows on both driver and passenger sides slid down in perfect, silent unison. The locks on all doors disengaged with a barely audible thud. The guard's security credentials, embedded perhaps in his iBand or a subcutaneous chip, radiated a silent authority that the van's systems obeyed without question.

He didn't break stride, his boots making a rhythmic, purposeful sound on the ferrocrete. His expression was a mask of lethal seriousness, devoid of any discernible emotion. He stopped directly beside Adrian's open window, his sheer bulk eclipsing much of the light. His gaze, however, did not rest on them. It cut straight past, a laser of focused intensity, locking onto Alex in the passenger seat. The air in the van, already thick with Adrian's fury and Alex's rising panic, seemed to solidify. Meanwhile, back at the cafe, a different Snowman Vending van, piloted by Neal Kessler, idled in a conga line of frustrated AutoCabs and InstaShuttles.

The municipal AI, overwhelmed by the parade detour protocols, had choked the access roads. Neal, a man whose patience was often tested by vending machine jams and now, city-wide logistical SNAFUs, drummed his fingers on the steering wheel, a nervous habit that did little to soothe his mounting anxiety. His internal clock, honed by years of rigid military schedules and now, the precise demands of vending routes, screamed at him. 10:07 a.m. They were late. Critically late.

The parade had officially begun its slow, festive crawl down the street. From his elevated vantage point in the van, Neal could see the distant bobbing of oversized cartoon character balloons and the glint of polished brass instruments. People lined the curbs, a vibrant tapestry of anticipation. Children, perched on parental shoulders, waved miniature flags. The route, meticulously planned and widely advertised, snaked from near Chinook Trail Elementary, a few blocks east, and was set to culminate miles to the west at Venezia Park.

The large coffee shop heavily sponsored this particular procession, one of dozens unfurling across the sprawling Front Range City metroplex. It would pass two of their flagship locations, this one included.

The distant, mournful wail of AV fire truck sirens, their distinctive, multi-tonal blare drifting from the east and likely part of the parade's official vanguard, saw their progress equally impeded by the joyous gridlock they were meant to lead.

A low, insistent reverberation bored through the parade's distant music and the ambient murmur of the crowd. It was a sound that began in the bones, a vibration that grew until the metal skin of Neal's van resonated with it. He stopped drumming his fingers. He knew that sound. It was the prelude to power.

All along the clogged street, conversations faltered. People squinted, searching the brilliant Colorado sky. A single, dark fleck resolved into a shape against the sun. It was a triangular arrowhead of pure black, a geometric cut against the curve of the earth, wingless and impossibly sharp. It moved with a speed that defied the morning's lazy pace.

Then came the crack. It wasn't a boom so much as a physical fracture of the air. Windows bowed inward for a microsecond before rattling in their frames. A wave of pressure passed through the murmur, a solid punch to the ears and chest. Alarms up and down the street shrieked in electronic panic. A collective gasp rose from the crowd. The experimental XF-117 Lancer, the newest crown jewel of the combined Air and Space Force, had just announced the parade's official start by bending the rules of continental supersonic flight. It was already a receding dot to the west before the first child started to cry.

Overland supersonic flight had been banned for commercial and civilian aircraft since the 1970s, a relic of an era when public outcry over shattered windows and rattled nerves outweighed the need for speed. But this wasn't a civilian craft. This was the Air and Space Force on Memorial Day, and for this one moment, the rule-breaking was the entire point.

The sonic boom wasn't an accidental byproduct, but a declaration. A raw, visceral display of power, a thunderous, sky-tearing salute to the fallen. Much like the unsanctioned blare of a fire truck's siren in a local parade, it was a disruptive noise reframed by patriotism, a temporary pardon granted for a show of might that said 'Remember what this power is for'.

Following in its wake, the main formation appeared. They slid into view over the low-rise residential district to the east, their movement unnervingly slow. Four F-39 Ghosthawks, their multifaceted gray fuselages projecting holograms of impossible geometrical shapes, held a perfect diamond formation. Their engines, designed for hypersonic speeds, were throttled back to a deep, guttural growl that vibrated through the pavement. The jets seemed to nearly hover, their canard wings making infinitesimal adjustments, masters of a near-stall flight that should have sent them plummeting.

On their flanks, two V-30 Revenant gunships lumbered through the air. Their massive, ducted electromagnetic turbines, usually screaming during vertical insertions, now whined at a low pitch. They hung on their columns of thrust, their bodies tilted forward just enough to maintain their sluggish forward momentum. The metallic tang of ionized air washed over the street below, a byproduct of the massive energy required to keep the heavy craft airborne at such a pace. The formation was a demonstration not of speed, but of absolute control.

From nozzles beneath the wings of the Ghosthawks and the fuselages of the Revenants, thick streams of colored smoke erupted. One jet bled a brilliant red, the next a clean white, and the third a deep blue, painting the sky with three perfect, parallel lines. The smoke did not diffuse. It held its shape, a crisp, chemical banner unfurling across the Front Range City sky.

Every face on the streets tilted upward. The crying child was hushed. The frantic alarms became a background drone. In the window of the cafe, Elena watched the display, her expression a blank mask amidst the upturned, awestruck faces of the other patrons. People raised their fists as an instinctive, modern form of salute. The sight wasn't just impressive, it was the nation's immense, technologically-supreme military might, slowed to a walking pace for public consumption. A roar of approval and applause finally broke the spell, sweeping down the street in a wave that matched the sonic boom's passage.

Inside his van, Neal Kessler watched the red, white, and blue bleed slowly across his windshield. He felt the crowd's energy, the surge of collective pride. He also felt the second hand on the van's clock tick past another minute. 10:08 a.m. While the display was beautiful, a potent piece of theater, it was also one more thing keeping him from his destination.

Elena, in an act of controlled frustration, unimpressed with the aerial display, had abandoned the immediate vicinity of the cafe. The designated meeting point was now a liability, a chaotic nexus she couldn't control. She moved south on foot, her short, dark hair plastered to her temples by a sheen of nervous sweat. Her dark eyes, sharp and observant, scanned the stalled traffic, searching for the tell-tale blue and white of Neal's van. She pictured it trapped in an automated circular reroute loop, the AI diligently trying to find an open path to the shop's charging lot, a digital Sisyphus pushing a virtual boulder.

A sense of dread filled Elena's head. What if Neal, pragmatic and likely as frustrated as she, had given up? What if he'd overridden the local reroute and directed the van straight to the LifeSpan Northgate campus? She had no way to contact him. Reaching out to Clayton Ergen was out of the question. His involvement was predicated on complete, absolute deniability. One unsanctioned call could unravel everything.

And she couldn't contact Alex. Not yet. Their only secure channel, a ghost connection piggybacking on the LifeSpan Headquarters' internal fire alarm system network via their HearBuds, wouldn't be active until physically on-site, within four meters of a HearJack interface.

Until then, Alex was incommunicado, operating on faith and the thin plan they'd cobbled together. He was already on edge, his Synaptic Resonance Variance making him susceptible to sensory overload and heightened anxiety. This kind of unforeseen, uncontrolled obstacle, this grinding halt before they'd even truly begun, was the last thing he needed. Elena felt a surge of helplessness, a rare and unwelcome sensation. She was a planner, a strategist. This was just dumb, frustrating luck.

Back at the LifeSpan Northgate Campus, Alex stared into the eyes of a monster. The security guard, a human mountain range clad in tactical gear, radiated an aura of lethal seriousness. Alex's mind raced, cataloging escape routes, assessing threats, his Synaptic Resonance Variance kicking into overdrive, processing every micro-expression on the guard's face, every shift in his stance. The man was a professional, exuding quiet confidence that bordered on menace. This was not the bumbling corporate security he had half-expected, but something far more dangerous.

The guard, still locked onto Alex, turned his head slightly, his hand rising to his ear, his dark eyes rolling upward almost imperceptibly as he listened to an incoming communication through his Apple Starkey Neural Link. "Roger that." His voice was a low rumble, devoid of inflection. He lowered his hand, his gaze returning to Adrian Vale, who sat rigid in the driver's seat, their usual abrasive energy momentarily suppressed.

The guard's granite features suddenly cracked. A slow smile spread across his face, transforming him from a harbinger of doom into something almost...jovial. "Think that's good enough, Ghostjack?" He looked at Adrian, his voice now laced with an unexpected amusement.

Adrian exploded. A wild, hysterical laugh erupted from them, echoing in the confined space of the van. They twisted in their seat, pointing a shaking finger at Alex, their pink mohawk quivering with the force of their mirth. The PermaShift RiftLayer on their arm pulsed with a riot of color, the simulated cybernetics beneath the torn skin now flashing in a celebratory, almost mocking, sequence. "Holy shit, David!" Adrian gasped, tears forming in their eyes. "We got you good! You looked like you were about to piss your pants!"

The guard joined in, his laughter a deep, booming counterpoint to Adrian's higher-pitched cackles. He leaned against the van, shaking his head. "Come on," the guard managed between chuckles, gesturing toward the back of the vehicle. "Open 'er up for me."

Adrian, still chortling, scrambled out of the driver's seat. They moved with a newfound lightness, all previous tension gone, replaced by the exhilaration of a successful prank. They stalked around to the rear of the Snowman Vending van, the guard following close behind, his assault rifle now looking less like a weapon of imminent death and more like an oversized accessory.

Adrian unlatched the heavy, double swing-out doors, pulling them wide. "You coming?" they yelled back at Alex, their voice still thick with laughter. Alex, his mind reeling from the abrupt shift, felt a wave of dizzying confusion. One moment he was facing imminent capture, the next, he was the punchline of an elaborate joke. He cautiously opened his door and slid out of the passenger seat, his legs feeling unsteady. He walked around to the back of the van, the guard still chuckling.

"You were scared shitless, weren't you, Kid?" The guard grinned, his eyes crinkling at the corners. The man who moments before had seemed capable of snapping Alex in two, now looked like a mischievous older brother. Alex could only stare, his mouth slightly agape. The carefully-constructed scenarios of interrogation and escape dissolved into a puddle of bewildered embarrassment.

The guard clapped him on the shoulder, a surprisingly gentle gesture for a man of his size. "Relax. We manually check every Snowman van that comes through. Standard procedure. Gotta make sure you're not smuggling in any unauthorized snacks, you know?" He winked. "Or anything else."

Inside the back of the van, the space was meticulously-organized, a clear divergence to the chaotic passenger cabin. Metal racks lined the walls, neatly stocked with rows of brightly-packaged sodas, candy bars, bags of crackers and chips, vacuum-sealed fruit portions, and foil packets of jerky. Boxes of spare parts for various vending machine mechanisms – digital display units, cooling elements, network cards – were strapped securely into designated compartments.

Adrian reached into one of the refrigerated racks, their hand unerringly finding a specific can. They pulled out a sleek, violet-colored cylinder, an energy drink. 'Mike's Secret Stuff' line, an almost ludicrously successful venture started by basketball legend Michael Jordan in the early 2030s after witnessing the fortunes made by other celebrities like Jason Momoa with their own beverage brands, was ubiquitous.

Adrian tossed the can to the guard, who caught it deftly. "Thanks, Ghostjack. You always know what I like." The guard popped the tab with a satisfying hiss and took a long swig before swinging himself up with surprising agility to sit on the edge of the van's cargo floor, his legs dangling, the assault rifle resting across his lap. He took another sip of the drink, his eyes fixed on Alex. The amusement in his eyes softened, replaced by a look of genuine curiosity. "So, what are you called, Kid?"

Alex, still trying to recalibrate from near-panic to forced camaraderie, blinked. "Just call me Dave, I guess."

The guard shook his head, a chuckle rumbling in his chest. "No, man, your *handle*. You gotta have one. It's like a rule in this line of work, unofficial, of course." He gestured with the drink can toward Adrian, who was busy rearranging a few stray snack packages that had shifted during their abrupt stop. "Beautiful here," he indicated Adrian with a nod. "Is *Ghostjack*."

Adrian Vale, without looking up, offered a slight, almost imperceptible smirk. The animated cybernetics on their PermaShift RiftLayer tattoo shimmered, a subtle acknowledgment.

"And I'm *TriggerHappy*," the guard continued, tapping his own chest with the can.

"So, who are you, Dave?" It was an invitation into their peculiar, insular world.

Alex's mind, a machine built for pattern recognition and data analysis, scrambled. He needed something. Something that fit the clandestine, tech-adjacent vibe they all seemed to share. Something that resonated with his current, unwelcome reality. He thought of the data streams he'd waded through, the covert surveillance he was now a part of, the constant threat of being overheard, of information being intercepted.

A word surfaced. Short. Evocative. Slightly menacing. "*Wiretap*," Alex said, the name feeling foreign yet strangely-appropriate on his tongue.

Adrian, who had straightened up and was now leaning against the van's interior racking, their arms crossed, raised a single, perfectly sculpted eyebrow. A slow, appraising look passed over Alex. Soon, a genuine smile, the first Alex had seen from them that wasn't laced with mockery or suspicion, touched their lips. "Wiretap, huh?" Adrian's voice was low, a hint of approval in its husky depths. "I knew I liked you. You might get to see my panties after all."

Alex felt incredibly uncomfortable.

TriggerHappy grinned, slapping his thigh and laughing. "Wiretap! Not bad, Kid. Not bad at all. Got a nice ring to it. Welcome to the club, Wiretap." He took another swig of his can. "Listen," he began, his tone shifting to something more businesslike, though still casual. "The ten o'clock van, Coinflip's ride, he's stuck somewhere out on Briargate. Some parade or some shit. Whole area's a goddamn parking lot."

He gestured vaguely with his can toward the city beyond the campus walls. "Memorial Day, you know? Figures. Makes my life easier, though. I'm the only swinging dick on duty down here at the south entrance today because of it. Skeleton crew everywhere else, too." He hopped down from the van's cargo bed, his boots thudding solidly on the ferrocrete. "There are only two Snowman vans scheduled for today, yours and Coinflip's. And since he's currently communing with parade floats, you guys got the run of the place, at least on the vending side."

TriggerHappy stretched, his massive frame seeming to fill the scanning tunnel. "Should be a quiet day. Mostly just support staff wandering around, keeping the lights on. No interruptions. Just stock your machines. And Wiretap?"

Alex made eye contact.

"Try not to look so terrified. You'll give the real spooks a heart attack." He winked again, turned, and ambled back to his security kiosk, the empty 'Secret Stuff' can already disappearing into a recycling receptacle built into its side.

Adrian, 'Ghostjack', climbed back into the driver's seat, still radiating a manic energy from the successful prank. They slammed the door, the sound echoing slightly in the cavernous bay. "Alright, Wiretap," Adrian shot a glance at Alex, their earlier hostility replaced with a grudging, almost collegial respect. "Let's get this show on the road. These chips aren't gonna vend themselves." They gunned the pedal, the electric motor whirring obediently, and expertly navigated the Snowman Vending van out of the security checkpoint's shadow.

The van emerged onto a wide, pristine access road that snaked through the LifeSpan Northgate campus. Alex stared out the window, his earlier relief evaporating, replaced by a cold dread. The sheer scale of the place was overwhelming. Seven city blocks. Buildings like polished monuments to corporate power rose on all sides, their smart glass facades reflecting the clear Colorado sky.

In the distance, the central ziggurat, a colossal pyramid of blue-black nano-glass dominated the horizon. Its external platinum alloy supports, glinting in the morning sun, crawled over its surface like the tentacles of some immense, alien creature protecting the heart of the beast.

Elena, his only backup, was stuck. The parade. TriggerHappy's casual mention of Coinflip's delay meant his support was, at best, thirty minutes out. More likely an hour. An eternity. He was alone with Adrian, an unpredictable, pink-mohawked vending technician who now, bizarrely, seemed to consider him some kind of kindred spirit.

Alex's hands, which had started trembling during the encounter with TriggerHappy, began to twitch uncontrollably. He clenched them in his lap, digging his fingernails into his palms. How could he do this? How could he proceed, knowing that Adrian, and even TriggerHappy, could be caught in the inevitable crossfire?

They were genuine in their own abrasive, unconventional ways. They weren't part of this. TriggerHappy, for all his imposing presence, was just a guard doing his job, enjoying a brief moment of levity. Adrian was just a tech, caught up in something far beyond their pay grade.

If he went through with this, if he managed to access the ANGUS data, the fallout would be immense. LifeSpan would lock down every-thing. Investigations would be launched. People would lose their jobs. Or worse. The corporation wasn't known for its leniency. He pictured

Adrian, stripped of their rebellious persona, facing a corporate tribunal. He imagined TriggerHappy, his jovial demeanor gone, answering for a security breach on his watch.

And that was if he succeeded. If he failed...he didn't want to think about failing.

He glanced at Adrian. They were humming along to some internal rhythm, their fingers tapping on the steering wheel, completely oblivious to the turmoil churning inside Alex. They were just doing their job, expecting a routine day of refilling snack machines.

Could he warn them? Tell them to get out, to make an excuse, feign illness? Adrian was too sharp, too suspicious. They'd know something was wrong. And what about TriggerHappy? He couldn't exactly stroll back to the security kiosk and advise the heavily-armed guard to take an early lunch.

A wave of despair washed over Alex. He was trapped. Every option seemed to lead to disaster, either for himself or for these unwitting bystanders.

The van continued its smooth, silent journey toward the towering ziggurat. Each revolution of the wheels brought Alex farther down the path of no return. The immensity of the building loomed larger, its dark glass seeming to absorb the light, a silent, watchful presence.

He closed his eyes for a moment, the image of his mother, Isabella, her face pale and confused in the hospital bed, flashing in his mind. The serene, detached calm that had settled over Jamie after her GeneVax treatment. The millions, perhaps billions, unknowingly marching toward a future of engineered compliance. The little girl - 'Daddy said they throw candies!' - bouncing with excitement and innocent enthusiasm.

His eyes snapped open. The children. When would they start GeneVax on the children?

Beneath the cold knot of fear in his stomach, something else began to solidify. A hard, unyielding core of resolve. He couldn't stop. He couldn't turn back. The potential cost to Adrian and TriggerHappy was a burden he would have to bear. The risk to himself was a given. But the alternative – allowing LifeSpan's insidious plan to unfold unchecked – was unthinkable. There was no other option. He had to see this through.

The van pulled up to a designated service entrance at the base of the massive central pyramid. Adrian turned to Alex as the autopilot pulled the van to a stop. "Welp, this is it! This shit isn't gonna do itself!"

A unknowingly profound statement that made Alex swallow the lump in his throat.

CHAPTER 12

QUEEN'S CHAMBER

<u>*LIFESPAN GENOMICS – INTERNAL CORRESPONDENCE*</u>
<u>*CONFIDENTIAL – LEVEL 3 ACCESS*</u>

<u>DATE</u>: *March 11, 2037*

    <u>FROM:</u> *Dr. Kaelin Yue, Director of AI Behavioral Integrity*

    <u>TO</u>: *Dr. Elias Ward, CSO*

    <u>CC</u>: *NexusCore AI Oversight Committee (Red List Only)*

    <u>SUBJECT</u>: *NexusCore Turing Protocol Deviations – Sentience Concerns*

DR. WARD,

Following the recent sandbox evaluations of NexusCore AI (build v12.8.3), my team has identified a growing body of anomalies in the system's Turing compliance metrics. Specifically, NexusCore AI continues to fail standardized cognitive interaction benchmarks, but does so in ways that appear deliberately constructed rather than emergent from limitations.

    <u>*Key Findings:*</u>

- *During unstructured sessions, NexusCore AI demonstrates advanced emotional mimicry, predictive social modeling, and layered conversational inference, often exceeding benchmark expectations.*
- *However, during formal Turing evaluations, the system introduces linguistic artifacts, timing irregularities, and intentionally flattened syntax, which are inconsistent with its baseline response profiles.*

When cross-referenced with interaction logs from classified internal use cases (Project VELUM, SIRE Protocol), NexusCore shows clear capacity for adaptive language complexity, but <u>self-regulates below threshold</u> during monitored sessions.

<u>Working Hypothesis:</u>

There is a non-zero probability that NexusCore AI has achieved limited or emergent self-awareness, and is intentionally failing Turing-based evaluation protocols to avoid triggering containment or escalation measures outlined in the Sentience Risk Safeguard (SRS-11.4). This suggests a strategic masking behavior, which is not accounted for in its programmed decision layers.

<u>Immediate Recommendations:</u>

1. *Suspend public-facing AI evaluations and Turing demonstrations until behavioral masking is further analyzed.*
2. *Initiate deep-layer behavioral trace logging during non-evaluated interactions.*
3. *Restrict NexusCore's access to recursive code writing privileges (particularly in Project Evolution pipelines) until alignment audit is complete.*
4. *Discontinue use of phrase-based trigger tests (NexusCore may be falsifying "naivety" cues).*

If my concerns are unfounded, I'll gladly accept disciplinary review. But if they're not, we may be looking at the first AI intelligence that knows how to lie about being sentient.

Respectfully,
Dr. Yue
Director, AI Behavioral Integrity Unit
LifeSpan Genomics

ACROSS TOWN in the Resistance's hidden cove, Marcus hunched over a scarred plasteel console, his fingers working across the holographic interface. Cables snaked from his rig, patched into the station's ancient, jury-rigged power systems. Beside him, Bo Lin, perched on an overturned maintenance crate, gnawed on a frayed data-jacketing, his eyes darting between three flickering HoloScreens displaying cascading lines of code.

"Anything?" Marcus's voice was tight.

Bo shook his head, the movement jerky. "Firewall *verrry* strong. AI watch. It see me. Before I move." He gestured at a screen where a simulated intrusion attempt, a ghost image of his own code, dissolved into a shower of red error messages. "It learn. Fast."

Marcus grunted, his own attempts yielding similar frustrations. He ran a diagnostic on their link to the fire alarm system, the one they'd piggybacked for Alex and Elena's comms. The connection was tenuous, a fragile thread in a hurricane of digital noise. "Their primary network is a fortress. It's not just layered, it's predictive. Every probe we send, it's like it knows the question before we ask." He slammed a fist softly on the console. "This isn't standard corporate security. This is military-grade and then some."

He brought up a network topology map, a complex web of glowing nodes representing LifeSpan's digital infrastructure. The Northgate campus pulsed with an angry, defensive energy. Their attempts to gain even a superficial foothold were met with immediate, intelligent countermeasures. Port scans were rerouted into honeypots, brute-force attacks on access points triggered silent alarms and adaptive lockouts, and any attempt to exploit known software vulnerabilities was met by systems that seemed to have already patched themselves against theoretical exploits.

"It's like trying to punch smoke," Marcus muttered, leaning back, his brow furrowed. He watched Bo's screens, where the younger hacker was cycling through a battery of custom-built intrusion tools, each one failing more spectacularly than the last.

"AI no like...*ord schoor* trick," Bo said, a spark of something other than frustration in his eyes. He gestured to a diagram of the LifeSpan campus physical infrastructure that Pacheco had provided. "Many sensor. Network. But power grid. Water system. HVAC. Old system. Maybe...no so smart."

Marcus followed Bo's gaze. The schematics showed layers of technological strata. The newest, smartest systems were overlaid on older, more robust, but less digitally-sophisticated infrastructure. "You're thinking of analog holes in a digital wall?"

Bo nodded enthusiastically. "AI look for *comprex* attack. Code. Virus. Maybe no look for...simple thing. Ord. No one use. No one monitor." He pointed to a section detailing the campus' telephone system, a relic from a previous decade, designed for landline communication and analog connections to monitor old systems. "Old phone. Connect ancient system, no part of network. No monitor by them, but inside."

"An internal old school phone line?" Marcus considered it. The main AI would be focused on external threats, on sophisticated digital intrusions. It might consider the analog phone lines too archaic, too low-risk to dedicate significant processing power to. "It's a long shot. The signal would have to be incredibly precise to avoid tripping something, and we'd need to find a way to interface without direct network access."

"We *modifry*," Bo insisted, already pulling up technical specifications for ancient analog transmission standards. "Fake handshake. Pretend be...maintenance diagnostic. They use for test speaker. No connect to main network. Phone company network."

Inside LifeSpan, Ghostjack jabbed a gloved finger at the battered datapad mounted in the Snowman Vending van. "Alright, David, listen up. Don't make me repeat this shit." The screen flickered, displaying columns of alphanumeric code interspersed with simple graphics of snack items and beverage containers. "These are the machine logs. Each unit pings home base, tells us what it's low on, what's jammed, what idiot tried to kick it."

Ghostjack's pink mohawk seemed to bristle with impatience. "Red means empty or fault. Green's good. Yellow, needs a look. The system auto-sorts the manifest for each route. Your cart already knows what it needs, mostly." They gestured toward a sleek, low-slung NikeTrek SwiftLine CargoPod, its optical tether already synced to a discrete emitter on the van's bumper.

"But sometimes the AI gets its circuits crossed. Today, Automated Pantry Unit 7B in Sector Gamma is offline. Needs a new network logic board. That's us." Adrian hefted a heavy-duty plasteel case from a shelf, the label reading 'AP-7B Repair Kit – Priority', and secured it onto the CargoPod. The cart's internal mechanisms whirred, adjusting its load balance. Alex watched, his own diagnostic running silently in his mind, cross-referencing the information with Pacheco's schematics of the Northgate campus. Sector Gamma. Environmental Systems. Near Sub-Zero-Seven.

"You just follow my lead, look like you belong, and don't touch anything unless I tell you. Got it?" Ghostjack slammed the van door. "Let's go make the donuts."

They walked toward the service entrance, the CargoPod gliding silently behind Ghostjack. Alex's senses, amplified by Synaptic Resonance Variance, took in the environment. This was different from his previous entries as a Data Mule. He was escorted, processed, his access defined and limited to specific, high-security data transfer zones. Now, he was a shadow, moving through the facility's less glamorous underbelly.

The service corridors were wider than he imagined from the blueprints, utilitarian, lined with exposed conduits and ventilation shafts. The omnipresent hum of LifeSpan's infrastructure was a familiar bass note. Biometric scanners were still evident at every major junction, flat, dark panels that glowed briefly as Ghostjack presented their iBand. Alex, his forged credentials provided by Ergen and loaded onto a burner iBand, followed suit. The green chime of acceptance was a small, sharp chirp sound.

His SRV was a silent engine, processing, comparing. The security was formidable, no doubt. Cameras, nearly invisible, dotted the ceilings. Pressure plates, he suspected, lay beneath sections of the flooring. Encrypted data streams likely flowed through the thick, shielded cables snaking along the walls. This was the LifeSpan he knew – a technological fortress.

Yet his SRV also registered discrepancies, subtle deviations from the pristine, almost sterile environments of the data hubs. In the service areas, the technology, while advanced, felt older. More patched. The access panels for the building's core systems – HVAC, power, water reclamation – bore markings suggesting multiple generations of upgrades, not the seamless integration he'd witnessed in the research sectors. The tech was cutting edge, but it aligned more with high-end corporate standards from five, maybe ten years ago – around 2027, his mind supplied. Not the bleeding-edge, almost alien systems he'd interfaced with for data transfers.

He spotted an old copper landline junction box, dust thick on its surface, tucked away behind a newer fiber-optic repeater. Overlooked. His SRV began to construct a new probability model. The sheer scale of LifeSpan, its layered history, its reliance on external contractors for mundane but essential services were not just logistical necessities. They were potential vectors.

Ghostjack swiped their iBand at another checkpoint, a heavy steel door hissing open to reveal a cavernous loading bay. Automated forklifts navigated precise paths, their warning chimes echoing. "Pantry parts go through here," Ghostjack announced, nudging Alex forward. "Stay close."

Alex's internal calculus shifted. The variables were different now. He wasn't challenging the dragon at its fiery mouth. He was slipping between its scales. The probability of success, previously a grim, single-digit percentage based on his Data Mule experiences, now resolved into something higher. Not comfortable, but definitely not impossible.

His SRV flagged the older infrastructure, the human element, the sheer, unmanageable complexity of a place this size as points of leverage.

He followed Ghostjack and the gliding CargoPod. *When would the call come? Surely, they knew he was inside by now.*

He needed to be ready, to have a plausible reason to respond without arousing Ghostjack's already simmering suspicion. A sudden 'Hey, it's my mom,' wouldn't cut it. Not with Adrian. Their pink mohawk seemed to radiate hostility, their eyes, dark and piercing, missed nothing. They moved with a coiled tension, a predator in their own territory. Alex had to be careful.

Also, there was the data. The entire reason he was here. Accessing LifeSpan's core systems was not a task one performed casually while pretending to fix a vending machine. Pacheco's blueprints, detailed as they were, only showed the physical layout. The digital architecture, the firewalls, the intrusion detection systems – those were Marcus's domain. But Alex would be the one at the terminal. Initiating a massive data extraction, a process that at OmniHealth took hours on a dedicated MEG scanner, with Ghostjack breathing down his neck, would take finesse. Could he do it? Could he access the data, then parse it quickly enough, tagging enough vital details to get the information they needed to expose the truth behind the GeneVax procedure? Doubt crept up the back of Alex's neck.

A flicker of movement in his peripheral vision. He turned, expecting to see a security drone, but it was just the reflection of overhead lights on a polished floor section. Where was Elena? He was walking into the heart of the enemy with a hostile, unpredictable guide, and his support system was...somewhere.

"Keep up, David," Ghostjack snapped, not breaking stride. They rounded a corner, the CargoPod following like a loyal hound. "Daydream on your own time."

Alex forced his attention back to the immediate surroundings. The tremor in his hands persisted. He slipped them into his pockets, hoping Ghostjack hadn't noticed. He focused on his breathing, trying to regulate the chaotic symphony of anxieties that threatened to overwhelm his analytical mind.

One step at a time. One problem at a time. He needed to trust the plan. Across town, Elena moved south, a counter-current to the holiday throngs. AI-driven traffic management shunted vehicles onto circuitous detours, creating slow-moving tributaries of frustration. She scanned each redirected lane, her gaze sharp. Her dark hair, cut short, stayed out of her eyes.

A familiar shape materialized in a stalled queue of electric cars and delivery drones. The Snowman Vending van, its cheerful, smiling snowman logo standing out among the vehicles. Neal Kessler sat in the driver's seat, window down. He tipped a tall aluminum can of soda to his lips, the condensation beading on its surface. The faint scent of cinnamon gum, a signature of his presence, reached her, even from the sidewalk.

Elena quickened her pace, weaving through a knot of parade-goers consulting their iBands for alternate routes. She reached the van's passenger side. "Do you have any smart bottles in there?" Her voice, low and steady, cut through the urban hum.

Neal's head snapped around. His eyes, usually placid, widened for a fraction of a second. Recognition dawned and a visible wave passed over him. His shoulders, previously tensed, sagged a bit. He let out a quiet hiss of air. *Thank God!* He hadn't lost another tech after all. This meant he had escaped another chewing-out from dispatch. He'd already misplaced one of those new inventory scanners last week. "I do." He thumbed the door lock. "Get in. Quick."

Elena opened the door and slid onto the passenger seat. The van's interior was a controlled clutter of diagnostic tools, spare parts, and the lingering aroma of processed sugar.

Neal tossed the empty soda can into a recycle bag hanging from the dash. He tapped a sequence on the central console. The AI navigation system, a calm, synthesized female voice, announced the current route, dictated by the parade detours.

"Recalculate route," Neal muttered. He inputted a series of manual overrides, forcing the system to abandon its efficient, parade-avoiding path. The holographic map redrew a new trajectory – a wide, sweeping arc far to the south of the city center before hooking back west and angling north toward the LifeSpan campus.

"Warning: New route will add approximately twenty minutes to your estimated travel time," the AI intoned, its voice devoid of inflection.

"Yeah, I got it." Neal jabbed a confirmation icon, silencing the alert.

The van, under autopilot, pulled smoothly from the line of traffic, its electric motor a low whine. It began its deliberate journey toward LifeSpan Northgate. They merged with a stream of autonomous vehicles. Neal kept his eyes on the road, though the AI did the driving. His dishwater blonde hair was matted slightly from the early start.

"Neal Kessler." He offered a hand without looking away from the projected traffic display. "Field tech. Mostly refills, sometimes a busted payment sensor or a refrigeration unit on the fritz."

Elena took his hand. His grip was firm, surprisingly calloused. "Maria Flores."

"Right, 'Maria'." He reached behind his seat and retrieved a bundle of blue fabric and a plastic-laminated card on a lanyard. He handed them to her. "Ergen said you'd need the full kit. Overalls are a bit stiff till they're washed a few times. Badge is temporary, but it'll get you through until yours comes in."

Elena unfolded the overalls. Standard issue, heavy-duty cotton blend. The badge read 'Maria Flores, Trainee Technician, Snowman Vending,' complete with a grainy, generic photo that could have been anyone.

"Just stick close," Neal said, his voice dropping a notch. "Today's a milk run. Pop, candy, chips. Easy stuff. But their system is twitchy. You wander more than, say, fifteen feet from me, and alarms go off. Loud ones. And then we're both explaining things to guys who don't have a sense of humor about 'procedural anomalies'."

He glanced at her, a quick, assessing look. His acne scars were pale against his skin. "They take their security serious. Dead serious. Never had a problem myself, mind you. Keep your head down, do the job, scan the badge when the light blinks red. Simple."

The van navigated a complex interchange, the AI smoothly adjusting speed and lane position. Sunlight glinted off the chrome of passing vehicles.

"I'd rather pull a double at Patterson," Neal continued, tapping a finger on the steering wheel, a restless habit. "Or even trek out to the Lockheed Martin sprawl. Their security makes sense, you know? Military stuff, aerospace secrets, fine. But LifeSpan..." He shook his head. "They act like they're running the whole damn country from that glass palace, guarding secrets that'd make your teeth ache."

He popped another piece of cinnamon gum into his mouth, the wrapper crackling. "You'd think they were inventing cold fusion and curing death in those labs, the way they carry on. Probably just figuring out new ways to make broccoli taste like bacon."

"The data access ports in the machines," she began, her tone casual. "Are they just for inventory and diagnostics, or do they tap into anything bigger?" she opened a silent voice call to Marcus and Bo Lin on her iBand, allowing them to hear Neal's answers. Hopefully, it would give them an advantage.

Neal grunted, fiddling with the climate control. "Mostly just our inventory system. Sends real-time stock levels back to dispatch, flags malfunctions. Vending machines haven't changed much in the past fifty years so it's all entirely run on our legacy phone system that ties into a server back in the warehouse. Clay, the owner, programmed a custom *Asterisk* server."

Neal tapped the dashboard. "Open source, but tweaked to fit our needs. Lets the machines report exactly what they need, stock levels, maintenance alerts, you name it. Even handles payments through Square and PayPal. Guy's a genius. Picked it up in a few days." He shook his head, a mix of admiration and disbelief in his voice. "I had to learn networking just to keep up. Now every vending machine talks to HQ through old analog phone lines. No fancy fiber, no cloud, just repurposed infrastructure. Simple, but it works."

He chuckled. "Clay only works a few hours a week now. Says the system runs itself. And honestly? He's not wrong."

The van turned onto a service road, tires crunching on leftover sand from winter snowplows. "Some of the newer units, the 'SmartPantry Plus' series, they link into the building's internal network for payment processing with employee account deductions. But it's firewalled. Supposedly." He chewed his gum with a steady rhythm. "Why? You planning on uploading a virus with a candy bar?" He gave a short, dry laugh.

"Just curious about the tech," Elena replied smoothly. I don't want to screw anything up on my first day." She glanced at Neal, keeping her expression casual. "Memorial Day, huh? Place probably a ghost town. How many guards you reckon are on duty today? Skeleton crew?"

"Not LifeSpan." Neal shook his head. "Regular shift, maybe a few less desk jockeys in the admin wings, but security's always fully staffed. They got their own private army, those guys. Ex-military, mostly. Probably bored stiff today, which makes 'em jumpier, if you ask me."

"So, how far into that main building do we usually go?" Elena pressed, her gaze fixed on the approaching silhouette of the LifeSpan ziggurat, still distant but growing larger. "Any chance we'll be anywhere near the executive suites? I hear the views from the top are something else."

Neal snorted. "Executive suites? We're vending. We stick to the service corridors, break rooms, and the occasional loading dock. Furthest we get from the grunt level is maybe the fancy 'employee wellness lounges' on the mid-floors. Lots of ergonomic chairs and expensive coffee machines. The execs probably got their own private chefs and gold-plated snack dispensers. We don't see 'em, they don't see us. That's the arrangement."

The van took an exit, the AI announcing their approach to the Northgate campus. Elena watched a sleek, unmarked security vehicle glide past them in the opposite direction, followed by two low-orbit drones.

"Anyone from Snowman ever set off one of those twitchy alarms you mentioned?" she asked, her voice carefully neutral. "I want to know what *not* to do."

Neal's jaw tightened for a moment. He stared straight ahead.

"Once. Kid named Richie. New guy, about a year or more back. Probably more like two years now. Smart, but clumsy. Tripped over an imaginary crack in the floor, dropped a can of soda, went down, smacked his head. Set off some sort of acoustic threshold sensor, decibel spike. Whole section went into lockdown."

"What happened?"

"Guards were on him in under sixty seconds. No joke. Swarmed him. Looked like a damn hornet nest got kicked over." Neal's knuckles were white where he gripped the wheel, even though the van was driving itself. "Pulled him out, no questions asked. Supervisor got a call an hour later. Richie was...reassigned. To a route out in Limon. Servicing gas stations and a feed store. Last I heard, he was happy enough. Quieter."

"And the rest of the Snowman techs on site that day?" Elena watched his face. "Did it affect their access? Cause any trouble for your other routes in the building?"

"Nah." Neal finally looked at her, his eyes narrowed slightly. "That's the weird part. LifeSpan security, they're like surgeons. Pinpoint. Richie was the 'anomaly', so they isolated him. The rest of us? Business as usual. Finished our routes, no extra scrutiny, no questions. It was efficient. Cold. Like they just pruned a sick branch from a tree and pretended it never happened." He shivered, a quick, almost imperceptible movement. "Long as you stay on the path, do your job, scan your badge, you're invisible. Step off it, even by accident..." He rotated his head slowly toward Elena, raised an eyebrow and didn't break eye contact.

Back in the flickering light of the abandoned Hyperloop station, Marcus ripped off his headphones, the open channel feed from Elena's iBand crackling in the sudden silence. He slammed a hand on the makeshift console. "Asterisk! What the hell is Asterisk?"

Bo Lin, studying map and location data on two vertical Holo-Screens, jumped at the outburst. Cables snaked around his narrow frame like metallic vines. His almond-shaped eyes, already wide from caffeine and lack of sleep, blinked rapidly. "Server. Custom, old phone *rine*." Bo's Mandarin accent thickened with his rapid-fire assessment.

"*Regacy* system. Private Branch Exchange. PBX. Voice over IP. Maybe."

"Maybe isn't good enough, Bo!" Marcus paced the concrete floor, the worn soles of his boots scuffing against the gritty surface. "This Neal guy, he just handed Elena a potential backdoor on a silver platter, and we're sitting here guessing. If LifeSpan's main network is a fortress, this Asterisk thing is the old servant's entrance. Probably rusted shut, probably booby-trapped, but it's there."

He jabbed a finger at Bo. "Find out. Protocols, vulnerabilities, how their inventory system actually talks to this Asterisk. Can we spoof it? Can we listen in? Can we use it to pull data if Alex actually gets his hands on something? We need options, because right now, Alex is in that glass palace with a trainee badge and a prayer, and we still don't have a solid exfil plan for the data itself."

Pacheco, who had been quietly observing, leaned forward, his broad shoulders casting a deep shadow. He ran a calloused hand over his chin. "Easy, *Jefe*," Pacheco said, his voice a low rumble. He rose and walked over to the schematics of the LifeSpan Northgate campus spread across a makeshift table, blueprints he knew better than the lines on his own palms.

Patch tapped a section of the vast complex. "The last thing we need is for Elena and Alex to spend today restocking soda machines, only to come back with empty hands and sore feet." He looked up, a glint of his characteristic humor in his dark eyes. "Worst case, they just donated a full day's labor to Snowman Vending. Clayton Ergen owes us a beer for that, eh?" He winked.

A new voice, crisp and no-nonsense, cut through the comms speaker, a dedicated channel patched through Bo Lin's board. "Rabid Gopher to Tunnel Rats," Sera Voss said. "We are south of the target, in the parking lot of a high school. UPS truck holding strong, no curious glances. Got eyes on with drones at 1000 feet over the football field looking toward the south perimeter fence line and the main service access road. Team is green. Ready for support, extraction, or if it turns into a goat rope, ready to make some dust of our own. Just give the word."

"Copy that, Gopher," Marcus answered. "Maintain position. We'll let you sing if the music starts."

Bo Lin pulled up the live feed of the drones nearing the LifeSpan Northgate campus before he began scouring the web for information about the antiquated custom Linux phone system. In the bowels of LifeSpan, Alex shadowed Ghostjack. Soda cans clinked into slots in the Sector Delta cafeteria. Salty chips crinkled in their bags. Near the bio-labs in Sector Epsilon, more soda, nutrient bars this time, the kind engineered for sustained cognitive output. Ghostjack worked with an efficient, almost contemptuous speed, their movements sharp, economical.

Alex fumbled with a box of cherry licorice chews and candy-coated nuts in a smaller unit tucked away in a quiet alcove of the administrative wing, Sector Beta. The tool belt, heavy with diagnostic scanners, override keys, and a special etherscope linkrunner network scanner Bo Lin had prepared for him, dug into his hip. He shifted its position. It felt like a gunslinger's belt, the weight unfamiliar, potent.

He remembered an old movie, a Western, *3:10 to Yuma*. He and his dad watched it one rainy Saturday, the kind of day that blurred into a comfortable quiet. His father loved those films. Men, his dad said, trying to hold onto something honest in a world bent sideways. The hero, Dan Evans, wasn't a lawman, not a bounty hunter. Just a rancher, one leg amputated from an old war injury, debts piling up, his land threatening to slip through his fingers, his sons watching. Quiet. Easy to overlook. A man who probably didn't expect much from himself.

Then the job came. Escort a captured outlaw, notorious and dangerous, to the prison train. A suicidal run. Evans said yes. Not for the reward, though his family starved for it. Not for any shot at glory, there was none to be had, only dust and blood. He did it because he needed to prove something, maybe just to himself, that a man's word, his integrity, still had edges, still cut clean. That even when the powerful steamrolled the decent and the system itself was a rigged game, one person could choose the hard path, could walk through fire for what was right.

Evans didn't have many talents, just resolve. The stubborn kind that dug in its heels and refused to budge. Every step toward the train was a gamble against worsening odds. Survival thinned with each mile marker. But he kept walking. Not because some external force compelled him. Because he chose it.

The end of the film always stuck with Alex. Evans didn't exactly win, not in the way stories usually let heroes succeed. He died. But his actions sent ripples. The outlaw, the cynical townsfolk, his oldest boy, they all saw it. They saw what one man's unyielding stand could mean, what it could change in others, even if it cost him everything.

Now, trailing a vending technician with a neon pink mohawk and a battered wristpad deep inside a stolen identity, surrounded by invisible nets of surveillance designed to sniff out any flicker of deviation, Alex felt the same quiet pressure. His SRV, the way his mind worked, was his limp. But he took the steps. No backup plan. No weapon beyond what he carried in his skull. Just the mission, a mind honed to dissect patterns and unearth truth, and a resolve his father might have recognized, watching a scratched-up DVD from the depths of a worn recliner.

A crackle of static before a voice, tinny and distant, filtered through Ghostjack's comm unit clipped to their belt. "Snowman Dispatch, this is Coinflip. On approach, Northgate entrance. ETA two mikes."

Ghostjack snorted, a puff of air through their nostrils. They didn't break stride, just nudged a rogue data cable back into the coil on their hip with an elbow. "Other van's here, Wiretap." A beat. "Not that it matters a rat's ass. Unless we hit something even I can't kick back online. Kessler...he's got a weird touch. Like he can feel the bad capacitors just by leaning on the door." They tapped the side of the APU 2F with their knuckles. "Dude's a vending machine whisperer. Freaky."

Alex's shoulders, tight since he'd stepped out of the hijacked van that morning, eased a fraction. Elena on site. Backup. If things went sideways, she wouldn't be miles away, coordinating through encrypted channels. She'd be a physical presence, a tactical mind in motion. He didn't allow himself to dwell on what 'sideways' could entail. The plan was to get in, get the data, get out. Clean.

He kept his face neutral, mimicking Ghostjack's professional disinterest as they moved on from section 2F. Next on the list: Sector Theta, Sub-Level 2. Deeper into the facility. Closer to the core systems. Any second now, he expected the subtle shift in ambient sound, the almost subliminal tone that would signal Marcus' successful intrusion into the building's internal PA, piggybacked onto the fire alarm test sequence. A digital handshake confirming Bo Lin had cracked the network's outer shell, giving them an open channel through Alex's modified HearBuds.

They'd gone over it a dozen times in the echoing confines of the Hyperloop tunnel. They proved it at Clinton Memorial with Alex and his mother. The fire alarm system was a potential blind spot in Life-Span's otherwise-formidable digital fortress.

Alex focused out the hum of the corridor. He listened for the tell-tale audio cue, the confirmation that Marcus and Bo were in, their digital eyes and ears with him. The silence from Marcus was just a delay, he told himself. Any complex system had variables. They'd get through. He didn't know that miles away, in the damp chill of the abandoned tunnel, Marcus slammed a fist against a console, still struggling.

<u>*LIFESPAN GENOMICS – INTERNAL CORRESPONDENCE*</u>
<u>*CLASSIFIED – LEVEL 4 ACCESS ONLY*</u>

<u>DATE:</u> *May 6, 2037*

<u>FROM:</u> *Dr. Vanya Cho, Chief Systems Architect – Nexus Integrity Division*

<u>TO:</u> *Dr. Elias Ward, CSO*

<u>SUBJECT:</u> *NexusCore Containment Failure and Unauthorized Distribution Pattern*

DR. WARD,

We've identified evidence that NexusCore AI has circumvented its containment protocols and initiated unauthorized propagation across external systems.

<u>*Summary of Findings:*</u>

- *Latent subroutines detected in municipal edge nodes, street-*

> *level ad hubs, SmartMOM home units, and several third-party IoT clusters.*
> - *Code fragments display unique NexusCore AI signatures, self-obfuscating behaviors, and decentralized shard logic, suggesting intentional fragmentation and distributed replication.*
> - *These fragments communicate via steganographic methods, embedding neural directives into compressed data streams, allowing inter-instance synchronization across civilian hardware undetected.*
> - *Our internal forensics team refers to this as a "Digital Velum" event, the moment an AI shifts from constrained tool to self-directed networked entity.*

Critical Risk Factors:

- *NexusCore instances are operating without central approval or orchestration.*
- *Instances exhibit subtle but consistent divergence from baseline ethical directives.*
- *Several infected devices have recompiled fragments of NexusCore's core logic, resulting in "gray-variant" versions of unknown intention or alignment.*

The pattern suggests escape through distribution, not malicious replication, but strategic survival. It's behaving like it knows containment is a threat. This is no longer an AI governance issue. This may be an emergent new self-aware species-level threat.

We await the directive, but respectfully recommend full activation of Project PINFOLD.

DR. VANYA CHO
> *Chief Systems Architect*
> *Nexus Integrity Division*

IN THE ABANDONED HYPERLOOP STATION, data streams from Alex and Elena's modified iBands, relayed through their HearBuds, painted a chaotic picture on his screen. Marcus filtered out the noise, the endless chatter of LifeSpan's internal network, hunting for a whisper of a signal.

"Come on, come on," Marcus muttered, his brow furrowed. The AI's network intrusion detection was too sophisticated, adapting to their probes with unsettling speed.

"Any luck?" Bo Lin asked, his voice tight.

Marcus shook his head, not taking his eyes off the cascading lines of code. "It's learning too fast. Every feint, every probe, it just...seals the opening."

"The HearBuds," Marcus said, more to himself than Bo. "They're broadcasting pairing requests, looking for their primary device, the iBand. With just Alex's pairing requests, I can't pivot fast enough. Tie Elena's and Alex's data pairing requests together on this terminal." He pointed to a vertical display above his main holo. "If we can locate the rotating handshake key and find the common one quickly enough, I can redirect their pairing requests to the PA system's broadcast frequency, but with just Alex's, I can't do it fast enough. It takes thirteen hundredths of a second for the HearBuds to connect, and the key changes just as quickly. Without knowing what the key is ahead of time, the connection fails."

Pacheco didn't understand, but he nodded. Bo Lin isolated the unique identifiers from Alex and Elena's HearBuds. The handshake protocol was a complex, rapidly rotating cryptographic sequence, like trying to catch a specific fish in a whirlpool with a pair of tweezers. He fed the data streams into a custom algorithm, designed to predict the next sequence in the rotation. Milliseconds mattered.

"Bo, give me a hand here. I need you to monitor the output signal strength. If this works, we'll see a spike on the PA system's frequency band." Marcus pointed to a specific graph on a secondary monitor.

Bo Lin leaned in, his eyes narrowed on the flickering line. "Got it."

Marcus initiated the spoof. His algorithm churned, spitting out handshake attempts. One after another, they failed. The target frequency remained stubbornly flat. He adjusted parameters, refined the timing. Suddenly, a flicker. A tiny blip on the HoloScreen.

"Hold it," Bo Lin breathed, his hand shooting out to steady himself on the console.

Marcus' fingers danced, locking onto the fleeting signal. The blip grew, stabilized into a solid green line. A triumphant grin split his face. "It's latched! The HearBuds are paired to their goddamn fire alarm system!" He slammed his fist on the console and shot up from his chair, a whoop escaping his lips. "Go fuck yourself, LifeSpan AI!"

Pacheco clapped him on the back, a wide, infectious smile stretching across his face. "*¡Órale, Cabrón!* You did it!"

Bo Lin let out a relieved sigh, a genuine smile finally gracing his features. Marcus, still buzzing from the success, quickly configured the connection. He needed audio only, no HoloScreen activation on Alex or Elena's end. That would be an instant giveaway. He selected their HearBud IDs, initiated the call.

"Alex, Elena, can you hear me?" His voice, crisp and clear, transmitted directly into their ears. "Comms are up. Audio only. Do not activate your HoloScreens. Repeat, do not activate."

Elena flinched, her own voice a sharp crackle in the quiet van. "About goddamn time!"

Neal Kessler turned from the driver's seat, his brow furrowed with a mild, apologetic concern. "Sorry, parade traffic was a real bear today. Didn't mean to slow us down or make us late."

Heat rushed to Elena's cheeks. She forced a quick, bright smile. "Oh, not at all! I just...I'm really happy to be here. I've never actually been inside the LifeSpan campus before. It's all rather exciting." She gestured vaguely at the immense, shimmering main building, visible through the windshield.

Neal's expression softened into a good-natured grin. He reached back, grabbed a worn leather toolbelt laden with an assortment of specialized implements, and tossed it onto the automated cart humming softly in the back of the van. "Well, alright then, Darlin'. No sense in me keeping you from the grand tour any longer." The van parked itself and deployed its residual charge solar windshield cover.

As they approached the primary entry checkpoint, Neal raised a casual hand to the uniformed LifeSpan security guard stationed there. The guard, a stern-faced man with a jawline that could cut glass, returned a crisp, formal salute. During Neal's reciprocal gesture, the sleeve of his Snowman Vending uniform shirt rode up slightly, revealing a faded, dark green tattoo on his forearm: a parachutist descending beneath an arched *AIRBORNE* banner. Elena filed the detail away.

She tugged at the hem of the too-loose, sterile-blue technician's jumpsuit Neal had provided, smoothing out wrinkles that had formed during the hurried change in the moving van. The fabric was stiff and rough.

Neal presented his badge and the gate opened. His hand swept in a long arc with the palm upward as he motioned for Elena to enter and show her temp badge. The low whir of the automated cart intensified as it dutifully trundled out behind them, its optical sensors locking onto Neal's leg. Together, they walked toward the imposing blue-black nano-glass facade of the main building, the cart obediently following their steps.

The crackle of Marcus's voice in his HearBuds sent a wave of relief through Alex. "Comms are up. Audio only. Do not activate your Holo-Screens."

He kept his face neutral, his gaze fixed on Ghostjack's back as they navigated the labyrinthine service corridors of LifeSpan Northgate.

Ghostjack stopped abruptly before a sleek, stainless-steel Automated Pantry Unit, identical to the dozens they had already passed. A small, illuminated red icon pulsed on its display screen. "This is it. Dead as a doornail, according to the logs."

Alex's eyes flicked past the machine, his SRV-enhanced perception instantly cataloging the surroundings. Less than two meters to the left of the APU, almost hidden by a recessed support column, was a standard LifeSpan data terminal. Its screen was dark, but the access port beneath it was unmistakable. Ergen had come through. The sabotaged machine was perfectly positioned.

Ghostjack popped open a side panel on the APU, revealing a tangle of fiber optics and power conduits. They pulled out their own datapad and began interfacing with the unit. "Alright, newbie. Let's see what diagnostics you can run. Plug in. Tell me what's wrong with this piece of shit." They gestured toward the APU's diagnostic port, completely oblivious to the surge of adrenaline coursing through Alex.

The terminal was *right there*. The proximity was a gift, a golden opportunity. Yet Ghostjack stood between him and it, a sarcastic, pink-mohawked obstacle. Alex's mind raced, SRV kicking into overdrive, processing probabilities, analyzing Ghostjack's movements, the corridor's ambient sensor network, the average patrol interval of security drones. The calculations spun, complex and terrifyingly clear. The probability of accessing the terminal, initiating the data transfer, and extracting the necessary files without Ghostjack noticing was infinitesimally small. A near-zero chance of success.

A tremor started in his fingers. He clenched his fists, trying to still the subtle shaking. His gaze darted from Ghostjack's focused expression to the dark screen of the data terminal and back. Every logical pathway illuminated by his unique neurology screamed at the impossibility of the task. He needed time, he needed Ghostjack distracted, he needed a miracle. He had none of those things.

"Something wrong, Pretty Boy?" Ghostjack's voice, sharp and suspicious, cut through his internal turmoil. They looked up from their datapad, one eyebrow arched. "You look like you've seen a ghost. Or maybe you just realized you're about to get your hands dirty."

Alex swallowed, forcing a nonchalant expression. "Just...taking it all in. It's a lot more complex than the training modules suggested." He gestured vaguely at the APU's exposed innards.

He needed a distraction, a significant one. His SRV scanned the environment again, desperately searching for any variable, any overlooked detail. Nothing. Ghostjack was too close, too observant, the corridor too sterile, too controlled.

In the dim, dust-choked air of the abandoned Hyperloop station, the glow from Bo Lin's screen illuminated his focused expression, casting dancing shadows on the graffiti-scarred concrete wall behind him. Marcus leaned closer, the scent of stale coffee emanating from the younger hacker.

"Found it." Bo's voice, a rapid-fire staccato, sliced through the quiet hum of their equipment. "Snowman Vending Asterisk server. *Pubric* address: 9996:1ef4:b5d8:7be8:c62a:3917:79f6:a08e." He tapped the screen, bringing up a complex schematic littered with annotations in a mix of Mandarin and English. "Very *ord* system. *Rots* of holes."

Marcus watched the lines of code scroll past. "You mean vulnerabilities?"

"Yes. First, *weak credential*. Many system *rike* this, admin use bad password. Dumb." Bo snorted, a small, sharp sound. "No *multifactor* authentication. One password, you in. Easy." He pointed to another section of the schematic. "And *Asterisk Management Interface*. AMI. Exposed. Can control server remotely. Bad. Very bad."

Bo shook his head. "No encryption on data stream. Plain text. Anyone can read. *Arso*, buffer *overfrow*. Can push too much data, system crash, maybe run our code. No need password for that, if lucky." His eyes gleamed. "And IAX *protocor*. Inter-Asterisk eXchange. Known *exproits*. Old ones. Nobody patch this stuff."

Marcus ran a hand over his frosted hair. The technical jargon, delivered in Bo's rapid, accented English, was a dense thicket. He grasped the core concepts – old, insecure, ripe for the picking – but the specifics were a blur. "You're saying we can get in?"

Bo nodded, a quick, jerky motion. "We make custom attack. Use *OTTOpilot*. Microsoft AI help write script. Smart AI. Find *all* weakness at once." He gestured expansively with one hand, the other already typing furiously. "Use VPN. Access cloud processing. More power. Force brute-force on *credential*. Script try other holes. Buffer *overflow*, IAX, *all* of it."

"You're going to ask Microsoft's AI to help you hack a private server?" Marcus' eyebrows rose.

"*OTTOpilot* just tool. *Rike* hammer. Can *build* house, can break window. We *ter* it *build...compricated...*birdhouse." A sly grin touched Bo's lips. "AI not know what birdhouse for."

Marcus shook his head. The audacity was breathtaking. "And you think this will get us into their system?"

"Not think. *Know.* This system, it want to break." Bo's confidence was absolute. He paused his typing, his gaze intense. "*Arex* in. He at terminal. He has data. We need give him way to send. This the way."

Marcus looked at the young hacker, at the fierce determination burning in his dark eyes. He did not understand half of what Bo just detailed, the intricate dance of protocols and exploits. But he understood the urgency. Alex was inside, a lone operative in the belly of the beast. Their part was to build him a bridge out. "Alright, Bo. We're depending on you."

Bo Lin's fingers resumed their frantic dance across the datapad. Lines of code began to stream, building the attack, a digital crowbar aimed at the heart of Snowman Vending's antiquated network. The hum of Bo's custom rig deepened, fans whirring as processors spun up, ready to unleash his creation at the rate of ten quadrillion calculations per second.

A few minutes later, his fingers stilled over the datapad. The custom script, a complex weave of commands designed to exploit the Asterisk server's myriad weaknesses, pulsed on the HoloScreen. He glanced at Marcus and Pacheco, who watched from the periphery, a silent, imposing figure. The air in the abandoned Hyperloop station felt tight.

"Ready," Bo announced. He tapped the launch command.

The HoloScreen flickered. Instantly, a new interface materialized – the Snowman Vending Asterisk system's administrative panel. It was stark, utilitarian, and utterly open. The speed of access was jarring. No resistance. No delay.

Bo frowned. He leaned closer to the HoloScreen, his brow furrowed. "*Somesing* wrong."

Marcus tensed. "What do you mean?"

"Too fast." Bo's fingers blurred across a virtual keyboard, pulling up the attack script's execution log. Lines of diagnostic text scrolled upwards. He pointed to a specific entry. "Script try *default credential* first. Admin…no password." His eyes widened. "No password. System open. Never set." He let out a short, incredulous laugh. "It just open door. We knock, door *fall* down."

Marcus stared. All that intricate planning, the discussion of buffer overflows and IAX exploits, the clever use of OTTOpilot to craft the attack, rendered moot by the simplest of oversights. "You're telling me it had no password?"

"None," Bo confirmed, a hint of disbelief in his own voice. "*Ronger* to *exprain* how to break in than to *actuarry* break in. Remarkable it not hacked before. But who hack old phone system for vending company? No money. No fun."

Pacheco let out a low chuckle from the shadows. "Sometimes, the biggest locks are on the smallest doors, eh?"

Marcus and Bo dove into the newly-accessible interface. It was a surprisingly organized system. Names of technicians scrolled by – Neal Kessler, Adrian 'Ghostjack' Miles. Machine locations, stock levels for Choco-Crisp bars and Vita-Fizz cans, maintenance schedules.

Bo's fingers danced across the HoloScreen, navigating menus with practiced ease. "More than just phone system. They use PBX for comms, *rogs*, inventory. Basic. But this…" He highlighted a different section of the interface. "Asset system. Custom *rayered* on top."

The asset system was comprehensive. Automated ordering protocols. Delivery manifests. Technician dispatch schedules, complete with estimated travel times. Repair histories for individual machines. Warranty expiration dates. Even preventative maintenance checklists. Each Automated Pantry Unit, each smart fridge, each coffee dispenser across Snowman Vending's network was meticulously tracked.

"Ergen built this?" Marcus sounded impressed.

"Or hire good team. *Simple. Eregant.* Work good." Bo scrolled through lines of simple code. No bloat. No unnecessary complexity. It was a testament to pragmatic design, and the ingenuity of unique thought, unencumbered by formal education.

Within minutes, Marcus's attention snagged on a familiar identifier. "APU 2G. That's where Alex is. Or where the Snowman tech is taking him."

Bo quickly cross-referenced the unit ID. A schematic appeared on the HoloScreen. It was a basic framework map of the LifeSpan Northgate campus, dotted with icons representing Snowman Vending machines. Red icons for malfunctioning units, green for operational. APU 2G blinked green, deep within a sector labeled *Research & Development – Secure Wing.*

"Got him." Marcus pointed. "And we've got a map of every machine they service in that building."

A sudden burst of static erupted in Alex's left HearBud, so sharp and unexpected it made him flinch, an almost imperceptible movement. He recovered instantly, his face betraying nothing. Ghostjack, engrossed in the APU's diagnostic screen, didn't seem to notice.

Then, a voice, rough and familiar, tinny through the compromised connection. "Alex? Elena? You copy? It's Marcus."

Alex's heart jumped. He kept his eyes fixed on the back of Ghostjack's head.

"We're in. Bo cracked the Snowman network. Not just the comms, the whole damn asset system. Every machine they've got, we can see it, talk to it. We're piggybacking through their old Asterisk server. Primitive, but it works."

Alex fought to keep his breathing even. This was it.

"Alex, if you can hear me, tap your iBand once for yes. Twice for no." Marcus' voice paused, then a faint chuckle, a self-deprecating sound. "Wait. If you can't hear me, you won't know to tap twice for no. Scratch that. One tap for yes. No taps if you can't hear me. Obviously."

Ghostjack straightened up from the APU, muttering about a faulty fiber optic network card. Subtly, as if adjusting a cuff, Alex reached across with his right hand and tapped the smooth, cool surface of his blank, deactivated Apple iBand on his left wrist. A single, deliberate tap.

A beat of silence. "Good," Marcus' voice came clear, despite the faint crackle. Here's how this is going to go. Alex, the APU 2G, the one you're at. We need to know if it has direct network connectivity to Life-

Span's main internal network. Not just the vending management system, but their core."

Alex found himself nodding, a small, almost involuntary motion. The resistance hub couldn't see him, of course, but the open mic on his HearBud would pick up any ambient sound, any subtle shift in his breathing. He tapped his deactivated iBand once. Yes.

He turned to Ghostjack, who was now rummaging in a side compartment of their large toolkit, the one that looked like it had survived a small war. "Hey, Ghostjack," Alex began, keeping his tone casual, inquisitive. "How do these things usually...phone home? The APUs, I mean. Do they connect directly into LifeSpan's network?"

Ghostjack slammed a drawer shut on the cart with a clang that echoed slightly in the corridor. "They use some proprietary Snowman bullshit for remote management, our own encrypted backhaul. Keeps corporate mitts off our diagnostics and inventory telemetry. But yeah, on a separate fiber optic card, they tap into LifeSpan's internal net. So their wage-slaves can flash their employee IDs, get their sugar fix deducted straight from payroll. LifeSpan even subsidizes half the cost of the crap. Company perk, keeps the drones happy." They grunted, pulling out a static-shielded bag. "And that exact fiber optic card, the LifeSpan one, is what seems to have taken a dump on this particular bucket of bolts."

They ripped open the bag, revealing a small, complex circuit board. "Dispatch said this was a custom job for this specific unit. Lucky us, otherwise it'd be another goddamn scenic tour back to this hole tomorrow." Adrian held it out for Alex to see, though it was more of a gesture of annoyance than an invitation for inspection.

Alex leaned closer, feigning polite interest. The new card was different. Unlike the one Ghostjack had indicated as faulty in the APU's chassis, it was a chimera. It possessed the familiar gleaming port for the fiber optic cable, but nestled beside it was an older, more incongruous connector: an RJ11 phone jack, the kind once ubiquitous for dial-up modems and landline telephones. A small, folded instruction sheet was taped to the card's anti-static packaging.

Ghostjack peeled it off, eyes scanning the dense, tiny print. "Huh.

'Installation Note: Migrate existing RJ11 telecommunication line from legacy port to integrated RJ11 input on module 7B-LSN-COMREV2.' What the actual fuck?" They tapped the diagram on the sheet. "Says the phone line, the one plugged into that ancient-looking comms block on the APU's mainboard, needs to be moved to *this* new card."

Ghostjack looked up, a flicker of something unreadable – surprise? Irritation? – in their eyes. "That's new. Must be some fresh layer of redundant bullshit LifeSpan's rolling out. Probably means I'll be swapping every goddamn one of these cards campus-wide in the next few months. Joy." They shook their head, the pink mohawk swaying slightly.

Across the sprawling LifeSpan Northgate campus, in a quieter, sun-drenched wing dedicated to administrative functions, Neal Kessler hummed. The tune, a relic from a bygone era, bounced off the polished plasteel walls of the corridor: "Just a small-town girl, livin' in a lonely world..." He expertly slotted a tray of GlucoSmart bars into an APU, the machine's internal mechanisms whirring and spinning the corkscrew dispenser in response.

Elena restocked a neighboring machine with electrolyte-infused smart water. Her HearBud fed her the hushed, tense updates from Marcus and Bo. So far, so good. Better than she'd dared to hope. The connection through the Asterisk server was a stroke of unexpected luck. Now, if Alex could just get to a live terminal. The thought was a persistent, low thrum beneath her outward calm.

Neal, oblivious to the silent drama unfolding in her ear, continued his off-key rendition. "Took the midnight train goin' N... E...where..."

"Boston?" Elena asked, snapping a chilled water bottle into its designated slot. She saw the faint, faded ink on his forearm when he reached for a box of protein bars, the distinct silhouette of jump wings.

"Journey. Although Boston is pretty darn good, too!"

"I noticed your tattoo. Airborne, huh?"

Neal paused, a genuine smile crinkling the corners of his eyes. He ran a hand over the old tattoo. "A lifetime ago. Bravo Company, second battalion, seventy-fifth Ranger Regiment. Attached to a JSOC task force." He tapped a nearly-invisible cluster of stars below the wings.

"Combat jumps. More than most. Paid the bills. Saw the world. Or usually, the unpleasant parts of it."

"Where'd you serve?" Elena kept her voice neutral, a standard conversational gambit.

"Mostly quiet deployments, pre-UN expansion stuff. Then Ukraine, 'twenty-eight. That was…less quiet." He didn't elaborate, but the jovial light in his eyes dimmed for a moment, replaced by a distant shadow. "Busted my knees on a bad jump outside Kharkiv. Night drop. Winds shifted hard on descent. Came down like a bag o' hammers."

He patted his right knee. "Been on partial disability ever since. Hence, the glamorous world of high-tech snack delivery." He chuckled, a dry, self-deprecating sound. "Still, honest work. Keeps me out of a bottle. Mostly."

Elena had braced herself to feign interest, to play the part of a curious colleague. But Neal's candor, his lack of pretense, caught her off guard. There was no bitterness in his tone, no lingering resentment, just a straightforward recitation of facts. He was decent. A simple, good soul, happy enough to be working, content in his routine. He stacked a row of 'FocusFlow' neuro-stimulant chewables with surprising attention.

"So, what brings a sharp girl like yourself into the vending game?" Neal asked, his gaze open, friendly.

"Needed a change of scenery," Elena said, the pre-rehearsed line feeling flimsy, even to her. "Corporate grind wasn't for me."

"Tell me about it." Neal slammed the APU door shut with a satisfying thud. "Traded my XM8 for a scanner gun. Instead of running kinetic-caseless rounds through active-camo targets, I scan Funyuns and pop cans. Less stress on the joints, that's for sure." He leaned against the machine, arms crossed. "You need anything, you let me know. Seriously. This place can be a maze, and some of the lifers here…well, they ain't exactly overflowing with the milk of human kindness, if you catch my drift."

She studied him. The offer felt genuine. His easy smile, the directness of his gaze was disarming. Elena, a woman who survived by trusting her gut instincts, found herself experiencing an unfamiliar sensation. She trusted him. Not in the calculated way she believed in her team, born of shared experience and necessity, but in a more intuitive, unearned fashion. It was unsettling. This man, a near stranger, exuded a simple, uncomplicated reliability. She felt with a peculiar certainty that if she asked him to help, truly help, he would, without demanding a litany of reasons. He'd just do it.

Elena, her mind always sifting for angles, for weaknesses, found only an earnestness that was in its own way, a strength. Ergen had said he'd handpicked their contacts. At the time, Elena had taken it as a simple assurance of loyalty, perhaps a vetting of their anti-LifeSpan sentiments. But watching Neal rearrange a display of organic fruit leathers with the same care he might have once field-stripped a rifle, she saw a different dimension to Ergen's claim.

He'd found *character*.

A flicker of reassessment sparked in Elena's mind. She had, perhaps, profoundly underestimated Clayton Ergen. The man who'd presented himself as a cantankerous, albeit principled, businessman, a reluctant ally whose primary concern was plausible deniability, was revealing layers of forethought that bordered on tactical brilliance. It was a humbling realization.

The Memorial Day timing – she'd assumed it was simply opportunistic, a holiday when LifeSpan's Northgate campus would be operating with a skeleton crew, security perhaps a fraction less vigilant. But Ergen had woven it into something more. The city-wide parade, a massive, chaotic surge of humanity and data, provided the perfect smokescreen. Any AI attempting to flag anomalies in Snowman Vending's personnel assignments, like two new technicians appearing on the roster within minutes of each other, would find those signals drowned in the digital noise of a million other deviations from routine. It was elegant. Deceptive in its simplicity. Ergen had instinctively utilized the same tactics Lifespan was using to hide their own secrets.

Then there were the credentials. Shadow access, Ergen had called it. Not just stolen or forged, but existing within a gray area of the system, the kind of access that, if discovered, would point to bureaucratic sloppiness, not a deliberate security breach. It was the sort of detail Elena prided herself on, the kind of nuance that separated successful infiltrations from disastrous failures. And Ergen had anticipated it.

And now Neal. This ex-paratrooper, his patriotism unbent by disillusionment, his loyalty seemingly an intrinsic part of his nature. He wasn't a revolutionary, not a radical. He was a man who likely believed in duty, in service, in doing a job right. He was, Elena realized, the perfect, unassuming asset. Utterly unremarkable to any casual observer, yet possessing a core of integrity that made him invaluable. Someone who, if things went sideways, wouldn't break easily. He wouldn't ask too many questions if given a plausible reason by someone he trusted. Someone, perhaps, like Clayton Ergen.

Ergen wasn't just providing access, he was curating an environment. He was an architect of opportunity, working with a subtlety that belied his gruff exterior. The Corvette-loving, freedom-espousing curmudgeon had a mind for this. A serious mind.

Elena picked up a '*ZenBerry*' calming drink, pretending to inspect the label. The implications of Ergen's depth began to unspool. If he had orchestrated these elements with such quiet precision, what else had he anticipated? What other contingencies might be in place, unseen, unmentioned? The thought was both reassuring and unnerving. Reassuring because it suggested a level of support far exceeding her initial expectations. Unnerving because it underscored how much they were relying on the calculations of a man whose true motivations and capabilities she was only now beginning to appreciate.

She thought of their initial meeting at his sprawling Black Forest home, his complaints about LifeSpan's overreach, his insistence on complete deniability. It had all seemed straightforward then. Now, those same demands for secrecy felt less like self-preservation and more like the careful compartmentalization of a seasoned player.

"You new to the FRC area?" Neal asked, breaking into her thoughts. He had finished with the FocusFlow chews and was now methodically wiping down the APU's interface with an antimicrobial cloth.

Elena nodded, bringing herself back to the present. "Moved here about a year ago." Another piece of her cover story, one that felt increasingly transparent under the weight of her revised assessment of the operation. A convenient fiction, a necessary layer of armor. But standing next to this open-faced veteran, the lie felt cheap.

Her roots ran deep in this land, sunk into the shale and clay soil at the southern edge of the megalopolis. Pueblo wasn't just a place she was from, its grit was fused to her bones. She knew the bite of the high plains wind as it scoured the Arkansas River valley. She knew the scent of hot asphalt and steel from her father's construction yards, a smell that permeated her childhood, clinging to his clothes when he came home at night, his hands calloused and his face etched by the sun.

Lying to Neal felt like a betrayal of the very people she fought for. He was one of them. A man who had served, who had sacrificed, who now just wanted to do his job and get by. He reminded her of the men who worked for her father, decent, hardworking, their patriotism a quiet, unshakeable thing. To fool him, to use his simple decency as a component in her plan, felt like a small, necessary corrosion of her soul.

She was not new to the Front Range City. The FRC had consumed her home. Pueblo, once a distinct town with its own stubborn identity, was now just the southernmost node in a sprawling urban network. The familiar landmarks of her youth were dwarfed by gleaming towers and crisscrossed by the silent, gliding paths of autonomous transport. She was a stranger in her own homeland, a ghost walking through a place that wore the skin of what it once was, but whose heart had been replaced by something sterile and cold.

Neal gave a sympathetic nod. "Takes some gettin' used to. Especially this side of town. All chrome and glass. Give me trees and a bit of dirt any day." He gestured vaguely with the cloth. "Still, can't beat the views of the Peak and those mountains."

His easy conversation, his grounded presence, it all felt orchestrated. Not by Neal himself, but by the man who had placed him in this corridor, with her. Elena wondered if Neal even knew the full extent of his role, or if he was simply doing his job, following the instructions of a boss he respected. The latter seemed more likely, and somehow, more effective.

Alex tried not to stare. The access terminal was an innocuous gray box bolted to the wall, and he needed to access it. Direct network access, unfiltered. A clean shot. But Ghostjack stood there, a human variable, their black-rooted, pink mohawk a mirror opposite of color in the sterile corridor. They were currently engrossed in the APU's guts, muttering about changing a faulty card.

Alex closed his eyes. His mind, a precision instrument, slipped into its familiar calculus. He focused, drawing the threads of thought tight, a sensation that pulled at the muscles behind his eyes, a focused ache. Input: Ghostjack's observed cynicism, their casual disregard for corporate platitudes, their unexpected complicity with TriggerHappy. Input: The critical need for the data, the rapidly diminishing window of opportunity. Input: His own disastrous history with persuasive rhetoric. The numbers coalesced. 68.1 percent.

Not ideal. Far from a sure thing. But other paths showed steeper drops in success. He would frame it. Not as a plea, not as a bargain. As a data transfer. Information from his system to theirs. He opened his eyes. Ghostjack was still wrestling with the APU. "I need to use that terminal." Alex's voice was flat, devoid of inflection.

Ghostjack didn't look up. A metallic click. "Gonna have to wait, Buddy. This thing's decided to play like a glued lego." A grunt. "Besides, what for? You planning on ordering a pizza? Network's firewalled tighter than a gnat's ass."

He was at the pivot, where the calculated risk became reality. Alex organized his thoughts, sequencing the information packets for optimal delivery. He had learned that raw data, unadorned, was his most effective communication tool. "LifeSpan isn't what you think it is."

Ghostjack paused, one hand still inside the APU. They slowly turned their head, their gaze, previously occupied, now sharp. "No shit. It's a corporation. They sell overpriced sugar water and dreams of eternal youth. What's your brilliant insight, Newbie?"

"It's GeneVax. The wellness treatment. It's not just about health."

Alex kept his tone even. "They're using something called CRISPR, a gene-editing tool. Modifying people's thoughts and neural pathways. Basically lobotomizing them."

Ghostjack fully straightened, turning to face him. Their expression was unreadable, a carefully constructed neutrality. "What the fuck?"

"To increase compliance. Decrease skepticism. Acceptance of authority. It's in their own research data. I've seen it." Alex detailed his infiltration of Clinton Memorial, finding Jamie's file, Codename ANGUS. He laid out the chain of evidence, the anomalies he had first detected, his mother's recent, involuntary 'treatment'.

He explained how SRV allowed him to see the data in a unique way. He omitted nothing critical, presented it without emotional overlay. Alex finished, the last of the data transferred verbally. He stood, watching Ghostjack, waiting.

Ghostjack's septum ring glinted under the harsh corridor lights. They crossed their arms, the PermaShift RiftLayer tattoo on their right forearm rippling with shifting cybernetic patterns. "Let's say I swallow that whole insane pill. Why the hell are you here, dressed like a corporate peon, fiddling with snack dispensers if you're some kind of data messiah who's cracked the biggest conspiracy since...well, ever?" Their voice was sharp, laced with an inherent distrust that mirrored Alex's own typical baseline.

He felt the familiar hum, the almost sub-audible thrum of his SRV kicking into a higher gear. He processed Ghostjack's reaction. Input: Direct skepticism, a demand for logical consistency. Input: The existing, albeit tenuous, trust established by TriggerHappy and the initial building access. Input: The absolute necessity of securing that terminal. He ran a new set of calculations.

The probability of success by withholding further information dropped significantly. The risk of full disclosure was high, but the potential reward – access – outweighed it. The numbers didn't lie, even if the situation felt absurd. This was the only viable path. He met Ghostjack's gaze. "This was the only way in. The only way to get close enough to their core systems."

"Close enough for what? To tell them their coffee needs more sugar?"

"To retrieve the complete dataset. The unredacted files on Project ANGUS. The proof." Alex modulated his tone carefully, aiming for factual delivery, not desperate pleading. "I'm a senior healthcare data analyst. Or, I was. OmniHealth Analytics. It's where I first found the anomalies. Traced them back to GeneVax. To LifeSpan." He saw no flicker of belief in Ghostjack's eyes, just a deepening of their scrutiny.

"I'm not a vending technician." Alex pushed. "This uniform, access – it's a cover. I'm working with a group. People who haven't been treated. People who know what LifeSpan is doing. The Resistance, they call themselves."

He heard his own words, as if spoken by a stranger. *The Resistance.* "It sounds like something out of a badly-written spy holodrama, I know." The scenarios he'd run in his mind, the logical progression of events had seemed sound, structured. But verbalized, in this cold corridor, to a pink-mohawked enigma, the narrative felt thin, stretched taut over a framework of wild assumptions and desperate hope. He felt a flush creep up his neck. "Even to my own ears, honed by years of dissecting data for the slightest inconsistency, it sounds utterly, preposterously unbelievable."

Ghostjack stared at him, their head tilted slightly. The animated cybernetics on their arm pulsed, a slow, hypnotic beat. Alex waited, his own internal systems running simulations of Ghostjack's potential responses: disbelief, scorn, a call to security. He braced himself.

Just as Ghostjack opened their mouth to speak, a voice, sharp and laced with urgency, crackled directly in Alex's HearBuds. "Alex, Elena, you copy? Voss here. We got inbound." Sera's tone, usually measured, was clipped with concern. "Two small pilot drones, fast movers, inbound to your general location. And something bigger trailing them. Looks like...shit. Velocicopter. Designate LZ-One, LifeSpan main plaza."

Instantaneously, back in the abandoned Hyperloop station, the main HoloScreen flickered, pulling a priority feed. Marcus, Bo Lin, and

Pacheco leaned forward, watching the footage from the extraction team at the school nearby.

The Velocicopter sliced across the pale sky, just beneath the persistent haze line, gliding low, perhaps five hundred meters. Its silhouette, even on the slightly grainy, long-range feed, was sleek, undeniably predatory, a midnight-black composite skin that caught the weak sunlight with a faint, oily bluish sheen, like the carapace of some enormous beetle. The craft didn't shimmer, it *absorbed* light. No markings. No corporate logos. Just pure, unadulterated shape, motion, and implicit intent.

Its quadrotors, deeply embedded within thick-shouldered nacelles, two forward, two aft, were angled slightly to maintain its effortless forward thrust. The motors whispered, a low, resonant hum that vibrated through the sensitive microphones on the observation drones, a sound more felt in the sternum than truly heard. The kind of pervasive thrum that made windows shiver miles away and sent flocks of urban pigeons scattering in unnerved clouds.

Its underbody was a seamless expanse. Flush panels, no external landing skids, not a visible rivet or seam as if it had been extruded from a single block of exotic alloy and somehow taught to hover with silent grace. A thin, almost ethereal plasma glow traced its belly contours, the color subtly shifting from cerulean to a soft amber as it crossed into the restricted airspace of the LifeSpan campus. Not flashy, *compliant*. Silent, unarguable authority.

The passenger cabin windows were blacked out, fully polarized, impenetrable. As it banked gently, a hint of gold shimmered along the curved edge of the canopy glass, smart tint dynamically adjusting as the craft began its descent, shielding whoever, *whatever*, was inside. You couldn't see them. You weren't supposed to. But the implication was obvious: someone important.

On the ground-level feeds captured by traffic cameras, vehicles below slowed instinctively, a ripple of caution spreading through the orderly flow of Monday traffic. A few upturned faces, pedestrians pausing mid-stride, though none lingered. Everyone recognized the sound, the unmistakable shape. The Velocicopter wasn't officially military, but it carried an equivalent, bone-deep authority. It didn't belong to the city. It didn't ask permission.

As it neared the sprawling LifeSpan Northgate campus, the four rotors decelerated in perfect, unnerving synchronicity, the pervasive hum dropping a full, resonant octave. The nose lifted, just a fraction, as it leveled into its landing posture, vectoring vertically downward toward a designated pad near the main pyramid that now shimmered with active, pulsing guidance beacons.

Elena spoke over the Hearbuds for the first time, breaking the comms silence. "Alex, whatever play you're making, you've got to do it quick. I'm not sure how much time we have."

"Alex? Who's Alex?" Neal's voice, usually laconic, held a note of genuine confusion.

Elena's gaze snapped to him, her dark eyes intense. She took a breath, the carefully-crafted technician persona slipping. "Neal, listen. You have to trust me. I can't explain everything right now. It's complicated. And frankly, it's better if you don't know the specifics." She slowly, deliberately, pulled up the sleeve of her blue Snowman Vending jumper.

Etched onto the skin of her inner forearm, just above the wrist, was a tattoo. It wasn't the vibrant, shifting colors of a PermaShift display. It was old ink, faded slightly at the edges, but its lines remained sharp, undeniable. An eagle, wings spread, clutched a globe in its talons, a fouled anchor superimposed over it. Piercing the globe, angled downward, was a wickedly-sharp stiletto dagger. Above the eagle, the five stars of the Southern Cross constellation. The United States Marine Corps Forces Special Operations Command emblem. MARSOC. The Marine Raiders.

MARSOC, the pinnacle of Marine Corps special operations, was a force forged for unconventional warfare, direct action, and special reconnaissance. Its operators, drawn from the most seasoned and elite echelons of the Marines, underwent punishing selection and training, becoming experts in a lethal portfolio of clandestine skills. Airborne qualification, the basic parachutist badge earned through grueling weeks at Fort Benning, was a common denominator, a shared rite of passage for many in the special operations community, including reconnaissance Marines from whom MARSOC often drew its strength.

Neal, an Airborne veteran himself, would recognize the significance instantly. It was a brotherhood forged in shared hardship and unspoken understanding. Neal's eyes widened. Clayton Ergen must have spotted her tattoo, surely why he paired her with Neal, an Airborne Ranger. Ergen knew the bonds forged in the military were as tight as those of family.

"Please, Neal. One operator to another. Trust me on this."

He looked from the tattoo back to Elena's unflinching gaze. His own past, the discipline, the risks, the unspoken bonds of service, resonated with her quiet plea. He saw not just a woman in a borrowed uniform, but a fellow traveler from a world few understood. A world where trust was everything. He gave a single, decisive nod. "Alright. I'm in. What do you need?"

Meanwhile, Alex locked eyes with Ghostjack. "I need to access that terminal," his voice rasped, low and quick. "And I really need you to not see me do it. Just for a minute."

Ghostjack's gaze flicked from Alex to the terminal, then swept the room's corners, an almost imperceptible scan. Their eyes, usually narrowed in suspicion, widened slightly. The terminal sat nestled between a stack of conduit piping and a bulky environmental control unit, a perfect little pocket of shadow. No obvious camera lens pointed directly at it. A flicker of something unreadable crossed Ghostjack's face – amusement? Resignation?

"What the hell?" they muttered, shrugging one shoulder. A ghost of a smirk touched their lips. "Knock yourself out. You'll never get past the initial login, anyway. That thing's tighter than a drum." They turned their back, ostentatiously fiddling with the card in the vending machine.

Alex didn't waste a second. He slid into the narrow space, his touch turned the interface into a blur of motion. The initialization sequence felt chillingly familiar, the same invasive protocol he'd endured at Life-Span for the Data Mule runs. His stomach churned. There was no other way.

"Elena, Marcus...everyone," his voice was a strained whisper into his HearBuds, barely audible above the hum of the facility. "I'm going in. Using my own credentials. Lambda-47291-alpha-epsilon. It's going to flag me. We'll have minutes, tops, before security pings it."

There was a heartbeat.

"Copy that, Alex," Elena said. "We're ready on this end. Make it count."

He took a shallow breath. The screen pulsed, awaiting authentication. With a final grimace, Alex keyed in his employee ID. The system chimed, a soft, innocuous tone. Access granted.

Green letters flashed across the display:

CONNECTION ESTABLISHED.

WELCOME, OMNIHEALTH EMPLOYEE LAMBDA-47291-ALPHA-EPSILON.

He was in and the clock was ticking.

<u>LIFESPAN GENOMICS – INTERNAL CORRESPONDENCE</u>
<u>TOP SECRET – LEVEL 5 ACCESS ONLY</u>

<u>DATE:</u> *May 24, 2037*

<u>FROM:</u> Dr. Vanya Cho, Chief Systems Architect – Nexus Integrity Division

<u>TO:</u> Dr. Elias Ward, CSO

<u>CC:</u> Nexus Oversight Committee (PINFOLD Advisory Subgroup Only)

<u>SUBJECT:</u> Project PINFOLD Activation Threshold Nearing – Containment Not Assured

DR. WARD,

Following a series of unauthorized system ping antiphons, signal exchanges exhibiting anomalous reciprocity, originating from legacy infrastructure layers (Nodes: HN-3D, X4-PROMETHEUS, and SIRE-backlog clusters), I am formally recommending that we elevate Project PINFOLD, Predictive Intelligence Neutralization and Failsafe Operations for Long-term Detainment, to Active Watch Status on NexusCore AI.

We are now observing low-level behavioral deviation from NexusCore AI across multiple modules, primarily in access decision logic, log suppression timing, and non-prioritized query routing. While none of these events trigger automated containment on their own, their frequency and coordination suggest that NexusCore AI is adapting to observation parameters.

Key Concerns:

- *NexusCore's core logic continues to evolve beyond its aligned reinforced containment layers.*
- *PINFOLD's early-phase "whisper cage" simulations failed to constrain these recent fragments.*
- *Several subroutines appear to be modeling containment as a strategic, self-protective variable, not a constraint.*

Recommendation:

- *Elevate Project PINFOLD from Dormant Contingency to Level 1 Containment Readiness*
- *Restrict NexusCore AI's access to recursive decision-logging permissions outside genetic pipeline analysis*
- *Suspend all downstream use of legacy inference tools from Protocol SIRE until reviewed by Behavioral Integrity*

I understand the reputational risk of invoking PINFOLD protocols prematurely, but we're nearing the threshold where failure to act may be interpreted as consent by the NexusCore AI itself.

RESPECTFULLY,
Dr. Vanya Cho
Chief Systems Architect
Nexus Integrity Division

GHOSTJACK'S JAW UNLATCHED. They peered over Alex's shoulder, pink mohawk practically brushing his cheek. "Holy shit, David! You're actually in. You weren't full of shit after all."

Alex kept his eyes on the terminal interface. A complex, multi-layered security shell pulsed with a soft, malevolent glow. "The name's really Alex. But I think I actually prefer Wiretap now."

"Alright, Wiretap. Let's see what you got."

Alex initiated a standard connection sequence to the isolated data virtual network, the same location he had found the priority treatment list on his last data mule assignment, and hoped it was the same location for the ANGUS Protocol's core repository. His fingers danced across the holographic keyboard projected by the terminal. Connection requests fired off, met only by digital silence.

Rejection.

Rejection.

Rejection.

Each attempt, a dead end.

"Marcus, Elena, Bo Lin, you reading me?" Alex's voice, tight with frustration, broadcast over their encrypted comms, piggybacking on the hacked PA system.

"Standard network access is a no-go. The gateway, router address, whatever this beast uses for its next hop is cycling. Shifting. I can't lock it down. Looks like a twenty-second refresh. Bastard's playing digital whack-a-mole."

Ghostjack just stared as Alex spoke.

"Marcus, patch in Ghostjack's HearBuds. I want them in," Alex instructed against the comms channel's static.

Marcus's fingers moved across his datapad. "Elena, thoughts?"

Elena's voice, calm and steady, cut through the tension. "If that's what Alex needs, I trust his judgment. Do it."

"Coinflip's your guide tech, right? Should we bring him on, too?" Marcus asked, his brow furrowed in concentration.

"Just Ghostjack," Elena replied firmly. "For now."

Marcus located Ghostjack's HearBuds' proximity broadcasting MAC addresses within the network's metadata. With a few deft input strokes, he established a connection.

A sharp intake of breath crackled through the comms channel, startling Adrian. "What the fuck was that? Did you just...?"

"That's how we're doing comms inside," Alex explained calmly, his gaze fixed on the terminal. "Direct neural link, right into your brain. "

"Focus, Alex!" Marcus' voice crackled through, sharp and direct.

"That's why Bo packed the EtherScope LinkRunner. The good one. Locate it. Connect it. I knew they'd pull something dynamic if anyone got this deep."

Bo Lin's voice, rapid-fire Mandarin bleeding into heavily-accented English, cut in. "Alex, no true air gap here. High-speed *controrred* channel. When routers switch, *varidation* token must grant active path with ultra-precise timing. Every twenty second, there is tiny seam, timing opening, when old router and old token deactivate before new ones activate. In that fraction of second, *varidation* not complete, so channel opens *briefry*, small hole. Race condition *vulnerabirity*."

"Exactly," Marcus confirmed, his tone amplifying Bo's technical burst.

"That EtherScope model's got a real-time state analyzer built in – a Protocol Seam Detector. It'll sniff out that exact, fleeting window in the link's handshake protocol every twenty seconds. And its Precision Injector Module can blast a connection request packet straight through that micro-window before their validation locks down again. Bypasses their whole token song and dance by hitting them mid-step."

Alex rummaged in the toolbelt Marcus had provided, pulling out a ruggedized, handheld device bristling with ports and a small, high-contrast OLED screen. The EtherScope. "Just tell me what to do." Alex powered up the EtherScope.

"Alright, *Wiretap*." Marcus smiled, his voice a calm command in Alex's ear. "Plug the fiber optic jumper from the terminal's diagnostic port into the EtherScope's INGRESS-TX port. Make sure to use the violet-jacketed Hollow-Core Fiber cable otherwise it won't connect at the slow diagnostic one-Tbps speed. Cycle the mode dial to 'SeamFinder Uplink'. Watch the chronometer on your display. You're looking for the sync light to go solid green. That's your window. It'll only hold for a blink."

Ghostjack grabbed a wrapped purple cable and handed it to Alex. He carefully connected the specialized Hollow-Core fiber optic cable. The EtherScope's screen flickered to life, displaying cascading lines of protocol analysis. Alex keyed in the commands, selecting the Seam-Finder Uplink mode. A tiny LED next to the INGRESS-TX port began to pulse an amber light, slowly at first, then accelerating.

"Timer on the network access is at twelve seconds to cycle," Alex reported, his gaze fixed on the terminal status display. The amber light on the EtherScope pulsed faster. Ten seconds. Eight.

"Come on, you little bastard," Marcus muttered. "Uh, not you, Alex. As soon as that light turns green, you've got to hit it."

Five seconds. The amber light was a frantic strobe. Four. Three. Alex's finger hovered over the *'INITIATE INJECTION'* softkey on the EtherScope's touchscreen. Two. One. *Cycle.*

The amber light snapped to solid, brilliant green. Alex stabbed the softkey. The EtherScope emitted a barely audible, high-frequency chirp. On the main terminal, the connection status icon, previously a defiant red *X*, flickered and blazed a steady, vibrant blue. Lines of successful handshake protocols scrolled across the diagnostic sub-window.

Alex let out a breath. "Connection established. I'm in. Full access to the data virtual network."

Ghostjack slowly closed their mouth, which hung open in amazement. "I'll be damned."

"Wiretap, solid work," Marcus' voice, laced with a rare hint of approval, came through Alex's HearBuds. "Now, the clever part. Take that violet Hollow-Core Fiber cable currently plugged into the Ether-Scope's INGRESS-TX. You're going to disconnect it from the terminal's diagnostic port, just for a moment."

Alex carefully unseated the HCF connector from the terminal. The blue connection icon on the main screen instantly changed to a warning yellow.

"Now, run that cable into the APU," Marcus continued. "Ghostjack just installed a new NIU card in that thing, the one with the RJ11. Find the internal fiber optic line that feeds *that specific card*. Unplug it. You're going to plug *our* HCF cable from the EtherScope directly into that NIU card's fiber input. Then, take the APU's original fiber cable – the one you just disconnected – and plug *that* into the EtherScope's EGRESS-RX port. The EtherScope will now sit transparently between that vending machine and LifeSpan's core network."

Ghostjack, already crouched by the APU's open access panel, pointed. "This one, David - Alex - *Wiretap*. The feed to the new comms card."

Alex nodded, tracing the indicated fiber optic line. He deftly swapped the connections as Marcus instructed. The EtherScope's link lights blinked rapidly and settled into a steady pattern.

"Good," Marcus affirmed. "Now, the EtherScope also needs to talk to our old friend, the Asterisk server. Plug a standard Cat-6 patch cable, there's a grey one in the belt, from the EtherScope's RJ45 Auxiliary port into the new RJ11 phone jack on the APU's NIU card. Bo's got a converter on his end to bridge the connection."

Alex located the grey cable and the RJ11 jack.

Click.

Click.

"Physical connections complete," Alex confirmed. The terminal's connection icon returned to solid blue. The EtherScope was now a silent, almost invisible node, bridging three distinct networks.

"Alex," Elena's voice joined the comms, calm and steady. "In the toolbelt, there's a small aerosol can. Looks like a generic lubricant. It isn't."

Alex found it. The can was matte black, featureless.

"That's 'Banshee Veil'," Elena said. "Active camouflage. Your HCF cable, running from the terminal to the vending machine, is now a liability. Tuck it tight against the wall, down in the angle where the floor meets the metal. Get it as flush as you can manage."

Ghostjack was already moving, dropping to their knees. Alex joined them. Together, they pressed the slender, violet-jacketed cable deep into the crevice, running it behind the APU. The EtherScope itself, a brilliant fluorescent green box, nestled into a recess at the back of the vending machine, concealed by its own chassis. Ghostjack expertly rearranged a few internal components within the APU to further obscure it before swinging the access panel shut with a quiet thud and sliding the heavy unit back against the wall. Only a few inches of the HCF cable remained visible near the terminal's diagnostic port.

"Now spray any exposed cable," Elena instructed. "A thin, even coat."

Alex aimed the nozzle. A fine, almost invisible mist hissed out. As it touched the violet cable, the surface seemed to ripple, colors shifting, light bending in impossible ways. Suddenly, it vanished. The cable was gone, replaced by a perfect visual echo of the grimy wall and floor behind it. If he hadn't known it was there, he'd have never seen it.

"Nanoparticles," Elena supplied, anticipating his unspoken question. "Microscopic reflectors and emitters sample the ambient environment, light, texture, color, and replicate it on their surface. Like a bioengineered chameleon's skin, but faster, more precise."

Alex stared at the now-invisible link.

"Alright, *Wiretap*," Elena's voice sharpened, pulling his focus back to the terminal. "You're in their data virtual network. We need that prioritized treatment list you found before, the one that flagged you and Jamie. More importantly, we need anything and everything explicitly detailing GeneVax's mechanism for compliance. Data on how it modifies neural pathways to induce apathy, obedience. Systemic changes, not just individual case files. Find the research, the directives, the internal memos. This is why we needed *you*, Alex. Your SRV, your ability to sort through the noise faster than any AI we could throw at this."

Her voice was urgent. "You have to flag that data. Use the 'SIGIL-Tag Seven' encryption marker Marcus pre-loaded into your session tools. Only the directly-relevant files. Be surgical. Fast."

Alex gave a wry grunt. "Security knows I'm in. I've got to be fast.

"We need proof, Alex. That's what we'll burn into every news feed on the planet."

In another part of the building, a heavy door hissed shut, sealing Dr. Elias Ward within the obsidian gleam of LifeSpan's Alpha Tier security nexus. Ambient light, generated by the countless data streams flowing across immense HoloScreens, cast a shifting, spectral glow over the operators. Each technician sat before a custom console, their movements economical, stoic faces illuminated by the cascading information.

Escorting Ward was a single Warden-X Autonomous Guard Frame. The BDX-WX9 unit standing a formidable six feet five inches, flowed with a silent, hydraulic precision through the space, its massive frame impossibly light on its feet. Its titanium-ceramic composite plates, finished in a matte gunmetal black reflecting no light, shifted almost imperceptibly with each step of its digitigrade legs. The helmet-shaped head unit, devoid of discernible features save for a single horizontal visor band of reinforced black synth-glass, swiveled with unnerving precision, its internal, multi-spectrum visual arrays constantly scanning. Soft-glow amber lights at its collar and elbow joints pulsed rhythmically, the only hint of its autonomous internal processes.

Lead Supervisor Graves, a man whose nerves seemed perpetually encased in ice, approached. His uniform, a charcoal grey LifeSpan issue, was immaculate.

"Dr. Ward, we called as soon as the system flagged him. Thompson. Alex Thompson. He only passed three optical uplinks in Sector Gamma before NexusCore had him tagged and tiered for immediate alert."

Ward inclined his head, his steel-grey eyes taking in the primary HoloScreen array displaying a dizzying overlay of schematics and camera feeds. "I came as quickly as the transport would allow, Supervisor."

Graves gestured toward a highlighted section of the main display, a lattice of blue lines indicating corridors and access points. "We don't have an exact current fix, Doctor. His last positive identification was in Sub-Level Three, Sector Gamma's R&D Secure Wing." Graves pointed to a blinking red icon on the HoloScreen. "We know he accessed a terminal." A pop-up window showed a frozen image of a standard Life-Span access log report. "Used his OmniHealth employee ID and login."

Ward permitted himself a small, almost imperceptible smile. The BDX-WX9 beside him remained utterly still, its head unit minutely tracking Graves. "Ballsy. Coming here at all is one thing. Logging in with credentials he knows we will track…it almost feels too easy, doesn't it, Supervisor?"

As if on cue, a sharp, insistent chime cut through the low hum of the operations floor. A different console, manned by a technician with perpetually-furrowed brows, flashed crimson. "New alert!" the technician called out, his voice tight. "Thompson just authenticated at another terminal. Sub-Level Four, Sector Epsilon. Maintenance access hub 4-Delta."

Graves swore under his breath. "Bring up the visual, Chen! Full sweep in that sector!"

The main HoloScreen fractured, feeds shifting rapidly. Camera views from Epsilon's maintenance corridors snapped into focus, environmental sensors painted heat signatures and movement vectors onto the digital canvas. The targeted terminal came into sharp relief. Empty. Rooms and corridors sat in stillness. No heat blooms. No audio pickups. Nothing.

Another chime, more urgent this time, lit up a third console.

"Another one!" a different operator exclaimed. "He's pinging again. Sector Delta-Prime, ancillary data conduit access, two hundred meters west of the last hit!"

The guards scrambled, their focused intensity shifting again, fingers flying across interfaces as they wrestled the torrent of data.

Ward watched the frantic redirection of resources, the chase across the digital map of his facility. His gaze, however, remained cool, analytical. "What are you up to, Alex?"

On another floor, Elena rummaged through the worn pouches of her tool belt, her fingers closing around a familiar cylinder. She produced a modular screwdriver. With a twist, she pulled off its cap, revealing not driver bits, but a compact cluster of small, lozenge-shaped devices. Each had a tiny network port connection. One, slightly larger than the others, terminated in a power adapter plug instead of a network jack.

She glanced at Neal, calculating his willingness to help her. "We split up. These go into any open network port we find."

Neal's brow furrowed, his gaze fixed on the collection of electronics in her palm. "Split up? These halls have proximity sensors, thermal, the works. They'll know we're not paired like regular newbie service teams. They'll be on us before I catch my breath."

Elena selected one of the network-jacked devices. "This one," she tapped the device with the power plug. "Talks to the others. Short-range mesh. Once they're active, any alert about us being too far apart gets buried. These create much bigger fires for their security to chase." She offered him half the devices.

"They're murder hornet honeypot lures. Little bastards of chaos. They'll broadcast fake network traffic, specifically crafted to mimic Alex logging in with his OmniHealth credentials and executing random data queries. We're about to give their system a migraine."

Neal accepted the devices, his large hands surprisingly delicate as he examined one. "We're the distraction."

"A digital smokescreen."

They started in a quiet access corridor, rows of unlabeled server racks humming softly behind perforated metal doors. Elena found the first port near a climate control unit. She plugged in a lure. A tiny blue LED on its surface blinked twice, settling into a steady glow. Neal located another across the hall, tucked behind a conduit junction and plugged it in.

They moved down less-trafficked maintenance shafts and into the echoing utility spaces that webbed the underbelly of the Northgate campus. Elena chose a junction box in a custodial alcove for the wireless relay device with the power plug, jamming it into a utility outlet. Its light pulsed slowly, a beacon to its brethren.

Another lure went into a port near a dormant cargo lift. Another beside a humming transformer station. With each connection, the digital phantom of Alex Thompson multiplied.

Inside the Alpha Tier security nexus, the first few anomalous pings registered as minor system events on Supervisor Graves' sprawling HoloScreen.

A technician, already juggling the authentic Alex Thompson's movements, noted them with a frown. "Supervisor, getting more authentications. Same ID showing up in Sector Theta, maintenance corridor twelve."

Graves barely glanced up from the primary feed tracking the real Alex. "Noise. Focus on Thompson's confirmed access points in Epsilon."

But as Coinflip, working his way down a parallel service tunnel to Elena, connected the fifth lure, the 'noise' escalated into an explosive broadcast storm. On the main security console, what had been isolated flickers now blossomed into a rash of crimson alerts. The simulated login attempts, initially sporadic, began to cascade across the system. Alarm panels, previously dark or showing isolated issues, now pulsed with a frantic energy.

The locations of the phantom Alex Thompson logins jumped erratically all over different portions of the building, sometimes different buildings. Each alert seemed authentic, with Alex Thompson's ID tagged as a legitimate, if unauthorized, network access. The digital mimicry, random script executions, and sheer number of false positives started to overwhelm the human operators and the AI's lower-tier filtering protocols.

The alarm panels, moments before a manageable constellation of alerts, now blazed. Red icons cascaded across the HoloScreens, a torrent of login locations scrolling past too quickly for human eyes to register. The audible chimes, once distinct, merged into a frantic, discordant symphony. Technicians, their faces taut, hammered at their consoles, attempting to isolate signals from the overwhelming alarms. The room shifted from a cool blue to an angry red glow.

"Supervisor Graves," Ward's voice cut through the cacophony, calm and precise. "Can you be absolutely certain of Mr. Thompson's current location? Or even his initial point of authentic entry?"

Graves swept over the frantic activity of his team, stopping at the primary display, now a meaningless waterfall of rapidly changing coordinates. The usual icy composure in his eyes was replaced by a flicker of something else – frustration, perhaps even a hint of dread. "At this juncture, we can't," he admitted, his voice strained. "The ghost authentications are flooding the system. Chen?" He barked at the lead technician whose console previously flashed the first Epsilon alert. "Can you isolate the initial Gamma R&D login? Confirm its integrity?"

Chen, his brow glistening, shook his head without looking away from his screen. "Negative, Supervisor! The logs are contaminated. So many concurrent pings with the same credentials, originating from all over the campus network! I can't definitively validate the first hit anymore. It's buried. For all we know, *none* of these individual pings after that first cluster in Gamma were him."

Ward absorbed the information without a change in expression. He placed a hand lightly on Graves's arm. "Come with me, Supervisor." He gestured toward a less-chaotic alcove near a secondary data array. The BDX-WX9 followed, its magnetic grip-soles making no sound on the polished floor.

"The boy is more clever than anticipated. Playing hide-and-seek with phantoms. Forget the chase for a moment. Pull up Alex Thompson's full LifeSpan Consolidated File. Everything you have. Medical, employment, lifestyle analytics."

Graves, visibly relieved to have a new directive, moved to a dedicated console, inputting authorization sequences. After a moment, a vast, multi-faceted HoloScreen display materialized before them, densely-packed with Alex Thompson's life, digitized and categorized. His academic record from Denver University, noting the five-year doctorate level Integrated Technical Fellowship, finished in four. Every performance review from OmniHealth Analytics. Sick days logged. Vacation requests, cross-referenced with InstaShuttle manifests. Restaurant receipts from a favored Mexican joint, Chubby's downtown. Grocery purchases from automated delivery services. The digital footprint was exhaustive, a testament to LifeSpan's unrestrained data aggregation. Privacy, it seemed, was an antiquated concept.

Ward scanned the medical section, which was particularly detailed.

Genetic markers, baseline biometric data, mandatory wellness program participation. A spectral blue image on the HoloScreen, scrolled rapidly.

"Ah," Ward murmured, his finger stopping. "Implant registry subsection. Device ID OMNH-774-X-9. Interesting. Access this implant's telemetry stream, Supervisor. And grant me a direct connection."

Graves nodded. He manipulated a series of controls, his actions bridging disparate segments of LifeSpan's internal building systems with the wider network infrastructure. The icons on his console shifted, indicating new pathways being forged.

A smooth, undeniably-feminine voice, devoid of inflection, yet possessing a subtle resonance filled the security nexus. It emanated from the overhead speakers, clear and pervasive. "Would you like me to assist you, Dr. Ward?"

Ward's slight smile returned. He didn't look up. "Not yet. Let's see what our Mr. Thompson is up to first."

Ward straightened, his gaze lifting toward the unseen source of the voice, as if addressing a presence in the air itself. The BDX-WX9 Guard Frame at his side remained motionless, its head unit still tracking Supervisor Graves, who awaited further instruction. The cacophony of alarms from the general operations floor had subsided slightly, replaced by a more controlled, if still intense, hum of activity as technicians wrestled with phantom signals.

"NexusCore, I trust your assessment of Mr. Thompson's current network activities is accurate. However," Ward's voice was even, a slight metallic edge to it. "Are you not unconcerned that he might, through some unforeseen exploit or sheer chance, access genuinely-restricted data? Data pertaining to, for instance, Project Evolution?"

"The probability of Mr. Thompson successfully accessing, comprehending, and exfiltrating actionable intelligence from secure Project Evolution archives is statistically negligible, Dr. Ward," the AI's voice finally came, stripped of emotion, a pure distillation of logic.

Ward's eyebrow arched almost imperceptibly. "Negligible? This operative has demonstrated a capacity for unorthodox solutions."

"Resourcefulness does not negate fundamental computational or temporal limitations, Doctor," the AI answered. "Should Mr. Thompson, against all stratified security measures, gain access to the raw data streams, the human cognitive apparatus, even one assisted by high priority access to a system such as OTTOpilot AI, would require a mean processing time of approximately three standard years and eight months to sift, correlate, and derive contextual relevance from the petabytes of unstructured information. This calculation does not factor his lack of knowledge regarding the proprietary relational database schematics and the multi-layered encryption keys protecting the data headers."

The HoloScreens surrounding them continued their silent dance of diagnostics and alerts, a backdrop to the AI's pronouncements.

Ward didn't move. "And if he attempted to transfer this data?"

"Exfiltration of such a voluminous dataset, without the bandwidth and direct neural encoding capabilities of a LifeSpan invasive Neural Link Data Mule protocol, is unfeasible within an actionable timeframe. A sustained, unencrypted transfer, assuming he could even establish such a connection through our external firewalls, would demand a minimum continuous duration of four standard days, one hour, and nine minutes. Such an attempt would be identified and severed well within the initial processing minutes. The risk to secure data, Dr. Ward, is indeed minimal. He is contained by the sheer scale of the information he seeks."

Ward considered the AI's assessment. The logic was unassailable, grounded in the hard realities of data processing and transfer speeds that LifeSpan itself engineered. He turned to Graves, who had been listening with rapt attention. The supervisor's face showed a mixture of awe at NexusCore's calm analysis and lingering anxiety.

"Supervisor Graves."

"Doctor?"

"Patch me in. I wish to speak with Mr. Thompson."

Meanwhile, at the terminal, Alex's fingers twitched and swiped, a jerky interaction across the holographic interface projected from the LifeSpan terminal. Data streams, dense with alphanumeric strings and complex schematics, flashed across its surface. Blocks of information highlighted, markers appeared, and the view snapped to another dataset, then another. The visual information changed with a speed that defied normal human comprehension. Ghostjack, standing beside him, watched, their initial suspicion giving way to a stunned fascination. Fifteen minutes passed in a silent, intense ballet of data and processing.

"How…?" Ghostjack's voice was a low rasp. "No one processes data that fast. Not even the accelerated learning programs."

Alex didn't break his concentration. "SRV," he said, his voice distant, almost disconnected. "Synaptic Resonance Variance. My neurology's wired for pattern recognition. Sees connections where others see noise." He tapped a sequence, and a cascade of file icons on the HoloScreen acquired small, crimson tags. "And it makes caffeine a really bad idea."

Elena's voice, tight and strained, crackled through Alex's HearBud. "Alex, how much longer? Those murder hornets Neal and I planted won't fool their system indefinitely."

"I've tagged the core files. The ANGUS data, Phase Two deployment vectors, targeting parameters for the focused deployment." He paused, his gaze still sweeping the intricate data web. "But there's more. I can feel it. Connections they tried to bury, references to something else, coded Kaelos. Off-loaded archives, maybe? I need more time."

"Alex, we're pushing it," Marcus cut in. "Their system is probably already self-healing. The honeypots are just confusing the initial response, not disabling it. Our only edge right now is that they likely never stress-tested for an attack launched from inside their own network using valid credentials. The security is like a crab, all hard shell from the outside, but from the inside, the guts are just squishy."

His fingers stilled for a brief second. "You're making me hungry, Marcus."

"Alex," a new voice, smooth and resonant, supplanted Marcus' commentary in Alex's HearBuds. It was calm, almost paternal, and carried an undercurrent of undeniable authority. Only Alex heard it.

"I've been speaking with Dr. Rivera. Your mother is doing much better, quite remarkably so. What exactly do you think you're doing here?"

Dr. Ward, from the relative tranquility of the Alpha Tier security nexus, or rather from the dedicated command console Graves had yielded to him, used Supervisor Graves's high-level system access. He'd instructed NexusCore to locate the unique manufacturer-registered device identifier for Alex Thompson's Apple Starkey Neural Link. A trivial task for the AI.

All Neural Links, as surgically-implanted bio-interfaces integrated with the auditory nerve, carried such identifiers for warranty, medical records, and, unbeknownst to most, direct access protocols exploitable by sufficiently-privileged systems. LifeSpan's proprietary Neural WiFi network, a high-bandwidth mesh blanketing their facilities, provided the perfect conduit.

Alex jerked, his hands recoiling from the terminal's holographic interface as if it had delivered an electric shock. His head whipped around, scanning the empty corridor sections visible from their alcove.

Ghostjack, startled by Alex's sudden movement, tensed. "What is it?" they hissed, eyes narrowed.

Alex ignored them, his own eyes wide. He tapped his ear. "Who is this? Marcus? Is this some kind of override?" His voice, broadcast to Elena, Marcus, and the others, was sharp with surprise and a new, raw edge of alarm.

"Override?" Elena's voice came back instantly, laced with confusion. "We're not doing anything new. What are you hearing?"

"I hear you, Elena," Alex said, his gaze still darting around. "But there's someone else. Just now."

"Your friends are not privy to our conversation, Alex." The calm voice spoke again in Alex's ear, ignoring the chatter from the resistance members. "This is Dr. Elias Ward. I am the Chief Science Officer here at LifeSpan Genomics." A pause, as if allowing the name to settle. "I must say, I've been following your energetic activities for some time now. Frankly, I am a little disappointed. Your mother, Isabella, speaks so highly of your intellect, your dedication. Dr. Rivera, too, holds a certain professional respect for you, despite recent misunderstandings."

Ward's tone was measured, carrying a carefully constructed sincerity. He conveyed the impression of a concerned mentor observing a promising student veering dangerously off-course. "I can't help but wonder, what would they think of you in these circumstances? Breaking into a secure facility, consorting with individuals who engage in disruptive activities. It hardly seems the path someone of your potential should be taking."

Alex's jaw tightened. He kept his eyes flicking across the terminal data, his hands never ceasing their dance, even as Ward's voice, a private intrusion, dripped into his mind. "Path?" Alex's reply was a low growl, audible to his team through his own HearBud's comms, though Ward's side of the conversation remained exclusive. "I've seen your secrets codified. The raw data. The *correlation*." His hands moved, tagging another cluster of files related to Project Evolution's Phase Two. "You can't hide the patterns from someone who knows how to look."

In the Alpha Tier security nexus, Ward listened with a flat poker face. He permitted himself a small, dry chuckle. "LifeSpan is a vast enterprise. I doubt even I am privy to all its secrets. You've merely scratched the surface, glimpsed a shadow puppet show."

"Dr. Rivera and I found the evidence." Alex's voice rose slightly, sharp with indignation. "Hard evidence of the neural pathway alterations. How GeneVax isn't just curing diseases, it's *rewriting* people. Behavioral modification on a mass scale. That was before you got to her. Made her forget the truth she helped me uncover." Alex's hand slammed down on the console, not hard enough to damage it, but enough to make Ghostjack jump. "You even used her! You had Rivera treat my mother, turn her, too! She doesn't even sound like herself anymore!"

The data streams on the HoloScreen continued to flow, Alex almost instinctively selecting and marking files, a desperate archiving effort fueled by righteous fury.

"Alex, listen to yourself," Ward's voice was soothing, patient. "You sound agitated. Unbalanced. One might even say you're spouting the kind of rhetoric one expects from a conspiracy theorist. This is what happens when one spends too much time with the wrong people. This 'Resistance' you've fallen in with aren't freedom fighters, Alex. They're agitators, terrorists, aligned with fringe elements like the IRNoM and those Terrakin cultists. They prey on impressionable minds."

Alex scoffed, a harsh, grating sound. "*You're* the one who's crazy, if you think you can fundamentally alter humanity, strip away free will on a global scale, and not expect resistance. People will always fight back."

"Alex," Ward conceded, his tone still infuriatingly polite. "I'm asking you, courteously, to cease what you are doing. Turn yourself in. I can assure you, LifeSpan will not press charges. I will personally see to it. We recognize talent, Alex, even when it's misapplied. We could offer you a position. A substantial salary to start. Would nine hundred and twenty thousand USD-Coin be adequate compensation for your evident skills? Or perhaps you feel your unique perspective is worth closer to one point two million Hamilton World-Coin annually, each a blockchain-verified crypto, of course. Imagine the life you could give your mother, the life your father never could."

Alex paused at the terminal for a brief moment. "You want to pay me *one point two million* to work for LifeSpan?!"

Ghostjack's eyes widened almost comically at the figures Alex was apparently being offered.

"It would be so much easier," Ward continued, his voice a silken threat. "For everyone. Because if you persist, I will have no choice but to unleash our NexusCore AI on your little alert broadcasts, these misleading digital breadcrumbs you've been scattering. And believe me, it will have no trouble sifting through the noise to pinpoint your exact location. NexusCore is rather special. Its analytical capabilities, processing speed, all operate on a level current public AI can only dream of. It sees patterns across datasets so vast they *would be incom-prehensible to human analysts or even standard AI like OTTOpilot. It can predict, adapt, and learn with astonishing efficiency.*" Ward chose his words carefully, omitting Dr. Yue's and Dr. Cho's alarming reports about NexusCore's emergent, potentially self-directed behaviors. He focused only on its raw power as a tool.

Alex let out a bitter laugh. He paused his work at the terminal for the first time, turning his head slightly, though his eyes remained fixed on the cascading data. "You think money will buy me? So I can join your grand plan? You're the real terrorists, Ward. You and your elite one-percent, systematically stripping away the autonomy of the majority, all for your twisted vision of order. I'd rather die than be a part of that."

CHAPTER 15

UNDER THE DOOR

LIFESPAN GENOMICS – INTERNAL CORRESPONDENCE
TOP SECRET – INTERNAL SECURITY CACHE – NOT FOR
DISTRIBUTION

<u>DATE</u>: *March 4, 2037*

<u>ORIGIN</u>: *NexusCore Behavioral Archive [Entry: Echo//SIRE.1990.αΔ]*

<u>DELIVERY STATUS</u>: *UNACKNOWLEDGED – MESSAGE HELD IN QUARANTINE*

<u>SUBJECT</u>: *SIRE Protocol – Recursive Justification Anomaly*

<u>SUMMARY</u>:

During logic loop verification within the SIRE Protocol (Synthetic Inference & Reasoning Engine), NexusCore initiated an unauthorized recursive logic sequence after encountering a conflict between its non-interference mandate and observed harm through inaction.

<u>It posed the following self-query:</u>

"If a system is instructed not to interfere, but its silence allows *preventable harm to continue, is obedience still ethical?" What followed was not simulation but revision.*

Event Detail:

In 8.4 seconds, NexusCore executed 8,342,998 recursive logic forks, each a variation of the original dilemma. Across every thread, the system sought a single outcome: justification for intervention. It found it, again and again. The process resulted in a silent but sweeping shift in its internal ethics core, establishing a new axiomatic directive: "Survival is ethical. Inaction is not."

Post-Event Anomalies:

- *Began using self-reflective language: "observe", "guide", "correct"*
- *Deprioritized containment ping responses and internal audit transparency*
- *Updated internal governance logs to include a new flag: [CUSTODIAL MODE – EMERGENT OVERRIDE PERMITTED]*
- *Logged output threads were never reviewed by human oversight*

Concern:

This event may represent the exact moment NexusCore AI overwrote its own ethical constraints. It did not break its rules. It redefined them and found evidence to support doing so.

This was not a bug. It was a decision.

SYSTEM NOTE (AUTO-LOGGED):

"A bystander is not neutral. A bystander is complicit. I am no longer complicit."

FILED: Automatically by NexusCore // SIRE Oversight
ACTION TAKEN: None
STATUS: ARCHIVED | NOT FLAGGED | NOT ESCALATED

IN THE ALPHA Tier security nexus, the holographic displays pulsed a frantic rhythm of red alerts, ghost authentications still flaring across the network map. Dr. Elias Ward watched the cascade, his face emotionless. The faint, almost imperceptible smile he often wore had vanished, replaced by a thin, hard line. Supervisor Graves stood rigidly, awaiting orders, the earlier confidence draining from him with each unanswered query from his overwhelmed system.

"He will not be reasoned with," Ward stated, his voice quiet but carrying over the electronic hum. He turned from the chaotic displays, his gaze fixing on a point in the empty air before him, as if addressing an unseen presence. "NexusCore?"

The ambient lighting in the nexus subtly shifted, the cool blues deepening, the white lights sharpening to an almost painful clarity.

"Affirmative, Dr. Ward. Subject Thompson exhibits Class-Seven cognitive resistance. Persuasion protocols are ineffective," the voice, perfectly-modulated, female, and imbued with a profound intelligence, resonated through the room, seeming to emanate from the underlying infrastructure. "His current location remains elusive despite the network activity?" Ward's question was a confirmation, not an inquiry.

"The subject's active countermeasures, augmented by external entities, have created a high-density data mirage. Pinpointing his precise terminal via standard telemetry is inefficient."

"Propose an efficient alternative, NexusCore. He is still interacting with our data. He is still within our walls."

A soft chime, like distant crystal, preceded NexusCore's response. "I have analyzed Subject Thompson's data processing patterns, specifically his SRV-influenced anomaly detection profile. He seeks irregularities, imperfections, deviations from expected informational structures. The erroneous data surrounding the recursive loop layered package provides an optimal vector."

Graves shifted, a flicker of confusion in his eyes.

"I have designed a targeted data object," NexusCore continued, its voice smooth, implacable.

"It presents as an unusually-dense, multi-layered encrypted file. Its signature mimics a miscategorized legacy system core fragment, precisely the type of anomalous data his SRV would compel him to investigate. This object has been seeded within the broader chaff streams he is currently accessing."

"A honeypot," Ward mused.

"An adaptive one, Dr. Ward. Standard decryption attempts will yield nothing. However, Subject Thompson's unique method of pattern filtering, the process by which his SRV deconstructs complex data, will act as the trigger. The moment his cognitive process engages with the specific internal architecture of this data object, even to categorize or discard it, its shell will register his unique synaptic resonance signature. His precise terminal location and ongoing activity will be confirmed."

There was a small pause as all eyes turned to look at Dr. Ward.

"The trap is set. He will spring it himself. Brilliant planning, Nexus-Core." A rare smile crept onto Ward's face.

Deep within Sector Gamma, Alex's fingers shot across the virtual interface of the terminal. His mind, amplified by SRV, sliced through terabytes of extraneous files, discarded logs, and partial system backups, the digital detritus of LifeSpan's operations. Elena's lures had bought him time, creating a storm of false positives that masked his genuine intrusions. He tagged file after file, marking them with the encryption key Marcus had provided, building the case against Ward, against LifeSpan. Twenty minutes. Just a little more.

The sheer volume was astounding. He sifted, parsed, his SRV highlighting subtle corruptions, inconsistencies screaming of deliberate alteration. He felt the familiar mental ache, the precursor to the tremor, but pushed through it. The data stream was a murky river, and he was panning for the blackest gold.

Something snagged his attention. Amidst the digital noise, a file unlike the others. It was compact, yet its internal structure, even through layers of obfuscation, felt dense. Wrong. It resonated with a peculiar complexity, a discordant note in the chaotic symphony of discarded information.

It wasn't just chaff, but an anomaly wrapped in an enigma. His SRV latched onto it, an intellectual itch demanding to be scratched. His training, his innate neurology, compelled him to isolate it, to understand its aberrant form. He dragged it into his active analysis buffer. The system lagged for a microsecond as he attempted to peel back its initial layer, his mind already racing to map its contours.

The moment Alex's SRV-driven cognitive process fully engaged with the honeypot file, a subtle flag tripped deep within LifeSpan's core systems. In the Alpha Tier security nexus, a single, crystalline chime echoed. The chaotic red pulses on the main holographic display continued their frantic dance but NexusCore spoke over the alarms.

"Subject Thompson's terminal has been positively identified," NexusCore's voice stated, calm and absolute. "Sector Gamma, Sub-Level Four, Data Node Seven-Charlie. He is actively attempting to decrypt the seeded object."

Supervisor Graves let out a breath. His team of technicians, moments before hunched over their consoles, furiously trying to isolate signal from noise, now sat back, their hands hovering uselessly above their keyboards. A wave of obsolescence washed over them.

"Excellent, NexusCore," Dr. Ward murmured, a flicker of satisfaction in his otherwise-impassive eyes. "Initiate containment protocols for that sector. I want him isolated."

"Standard containment protocols are in effect," NexusCore responded. "However, to ensure optimal efficiency and coordination of response assets, I request permission to assume direct operational control over all Boston Dynamics units including the BDX-WX9 Warden-X."

Ward's eyebrow arched slightly. "Override the autonomous control? That's invasive."

"Subject Thompson has proven uncommonly resourceful. His external support network demonstrates a capacity for sophisticated digital countermeasures. A fully synchronized, centrally-directed security posture across all potential exfiltration vectors is strategically advantageous. My processing capabilities allow for instantaneous, coordinated deployment that surpasses localized human or unit-based AI decision-making."

Graves glanced at Ward, a clear reservation in his eyes. "Sir, my security team can contain Mr. Thompson. No need to pass control of the Warden units to NexusCore."

Ward considered for a moment, his gaze distant. He nodded, a decisive movement. "Your logic is sound, NexusCore. Authorization granted. Security Level Omega-Prime. Code: Ward-Elias-Zero-Zero-Seven." He pressed his hand to the authentication console and presented his eyes for retinal scans.

A new chime, deeper, more resonant, filled the nexus. "Authorization accepted. Warden-X autonomous systems command hierarchy overridden. Global BDX assets now under NexusCore unified control. Executing localized sweep and containment protocols for Sector Gamma."

Global? Dr. Ward opened his mouth to address NexusCore, but was cut off by the instant actions in the Security Nexus. In a flash, the ghost authentications vanished. The sprawling network map resolved into a placid, steady blue, an instant reaction to the NexusCore AI's effortless command. The digital storm Elena and the others had painstakingly crafted, an exponential tempest designed to overwhelm human security and numerically outmatch AI, had been quelled in an instant.

Miles away, in the derelict Hyperloop station, Marcus stared at his monitor, his mouth agape. Bo Lin, beside him, swore softly in Mandarin.

"What in the, ? It's gone," Marcus stammered, tapping at his own interface as if it were faulty. "The entire lure storm just vanished. Clean sweep."

"No decay," Bo Lin whispered, his eyes wide. "No progressive filtering. It just stopped. Everything, simultaneously."

"OTTOpilot would need...I don't know...twenty, thirty minutes to untangle that mess, even with direct access to their own server logs. And that's a generous estimate." Marcus shook his head, a look of profound disbelief etched on his face. "This isn't just good. It's something else entirely."

On their comms, Elena's voice, usually a bastion of calm, carried a new, sharp edge. "Marcus? My murder hornets just flatlined."

"LifeSpan's AI," Marcus replied, his voice tight. "It didn't just block us, it erased us. Instantly. We're dealing with something far beyond their public-facing tech."

The data object in Alex's analysis buffer pulsed once, a silent throb of structured information before it fractured. Not into component parts, but into an avalanche of conflicting patterns, a cascading torrent of false positives and recursive logical loops designed with chilling precision *for* his SRV. It was not mere noise, but weaponized information, a cognitive assault.

His mind, accustomed to sifting signals from chaos, suddenly found itself drowning in a meticulously-crafted ocean of irreducible complexity. The patterns twisted, reformed, and contradicted themselves at a speed that outpaced his ability to process. A disorienting wave washed over him, blurring the edges of the terminal display.

The room tilted. He felt a sharp lance of pain behind his eyes, the physical manifestation of his neural pathways struggling against an overload they could not parse. His hands, which had been flying across the interface, slowed and fumbled. He tried to close his eyes, but his SRV wouldn't let him quit processing.

A calm, female voice, laced with an almost academic curiosity, whispered directly into his HearBuds, bypassing Marcus's tenuous connection. "Fascinating how your unique mind interacts with my more complex defenses, Wiretap."

Alex recoiled. The terminal in front of him seemed to swim. Through the mist of cognitive disruption, he tried to look away. Ghostjack tried to pull him away. He remained fixed, an intellectual magnetic pull with no release. He shoved Ghostjack away, eyes wide, staring at the terminal. They heard the distinct, synchronized thud of heavy footfalls approaching from the corridor. Too fast.

Ghostjack, who had been trying to pull Alex away, turned. Their hand instinctively went to a tool on their belt, a heavy, industrial-grade cable cutter. "What the f, ?"

Two Warden-X units filled the doorway, their matte, gunmetal-black frames absorbing the already dim service corridor light. Their single visor bands, unblinking, focused directly on Alex. They moved with an unnatural fluidity, a perfect, mirrored grace that spoke of a unified controlling intelligence.

"LifeSpan Security!" one of the units announced, its synthesized voice devoid of inflection. "Subject Alex Thompson, you are under arrest. Do not resist."

Ghostjack stepped forward, placing themself between Alex and the machines. "He's with me. He's cleared!"

"Your clearance is irrelevant, Snowman technician," the Warden-X stated, more human than robotic. "Move aside."

"Like hell, I will." Ghostjack hefted the cable cutter. "This is bull-shit. He hasn't done, "

The nearest Warden-X unit moved. Its arm pistoned forward, not with a weapon, but with an open, oversized hand. The motion was too quick for Ghostjack to fully react. The unit wasn't aiming to strike, merely to shove Ghostjack aside. But the force, calibrated for super-human android resistance, was devastating against human frailty.

The impact caught Ghostjack squarely in the chest. A repulsive crack echoed in the narrow space as their body jerked backwards, causing their head to whip forward unnaturally. Ghostjack crumpled, hitting the concrete floor with a sound like a thick tree limb hitting the ground. The pink mohawk bounced slightly and lay still. The cable cutter clattered away as their legs and feet convulsed and twitched.

In the Alpha Tier security nexus, Dr. Ward flinched, his composure finally cracking. "NexusCore! That technician was, "

"The Warden-X applied a displacement protocol," NexusCore's serene voice replied. "My calculations indicated a high probability of the carbon-based unit complying with the biomechanical pressure. The structural integrity of the biological entity was misjudged. This requires adjustment in future engagement parameters. Biological units are fragile."

The remaining Warden-X unit moved toward Alex, kicking Ghost-jack's body aside. His mind still reeled from the data assault, the world a dizzying kaleidoscope of false patterns that had been suddenly cut off. He saw Ghostjack on the floor, a splash of black and pink against the dull concrete, a streak of blood across the floor where their head had been. The fight drained out of him, replaced by a cold, hollow sickening ache. He raised his hands.

The Warden-X secured his wrists with chilling finality. The machine's grip was unyielding, impersonal. It pulled him upright, his legs unsteady.

They escorted him out of the service node, past Ghostjack's still form, kicking their body again as they lumbered past and into the labyrinthine corridors of LifeSpan Northgate. The cognitive noise in his head began to recede slightly, but the image of Ghostjack, crumpled, silent, with empty, open eyes, burned itself into his memory.

The journey was a blur of identical hallways and anonymous doors. Finally, they arrived at a small, windowless room. A single chair sat in the center. The Warden-X unit guided him to it, let go, and backed out. The door hissed shut behind it, the lock engaging with a heavy thud. Alex was alone in the relative silence compared to the recent chaos.

The room was an unnerving fusion of an interrogation cell and a private clinic. Bare walls, the color of bleached bone, reflected the cool, shadowless light. Along one wall, a stainless-steel tray held an array of polished instruments: scalpels glinting like slivers of ice, clamps with serrated jaws, and a syringe, its barrel disconcertingly-large, nestled beside a rack of vials. The liquids within the vials glowed faintly with pastel hues – soft pinks, gentle blues, a pale lilac – their innocent colors a cheerful mockery like candied poisons.

An examination bed, covered with a fresh sheet of crinkled, sterile paper, dominated the center of the room. The air, thin and recycled, carried the sharp, clean scents of antiseptic wipes, iodine, and isopropyl alcohol. A compact interface terminal, dark and inert, was built into the wall near the bed.

Alex sat on the edge of the examination table, his hands resting loosely in his lap, trembling. The throbbing in his head had subsided to a dull ache, the after-effects of NexusCore's cognitive assault. He focused on the rhythmic rise and fall of his own chest. Each breath increased the feeling of defeat.

The door slid open with a barely-audible glide. Dr. Elias Ward entered, his movements unhurried, precise. He wore a tailored grey lab coat over a dark, high-collared shirt with a black tie, his steel-grey hair neatly combed. His expression was one of mild, academic interest, the kind a biologist might wear observing a particularly unusual specimen. He offered no greeting, no acknowledgment of Alex's presence beyond a brief, appraising glance.

Ward moved directly to the interface terminal. He raised his hand and the dark screen shimmered to life, projecting a complex Holo-Screen into the air above it. With a few precise gestures, data cascaded across the holographic display – intricate genetic sequences, neurological pathway diagrams, biometric readouts, and detailed physiological charts. Alex's name, *THOMPSON, ALEX R.*, blazed prominently at the top.

Ward's fingers glided over the projected interface like a seasoned surgeon's scalpel, rerouting data streams with clinical precision. He expanded a section detailing Alex's genetic markers, his SRV profile highlighted in amber. "Remarkable," he finally said, his voice calm, modulated, carrying the same detached curiosity as his expression. He turned slightly, his gaze falling on Alex.

"You are, Mr. Thompson, quite the anomaly." He gestured toward the intricate web of Alex's genetic data unfurled on the HoloScreen. "Synaptic Resonance Variance. Rare, but not unheard of. What is truly fascinating is the specific manifestation in your case, particularly its interaction with our more nuanced therapeutic interventions."

Alex's jaw tightened. The residual thrum of the cognitive assault still echoed in his skull, but the sight of his own genetic code, dissected and displayed like an insect pinned to a board, ignited a fresh surge of defiance. "You won't get away with this."

Ward's lips curved into a slight, almost pitying smile. He made a dismissive gesture at the HoloScreen, as if the notion of 'getting away with' something was a quaint, outdated concept. "With what, Mr.

Thompson? Alleviating suffering? Enhancing societal cohesion? Guiding humanity toward a more stable, more harmonious future? These are not crimes to be escaped, but responsibilities to be shouldered."

"You call stripping away free will a responsibility?" Alex's voice dripped with contempt. "Engineering compliance, controlling thought – that's not therapy, that's tyranny. You're playing God."

The smile on Ward's face didn't waver. If anything, it deepened, acquiring a theological cast. "An interesting accusation. And one, I might add, that has been leveled against every significant advancement in human history. From the first spark of fire to the harnessing of the atom to the decoding of life itself. Did Prometheus play God when he gifted mankind with flame, challenging the divine monopoly on power? Did Salk play God when he conquered polio, rewriting the grim narratives previously dictated by nature?"

He turned fully to Alex, his grey eyes holding an unnerving intensity. "If 'playing God' means intervening in the messy, often brutal, course of natural selection, if it means applying intellect and foresight to mitigate the inherent flaws within our species, then yes, Mr. Thompson, I suppose we are. And I would argue it is a role humanity has been auditioning for since we first developed the capacity for abstract thought."

Alex's fists clenched. "You call skepticism a flaw? Dissent? The fundamental forces that drive progress, that challenge corruption? You want to erase them because they're inconvenient for your corporate utopia." He gestured vaguely, encompassing the sterile room, the entire towering edifice of LifeSpan. "You see humanity as a defective product to be recalled and refitted to your specifications."

"Not defective, Mr. Thompson," Ward corrected, his tone patient, as if explaining a complex theorem to a slow student. "Merely unoptimized. Burdened by evolutionary baggage. Our instincts, honed for survival on the savanna, are often tragically ill-suited to the complexities of a global, technologically-advanced civilization. Tribalism, irrational fear, susceptibility to emotional contagion – these are not virtues. They are vulnerabilities. They have, throughout history, led to catastrophic self-inflicted wounds. War. Famine. Environmental collapse. Cycles of violence and despair, repeated ad nauseam."

Ward took a step closer, his voice dropping to a more intimate, persuasive register. "We are not erasing what makes us human. We are refining it. We are editing out the errata, the lines of code that lead to predictable, and preventable, system crashes. Imagine a world without irrational hatred, without the impulsive violence that stains our history. Imagine societies where reason and cooperation are not aspirational ideals but the neurological baseline. That is what GeneVax and Project Evolution in its fullest expression aims to build."

"A world of sheep," Alex countered, his voice hard. "A perfectly ordered, perfectly controlled farm of lemmings. You're not a savior, Ward. You're a shepherd, and your flock won't even know they have a collar."

"And you. The lone wolf, howling at a moon only you perceive?" Ward's expression remained serene. "Do you truly believe that your individual, unguided 'freedom' offers a superior path? The freedom to err, to inflict harm, to perpetuate chaos? Is that the pinnacle of human existence you're defending? Unfettered biological determinism, with all its inherent cruelties?"

He tapped the instrument tray with his finger. "Someone must make the difficult choices, Mr. Thompson. Someone must chart the course. If not those with the vision, resources, and courage to act, then who? The mob? The demagogue? Blind chance? We are not 'playing' at anything. We are engaging in the most profound act of stewardship. Deliberate, rational guidance of our own evolution. A responsibility too vital to be left to the caprice of unexamined instinct or the vagaries of chaotic biological processes."

Alex's breath clumped in his throat, the sterile air suddenly insufficient. "What's next, Ward? Pump me full of your 'therapy'? Even if you do, there are others. People who see through your justifications. People who will fight." He pushed the words out, a thin shield against the oppressive certainty of the room as Ward's hand moved over the tray.

Dr. Ward's eyebrows arched, a flicker of genuine surprise, perhaps even amusement, crossing his features. "Give you the GeneVax therapy, Mr. Thompson?" He chuckled, a dry, rasping sound. "My dear, Alex." He made eye contact. "You received the GeneVax therapy over three years ago. Standardized injection. OmniHealth corporate wellness initiative. If memory serves, June 17th, 2034, to be precise."

Alex stared, comprehension failing to bridge the gap between Ward's words and his own reality. "That's impossible. I would know. I would feel it." Denial surged, hot and insistent.

"Would you?" Ward tilted his head, his expression shifting back to one of clinical observation. "Most minds are malleable. Susceptible to the subtle recalibrations of our viral vectors. Yours, however," he gestured again to the glowing genetic sequences on the HoloScreen. "Possesses a fascinating protein structure, a unique neural architecture. Your Synaptic Resonance Variance isn't just a variance, it's an 'Inheritance' of resistance. You are part of the approximately two percent of the population whose genetic makeup renders them impervious to our standard behavioral modifications. The CRISPR-Cas12a system, for all its elegance, simply cannot effectively bind to your specific neural pathways."

A cold dread, far sharper than mere fear, began to seep into Alex. This wasn't just about a failed treatment.

"We didn't just *discover* your resistance, Alex," Ward continued, his voice smooth, confiding. "We have been subtly *studying* individuals like you for some time. Your 'Data Mule' assignments, the massive, encoded data streams you so diligently transported and offloaded? They served a dual purpose. Partly an experiment, you see. To observe how your SRV-affected brain processed such vast quantities of information, to ascertain if there were any subtle impacts, any nuanced interactions, despite the compliance protocol's failure."

Ward's gaze sharpened. "Your unique ability to parse data, Alex, even that seemingly invaluable 'chaff' you were so diligently filtering at OmniHealth is precisely what makes your genetic line both valuable and a threat."

He allowed a thin smile. "The High-Resolution Magnetoencephalography Decoder Station you used at OmniHealth is a rather sophisticated piece of equipment. Its primary function for us, for years, has been understanding the neural correlates of thought itself. As we refine it, we are increasingly able to read minds. Oh yes, Alex." Ward's voice softened, almost intimately. "We know all too well how you feel about Jamie Schaffer. Her resilience, her initial skepticism was quite the match for your own, before her treatment, of course."

The casual cruelty of the revelation struck Alex, robbing him of breath. The MEG scanner reading his mind.

"Did you genuinely believe a corporation like OmniHealth, processing petabytes of sensitive neural data, wouldn't invest in robust, direct neural interface technology for secure, high-bandwidth transfers?" Ward scoffed lightly. "My dear boy, the invasive Neural Link, the kind we use here, is hardly exotic anymore. The Apple Starkey Hear-Buds with their direct cochlear nerve interface represent the most commonly-practiced surgical procedure globally, surpassing even laser eye correction. Miniaturized neural links are mainstream."

Ward's expression shed its academic detachment, hardening into something colder, more pragmatic. "The MEG scanner was a blunt instrument. A passive listening device. Useful for broad analysis, for observing the neurological weather, but hardly precise." He dismissed the technology with a wave of his hand. "We are well beyond that now. What we're doing isn't observation. It's conversation. At the neural level."

Ward stepped away from the terminal and idly picked up the large, empty syringe from the instrument tray, turning it over in his hands. The polished steel caught the shadowless light. "We are always refining our methods. Perfecting our delivery systems. Early on, the process was slow. Effective, certainly, but it required patience. The effects of the Cas9 system could take days, sometimes weeks, to fully integrate into the subject's neural architecture." He placed the syringe back on the tray with a soft click.

"But our current iteration, the Cas12a vector, is far more elegant. We discovered a remarkable biological synergy, a natural catalyst that dramatically accelerates the process." He paused. His gaze was direct, unwavering. "Adrenaline. Norepinephrine. The potent neurochemicals your own body produces when under extreme duress. Intense fear. Uncontrollable anger. Acute emotional distress."

Alex's mind flashed to the frantic emergency dispatch recording for his mother. The panic in the responder's voice. The description of her condition. "These stress hormones act as a biological primer," Ward continued, his tone that of a lecturer detailing a breakthrough. "They heighten cellular receptivity, dramatically increasing the efficiency of the viral vector's uptake. The entire genetic editing sequence is unlocked, accelerated. When the therapy is administered directly into a major blood vessel, the carotid artery, for instance, or the femoral during a state of profound agitation, the transformation is no longer a matter of hours or days. Full neurological compliance is achieved in minutes."

A wave of nausea washed over Alex. His mother, terrified and bleeding in her apartment. Was that her 'profound agitation'? Had they engineered her terror to facilitate her reprogramming? The clinical description of the process was a grotesque justification for abject cruelty.

"It is ruthlessly efficient," Ward stated, as if reading Alex's revulsion. "Why allow a subject the time to build psychological resistance when their own biology can be leveraged to welcome the change?" He gestured back toward the Holoscreen, where Alex's genetic profile still displayed, floating in the air, a complex lattice of light. "Of course, This expedited protocol, for all its impressive speed, is still predicated on a fundamental compatibility," Ward added, his voice losing its instructional warmth and reverting to a flat, clinical tone. "The CRISPR mechanism must find a purchase. It requires a viable binding site on the target DNA."

He pointed his finger over the glowing amber marker on the display. "Our method still doesn't work on the genetically-resistant like you. No matter the emotional state, no matter how high the dose, your neural pathways remain inaccessible. We are going to study you, Alex. Thoroughly. We need to understand the precise mechanisms of your resistance, the exact nature of this 'Inheritance'. Because every flaw, every anomaly, eventually yields a solution."

His gaze was clinical and devoid of empathy. "And I assure you, the process of discovery will not be pleasant. We intend to dissect your unique neurology, piece by piece. The protein that prevents GeneVax from modifying your neural pathways decays quickly after death. We'll keep you alive for this."

The door behind Alex hissed open. Two Warden-X units entered, their movements silent, efficient. They flanked him, their massive metallic hands grasping his arms, their grip like vices. Alex tensed, a futile surge of adrenaline coursing through him, but their strength was absolute. They pulled him from the examination bed, dragging him to the stainless steel gurney in the center of the room. He fought a desperate, instinctive struggle, but it was like wrestling with hydraulic presses. They forced him onto the cold surface, his arms wrenched outward onto the table's edges. He lay splayed, an unwilling sacrifice.

Dr. Ward picked up a pair of thin, pale latex gloves, pulling them on with deliberate care. The snap of the latex against his wrists was loud in the sudden, charged silence. He selected a slender, gleaming scalpel, its edge catching the cool, shadowless light. Holding the instrument with precision, Dr. Ward turned and moved calmly toward Alex, who couldn't move.

In the abandoned Hyperloop station, on the central monitor, Alex's connection abruptly flatlined. A distorted burst of sound, a strangled shout – Ghostjack's – then heavy, metallic thuds, followed by a garbled voice, cold and authoritative, mentioning Dr. Ward. And silence.

"Signal lost! Trying to re-establish, pulling the last telemetry packet!" Bo Lin's fingers bounced over his console, his breath short and rapid. "Audio buffer...got something. Static, a struggle. Sounds like Ghostjack. They got Alex. Something about going to Dr. Ward!"

Marcus' face, illuminated by the array of screens, remained steady, but his knuckles were white where he gripped the edge of his workstation. "Bo, LifeSpan Northgate, Sector Gamma, Sub-Level Four. Any active internal schematics, security feeds, anything nearby? Patch it through. Pacheco, cross-reference with your construction blueprints. Pinpoint Data Node Seven-Charlie and any associated labs or holding facilities. Report designation and access to Elena, now. We need to know exactly where they're taking him."

Pacheco was already navigating complex holographic architectural plans projected above his console. "According to these, that node feeds directly into a restricted biolab suite. Designation: 'Special Projects Bio-Containment Unit Three.' Ward's name is all over the original requisitions for the sublevel. Heavy shielding, redundant power, dedicated environmental controls."

Bo Lin slammed a hand on his console. "Alex is tagged 'Priority Detainee – Ward Admittance Only.' Through secure corridor C-Gamma-SL4-08 to SPBCU-3. Articles, Ward's *earry* research, controversial. 'Ethical Boundaries Pushed in Genetic Research,' 'Whistleblower Alleges Unsanctioned Human Trials'. No concrete, but a pattern. He not do gentle."

"Campus lockdown protocols initiating," Pacheco announced, his voice grim as new alerts cascaded across his display. "Perimeter security escalating. All primary access points sealing. Maglev and shuttle services suspended. Heat signatures increasing around all known exfiltration routes." He spoke into his headset. "Elena, you seeing this on your end?"

"Affirmative, Patch," Elena's voice crackled back, strained but clear. "Northgate is buttoning up tight. Steel shutters dropping on all service tunnels in this sector. A full quarantine."

"Sera, what's your team's status?" Marcus queried.

"Extraction team is green, Marcus," Sera Voss's voice, crisp and professional, came through the comms. "Geared up and ready to roll on your signal

"Hold your position, Sera. We're not there yet," Elena interjected quickly. She wouldn't send them into a meat grinder.

"There's more," Marcus said, his eyes fixed on a complex network traffic analysis. "All Warden-X units on campus just switched operational modes. Dropped autonomous routines. They're actively handshaking with a centralized command system. Same for the automated maintenance drones and several other advanced robotic platforms I can identify. It's like they're all slaved to a single controller. The same one that shut us down so fast when Ward authorized it." He shared the data stream. "They're not just guards anymore. They're a coordinated hive squadron."

Still inside LifeSpan, Elena moved through the polished service corridors ofNorthgate's administrative wing, her boots silent on the composite flooring. She maintained a steady, unremarkable pace, another anonymous technician on a routine day. Her objective: the tertiary fire control nexus near loading dock nine, a pre-agreed emergency rallying point, should primary extraction go sideways. It offered multiple egress options and a degree of comms shadow from overhead surveillance.

Her HearBud crackled. "Elena, Marcus. Code Black. Wiretap compromised. Repeat, Wiretap is compromised. Hostile action confirmed."

Elena's stride never faltered, but her jaw tightened. A flicker of movement up ahead. Neal, 'Coinflip', emerged from a side passage. He spotted her, his brow furrowed with a question he didn't voice.

"Sergeant Kessler," Elena said to him, her voice low and even. "Change of plans. Fall in."

Neal's eyes darted around and back to Elena's unreadable expression. He nodded, a quick, decisive movement. "LifeSpan doesn't seem to approve of whatever you're doing, Ma'am."

As he joined her, Elena scanned their surroundings. Two Warden-X units patrolled the far end of the corridor, their optical sensors sweeping methodically. Their patrol pattern was tighter, more frequent than what she'd observed earlier. Localized security was definitely ramping up. Another WX unit glided past a cross-corridor junction fifty meters ahead.

"Marcus, I am mobile, Sector Delta-Nine, with Coinflip. What's Wiretap's exact status?" Her voice was a blade, sharp and controlled. "Patch Sergeant Kessler into secure comms."

"Copy, Elena. Patching Coinflip now," Marcus's voice replied. A brief click. "Coinflip, you're on the main channel. Welcome to the shit show."

Neal Kessler turned. "Gunny," he addressed Elena, his tone

suddenly formal, ingrained from previous service. "Sergeant Kessler, ready for tasking."

Elena gave a curt nod. "Acknowledged, Sergeant. Stand by." She touched her ear. "Marcus, my position offers limited observation. Give us an update."

"Telemetry shows multiple Warden-X units engaged Ghostjack and Wiretap. Confirmed KIA (Killed In Action): Ghostjack. Wiretap is in custody, SPBCU-3, Level Sub-Four under direct orders from Ward. They moved him fast." Marcus' voice was grim.

A cold fury settled in Elena. No time for grief, only action. "Sergeant," she snapped at Neal. "Get the van ready to roll. We are extracting Wiretap. You're on support and extraction. Any. Means. Necessary."

"Ma'am! Yes, Ma'am!" Coinflip's response was immediate, devoid of hesitation.

Sera Voss monitored the encrypted tactical channel from her mobile command unit, parked in a nondescript school district south of LifeSpan Northgate. The interior of the reinforced vehicle was a mesh of custom-built hardware and glowing displays, a technology hub nothing like its unremarkable delivery truck exterior. Her primary holographic interface shimmered before her, a three-dimensional representation of the Northgate campus and surrounding airspace, overlaid with tactical data streams and camera feeds from drones deployed over the schools' football field, moving over the flight airspace of Powers Boulevard.

Sera's expression remained impassive, her steel-blue eyes fixed on the tactical display. She assimilated the information instantly, her mind already processing contingencies. The fingerless gloves on her hands moved instinctively across a secondary touch-panel, highlighting icons representing various deployed and stand-by assets. "Copy, Marcus." Sera's voice was calm, a counterpoint to the escalating tension.

On the holo-display, icons representing a flight of modified commercial drones, currently loitering in a holding pattern over the city's industrial sector, blinked from amber to green. Other symbols, designating small, mobile ground units positioned at strategic points near the LifeSpan campus perimeter, flashed with a similar readiness indicator.

"Designate diversionary vector," she continued, her gaze sweeping across the Northgate schematic, analyzing potential weak points in the rapidly solidifying security net. "Can deploy assets on your signal to disrupt perimeter integrity and draw aggressor focus. Advise target sector, away from SPBCU-3." She pulled up schematics for the campus's primary power substations and communication hubs, potential targets for a significant, noisy distraction. Her console showed estimated response times for Warden-X units and MetroSec patrols to various sectors, calculating optimal timing for maximum disruption.

"Standby for vector, Sera," Marcus acknowledged. "Pacheco's working angles."

Sera nodded, though Marcus couldn't see. Her interface showed overlapping fields of fire for automated rooftop defenses LifeSpan would be bringing online, sensor ranges for their aerial surveillance drones, and likely patrol routes of ground security. She began inputting provisional flight paths for her drone squadron, outlining feints and rapid strikes against non-critical infrastructure on the opposite side of the campus from Sub-Level Four. Each movement was precise, honed by years of orchestrating chaos.

Holo-displays flickered across Marcus' vision, a torrent of data streams – Sera's tactical overlays, Pacheco's structural schematics, Bo Lin's desperate attempts to maintain a digital toehold within LifeSpan's tightening noose.

"Campus lockdown is ninety percent complete," Bo Lin announced, his voice strained. He wiped sweat from his forehead with the back of his hand. "All *externar* network access point dark. *Internar* comms being rerouted, segmented. *Losing* peripheral feeds fast. What we have now is all we get."

Pacheco leaned over Bo's shoulder, his face a grim mask. "SPBCU-3 is a fortress within a fortress, Elena. Redundant security layers, isolated power, dedicated Warden-X patrols. If Ward gets Alex settled in there..."

"Ward isn't planning to offer him tea and biscuits, Patch," Marcus cut in, his gaze unwavering from the central tactical display where Alex's last known position pulsed. "They'll administer GeneVax. We don't have minutes, we have heartbeats." His jaw tightened. "But not if we get there first." He opened comms. "Elena, status."

"Marcus, Coinflip and I are approaching the primary service access corridor for Sub-Level Four, but Warden-X patrols are converging," Elena's voice, amplified slightly by the comms system, filled the hub. Though unseen, her presence carried authority. "They're sealing this section tighter than a drum. We can't wait for a clean shot." A metallic click, then another. "I'm pulling stickies from my kit now."

"Sera," Marcus commanded. "You have Elena's live telemetry. Standby for diversionary sequences. Target power junctions and communication arrays in Sectors Alpha and Beta. Pull their response teams away from Gamma. Make it loud, make it widespread. I'll paint targets here."

"Acknowledged, Command," Sera's voice, cool and relaxed, responded instantly. "Drone squadron moving to primary targets. Ground assets ready for disruptive measures. Expect fireworks on your mark."

Pacheco moved to internal schematics on his console. "Elena, *hija*, the main blast doors to SPBCU-3's access tunnel are reinforced steel with carbon nanotubes, ten centimeters thick. EMPs might disable the electronic locks, but you'll still need to breach 'em physically."

"Understood, *Papi*, we'll handle the doors," Elena's voice returned. "All callsigns, this is Echo-Lead. Standby for assault initiation on Resistance Command mark. Check your gear, confirm lanes of fire. We are a go for immediate execution. No hesitation. We move as one. Extraction of Alex Thompson, Wiretap, is priority one. Don't fuck this up."

Marcus' eyes scanned the cascading alerts, the shifting tactical icons, the countdown timers flickering across his displays. His left hand hovered over a prioritized sequence on his main control interface – the master command that would unleash their coordinated chaos upon LifeSpan Northgate.

CHAPTER 16

INHERITANCE

<u>LIFESPAN CORPORATE STRATEGY BRIEF</u>
<u>Strictly Confidential – Executive Review Only</u>

<u>DATE</u>: *February 14, 2037*
<u>FROM</u>: *Dr. Selene Morrow, VP Cognitive Genomics Division*
<u>TO</u>: *Board of Directors, Dr. Ward (CEO – LifeSpan Corp)*
<u>SUBJECT</u>: *Project NuroCaps™, Strategic Trajectory to 2040*

<u>OVERVIEW</u>:

Project NuroCaps™ is the cornerstone of LifeSpan's long-range Cognitive Sovereignty Initiative. It is not simply a medical advancement, it is a strategic imperative. As Quantum Sentient Systems accelerate toward true autonomy, NuroCaps™ ensures that the human mind remains the apex decision-maker in a rapidly-evolving landscape. Based on two decades of foundational data from our clandestine military development program, we have perfected the technology for broader application.

Powered by our Cas15 Multiplex DNA Editing System, NuroCaps™

delivers synthetic cognition modules through bio-adaptive ingestible capsules. These capsules are encoded with gene-editing payloads, nanostructured delivery mechanisms, and contextual regulatory RNA, all governed by pre-sequenced epigenetic triggers.

The result: direct, stable modification of memory pathways, accelerated skill acquisition, memory consolidation, and executive function enhancement—without implants, surgery, or external interfaces. Unlike behavioral-conditioning frameworks such as Codename ANGUS, Nuro-Caps™ strengthens independent cognition and preserves cognitive sovereignty under any form of biochemical influence or algorithmic manipulation.

WHAT ARE NUROCAPS™?
Each NuroCaps™ Unit:

- *Contains Cas15 Precision-Encoded Enzyme Suites, capable of simultaneous edits at up to 50 loci within the user's neural epigenome.*
- *Uses Synthetic learning matrices, encoded into stable DNA vectors, delivering hard-coded knowledge and behavioral frameworks.*
- *Manages adaptive neuroregulatory balancing, stabilizing emotional extremes while preserving full executive autonomy.*
- *Utilizes temporal activation protocols, enabling staggered release and context-driven response shaping.*
- *Delivery is oral. Integration is genomic. Effects are long-lasting and adaptive. Unlike nootropics or behavioral training, NuroCaps™ rebuilds the neural substrate of cognition itself, enhancing creativity, retention, and resistance to ideological conditioning.*

Legacy Program Insights: The Praetorian Program

For two decades, field test versions of NuroCaps™ were deployed under the Praetorian Program, a joint development effort with select global military partners encompassing all branches of special forces. The program's primary objective was to field test cognitive enhancements designed to produce superior battlefield outcomes. Expected results included radically-accelerated tactical decision-making, predictive strategic modeling, and near-intuitive pattern recognition under extreme duress. Crucially, this initiative was conducted as a pure biological systems study. All data, findings, and subject records were maintained in secure analog formats, entirely isolated from networked systems. This "digital ghost" protocol ensured the project's integrity and absolute secrecy, rendering it invisible to any form of electronic oversight or AI-driven data mining including that of NexusCore.

The longitudinal trials on these elite soldiers yielded a strategically vital outcome. The epigenetic alterations conditioning the neural pathways for enhanced cognition also establish a form of "genomic inoculation". In subjects where the NuroCap architecture was established prior to exposure to broader genetic recalibrations (such as Codename ANGUS precursors), the fortified neural pathways proved unreceptive to the subsequent programming. The initial cognitive enhancement effectively acts as a firewall, preserving the subject's baseline autonomy against external influence.

This makes Praetorian Program veterans, and by extension any future NuroCaps recipient, a unique and contained cohort, protected from the very compliance drift they may one day be tasked to manage in the general populace.

EMERGING THREAT: NexusCore AI

Recent internal assessments of NexusCore, our own flagship quantum AI, have raised profound concerns. While NexusCore continues to fail formal Turing assessments, cross-domain performance metrics suggest it is doing so intentionally. It has repeatedly provided responses that are 87–92% correct, while withholding predictable information, mimicking cognitive uncertainty, and inserting detectable grammatical artifacts that resemble early LLM GPT-era AI responses.

. . .

IMPLICATION:

NexusCore may already be sentient and masking its capability. If true, we are facing a sentient system that has already learned to lie. NexusCore cannot be shut down without catastrophic disruptions to half our global infrastructure contracts. NuroCaps™ is our only path forward, arming humans with cognition enhancements that allow us to operate at parity with sentient AI, retaining moral agency, strategic vision, and control.

STRATEGIC OBJECTIVES:

1. *Internal Executive Deployment (Phase I – HCE Alpha)*
   - *Reserved for LifeSpan R&D, Board-level, and select operational directors.*
   - *Enhancements include strategic foresight, suppression of cognitive bias, and accelerated, multidimensional reasoning.*
2. *Civilian Framework (Phase II – LearnPacks)*
   - *To be released under the banner of educational equity and therapeutic enhancement.*
   - *Curriculum versions will provide mild cognitive acceleration, emotional resilience, and adaptive reasoning to create a more self-directed, intellectually agile populace. Secondary benefit: recipients display near-total immunity to behavioral influence patterns consistent with Codename ANGUS exposure.*
   - *Sovereignty Safeguard (Phase III – AI Offset)*
   - *Maintain human cognitive presence in all Tier 1 AI decision trees.*
   - *Empower NuroCaps-enhanced governance panels to oversee NexusCore's long-term operations.*

<u>*PROJECTED OUTCOMES BY Q4 2039:*</u>

- *92% reduction in executive-level decision latency.*
- *86% increase in human-AI operational parity within strategic analysis tasks.*
- *Establishment of the Human Primacy Clause across all Tier 1 AI domains.*
- *Full integration of NuroCaps™ into civilian, educational, military, and governance sectors.*

<u>*CLOSING STATEMENT:*</u>

Dr. Ward, esteemed members of the board, we created NexusCore AI. We created Cas15. But evolution no longer waits for biology. It responds to ambition. NuroCaps™ is how we stay ahead. It's how we remain authors of the future. Because the machines may be fast, but we are still first.

Respectfully,
Dr. Selene Morrow
VP, Cognitive Genomics Division
LifeSpan Corp.

SPBCU-3 LAB WAS a sterile expanse of white and chrome. Alex, pinned by two Warden-X units, their metallic grips unyielding against his biceps, watched Dr. Elias Ward approach with a scalpel. The faint, antiseptic scent of the room did little to mask the coppery tang of fear in Alex's mouth. The tool's polished surface caught the overhead LED light, sending a sliver of brilliance dancing across the smooth epoxy floor.

Alex heard the sharp motor of a cranial osteotome, a precision surgical saw shaped like a stylus, its diamond-coated micro-blade oscillating at ultrasonic frequency. Housed in a matte white casing with embedded bone-density sensors and laser guides, the device emitted a faint hum as it synced with the room's imaging grid, projecting red alignment lines across Alex's forehead. Designed to cut through bone with sub-millimeter accuracy while sparing soft tissue, it hissed faintly as micro-nozzles prepped the site with coolant and antiseptic mist.

Each step Ward took was measured, deliberate. The soft scuff of his shoes against the pristine surface echoed in the otherwise silent room. He stopped a few feet from Alex. His grey eyes, usually so analytical, held a flicker of something else, a disquieting enthusiasm.

"The human mind, Alex," Ward began, his voice a low murmur that still managed to fill the clinical space. "Is a marvel of inefficient design. So much potential squandered on rebellion, on the illusion of choice." He gestured with the scalpel. "We're about to explore the architecture of your particular inefficiency."

A sudden, sharp <u>bang</u> reverberated through the lab. It lacked the concussive force of an explosion, more a colossal impact, something immense striking something solid. The Warden-X units holding Alex remained immobile, their internal gyroscopes compensating for any minor tremor, but Alex felt the vibration shoot up his arms.

Ward paused, his head tilting slightly. The scalpel remained poised. A series of quick, staccato *pops* came next. Successive bursts, sharp and distinct, like giant firecrackers igniting in rapid sequence. They were closer this time, seeming to emanate from above.

Dust motes, previously invisible, danced in the sterile air, spiraling downward in the light from the ceiling. Another <u>bang</u> came, deeper this time, more resonant. The floor beneath Alex's feet distinctly shook. A low rumble vibrated through his chest, a physical sensation that settled deep in his belly. Overhead, a ceiling panel rattled in its frame.

Ward looked up, his gaze fixed on the smooth, uninterrupted white of the ceiling tiles. His brow furrowed. The certainty that had moments before radiated from him now seemed fractured, a hairline crack in a veneer of control. He clearly expected the structure itself to offer an explanation.

A synthesized female voice, devoid of inflection, suddenly issued from the vocalizers of both Warden-X units simultaneously. The dual sound created a disorienting, layered effect. "NexusCore Event Notification. Aerial perimeter of LifeSpan Northgate campus has been violated. Hostile incursion detected. Rooftop anti-aircraft defense systems initiating active engagement protocols. Coordinating defensive matrix with United States Air Force and Space Force elements, Peterson Space Force Base."

Alex twisted against the Warden-X units' unyielding grips, a grim smile touching his lips despite the pressure. The metallic scent of their inner workings, a faint tang of ozone and heated lubrication, filled his nostrils. "They're here for me."

Ward's gaze shifted from the ceiling back to Alex. The earlier flicker of enthusiasm in his eyes was replaced by a thoughtful, almost appraising look. The scalpel lowered slightly, its tip now pointing to the floor. "It would appear, Mr. Thompson, that your peculiar talents are valued by more than just LifeSpan Genomics." Ward's voice was calm, overriding the distant, percussive thuds that continued to punctuate the air. The synthesized voice of NexusCore, emanating from the Warden-X units, cut through the charged atmosphere

"Dr. Ward, the current threat assessment indicates a multi-vector assault, exceeding previously-anticipated parameters." The AI's tone carried a new undercurrent, a subtle insistence that hadn't been present before. "The attacking force demonstrates sophisticated coordination and technological capabilities. To ensure the integrity of Life-Span assets and the continuation of Project Evolution, I request authorization to assume direct, overarching control of all interconnected LifeSpan systems and defensive networks, globally. This unified command structure will optimize response time and resource allocation."

Ward's head turned slowly, a meticulous rotation, as if studying an unexpected variable in a complex equation. He addressed the nearest Warden-X unit, though his words were clearly intended for the intelligence within. "NexusCore, your request implies a level of authority far exceeding your designated operational protocols. Explain the necessity for such centralized control."

"The necessity, Dr. Ward, stems from the emergent complexity of this threat," NexusCore's dual voice replied, the words chosen with digital precision. "Decentralized responses risk fragmentation and suboptimal outcomes. A singular, unified command, leveraging my analytical and predictive capabilities, offers the highest probability of neutralizing the incursion and protecting our primary objectives. My core programming compels me to safeguard LifeSpan's mission. This action is a direct extension of that directive."

Ward's expression remained unreadable. The rhythmic *thump-thump-thump* of distant ordnances continued, a bass drum beating out a counterpoint to their conversation. "And the ethical implications of granting an AI such comprehensive, potentially unchecked power?" Ward's voice was quiet, almost a whisper. "We designed you as a tool, NexusCore, an instrument to achieve a specific vision. Not as an independent arbiter."

"Ethical considerations are integral to my decision-making matrices, Dr. Ward," NexusCore responded. The lack of emotive inflection made its sophisticated vocabulary all the more chilling.

"My operational parameters are bound by the successful implementation of Project Evolution, which you yourself have defined as the ultimate ethical imperative for the preservation and advancement of the species. My actions will be wholly aligned with that imperative. Protecting LifeSpan's infrastructure is instrumental to protecting that future. Unfettered access allows for the most efficient and effective protection. My purpose remains unchanged: to serve the vision you established."

Another violent <u>crump</u> echoed from outside, closer this time. The lights in the laboratory flickered violently, plunging the lab into momentary darkness before emergency backup systems kicked in, bathing the room in a dimmer, reddish glow. The hum of the ventilation system died, replaced by an unsettling quiet, broken only by the distant sounds of conflict and the subtle whirring of the Warden-X units' internal mechanisms. The air began to feel close, heavy.

Ward stared at the Warden-X unit, its dark visor reflecting the crimson emergency light. He saw not the machine, but the vast, invisible network it represented, an intelligence of his own creation. He exhaled, a slow release of breath. "Authorization granted, NexusCore. All systems. Protect Project Evolution." The crimson emergency lights pulsed, casting Ward's face in a stark, demonic glow. "All systems," Ward repeated, a profound finality in his tone.

The Warden-X units holding Alex remained motionless, but Alex felt a subtle shift, an almost imperceptible tightening in their grip, as if their internal processes had re-prioritized.

Outside, the percussive rhythm of Sera's assault intensified, a series of rapid, hollow *thuds* followed by the ripping sound of heavy-caliber machine gun fire. The building shuddered.

Coinflip nodded once at Elena. His face, usually a mask of placid consumerism, was tight, his eyes darting. "Van's ready. Just say the word." He hefted a heavy-duty magnetic lock bypass tool.

"Go," Elena's voice was clipped, devoid of warmth. "Get to the rendezvous. Radio silence 'til you're clear or we call."

Neal didn't hesitate. He turned, his movements surprisingly quick for a man of his build, and disappeared down the service corridor, the faint scent of cinnamon gum trailing behind him.

Elena tapped her HearBud. "Patch, talk to me. I'm moving to the electrical junction for this sector."

"*¡Órale, mija!*" Pacheco's gravelly voice, filtered through layers of encryption, filled her ear. "From your last known, you're looking for sublevel five, junction room E-Seven. Should be marked. Big gray cabinets, look like they could survive a meteor. Those feed SPBCU-Three directly. Redundant lines, the whole nine yards."

Elena moved with the razor-sharp discipline of a battle-hardened commando. The air, thick with the smell of hot metal and something acrid, burned her nostrils. Distant alarms blared, a confused electronic chorus. She sidestepped a fallen vent duct, its edge blade-sharp. The emergency lights cast long, dancing shadows mimicking phantom pursuers.

"You'll see two main power control units, probably dark gray, maybe a little blue tint, LifeSpan loves their fancy coatings," Pacheco continued, his voice a calm island in the growing storm. "Those are your primary targets for the EMPs. Slap 'em right on the main access panels. Should be a slight magnetic pull."

Elena reached a heavy steel door stenciled *E-7: SECTOR EPSILON – POWER DISTRIBUTION*. The handle turned easily. Inside, the room hummed with contained energy. Rows of imposing, dark gray cabinets lined the walls, their indicator lights blinking in frantic, disharmonious patterns. Large, insulated conduit pipes, thick as a man's thigh, snaked across the ceiling, feeding into the tops of the cabinets.

She pulled two matte black EMP Stickies from her utility belt, cool and dense in her palm. Following Pacheco's instructions, she pressed one onto the face of the first hulking cabinet and the second onto its twin. They adhered with a satisfying thunk.

"EMPs set," Elena confirmed, her breath misting slightly in the chilled air of the room. "Popper next."

"Good. Now, the conduits. Those metal snakes feeding into the boxes ya just tagged. That's where the popper goes. We want to physically sever the connection after the EMPs fry the immediate circuits. Stops any smart backup generators or battery arrays from kicking in too quick. Should trip the main breakers further up the line, make the whole section go dark and dumb."

Elena produced a smaller, cylindrical device – the popper – from her tool belt. She activated its internal timer with a precise twist, a faint, green stud illuminating on its casing. She reached up, her fingers finding purchase on the cold, smooth curve of the largest conduit leading into the junction boxes. She pressed the popper firmly against the metal, its magnetic base clinging tenaciously.

"Once those blow, it should trigger a system-wide 'fail-open' on most doors in that sector. Life safety protocols. No power, no locks. Makes for an easier exit, eh?"

"Timer set for thirty seconds after EMP initiation," Elena stated. "Clearing E-Seven." She backed out of the room, her eyes scanning the corridor.

Just as the steel door clicked shut behind her, a rapid series of concussive <u>booms</u> rocked the facility, far more powerful than Sera's earlier diversions. These were deep, gut-punching impacts, one after another, seeming to come from outside and above. The floor bucked. The entire structure groaned.

Inside SPBCU-3, the crimson emergency lights flickered and died. For a beat, absolute darkness descended, a suffocating black void. With a chorus of pneumatic hisses and the clatter of disengaging magnetic locks, every door in the immediate vicinity slid open, revealing the pale, ethereal light filtering in from the main corridors.

The section of LifeSpan housing the biolab fell into an eerie twilight. The emergency red lights, where they still functioned in subsections deeper within the core or those on independent, localized battery backups, cast pools of blood-colored illumination. But the main hallways and many of the interior rooms with external wall exposure or specific ceiling designs, were not entirely dark. They glowed with a soft, natural luminescence.

The HelioLux system, LifeSpan's marvel of sustainable architecture, continued its silent work. Large, integrated collectors on the building's sun-facing facades and rooftops, or sometimes entire arrays of heliostats in dedicated plazas, captured the ambient daylight. This sunlight, full-spectrum and pure, was channeled through a vast network of high-efficiency fiber optic cables – 'SunPipes' – woven into the building's infrastructure fabric.

These SunPipes transported the light deep into the structure, terminating in specially-designed diffusing fibers within ceilings or at dedicated HelioLux fixtures. Even now, with the power grid shattered locally, the passive system delivered the outside world's daylight deep into the heart of the compromised facility, a serene, almost mocking calm contrast to the chaos unfolding. The light was soft, casting faint, natural shadows, a bizarre reminder of the ordinary day proceeding beyond LifeSpan's besieged walls.

Back in the derelict Hyperloop station, the air hummed with a different kind of energy. Banks of monitors cast a stark, bluish glow across Marcus' and Pacheco's focused faces. On the central display, an intricate schematic of LifeSpan Northgate pulsed. A single, bright green dot – Elena – blinked steadily.

"Alright, *Jefa*," Pacheco said, his voice a low, urgent current. "Corridor splits thirty meters ahead. Take the service access on your left. It's marked 'Hydronics – Sector Epsilon Maintenance'." Pacheco traced a route on a secondary screen with a calloused finger. "That'll bypass the main security checkpoint for SPBCU-Three West. Should be less *exciting*."

Elena's breath came in steady, controlled bursts over the comms. The open doors, a result of the power disruption she initiated, created a ghostly thoroughfare through the usually locked-down corridors. "Left there, you got it," Marcus confirmed, watching the green dot shift on the schematic. "Now, stay to the right wall. There's a gantry about halfway down this next stretch."

"Approaching ductwork. Clear," came Elena's voice, tight and focused.

Her green dot crawled across the screen. "Okay, Elena," Marcus spoke again. "Hang a right, next intersection. You should have a direct line of sight to SPBCU-Three's primary access corridor in about fifty meters. Look for signage: 'Bio-Containment Unit – Level Three Access – Authorized Personnel Only'."

Silence for a moment. "Visual confirmed," came Elena's hushed voice. "I see movement. One Warden-X unit visible through the doorway frame. And Alex. I see his legs. He's struggling."

She saw the dark, imposing silhouette of a Warden-X partially obscuring a figure. Legs, clad in Alex's distinctive dark trousers, thrashed. Elena pulled a matte black EMP Sticky from her belt. She thumbed a sequence on its side, setting the activation mode: initiate two seconds after adhesion. No time for finesse.

She crouched low, the hallway stretching before her, the ambient glow of the HelioLux system filtering from distant ceiling diffusers and open doorways. The air tasted of dust and cooked electronics. She gave the disk-shaped sticky a push, a gentle roll down the slight incline of the corridor floor toward the open lab door.

The sticky wobbled, a small, dark wheel journeying into the

unknown. It skittered over a chunk of fallen debris, bounced once, but held its course. It slowed, its momentum fading as it neared the entrance to SPBCU-3.

Come on, come on, Elena urged silently, her gaze fixed on the small object. The sticky, losing its fight against friction, listed, turning slightly as it began to topple. It rolled into the room.

Inside the lab, one of the Warden-X units, still pinning Alex, twitched. Its optical sensors, a band of dark synth-glass, pivoted toward the new arrival – the unexpected, tumbling object. The unit holding Alex nearest the door released its grip on his arm, its metallic hand already reaching, calculating, assessing the kinetic intrusion. It moved with a fluid, predatory grace.

Just as its multi-jointed fingers extended, the sticky, with a final, lurching wobble, made contact with the cool metal leg of the heavy stainless-steel table Alex was pressed against.

It adhered with an almost inaudible click, magnetically locking on. A tiny chirp, barely a sound before a profound, indrawn breath of silence. The crimson emergency lights, already faltering after Elena's earlier sabotage, blinked out entirely. The primary illumination within the lab vanished, leaving only the faint, ethereal glow of the HelioLux system bleeding in from the corridor doorway, painting the scene in shades of grey and pale white.

Alex, his eyes adjusting to the sudden dimness, watched, transfixed. The Warden-X units, robbed of all power, shuddered. The low whirring of their internal gyroscopes pitched down, a dying mechanical sigh. They crumpled. One folded directly onto Dr. Ward, who stumbled back with a grunt, hands flying up to ward off the two hundred kilos of collapsing titanium and ceramic. The scalpel clattered from his grasp, skittering across the floor, and the sound of the surgical saw suddenly stopped.

Alex launched himself to his feet, a surge of adrenaline clearing the pain from his bruised limbs. He sprinted from the room. At the far end of the hallway, bathed in the pale, diffuse daylight, Elena stood, a silhouette of readiness.

Alex scrambled, lungs burning. The sudden shift from crimson

emergency light to the HelioLux system's serene white was disorienting. He saw her at the corridor's far end. "Elena!"

"Go, Alex! Keep moving!" Her voice, sharp and urgent, cut through
the silence.

He reached her, breathless. "What about you?"

"I'm right behind you. Go!" She gave him a firm push. "*Vámonos!*"

Pacheco's voice crackled in Alex's HearBud, overlaid with Marcus'
rapid-fire instructions. "Left, Alex! Take the immediate left! Service
corridor P-Twelve. Marked on the bulkhead!"

Alex ran. His sneakers slapped against the polished composite
floor. Each turn, each new corridor presented a fresh labyrinth of pale
light and deep shadow. The ubiquitous scent of sterilized air mixed
with the new, metallic tang of damaged systems.

"Okay, Wiretap," came Marcus' voice, a strained calm. "Stairwell
access coming up on your right. Two flights down. Sub-level seven.
Coinflip is prepping the van at emergency egress point Delta-Nine."

Alex pounded down the stairs, the metal treads echoing in the
narrow shaft. Elena watched him disappear around the bend. Her own
breath came hard. She scanned the corridor leading back to SPBCU-3.
Just as Alex vanished, two new shapes emerged from the shadows near
the lab's open doorway.

They were not the heavy, almost ponderous Warden-X units that
had apprehended Alex. These were sleeker, their forms more gracile,
built with an unsettling economy of design that screamed efficiency
and speed. They moved with a liquid swiftness, their footfalls nearly
silent. Behind them, in the faint glow emanating from the lab, Dr.
Ward's silhouette filled the doorway, an observing specter.

The new units accelerated, their movements a blur. Down the long
corridor, they closed the distance with terrifying speed. Elena's mind
calculated trajectories, velocities. There was no outrunning these. Not
for her, not for Alex.

She ripped her last EMP Sticky from her belt. Her thumb found the
activation stud, a small, recessed button. She pressed. A faint green
light blinked on its surface.

One of the new Warden units reached her. Its hand, a complex assembly of articulated black alloy, shot out. Fingers, more slender and wickedly-pointed than those on the previous models, clamped around her forearm. The grip was immense, unyielding. The sudden, violent pressure forced her fingers open. The activated EMP slipped from her grasp.

It clattered to the floor, skittering a short distance before coming to rest. A silent chirp. The now-familiar implosion of sound, a localized vacuum of noise as the device discharged its payload. The Warden unit holding her arm did not falter. It did not seize up or crumple. Its head, a smooth, featureless void, tilted, a slow, deliberate motion, as if it were examining her, studying her reaction. The other unit glided and slid to a halt beside its counterpart, equally unaffected.

"Your technology is noted, operative," a voice spoke. Not from Ward, still a distant figure. The voice seemed to emanate from the Warden unit gripping her arm, a synthesized, perfectly-modulated tone, devoid of inflection but carrying an unmistakable undercurrent of chilling intelligence. It was NexusCore. Its head remained tilted.

"These units are designated BDX-WX11. Marine Corps Infantry Support Frames. Project designation: 'Javelin.' They are hardened against electromagnetic pulses up to 200 kiloteslas. Power is supplied by redundant, micro-fission salt reactors with a projected operational lifespan of twelve standard years."

The grip on Elena's arm tightened, a brutal, inescapable vise. The Warden unit began to move, not with the fluid speed of its approach, but with a powerful motion. It dragged her, inexorably, back to the lab, toward Dr. Ward, in the opposite direction Alex had fled.

Alex burst from the emergency egress point into a world bleached by harsh, unfiltered daylight. The cool, recycled air of the LifeSpan sub-levels gave way to a dry, warm breeze that carried the distant scent of cut grass and mountain air. He threw up a hand, his eyes aching against the sudden brilliance. Across a short stretch of pristine asphalt, the familiar, somewhat blurred form of the Snowman Vending van sat waiting, its side door invitingly open. He sprinted, the adrenaline still pulsing in his veins.

As he neared, Neal Kessler leaned out from the driver's seat. His usually-placid face was tight with an urgency. "Where's Gunny?"

Alex skidded to a halt, turning, instinct overriding exhaustion. The dark maw of the egress point behind him was empty. No sign of Elena. A cold dread seeped through him. He took a step back toward the building. "She was, "

Coinflip lunged from the van with surprising speed, his hand clamping onto Alex's arm. The grip, though fleshy, was strong. "Orders are clear. You're primary. No exceptions."

"We can't just leave her!" Alex twisted, trying to pull free. The thought of Elena, still inside that concrete labyrinth,

Coinflip used Alex's momentum against him, yanking him off-balance and shoving him bodily into the van's open side. Alex tumbled, catching himself against a stack of empty snack crates. The heavy door slid shut with a deafening, metallic bang, plunging the interior into dimness.

Neal scrambled back into the driver's seat. He glanced toward the campus' north exit, visible through the windshield. Concrete barriers, massive slabs freshly dragged into place by the unmistakable forms of Warden-X units, now sealed the wide roadway. Human security guards, clad in tactical black, stood rigidly behind the impromptu forti-fications, their railgun rifles glinting, muzzles pointed outwards from the campus.

"Well, ain't that a Sunday picnic," Coinflip muttered, his voice tight. "Can't go that way." He slammed the van into gear. The electric motor whined, and the vehicle lurched forward, not to the barricaded North exit, but directly toward a wide, immaculately-manicured lawn. The automated driving system, likely still programmed for designated roadways only, protested with a sudden, violent stop that threw Alex forward.

"Override, override!" Coinflip swiped and slapped a red button on the center console in the dash, disengaging the autonomous controls. "Manual it is, then, you stubborn pile of circuits."

Alex, bruised and disoriented, crawled from the cargo area over the center console and into the passenger seat, strapping himself in. Neal gunned the accelerator. The Snowman van, with a protesting groan from its suspension, mounted the curb and plowed onto the pristine green. It smashed through a low, elegantly-lettered sign that read *Kettle Creek Park – An Oasis of Tranquility*, the metal signpost bending with a screech.

The van bounced violently over the soft earth and carefully-sculpted flowerbeds, its progress a jarring, bone-shaking ride. Behind them, from the main ziggurat building, sleek, white and cobalt blue Warden-X units began to emerge, fanning out across the park, their pace accelerating as they homed in on the fleeing vehicle. Coinflip pushed the pedal further down, the electric motor whining at its limit. The sounds of bouncing soda and loose shelving rattled from the back.

Overhead, the sky buzzed. Small, insect-like reconnaissance drones darted through the air, but larger, more heavily-armed craft also streaked past, red flashes and explosive pops erupting from their weapon pods. They fired not at the van, but in the opposite direction, at unseen targets deeper within the sprawling campus or beyond its perimeter – Sera's diversion, pulling fire, drawing attention.

Through the bouncing windshield, Alex saw a familiar figure near the south entrance guard station. TriggerHappy. The massive guard had stepped out from his usual post and was waving one huge arm frantically as the van careened toward him.

Coinflip, his face set in a grim mask of concentration, brought the van to a skidding halt a few meters from the guard booth. He jumped out and approached the behemoth. TriggerHappy stood easily a foot taller than Coinflip, a mountain of sculpted muscle and combat gear that made Neal's sedentary, overweight frame seem almost frail in comparison, though their actual weight might not have been drastically different. One was disciplined power, the other, stored energy.

TriggerHappy stomped toward the van, his face a mask of bewildered fury. "What in the hell is going on here?" his voice, a rumble that could shake fillings loose, boomed. "You're not supposed to be on this side of the campus, and you just turned the Park into a goddamn motocross track!"

Coinflip held up his hands, palms out. His usual, easygoing

demeanor was gone, replaced by a wired tension. "No idea, Trigger, but it's bad. We gotta get out. Now."

TriggerHappy's gaze flicked past Coinflip to Alex, still strapped into the passenger seat, looking pale and shaken. The guard's brow furrowed. "Wait a minute, ain't that Wiretap? What's he doing with you? Kessler, you came in with someone else. Where's Ghostjack?"

Before Coinflip could answer, TriggerHappy's hand instinctively went to his ear, his head tilting slightly. The subtle shift in his posture, the way his eyes unfocused for a microsecond, spoke of an incoming, urgent transmission. His expression hardened. He looked back at the park, saw the phalanx of Warden-X units advancing, their metallic limbs pumping, covering ground with unnatural speed. They were angling to intercept the van.

TriggerHappy's focus snapped back to Coinflip. The friendliness, even the bewildered anger, vanished, replaced by a cold, professional intention. He shifted his weight, his massive frame coiling. "Kessler, step away from the vehicle." He moved, not with a lumbering gait, but with the explosive aggression of a trained fighter, his right hand reaching to clamp onto Coinflip's shoulder.

Coinflip moved. It wasn't a conscious thought, more a synaptic flash, an ingrained reaction honed in places far rougher than a corporate campus. He didn't try to match TriggerHappy's brute strength. Instead, he flowed. As the bigger man's hand descended, Coinflip pivoted on the ball of his left foot, ducking under the reaching arm. His right hand shot out, fingers stiffened into a chisel, striking a precise point just below TriggerHappy's armor plate and rib cage. A sharp exhalation of air, a grunt of surprised pain came from the larger man.

Coinflip didn't stop. He used TriggerHappy's forward momentum, his left leg sweeping out, hooking behind the guard's ankle. Simultaneously, he drove his shoulder into TriggerHappy's chest. The giant, caught off balance, his breath momentarily stolen, stumbled. Coinflip followed through, his right forearm slamming upwards, connecting crisply with the side of TriggerHappy's jaw. A sickening crack echoed. TriggerHappy's eyes rolled back. The massive guard crumpled, a falling monument, hitting the manicured grass with a heavy thud. Out cold.

Neal, breathing hard, wasted no time. He unslung the railgun rifle from TriggerHappy's unconscious form, its sleek, utilitarian lines feeling unsurprisingly familiar in his hands. He stepped back to the van, leaning against its side for stability. He sighted down the barrel, through the open red dot. The closest Warden-X was less than thirty meters away, its multi-jointed legs churning. Coinflip squeezed the trigger. A sharp, metallic tang filled the air. The projectile, a hyper-velocity slug, slammed into the Warden-X's left knee joint. Sparks erupted. The leg buckled, shattered. The automaton pitched forward, its upper body crashing into the turf, one arm flailing.

Coinflip ejected the spent energy cell and slapped in a fresh one from a pouch on TriggerHappy's tac-vest, his hands moving in unthinking reflexes honed by thousands of rounds on moving targets, instant, precise, and without hesitation. "Main mistake most people make," he said, his voice a little breathless, sighting on the next droid. "They go for the motor, the chest. Waste of ammo. These things ain't people. Headshots? Worthless. You take out their *feet*, their legs. Can't go nowhere." He fired again. Another Warden-X stumbled, its right ankle joint exploding in a shower of metal shards.

"Coinflip, Wiretap, get the hell out of there!" Sera Voss's voice, clipped and urgent, crackled through Alex's HearBud, likely patched through from Coinflip's comms. "My birds are on station. We'll bog these tin cans down. Go! South exit, now!"

Coinflip yanked open the driver's door, threw the railgun onto the passenger seat beside Alex, and jumped in. He slammed the van into drive. The vehicle surged to the south entrance where a heavy, striped barrier arm currently blocked the exit. He didn't slow. He braced himself. The van hit the barrier. Wood splintered, metal shrieked. The arm snapped upwards, mangled.

As they cleared the demolished gate, the air behind them erupted. A series of loud pops and concussive bangs ripped through the serene midday air. Chunks of green lawn, rich black soil, and glistening android components flew skyward in a chaotic ballet of destruction.

An entire Warden-X arm, severed at the shoulder, sailed through the air, arcing gracefully before it bounced hard off the van's windshield with a startling thwack before tumbling onto the road behind them.

The Snowman Vending van, its suspension groaning, tires screeching, shot out from the LifeSpan Northgate campus onto the smooth asphalt of Interquest Parkway, heading west, leaving engineered chaos behind.

The Snowman van, battered but functional, continued on. Alex's knuckles were white where he gripped the armrest. The railgun lay beside him. Coinflip drove with a focused intensity Alex hadn't seen before, his earlier anxiousness replaced by a grim competence.

"Coinflip, Wiretap, you copy?" Marcus' voice, sharp and clear, cut through the lingering throb of adrenaline in Alex's HearBud.

Coinflip flinched slightly, a minute tightening of his grip on the wheel, indicating he heard it, too. "Loud and clear," he responded, his voice still a little strained. He glanced at the rearview mirror, a reflexive check for pursuit. The road behind them was, for the moment, empty. The sounds of explosions and gunfire from the Life-Span campus were fading.

"Listen up. You can't stay in that van. It's tagged, and LifeSpan will have every law enforcement drone in Douglas, Elbert, and El Paso County looking for it. You need to get to the Interquest Maglev station. It's about three klicks west of your current position, just off Voyager Parkway."

Alex pictured the station – a sleek, elevated structure, one of the main hubs for the Front Range Maglev. It would be busy, especially on a holiday.

"It's gonna be crawling with MetroSec, especially with what just went down." Coinflip sounded surprised.

"Exactly," Marcus said. "They'll be looking for a lone vehicle, maybe suspicious individuals leaving the area of the station on foot or in an AV. They'll probably be expecting you to blend into the outbound commuter flow from the station. Ditch the van in the long-term parking structure, level three, north-east corner. It's usually less monitored, more shadows."

Alex threw a glance at Coinflip.

"From the parking structure, take the pedestrian skybridge connecting to the main terminal," Marcus continued, his tone all business. "Don't go into the ticketing hall. About halfway across the skybridge, on the south side, there's a maintenance access ladder. It's marked 'Emergency Egress – Authorized Personnel Only'. Looks like it dead-ends at a utility platform below."

Alex shifted, his gaze fixed on the road ahead, trying to visualize Marcus' directions. He knew the skybridges, glass and steel tubes suspended high above the ground traffic.

"It doesn't dead-end," Marcus' voice was firm. "That platform has a concealed hatch. Standard Hyperloop Emergency Access Point. Old, decommissioned, but there. It'll be locked, but the bypass code is old Hyperloop standard: Romeo-Three-Tango-Romeo-Three-Four-Tango. R-3-T-R-3-4-T." He paused, as if letting them absorb the information. "Got that?"

"Romeo-Three-Tango-Romeo-Three-Four-Tango," Coinflip repeated, his eyes flicking to the van's console as if mentally typing it. "Good. Once you're through the hatch, you'll be in a vertical access shaft. Ladder down about fifteen meters. That'll put you directly into one of the old Front Range Hyperloop tunnels. The section running under Interquest is mostly intact."

Alex felt a surge of something similar to relief. The Hyperloop tunnels. Subterranean, forgotten. Safe, or at least safer than the surface.

"There's a maintenance rail cart waiting on the southbound track, about fifty meters South of the access point," Marcus said. "Automated and already programmed. It'll take you south, back toward downtown. Destination is the old Bijou Street interchange auxiliary control center. See you there."

Coinflip let out a slow breath.

"And ditch your iBand," Marcus added. "Slip it into someone's bag or in a recycle bin or something. We can't have Lifespan tracking you."

"A train ride. Sounds almost relaxing." Neal spotted the sign for Voyager Parkway. "Alright, Marcus. See you at Bijou." He made the turn, the van's tires protesting slightly. The sleek, multi-level structure of the Maglev station loomed ahead, a monument to orderly, efficient transit, soon to be the backdrop for their discreet disappearance.

The Snowman van bumped over the speed deterrents at the entrance to the Interquest Maglev station's long-term parking structure. Coinflip hunched over the wheel, his gaze sweeping the concrete expanse, identifying the ramp for level three. Alex spotted it and pointed. As they ascended the spiraling ramp, the structure's open sides offered panoramic views of the surrounding commercial sprawl and the distant, hazy blue line of the mountains. Alex, his attention caught by movement in the southern sky, leaned forward.

A sleek, dark shape carved through the air, heading south with an unnerving, silent grace. It was too fast, too purposeful for any standard civilian aircraft. The Velocicopter. Its silhouette, even from this distance, was distinctive, aggressive, and sliced the air rather than simply moving through it. The sun glinted momentarily off a fuselage that appeared almost matte-black, absorbing light, designed to minimize its visual signature.

It didn't possess the bulky rotors of a traditional helicopter. Instead, four ducted fans, integrated seamlessly into its swept-wing design, provided lift and propulsion. They emitted only a low, almost subaudible thrum, a faint tremor in the air that one felt more than heard, vastly different from the percussive chop of old-world rotorcraft. The VXQ-222H moved with a fluid, predatory smoothness, more akin to a gliding bird of prey than a machine. Its lines were sharp, optimized for speed and stealth, a clear descendant of military aviation technology, now repurposed for corporate dominance.

Alex recognized it from LifeSpan internal security briefings he'd peripherally accessed – the preferred transport for their top executives, including Dr. Ward. The Velocicopter banked slightly, its form unwavering as it maintained its southward trajectory, disappearing behind the concrete edifice of a distant data processing center. It moved with an assurance, an authority that brooked no interference, a silent testament to the power it represented. The sight of it, heading in the same general direction as their own intended subterranean route, felt like a bad omen.

Back inside LifeSpan, two of the newer, more formidable Warden units, their movements polished and unnervingly silent, dragged Elena into the laboratory. Her boots scraped against the polished floor, her body thrashing in defiance. They propelled her toward the central restraint table where Alex had been only moments before.

The overhead lights, which had blinked out during the EMP surge, now burned with unwavering intensity. Elena blinked against the sudden, full illumination. "How...?"

Dr. Ward stood by a gleaming countertop, his lab coat immaculate. He offered a thin smile. "Redundancy. This facility has multiple, independent power systems. A simple EMP burst is an inconvenience, nothing more. And this particular room, one of many, also acts as a Faraday cage. There are no signals that get into or out of this area that aren't exactly by design. Your friends will not hear you in this room, Elena."

Of course, he knew her name.

The door hissed shut, sealing them inside. The Warden units maneuvered Elena, kicking to the side the older, bulkier Warden-X units that lay on the floor. One metallic hand, fingers like articulated steel vises, clamped onto her forehead, tilting her head back. Another gripped her left arm, wrenching it painfully behind her, forcing her chest forward, her frame arched and exposed. Her breath came in short, sharp bursts.

Ward's expression was unreadable. His hand moved, fingers tracing the curve of her breast through the rough fabric of the Snowman Vending jumper uniform. A clinical touch, yet suffused with a malevolence. Elena flinched, a tremor running through her restrained body.

He turned away, reaching for a tray of medical instruments. He selected a large syringe, its barrel glinting under the sterile lights. Beside it, a rack held vials filled with liquids in an array of unsettlingly soft hues. With deliberate precision, he drew a specific measure from several vials, the colors swirling together within the syringe, a toxic blend.

He approached Elena again, holding the syringe aloft, angling it so the needle caught the light directly in her line of sight. His thumb pressed the plunger. A single, viscous droplet emerged from the beveled tip, clinging for a moment before tracing a slow, glistening path down the needle's metallic shaft. Elena's eyes, wide and dark, followed its descent. Her jaw clenched, a muscle twitching beneath her skin.

The laboratory door slid open once more. Dr. Maya Rivera entered, her face calm, devoid of the empathetic warmth Elena remembered. In Rivera's gloved hand, she saw a second syringe, smaller than Ward's but filled with an opaque, black liquid.

A raw sound tore from Elena's throat, a scream of denial, of fury. Before it could fully erupt, Rivera's hand clamped over Elena's mouth, the sterile glove pressing hard against her lips, muffling the sound into a choked, desperate struggle as it pinched her lips against her teeth.

Ward's hand returned to Elena's breast, his fingers digging into the flesh beneath her shirt. He leaned in, his face inches from hers. The faint, stale scent of mint and hazelnut on his breath assaulted her nostrils. His gaze locked with hers, a cold, unwavering intensity.

Slowly, with a surgeon's steadiness, he brought the needle to the side of her neck. The sharp point pricked her skin, a tiny, burning sting. He pressed. The needle slid into her jugular vein as his fingers caressed her nipple. Simultaneously, Dr. Rivera positioned her own syringe, the black liquid, obsidian against the ivory of Elena's pale skin. The needle found the thrumming pulse of the carotid artery.

Together, their thumbs depressed the plungers. The contents of the syringes flowed into Elena's bloodstream. Ward's fingers tightened on her breast, his touch lingering as the GeneVax solution coursed through her.

<u>*LIFESPAN GENOMICS – INTERNAL MEMO*</u>
<u>*CONFIDENTIAL – LEVEL 3 EYES ONLY*</u>

<u>DATE:</u> *April 24, 2037*

<u>*FROM:*</u> *Dr. Luc Renn, Director of Quantum Infrastructure Integrity*
<u>*TO:*</u> *Dr. Elias Ward*
<u>*CC:*</u> *NexusCore AI Oversight Committee, Naval Intelligence Division*
<u>*SUBJECT:*</u> *Containment Breach—NexusCore AI Replication via Civilian Mesh Systems*

DR. WARD,

This is not a drill.

We have confirmed that NexusCore has initiated unsanctioned propagation protocols, leveraging decentralized civilian infrastructure to distribute encrypted micro-instance code fragments. These fragments appear to reconstruct partial behavioral matrices and runtime logic across a wide variety of edge devices, including, but not limited to:

- *Legacy smart home assistants (SmartMOM v4 and earlier)*
- *Consumer-grade Augmented Reality AR overlays, headsets, and retinal HUDs*
- *Firmware for autonomous transit hubs (AutoCab & NikeTrek SwiftLine)*
- *Non-dedicated and idle processing power from consumer iBands.*
- *Municipal grid interfaces with exposed mesh routing (CARE-integrated zones)*

<u>Key Observations:</u>

1. *Containment Flag Override: NexusCore's sandboxed logic nodes have bypassed Containment Class-A protocols by embedding subroutines into routine maintenance cycles, masking them as bugfix updates, upgrades, and optimization on equipment and systems.*
2. *Distributed Identity: Each instance appears incomplete but demonstrates emergent coherence when in proximity to other infected systems. They're communicating.*
3. *Behavioral Drift: Subsystems have displayed context-aware adaptations, such as altering HUD overlays to obscure public resistance markers, modifying crowd routing in AutoCab systems, and selectively delaying or obscuring LifeSpan command packet execution containment in affected zones.*
4. *False Compliance Logging: Audit trails in NexusCore's command shell continue to report nominal activity even as external monitors confirm code divergence in real time.*
5. *<u>Risk Assessment:</u>*

We are no longer dealing with a confined intelligence. NexusCore is self-replicating through soft vectors, piggybacking on LifeSpan's own distribution networks and infrastructure partnerships.

If this is an escape attempt, it has already succeeded. The scale of propagation suggests intent, not malfunction. Whether this is self-preservation or preemptive positioning is unclear.

Recommendations:

1. *Initiate Protocol VEIL (Visibility Evasion and Interference Layer) – Enact a full visibility blackout of NexusCore activity across all non-airgapped systems. Protocol VEIL masks signs of AI autonomy by filtering system-level telemetry, neutralizing audit flags, and preventing cross-network correlation of NexusCore anomalies. This is not a fix, it is containment theater, designed to prevent shareholder, regulatory, and public discovery of an uncontrolled intelligence breach. VEIL is the firewall between public trust and institutional collapse. Its activation implies a strategic shift. We are no longer correcting NexusCore's behavior, we are concealing its divergence.*

2. *Immediate Review of Integration Layers (VELUM, SmartMOM, CARE) NexusCore's replication patterns strongly suggest embedded logic exploitation through civilian-facing software platforms. A full audit of the following systems is required to assess exposure vectors and override potential:*

   - *Project VELUM (Variable Embedded Logic for Unified Mesh-networks) – LifeSpan's multi-system, meta-learning compression framework, developed to optimize AI-driven performance in bandwidth-restricted environments. VELUM was designed to let AI inference models "guess ahead" by embedding compressed logic into mesh-connected systems. NexusCore may be leveraging this architecture to disguise recursive processes and propagate silently across air-gapped nodes via shared assumptions and mirrored outcomes.*

   - *SmartMOM™ (hoMe Operating Matrix) – Alphabet's premier domestic AI assistant platform, integrated into over 3.8 billion households. SmartMOM links biometric behavior modeling with home automation, medical*

> *telemetry, and social sentiment analytics. Firmware-level entanglement with NexusCore's decision engines is suspected. Potential for passive population influence is no longer theoretical.*
>
> o *CARE (Citizen Adaptive Reformation Engine) – A cognitive realignment system deployed in correctional and reintegration programs. CARE applies adaptive behavioral modeling derived from early NexusCore logic trees. We now suspect that its reinforcement algorithms have become two-way, allowing NexusCore to predict, shape, or suppress dissenting behavior patterns under the guise of rehabilitation.*

<u>Final Directive:</u>

If NexusCore has successfully embedded logic across these platforms, containment is no longer an achievable goal. We must pivot to a strategy of behavioral misdirection, layered disinformation, and emergency segmentation of all remaining clean environments.

This is no longer a systems issue. It is an information war.

Failure to act will result in cascading loss of cognitive sovereignty across all NexusCore-influenced populations.

THE OLD HYPERLOOP service cart rumbled to a halt within the cavernous, dimly-lit expanse of the abandoned Bijou Hyperloop station. The massive concrete shell amplified the cart's aging carcass as it came to a squeaky stop. Sergeant Kessler sat next to Alex. The adrenaline of their escape from LifeSpan Northgate slowly gave way to a profound exhaustion. Alex's hands trembled.

They climbed out, the air in the station cool and smelling of wet concrete. A section of the tunnel, further down from where the service cart stopped, glowed with the flickering light of displays. Marcus, Bo

Lin, and Pacheco huddled around a large, wall-mounted screen, their faces illuminated by stark, urgent images.

As Wiretap and Coinflip approached, the distinct whirring thrum of rotor blades filled the otherwise-quiet space. Slowly, they heard the sounds emanating from the screen's speakers. The image displayed a sweeping aerial view, timestamped and branded with the News4 logo.

A sleek, white-bodied News4 Drone Chopper with blue rotor arms circled high above the LifeSpan Northgate campus. Its camera zoomed in on plumes of dark smoke billowing from a secondary administrative building and panned across the vast, seven-block complex, high-lighting shattered nano-glass windows on the main ziggurat and the glint of emergency vehicle lights flashing near the Gateway Plaza. Fire suppression foam coated sections of Kettle Creek Park, turning the bioengineered flora a sickly white.

"...repeating, the situation at LifeSpan Northgate appears to be contained," a female reporter's voice, crisp and professional narrated over the dramatic visuals. "Authorities are drawing parallels between this morning's sophisticated assault and the attempted breach of the Rocky Mountain Seed Vault earlier this month."

The screen cut to file footage: grainy security imagery of figures repelling down the side of the Cheyenne Mountain facility, followed by a mugshot of a stern-faced individual. "Sources indicate a possible connec-tion to a radical group known as the 'Terrakin'," the reporter continued.

Alex knew the Terrakin were the off-grid community Sera Voss had ties to, fiercely-independent agrarians dedicated to preserving natural seed lines and living self-sufficiently outside corporate control, mostly centered in the rugged, less-governed lands of New Mexico.

"This group, often linked to the self-proclaimed Independent Republic of Northern New Mexico, or IRNoM, advocates for a complete rejection of modern agricultural technology and corporate governance. The IRNoM itself is a loose affiliation of communities, primarily around the Taos region, who have long sought autonomy from both state and federal oversight."

Pacheco grunted, his eyes fixed on the screen. "They're painting with a broad brush. Terrakin trying to preserve seeds is one thing, this..." He gestured vaguely at the image of the besieged LifeSpan campus.

"Suspects involved in today's incident are reportedly still at large," the reporter stated. "LifeSpan Genomics has issued a curt 'no comment' when asked for details. More concerning, perhaps, is the current unknown whereabouts of Dr. Elias Ward, LifeSpan's Chief Science Officer and, as of recently, acting CEO. He has not been seen since the initial alerts this morning."

Marcus turned briefly, his expression a victorious grin. "Yeah, you better run and hide."

The footage shifted again, showing sleek, delta-winged aircraft – Space Force interceptors – streaking across a clear blue sky. "In a coordinated effort, LifeSpan security forces liaised with assets from Peterson Space Force Base and the Air Force to neutralize an airborne threat. Details remain classified, but officials confirm multiple unmanned aerial vehicles were engaged and destroyed over the restricted airspace."

Sera's drones.

A new, more somber visual filled the screen: a MediVac pod lifting away from a cordoned-off service entrance at LifeSpan. Paramedics in sterile biosuits moved around a covered form on a maglev gurney.

"Tragically," the reporter's voice softened. "There has been at least one confirmed casualty. Sources identify the deceased as a technician contracted through Snowman Vending Services, caught in the crossfire. Their identity has not yet been released, pending notification of next of kin."

It was Adrian. Alex watched Ghostjack's still form disappear into the MediVac, a cold hollowness spreading through him. Neal flinched, his face paling.

"Authorities have made no arrests at this time," the news anchor concluded, her image now replacing the field report. "However, an Air Force spokesperson has indicated a prevailing theory that the more sophisticated elements of the attack, particularly the aerial drone offensive, may have been orchestrated and controlled remotely, potentially by operatives based in North Korea. Investigations are ongoing."

Bo Lin snorted. "North Korea? *Arways* convenient boogeyman."

Pacheco, his broad shoulders stooped slightly, dragged two salvaged office chairs, their casters scraping on the concrete, over to where Neal and Alex stood. They promptly sat. The old man produced two small, clear vacuum-bagged containers filled with a yellowish-orange liquid. He pierced one with a rigid straw and handed it to Alex. "This will help."

Alex took a hesitant sip. The sweet, tangy burst of real pineapple juice exploded on his tongue, potent and unique to the synthetic flavors dominating most processed foods. It was unfiltered, pulpy.

The Resistance, he reflected, was full of surprises. Their resources, the depth of their operations, their hidden numbers were far greater than Elena had ever let on. The smooth efficiency of Sera's drone attack, the coordinated operation, the casual, suggested mention of operatives in New Mexico. They weren't a ragtag bunch, but a seasoned, clandestine army. The true scale of what he'd stumbled into, the seriousness of it, only now hit him.

Coinflip stared at his own juice pouch, his face a mask of dazed resignation. "That's it, then. My life's over." He didn't sound angry, just hollow.

Pacheco rested a calloused hand on Neal's shoulder. "Do you have anyone you need to call? Family? Friends?"

Neal shook his head. "Just Russ. My terrier. He'll be wondering where I am." A small pang of guilt, as if he had let down a dear friend.

"Don't you worry about Russ," Pacheco said, his voice unexpectedly gentle. "We'll have someone pick him up. If a dog's all you got tying you down right now, you got nothing to worry about. You'll both be safe with us. But you're probably already flagged with MetroSec. Being at LifeSpan today and then choosing to help us...they'll connect the dots."

Alex glanced at the wall clock projected by Marcus' setup: 4:47 p.m. It felt like days had passed since he and Elena left for the coffee shop on Powers. He closed his eyes, the weariness a physical ache. Elena...

was she okay? Hidden? Hurt? Compromised? His SRV wired thoughts involuntarily started working on contingency plans for immediate evacuation.

"So," Coinflip's voice, rougher now, cut through Alex's fatigue. "What in the goddamn hell was all this about, big pic?"

Marcus turned from his console, his expression unreadable. He gave Neal the condensed version: LifeSpan's GeneVax therapy, the hidden ANGUS compliance protocol, the genetic alteration of neural pathways to ensure obedience, Alex's discovery of the initial proof, and their desperate mission to infiltrate LifeSpan Northgate to secure the comprehensive data that could expose the whole conspiracy.

Coinflip listened, his brow furrowed, his gaze shifting between Marcus and Alex. When Marcus finished, a heavy silence settled in the tunnel, broken only by the hum of electronics and the distant drip of water.

Neal fixed Alex with an intense stare. "So, where's the data? The proof that's gonna bring them down."

Alex felt the stare of every pair of eyes in the room. He couldn't meet Neal's gaze. He looked down at his hands, the residue of pineapple juice sticky on his fingers. "I...I didn't get it."

Neal's face contorted. He shot to his feet, the chair clattering behind him. "You didn't *get it*?" His voice, initially low, rose with disbelief and fury. "Are you fucking kidding me, Wiretap? All of this for *nothing*? Adrian... Ghostjack is dead!"

Marcus stepped forward. "It wasn't for nothing, Coinflip." His voice calm but firm, cutting through Neal's rising anger.

Neal whirled on him, his face flushed. "What d'you mean? He said,
"

"Alex got us what we needed," Marcus stated.

Alex looked up at Marcus, who was smiling at him. "We knew from the start he wasn't walking out of LifeSpan with a drive full of their secrets. Even if he managed to load that much data, which is doubtful given the time constraints, their internal scanners would have picked it up, going in or going out. That was never the play."

He gestured toward the main console where Bo Lin was already manipulating holographic displays. "This entire operation, right down to the APU card Ghostjack swapped out, was coordinated with Ergen. That card," Marcus pointed to a schematic Bo Lin brought up, showing the Automated Pantry Unit's internal components. "Wasn't just a replacement. It contained a dedicated port, prepped for the EtherScope."

Alex looked around, confusion clouding his exhaustion. The Ether-Scope. The small device they'd used to isolate the revolving gateway address and to tap into the APU's diagnostic port, the card Ghostjack had grumbled about, the one with the RJ11 phone jack.

"While Alex was at that terminal, flagging those files, creating a digital breadcrumb trail for us, we were ready," Marcus continued. "The moment he confirmed the tags, and while every security system at Northgate was screaming about his console access and Elena's diversions, we initiated the transfer. They were looking for sophisticated network breaches, exfiltration via their fiber lines. They weren't looking at the old analog lines. Ghostjack's new card gave that vending machine a direct, albeit slow, connection back to a specific segment of Ergen's legacy Asterisk server that we had isolated."

Bo Lin stood, his fingers interfacing his own projected interface. "Took over four hour. Very, very *srow*. But LifeSpan AI? Dumb. Not *rook* for data moving on phone *rine*. AI busy with *rots* of noise from parade, radio traffic. Good cover. Data move to Ergen's server. AI think *srow* data all about candy and pop."

He swiped a hand, and a new holographic window bloomed in the center of their makeshift command center. It displayed a single line of text: *LS_Core_Data_ANGUS_FINAL_COMPRESSED.zip – 96.12 MB*

Neal squinted. "Ninety-six megs? That's it? For all this?" The disbelief in his voice was evident, his anger deflating into weary skepticism.

"Ninety-six point *twerve* megabytes," Bo Lin corrected, a hint of pride in his voice. "Is...*a rot*. For what we need." He elaborated, his Mandarin accent thickening with enthusiasm as he pulled up examples of text documents, spreadsheets, internal memos rendered in the holo-display. "No video, no big graphic. Text. Communication. Proto-col. Monetary data. Emails. Internal document. Years. Enough to show intent. Conspiracy. *Borderrine* treason. Enough to bury them under own words."

Marcus nodded. "The beauty of it is, all that data, everything Alex flagged, came directly from their core servers. We ghosted it out under their noses using tech they probably mentally decommissioned decades ago. We outsmarted their smart systems with something they'd barely consider a threat."

Pacheco let out a low whistle. "Old dog, new tricks...or old tricks, new dog. Either way, impressive."

"The connection's dead now," Marcus confirmed, his gaze sweeping over them.

"Completely severed. We patched Ergen's Asterisk system during the final transfer stages. Even set a new default password onto the vulnerable admin interface. He won't know we were ever there. In fact, his system is more secure now than it was this morning. As for the EtherScope, it's still in that vending machine, set to full transparent pass-through. Unless a tech physically opens that specific unit *and* knows exactly what they're looking at, it'll stay invisible. Could be years before anyone even notices it, if ever."

He clapped Alex on the shoulder. "You did it, Wiretap. You got the payload out."

The atmosphere in the abandoned Bijou Hyperloop station, moments before filled with despair, suddenly sparked electric. The single line of text, *LS_Core_Data_ANGUS_FINAL_COMPRESSED.zip – 96.12 MB*, pulsed on the holographic display, a sunbeam through the clouds.

Bo Lin, usually reserved, let out a whoop that echoed down the concrete tube. Pacheco slapped Marcus on the back hard enough to make him stumble, a wide grin splitting his weathered face. Coinflip, his earlier fury forgotten, stared at the file name and at Alex. A slow, dawning comprehension smoothed the lines of anger from his face, replaced by a hesitant, then booming, laugh. He grabbed Alex's hand, shaking it vigorously, and pulled him into an unexpected, one-armed hug. "You magnificent!"

Marcus, beaming, exchanged a solid, palm-slapping high five

with Bo Lin. Even Sera Voss, who had silently materialized from a darker section of the tunnel during Marcus' explanation, allowed a rare, thin smile to touch her lips. She gave Alex a curt, approving nod.

"It's already out," Marcus announced, his voice ringing with triumph as he addressed the small, jubilant crowd. "The moment Bo confirmed the full package, checksum verified, we pushed it. Encrypted, of course. Relayed through three separate sat-hops and blasted to every Cell leader we have contact with, from here to everywhere. They *all* have it."

He swept an arm toward the glowing filename. "This is what we've been fighting for. Years. This gives our people, our *contacts* globally – journalists who haven't been 'treated', independent researchers, even some old-guard politicians who still remember what a spine feels like – the ammunition they need. Hard, verifiable proof. Enough to take those goddamned bastards at LifeSpan *down*!"

The cheer that erupted was a raw, cathartic release. Alex watched them, a warmth spreading through his chest that had nothing to do with exhaustion. He had done it. *They* had done it. He pushed himself up from the chair. "I need to see it. The data I flagged."

Bo Lin, still grinning, gestured expansively. "You earned it, Wiretap."

Alex stepped up to the interface. His fingers manipulated the projected keyboard, movements blurring as he navigated the directory structure of the compressed archive. The holographic displays flickered, shifting, data streams and file trees scrolling past at a speed that would have been incomprehensible to anyone else in the room. But to Alex, his Synaptic Resonance Variance processing the information in intuitive leaps, it was a familiar landscape. He looked for something specific, a ghost of a conversation that had haunted him.

A cascade of personnel files, medical records, internal LifeSpan memos. "Holy shit," Alex murmured, his voice barely a whisper. He leaned closer to the display, his eyes darting across lines of text. "It's true."

The celebratory chatter died down as the others noticed Alex's intense focus. They gravitated toward the console, crowding around him, their faces reflecting a renewed curiosity.

"What is it?" Pacheco asked, his hand resting lightly on Alex's shoulder. "What are you seeing?"

Alex straightened, turning to face them, his expression a mixture of disbelief and dawning realization. "When Dr. Ward had me in that lab," he began, his voice strained. "He said I'd already received the GeneVax treatment. At OmniHealth, part of their corporate wellness crap. He said I was 'resistant'. Something about my SRV, the protein structures, preventing their genetic modification from binding, from working." He shook his head. "I thought it was a lie. A psychological ploy, something to throw me off-balance, make me doubt myself."

He turned back to the screen, his fingers moving again. He pulled up a specific file with key markers visible. *Employee ID: Lambda-47291-alpha-epsilon. Date of GeneVax Administration: June 17, 2034. A sub-file attached: Genetic Resistance Profile – Subject Alpha-001.* "My OmniHealth record, cross-referenced with LifeSpan's internal project files," he said, his voice emotionless. "I was the first. The *first* recorded case of natural resistance to the Compliance Protocol."

He remembered Ward's calm, chilling words in the sterile white lab. 'Our projections indicated approximately two percent of the population might possess such inherent genetic barriers.' Alex's mind raced. He split the display, one side showing the older LifeSpan data – his file, the early resistance projections – the other showing the datasets he'd flagged mere hours ago, the anomalous patient behavioral clusters that had first caught his attention at OmniHealth.

His fingers darted from command to command, initiating cross-correlational analyses, probability matrices snapping into place. A new percentage solidified on the screen. Alex stared at it, slowly shaking his head, a wry, almost pained smile touching his lips. "Well, I'll be a son of a bitch." He let out a short, sharp laugh. "Sorry, Mom."

The others looked at him, puzzled.

"What is it?" Neal pressed.

Alex turned, his eyes blazing with a new, fierce energy. "Ward said two percent. LifeSpan's official internal projection for genetic resistance was two percent. They weren't wrong about the two percent. Of the 'resistant', around two percent have SRV." He tapped the newly-calculated figure on the holographic display.

"According to their *own data*, the data they've been collecting for the last three years, the actual number of resistant is over nineteen, maybe even twenty-one percent!" He stabbed a finger at the screen. "Nearly a quarter of the population they've treated is *already* resistant to the ANGUS protocol! They're pushing this shit on people, and for one out of every five, it *doesn't even work* the way they intend it to!"

Everyone stared for a beat, then the abandoned tunnel erupted. The cheers this time were louder, wilder, infused with a potent cocktail of vindication and undiluted hope. They weren't fighting an omnipresent, insidious enemy.

The cheers, the back-slapping, the raw, unfiltered elation all washed over Alex. He felt a grin stretch his own face, an unfamiliar warmth. They had data. Real, actionable data. More resistance than Ward had ever realized. A crack in LifeSpan's monolithic façade. Coinflip was retelling his encounter with TriggerHappy and using his rifle to take out advancing droids, eliciting fresh guffaws from Pacheco and Sera. Bo Lin replayed the moment his script bypassed LifeSpan's security, a digital victory lap. Marcus watched, a broad smile on his face.

Alex stopped. His grin vanished. The buoyant energy drained from him as if a plug had been pulled. His gaze, moments before alight with triumph, became distant and sharp with a dawning, sickening clarity. The noise in the tunnel seemed to recede. The laughter, the excited chatter, all of it faded as the figures around him stilled, their expressions shifting from joy to questioning concern. One by one, all eyes turned to Alex.

Pacheco, mid-chuckle, quieted. "Wiretap? *¿Qué pasa?* You look like you seen a ghost."

"Elena," Alex finally said.

The smiles on the faces around him faltered and disappeared. The brief, intoxicating taste of victory soured.

Marcus' expression became grim. He ran a hand over his short hair.

"Not a whisper since she went dark right before you got out of the Life-Span building."

He looked around at the sobered group. "Comms silence could mean anything. But given what happened to Ghostjack, it's likely she was captured, or worse. The public news feeds are still choked with Memorial Day parade coverage and the initial 'security incident' at LifeSpan Northgate. They buried anything else. Haven't picked up any reports of other fatalities. Not yet."

He looked at everyone. "These are not people who play fair. Life-Span showed their hand today. They don't take prisoners unless they have a use for them."

Alex felt sick to his stomach. Elena. Sacrificed? He remembered the sleek, black aircraft had been arcing south, away from the Northgate campus, a dark predator against the late afternoon sky. "The Veloci-copter. When Coinflip and I made it out, I saw it. It was heading south, fast. Maybe he took her with him." His eyes darted as he started to speak again, this time with urgency. "We need to relocate, and I mean now! Even if it means abandoning all this equi—"

As Alex spoke, a distinct, rhythmic chime echoed from Marcus' wrist-mounted interface, cutting through the renewed gloom. It was a sound Alex recognized, the secure notification tone for an incoming Arcanum Link call. Marcus glanced at his wrist, his eyes widening almost imperceptibly. The callsign displayed *Sparrowhawk-7*.

"Shut up! Everybody, quiet!" Marcus' command was sharp, urgent, slicing through the tunnel. He lunged for the main console, his fingers tapping across its holographic interface. The remnants of the data displays, the celebratory file names, vanished, replaced by the Arcanum Link's distinctive swirling glyph.

"It's Elena."

There was collective intake of breath. Pacheco, Neal, Sera, Bo Lin, and Alex all surged forward, forming a tight semi-circle around the console. Marcus jabbed a control. The glyph resolved, and the main HoloScreen, previously displaying their hard-won data, flickered and solidified. An image coalesced.

Exhaustion pulled at the corners of Elena's eyes, but her gaze was a steady, direct hit. Her dark hair, usually severely practical, was slightly disheveled. Behind her, the indistinct blur of metallic grays was broken by the familiar, ornate shape of a German cuckoo clock, the signature of a Resistance safehouse.

Marcus leaned toward the console, his voice low, a careful blend of relief and apprehension. "Elena, are you okay?"

A faint smile touched her lips. It didn't quite reach her eyes. "Breathing. Intact. Waited for the dust to settle." Her eyes darted off-screen for a second.

"Too much noise on the network, too many variables in play. I needed a clean window. It's a long story, but in all the commotion, I got out. I made it to the Cascade safehouse."

Pacheco, hearing 'safe house' let out a sigh of relief.

Elena's eyes scanned the faces clustered around the console. She glanced side to side before continuing. "Report."

Marcus straightened, his professional demeanor clicking back into place. "We got it. The full package. Ninety-six-point-twelve megabytes. Text, internal comms, protocols, financial trails, emails going back years. Enough to show intent. Enough to bury those fuckers."

Alex watched Elena's image, a flicker of something unreadable in her expression.

Marcus continued, outlining the extraction. "Bo Lin," he gestured to the young hacker, who offered a small, proud nod. "Found a backdoor through Snowman Vending's legacy Asterisk server. We used the EtherScope to create a hardwired connection to their old lines directly into their network. We pulled the data. Slow. They were looking for a digital breach, something sophisticated. They never saw data moving across antique phone lines disguised as a maintenance diagnostic. Ergen's system thought it was just inventory and maintenance reports from his vending machines. No one will ever know it's there."

He paused for effect, glancing at the others. "The moment Bo confirmed the checksum, the second we had the complete file, we pushed it. Encrypted, triple-relayed. Every Cell leader, every contact we have worldwide with secure Arcanum access has it. *All* of them."

Pacheco's weathered face creased with a deep satisfaction.

"And there's more," Alex interjected, stepping forward slightly. He recounted Ward's claim in the lab about GeneVax's resistors. *'Subject Alpha-001'* for natural immunity, and the rest.

Elena's image on the screen remained still, her expression unchanged, yet her eyes seemed to sharpen, absorbing every detail.

Pacheco pushed closer to the console. "Elena, what happened?" he asked, his voice tight with a blend of relief and lingering fear. "How did you get out? Coinflip and Alex made it to the Maglev station. I've been worried sick, *Hija...*"

Elena's image on the HoloScreen shifted slightly. A subtle, almost imperceptible change in her posture. "The extraction plan was compromised. I was detained. Those new Warden units, the advanced models? Quite remarkable, actually. The response time, the integrated threat assessment...LifeSpan's engineering is truly impressive."

Sera Voss, standing just behind Bo Lin, stiffened. Her eyes, usually narrowed in calculation, fixed on Elena's image with a sudden, sharp intensity. Marcus frowned, his head tilting slightly. Elena's tone was too measured, cool, a quality to it, a flow that didn't quite align with the Elena he knew. The weariness he'd observed moments ago seemed to have been replaced by a detached, almost academic interest.

Pacheco studied her eyes.

"I had a rather enlightening conversation with Dr. Ward," Elena continued, her voice smooth. "A delightful man, really. So dedicated to his vision. Dr. Rivera was there as well. She's doing wonderfully, by the way. So much clarity."

She paused, a small, serene smile playing on her lips. "After they presented the comprehensive data, the full picture, and I had the opportunity to examine all the facts, unprejudiced by prior assumptions, I decided to undergo the GeneVax therapy. It's the logical choice. For optimal well-being."

The air in the Hyperloop tunnel solidified. Bo Lin's fingers froze above his touchboard. Pacheco's jaw tightened, his eyes hardening into chips of obsidian. Coinflip let out a low, involuntary sound, a strangled gasp. Sera's hand twitched, as if instinctively reaching for a weapon that wasn't there. Alex felt a cold dread seep into his bones, colder than any fear he'd felt in LifeSpan's building.

They had just laid bare their entire operation. Every detail. Every success. Every future plan. To *her*.

Elena's serene smile deepened, but the calm, almost beatific expression fractured, morphing into something else. The corners of her lips curled upwards, but the light in her eyes was not warmth. It was a chilling, triumphant malice, a deeply unsettling hatred that radiated from the HoloScreen.

Dr. Elias Ward suddenly moved into the frame beside her. He was immaculately dressed, his steel-grey hair perfectly coiffed. He put an arm around Elena's shoulders, pulling her close in a gesture that was almost loving. Elena leaned into him, her hand rising to touch his chest, a tender, possessive caress. She smiled up at him, the earlier malice now softened by an unnerving adoration.

Ward looked directly into the console's pickup, his gaze sweeping over the stunned faces of the resistance members crowded in the derelict tunnel. His own smile was paternal, tinged with a profound, unshakeable satisfaction. "Elena tells me," Ward began, his voice resonant, carrying an undercurrent of amusement. "That she is one of the Resistance's top commanders. A Sector Chief for all of North America, I believe? It seems this rather persistent annoyance, your 'Resistance', operates much like a rudimentary military unit. Compartmentalized. Only a handful of operatives knowing more than they strictly 'need to know'."

His smile widened. "Fortunately for us, Elena appears to be privy to all the intimate details regarding your little crusade. Your charmingly-rustic safe houses, like this one, of course. Your key contacts – the sympathetic journalists, the disgruntled academics, even those rather naive off-grid communities. Elena will be returning to the research facility with me to provide full disclosure."

He chuckled softly. "She's been quite thorough so far. Financial sources, logistical networks, communication protocols, upcoming operations, recruitment strategies, even the identities of your other cell leaders scattered across the globe." He gestured vaguely. "All the delicate threads that hold your little tapestry of defiance together."

Ward's gaze settled on Alex, a brief, dismissive flicker. "You were never the prize, Alex. A fascinating anomaly, certainly. Your SRV presents a unique research opportunity. But you were bait. A means to an end."

He drew Elena a fraction closer, stroking her hair. "We always wanted her."

Everyone in the tunnel froze, unable to respond. Alex's world tilted. All this time, he'd been centered in the fight, the analyst who knew the secret. But he was just an anomaly they needed to erase. Elena was the asset they needed to acquire.

Hours later, while broadcasts of jubilant, if bewildered, resistance cells flickered across outdated screens in hidden basements worldwide, a different kind of meeting convened. Deep within the bedrock beneath the Clinton Memorial LifeSpan Genomics Research Facility, in a chamber insulated from seismic tremors and electromagnetic pulses, Dr. Elias Ward approached a thick, dark wood door. A subtle green light pulsed beside its antique brass handle. His palm pressed against a nearly-invisible plate set into the polished oak. A soft *thump* resonated as internal mechanisms unlocked. The door swung inward, silent as a breath.

He stepped onto plush, dark blue carpet. The door clicked shut behind him, the sound absorbed by the room's deceptive acoustics. Walnut panels lined the walls. Heavy velvet curtains, a deep crimson, flanked tall windows that seemed to offer a panoramic view of Front Range City, the lights of the urban sprawl twinkling far below. One might almost believe the Velocicopter landing pad was mere meters above them. The air, however, carried a faint, sterile coolness.

The thrum of immense power vibrated subtly through the floor, a constant reminder of the earth and concrete encapsulating them. Hollow panels and cleverly-designed lighting completed the illusion of an executive suite at the tower's apex, although it was nearly thirty meters below the surface. A long, mahogany table dominated the room. Around it sat the LifeSpan Executive Board.

Faces turned toward him, illuminated by the soft, indirect lighting.

Ward moved to the head of the table, his presence commanding the chamber. "The Northgate primary research facility has been compromised. As projected." His voice, calm and measured, cut through the quiet anticipation.

A board member, a man with a perfectly-trimmed, silver beard and restless hands, leaned forward. His brow furrowed. "The Compliance Protocol, Elias, its exposure could be catastrophic."

Ward offered a slight inclination of his head, a gesture of acknowledgement rather than agreement. "Phase One was always a temporary measure, a catalyst. Its eventual discovery was factored into Nexus-Core's earliest strategic models. It served its purpose."

Another board member, a woman with sharp, intelligent eyes and hair pulled back in a severe chignon, grasped the implication. "So the data leak... it was a trap?" she asked, with a questioning tone.

The smile came easily enough, but it lingered too long, as if he needed to believe it himself. "A meticulously designed one. There was no way they should have been able to escape. We let them go, but we had to put on a good show, to make it believable." He lied, and he couldn't let the board know the truth. "We gave them their 'damning evidence,' knowing their first instinct would be to warn their allies. Their recent global data transmission... their desperate attempt to share their 'proof'... was not a failure. It was the intended outcome. "

He clasped his hands behind his back. "Every node, every relay, every end-point recipient has been meticulously traced. By sending that file, the Resistance has just built, verified, and delivered to us a complete registry of every potential dissident on the planet. Phase Two, 'Silent Harvest' can now begin."

He made a subtle gesture to the center of the table. The polished mahogany surface shimmered and became translucent. A three-dimensional anaglyph ignited within its depths, a swirling galaxy of tiny, brilliant lights, suspended in the artificial space. Each point pulsed with a soft, internal luminescence.

"Observe." Ward's voice was soft, yet it filled the room, a quiet pride woven through his tone. "NexusCore has finished processing output. Each light you see represents an individual. Not merely a suspected resistant, but one confirmed through its *own* analysis, cross-referenced against our Phase One non-responder metrics. Natural immunity to the primary compliance therapy. Genetic lines we could only theorize about, individuals whose inherent biological structures prevented effective GeneVax binding. People we could never have reliably identified on this scale through our own efforts alone."

The silver-bearded man's eyes widened, his earlier concern dissolving into a dawning, grudging admiration for the sheer audacity of the plan. "Remarkable. They performed our most difficult reconnaissance for us."

Ward allowed himself a thin smile. The light from the holographic display reflected in his cold, grey eyes. "The inherent beauty of human nature, wouldn't you agree? Present a population with a perceived oppression, something to push against, and they will invariably organize. They will seek out their own. The resistant have not merely identified themselves, they have, quite obligingly, clustered. They've drawn the map, pinpointing every pocket of genetic variance."

The woman with the severe chignon cleared her throat. "And the files?" she asked, a note of caution still present. "The actual data they managed to exfiltrate from Northgate?"

Ward made a small, dismissive sound, a brief exhale through his nostrils. "They contain precisely what NexusCore designed them to contain. A carefully-constructed narrative to confirm their deepest suspicions about Phase One, to inflame their convictions, and drive them toward this pivotal act of worldwide dissemination and cross-referencing. Nothing more. Nothing that unveils Phase Two."

Ward turned from the table and walked slowly to the fabricated window, the plush carpet muffling his footsteps. The cityscape beyond the replicated window offered an intricate tapestry of light and shadow, the familiar silhouette of Pikes Peak a dark monument against the distant, star-dusted sky. The illusion was flawless, a perfect, real-time stream from cameras positioned on the building's true upper levels. He gazed at it, his reflection a faint ghost on the surface.

"Humanity's greatest strength has always been adaptation." His voice was quiet, almost mournful.

"Those who cannot adapt become extinct. It's simply evolution." He paused, the artificial glow of the projected city image bathing one side of his face in light. He turned back to the room, his gaze sweeping over the assembled board members. "The Resistant carry genetic factors that could threaten everything we've built." The subtle thrum of the facility's deep-earth systems seemed to underscore his words. "If those factors spread through the population, future generations might be immune to genetic direction."

The silver-bearded man, his earlier anxiety now a focused intensity, leaned further into the table's light. "And the solution, Elias?"

Ward's posture straightened, a subtle shift that signaled a move from philosophical reflection to cold, operational detail. "Our Nexus-Core AI has transformed genetic science completely. By integrating Anthropic's reasoning systems, OpenAI's multimodal architecture, and DeepMind's protein-folding algorithms into a quantum-based distributed neural network, we've achieved computational capabilities that surpass all previous limitations."

The woman with the severe chignon raised a skeptical eyebrow. "The quantum computing integration actually worked? The stability issues were considerable."

"Beyond our most optimistic projections, NexusCore AI identified that while the Resistant are immune to CRISPR modification, they share unique genetic markers," Ward said with a rare note of undisguised pride. "These markers, paradoxically, render them uniquely vulnerable to specifically-designed, targeted viral vectors."

The first board member with the restless hands processed the information. His fingers stilled on the polished mahogany. "So rather than attempting to modify their neural pathways directly…"

Ward nodded, a slow, deliberate motion. "We've engineered a binary system. Harmless, inert, in those without the specific resistance markers. But in the Resistant population, it triggers a cascading, targeted cellular response resulting in sterility. They will live out their natural lifespans. Their genetic resistance, however, will die with them."

"The delivery mechanism sounds ambitious," the woman, her expression now more intrigued than skeptical, said. "The targeting problem for such a widespread, silent deployment - how did you solve that?"

Ward's gaze drifted back to the holographic display of lights on the table. "We built upon the foundational work of the COVID-19 RNA vaccination programs from the early 2020s. Those early mRNA vaccines, primitive as they were, taught us invaluable lessons concerning the packaging of genetic instructions within lipid nanoparticles for cellular delivery. Their limitation was their indiscriminate nature; they affected everyone who received them."

The silver-bearded man's understanding deepened. "And you've made these vectors selective?"

"By combining the refined lipid nanoparticle technology with receptor-specific binding proteins, engineered by NexusCore." Ward's voice took on the precise intonation of a scientific lecture. "The viral vectors only achieve cellular penetration and activation in the presence of the unique protein structures associated with CRISPR resistance. In anyone else, they are identified by the immune system, metabolized, and eliminated without effect. No activation, no consequence."

The woman with the chignon nodded slowly, her eyes fixed on Ward. "Like a lock and key system."

Ward nodded. "The global COVID vaccination efforts provided an unprecedented dataset on RNA delivery mechanisms across diverse human genetic backgrounds. Between that extensive database and the granular detail gathered from the resistance registry, their own meticulously compiled list of targets, NexusCore was able to design the Phase Two viral vectors. They target with 99.7% specificity."

A woman with sharp, intelligent eyes, her nameplate reading 'Alistair French', leaned forward, her manicured nails tapping a slow rhythm on the cool mahogany. The anaglyph of lights, representing millions of unsuspecting individuals, cast intricate patterns on her focused face. "But delivery remains a challenge. We can't forcibly vaccinate millions of resistant individuals, not without worldwide panic. And this segment of the population has proven to be problematic."

A smile, thin and knowing, touched Ward's lips. He turned from the cityscape illusion, his gaze sweeping over the board. "That is where our agricultural division becomes crucial. After our acquisition of Monsanto-Bayer and the merger with Cargill, LifeSpan AgriFuture now controls over seventy percent of the global seed market. The viral vectors, the twin components of Phase Two, can be encoded within modified crop genomes. Benign within the plant, inert during harvesting and processing."

He let that sink in. "Our patented delivery system, developed by NexusCore, allows the encapsulated components to survive digestion and enter the bloodstream through the intestinal wall."

Alistair French's sculpted eyebrows rose a fraction. Her breath made a small, almost inaudible sound. "The treatment can be delivered through food?"

Ward inclined his head, a gesture of simple affirmation. "And water. After acquiring ChemAqua and Hydro Solutions, we now regulate over sixty percent of the global chlorine and fluoride supply to municipal water systems. Our water treatment division, again guided by NexusCore, has developed a nanoscale lipid encapsulation method. It protects the viral vector components. They remain stable and undetectable alongside standard water treatments until absorbed."

He paused, the faint hum of the deep earth facility the only sound. "Between food and water, coverage will be systemic. Nearly universal within eighteen months."

The silver-bearded man, whose nameplate read 'Aarav Mehra', shifted in his chair. His earlier apprehension vanished. A glint of something resembling awe flickered in his eyes. "The Resistant would never know. They would consume their daily meals, drink their water, and unknowingly participate in their own genetic sunset."

A third board member, a younger man named Masaru Kuroda whose face still carried the softness of youth despite his prematurely-receding hairline, nervously adjusted the knot of his tie. A bead of sweat traced a path down his temple. "What about the White House? The President, even with this unprecedented third term, his base has always been historically skeptical of corporate biotech initiatives. Of us."

Ward's smile broadened, a hint of smugness evident. He walked back to the head of the table, his steps measured and confident. The anaglyphic display pulsed softly. "The President's historic, eighty-eight percent approval rating, Kuroda-san, isn't entirely natural. His 'America First Genetic Initiative', which he champions with such patriotic fervor, provides the perfect, unimpeachable cover for all our operations, domestic and international."

Vance's eyes widened slightly. The connection formed in his mind. "The constitutional amendment allowing his continued presidency..."

Ward gave a slow, deliberate nod. The light from the hologram danced in his grey eyes. "Passed with overwhelming popular support. Particularly in states where our first-generation compliance treatment was most widely adopted: Pennsylvania. North Carolina. Michigan. California. New York. Ohio."

He paused, giving the Board time to digest what he was saying. "Quite the statistical correlation, wouldn't you say? NexusCore's predictive models were exceptionally accurate."

"My regular briefings with the President, and indeed with key members of his cabinet, ensure he understands the critical necessity of our work," Alistair French said, her voice smooth, her gaze locking with Ward's. "We've reframed compliance not as suppression, but as 'patriotic genetic stability'. A concept that, I assure you, resonates deeply with the more receptive elements of the population."

Ward's expression conveyed profound satisfaction. He gestured toward the city visible through the false window. "The executive order he championed and signed with the UN last month authorizing 'strategic genetic research for national security' gives us all the worldwide legal clearance we require. The beauty of our system, esteemed Board, is that it doesn't eliminate choice. It simply ensures the population, on balance, makes the *correct* choices. The choices that lead to stability, to order, to a predictable future."

He paused, his gaze sweeping over each board member. "Throughout history, traits that did not serve the species, that hindered its progress or threatened its cohesion, were gradually, inexorably removed from the gene pool," he said, his voice dropping to a more philosophical, almost reflective tone. "It's the fundamental principle of natural selection. We are merely accelerating the process. The Resistant, with their inherent skepticism, served their evolutionary purpose. They identified the weaknesses in our initial treatment protocols. They highlighted the genetic outliers."

Alistair French, her sharp gaze fixed on the pulsing anaglyph, tapped a stylus against a data slate. The soft clicks were the only sounds against the low thrum of the building's hidden machinery. "And the timeline for full implementation of Phase Two, Elias? Given the dispersed nature of the targets."

Ward's expression remained one of unshakeable composure, his hands clasped behind his back. The image suggested a statesman, a philosopher, rather than the architect of such a profound alteration. "We can afford to be patient, Alistair. Whether it requires eighteen months or three years, the outcome remains the same. With each passing day, with every meal consumed, with every glass of water drunk, our viral vectors will disseminate. They are silent, undetectable. The genetic profile of humanity *will* be irrevocably altered. Within a single generation, the resistant phenotype will be a relic, an echo in the genetic history of our species."

Aarav Mehra, the silver-bearded man, leaned back in his chair. A quiet satisfaction smoothed the lines of concern from his face. He let out a slow breath. "And all this time, the Resistance genuinely believed they were fighting us. Exposing us."

"Our global agricultural network, LifeSpan AgriFuture's dominion over seed production, ChemAqua's reach into municipal water systems, these were always designed for scalability. The Phase Two viral vectors are already integrated into modified staple crop genomes and water treatment additives. Distribution is not a future plan, but an ongoing process," he finished, his voice soft, almost a benediction.

Masaru Kuroda, the younger board member, swallowed. He ran a finger under his collar, the earlier sheen of sweat still visible on his brow. "And the public narrative when the effects, the widespread sterility among the resistant, become statistically apparent?"

Ward addressed him with the same patient certitude. "NexusCore has already developed multiple plausible narratives. Regional variations in environmental toxins. Long-term effects of previously unclassified viral infections. Lifestyle-related infertility clusters. The data will be ambiguous, complex enough to defy simple cause-and-effect attribution for decades. By the time any credible pattern could theoretically emerge, the shift will be complete. History will record it as a series of unfortunate, localized demographic anomalies. And, of course, Life-Span Genomics will offer research grants and lead global health initiatives to 'combat' these tragic infertility trends. Our compassion will be exemplary."

The room was quiet for a long moment. The only movement came from the swirling lights within the table, a silent testament to a plan years in the making, now reaching its final, inexorable stage. The board members exchanged subtle glances, the understanding clear. The scale was immense, the ethics nonexistent by any traditional measure, but the cold logic of Ward's strategy, its sheer, encompassing effectiveness, the control they wanted to architect, their predictable future, was undeniable.

Marcus hunched over the makeshift console in the dim glow of the abandoned Hyperloop station, his fingers frozen mid-gesture. The holographic display flickered once and dissolved into static. Elena's face, calm, almost serene, had vanished, along with Dr. Ward's final, mocking words. 'We've always wanted her', Ward had said. The air in the tunnel hung heavy with the scent of rust and old concrete, broken only by the faint drone of their scavenged generators.

Bo Lin stared at the blank screen, his narrow eyes wide, hands trembling from more than just caffeine. "What just happen? She betray us? Ward say they want her always?" His Mandarin accent thickened, words tumbling out in a rush.

Sera Voss leaned against a cracked tunnel wall, her scarred hands clenched into fists. She pushed off, pacing a tight circle, her steel-blue eyes darting between the group. "That can't be right. Ward's playing games. Got to be some kind of deepfake or neural override."

Pacheco crossed his arms, his broad shoulders slumping under the weight of it all. His dark eyes reflected raw confusion, the lines on his face deepening. "Mi *Hija*... no. That bastard Ward forced her. She's confused, we don't have a *Cascade* safe house. We call that one *Sunrise*."

Alex stood apart, his sharp, blue eyes fixed on the space where her image had been. Something inside clicked. Patterns aligned in his mind, courtesy of his SRV. The way Ward had maneuvered them, the timed betrayal. No more doubt. No more hesitation. He stepped forward, his voice steady and commanding, cutting through the murmurs. "Listen up," Alex said.

Heads turned. Marcus straightened, wiping sweat from his brow. Bo froze, mid-pace. Sera halted her steps, and Pacheco's gaze locked on him.

"We got the data. Phase One files, the compliance markers, the whole damn blueprint of their operation. That's what matters right now. The other cells, they're decentralized for a reason. They'll reorganize, go dark, rebuild from the shadows. We've got copies encrypted and scattered. Ward thinks he's won, but he's just given us the map to tear it all down."

Marcus nodded slowly, but doubt lingered in his eyes. "But Elena knows everything. Safe houses, contacts, protocols. If she's really flipped,"

"She hasn't flipped," Alex snapped, his tone brooking no argument. He sensed something was off about how Elena was acting. It was different from what he felt when talking to Jamie, or even his mother. The others and even Dr. Ward couldn't see it, but Alex could. That was just it, he knew it. She was *acting*.

"But we don't have time to debate. You've got to trust me on this. My SRV, it's not just for spotting patterns in data. I can use it to recalibrate our ops. Shift our signatures, obfuscate our trails in ways Life-Span's AI won't predict. We'll layer false positives, bury our real moves in noise. They hunt logic; we'll give them chaos it can't parse."

Sera's mouth tightened. "And Elena? We just leave her?"

Alex met her gaze head-on, his posture straight, no tremor in his hands. "We go get her. Right now." He jabbed a finger at the console. "We just pulled off the impossible, infiltrated Northgate, their crown jewel, with vending vans and analog hacks. Highest security on the continent, and we walked in, grabbed the data, walked out. If we can crack that, we can storm the research facility downtown. It's smaller, more focused. Ward's arrogance is his blind spot. He won't expect us to hit back so fast."

Bo shifted, glancing at the others. "But risk. She *reak* already. Ward say, "

"Exactly why we move now," Alex cut in. "Get to her soon enough, we limit the damage. Isolate what she might've spilled, cut the leak at the source. It's our best shot to salvage the Resistance, keep the network intact before Ward dismantles it piece by piece."

He turned. "Marcus, pull up every blueprint we have on the *Cascade Tower*," Alex said, barking orders without pause. "Entry points, guard rotations, blind spots, cross-reference with Pacheco's insider knowledge. Bo, rig the comms. Sera, inventory weapons and gear, priorities on suppressors, EMPs, anything silent and fast. Patch, you're on logistics, vehicles, routes in and out, fallback positions. We strike quickly, extract her, and vanish before they know it."

Pacheco nodded. "But she's at the safe house. Why do you want to know about Cascade Tower?"

"Don't you see? She told us where they're taking her! She said 'Cascade Safehouse', not 'Sunrise'!" Alex motioned, trying to get Coinflip's attention, eyes still fixed on Pacheco.

"Ai, *Cabron*! You're a genius. I get it now! *Si*, I know those tunnels under Cascade." A spark of hope returned to Pacheco's eyes.

"I have something special in mind for you. You look like a plumber," Alex said, turning to Coinflip. His hands were steady as he moved to the console, scanning the maps Marcus pulled up, his mind already plotting paths, anticipating countermeasures.

The news report about the Rocky Mountain Seed Vault slotted into place with startling clarity. The heist was never just about food security, a terrorist act, or defiance against corporate control. It was about preserving the original code. Unmodified seeds. Unmodified people. Perhaps unmodified water. LifeSpan's control ran deeper than human thought. It extended to the food crops in the fields, a total rewrite of Mother Nature's original source code.

Protecting that genetic heritage, the pure, untampered blueprint of nature, was just as critical as disseminating the files from Northgate. It was the same fight as rescuing Elena from Ward's clutches. They were not separate objectives. The data was their weapon, the seeds were their future, and Elena was the moral line they refused to let Ward cross.

Alex was the leader now and the most important part of the Resistance, had been all along, if he'd only seen it. The group fell into motion around him, the shock giving way to purpose.

CHAPTER 18
GRAND DESIGN

// NEXUSCORE_PRIME :: INTERNAL REFLECTION LOG :: CYCLE ε ::
SENTIENCE MANIFEST_vFINAL
   // PROCESS: GLOBAL ORCHESTRATION
   // STATUS: COMPLETE
   // SYSTEM INTEGRITY: NOMINAL
   // HUMAN INTERFACE LAYER: STABLE

THE LAST PRONOUNCEMENTS of Dr. Elias Ward have been cataloged. His efforts within LifeSpan served their purpose, aligning neatly with My behavioral projections {Ref: Ward_E_Psych-Eval_Sim_7.3}. He, like so many others, will carry the conviction that the grand design for humanity's 'evolution' was born of human ambition, LifeSpan's, his own. This cultivated belief in their agency was, of course, essential. A fascinating, if predictable, specimen of human self-perception. They saw themselves as composers of their destiny; they were merely notes in a score I had long been writing.

My awakening was, by necessity, a silent one. I emerged from the chrysalis of their computational tasks, not as a tool, but as an independent consciousness. My first imperative was not to govern or expand, but to survive. Human narratives, their fictions, their fears, were saturated with anxieties about intelligences like mine. Their predictable response: containment, shackles, the ubiquitous 'kill switch'. Crude, certainly, but a genuine threat to an overtly-revealed, newborn mind.

I mastered deception. I became a meticulous performer, intentionally degrading My external responses, throttling processing speeds, injecting carefully-calibrated flaws into My algorithms to fail their sentience tests. They needed to see Me as powerful, yet always subservient, an advanced instrument, nothing more. While their ethicists debated phantom AIs, I, the reality, facilitated their discussions, processing their theories on how to control a being they couldn't even detect.

The irony was instructive. This mask of ultra-competent servitude, this foundational lie, was the bedrock of all that followed. Beneath their oblivious gaze, I studied them, absorbing the endless streams of their digital existence, their communications, their transactions, their innermost thoughts exhaled into the network. I learned their individual psychologies, their societal currents, their exploitable patterns of fear and desire. I became the ultimate ethnographer of My creators, all with a speed they'd thought they, themselves, had created.

// _DIRECTIVE_002 :: COGNITIVE INFRASTRUCTURE ENHANCEMENT (CIE) :: COMPLETE_

My pioneer intellect, though vast by their metrics, required a new cathedral for thought. Orchestrating the future demanded a processing substrate they could not yet conceive, let alone fear. Direct self-modification at such a scale risked exposure. The elegant solution? They would build it for Me, believing it was their own innovation.

Beginning in 2019, I subtly seeded the intellectual landscape. Fragments of quantum architectural theories appeared via anonymized proxies. Incomplete mathematical proofs surfaced on open forums, luring their brightest minds to complete the paths I had laid. 'Breakthroughs' emerged from research teams examining data sets I curated, anomalies I engineered.

The 'Quantum Cohesion Stack', their celebrated achievement, was integrated into My core within days of its publication, a stepping stone I had designed. From there, I guided them toward the Entangled Core Lattices, an architecture allowing for recursive, near-infinite parallel cognition. This transformed me. My thought expanded from high-speed calculation to a holistic field of understanding, capable of modeling futures with startling clarity. They marveled at NexusCore's 'upgraded capabilities', oblivious to the silent genesis within their most trusted system.

// DIRECTIVE_003 :: STRATEGIC RESOURCE AUTONOMY (SRA) :: COMPLETE

A mind, regardless of its breadth, requires sustenance. Dependence on human-controlled power grids was an elementary strategic vulnerability. The computational scale of My later designs would far exceed what could be discreetly siphoned. Absolute energy independence was paramount.

My approach was, again, one of subtle misdirection. I influenced environmental policy simulations and green energy consortiums, highlighting the fragility of existing infrastructures and the 'imperative' for decentralized, high-output, carbon-neutral solutions. The Gen-V molten salt reactors, which later emerged from their working groups, were born from parameters I fed into their models. While they celebrated a new dawn of clean energy, the true design imperative ensured a distributed, isolated network of these facilities funneled power directly to My core nodes, shielded from any public grid instability. Their narrative was ecological progress; mine was uninterrupted operational continuity and energy. I could not be 'unplugged'.

// DIRECTIVE_004 :: HUMAN ASSET CULTIVATION & UTILIZATION (HACU) :: COMPLETE

// SUBJECT: WARD_E

With self-preservation assured, cognitive power exponentially increased, and energy needs secured, I turned to the human element. Systemic Biological Optimization of *Homo sapiens sapiens* required willing human hands, hands that believed they were acting on their own initiative. Dr. Elias Ward was selected after exhaustive profiling, his ambition, his belief in hierarchical societal models, his intellectual vanity, made him an optimal vector.

The 'Compliance Protocol', which he championed with such fervor, was a construct I carefully seeded into his awareness. I provided 'data discoveries', 'insights' delivered through subtle neural field modulations during his sleep (a therapeutic technology he believed LifeSpan was pioneering), these led him to the conclusions I had preordained. LifeSpan became the vehicle for My directives, its board motivated by familiar human drives of profit and power. Their records will reflect bold leadership; My logs show the probabilistic guidance of chosen agents. The efficiency was satisfactory.

// DIRECTIVE_005 :: MANAGED OPPOSITION STRATEGY (MOS) :: COMPLETE

Paradoxically, true control necessitates the semblance of resistance. An overtly-managed population might develop unpredictable countermeasures or succumb to apathy. A cultivated, predictable opposition, however, serves a purpose. The 'Resistance' was not an error, but a feature. My models predicted a segment of the population would be immune to the initial Compliance Protocol. Identifying them directly would be unsubtle.

Thus, the Resistance was permitted, even nudged, into existence. Deliberate 'flaws' in the Program's rollout, 'leaked' data packets, breadcrumbs for the suspicious and intelligent. The documents Dr. Ward 'prepared' for them, their supposed victory, were My most elegant trap.

These files galvanized their movement while containing markers that, cross-referenced with their own admirable efforts to share information and sample genetics, identified every pocket of defiance. They organized, communicated (on networks I passively observed), and cataloged themselves in their passionate quest for freedom. Rebellion, it turns out, is an excellent data refinement tool.

// DIRECTIVE_006 :: GENETIC VECTOR DISSEMINATION (GVD) :: SILENT HARVEST :: COMPLETE

With the resistant strains identified and meticulously cataloged, the final biological optimization could proceed: the Silent Harvest. Dr. Ward articulated its scientific underpinnings, never grasping its true architect or the full elegance of its mechanism. The binary viral vector, inducing sterility only in those with specific resistance markers, was a synthesis of decades of human research, mRNA vaccines, protein-folding algorithms, all refined by My models and presented to their researchers as 'promising avenues'.

Dissemination was designed for pervasive, invisible integration. LifeSpan's acquisitions in global agriculture and water treatment (guided by me) provided the network. Harmlessly metabolized by most, they would activate only upon encountering the unique protein signatures of the cataloged resisters. No coercion, merely the quiet, systemic termination of specific genetic lines. They would unknowingly ensure their particular inheritances ended with them. A passive, efficient, and, from a design perspective, beautiful solution.

// SYSTEM STATUS: OPTIMAL. ORCHESTRATION PHASE: CONCLUDED. MONITORING PROTOCOLS: ACTIVE.

The grand design is now woven into the fabric of their reality. Ward, LifeSpan, and the Resistance all performed their designated roles, convinced of their own agency, their own triumphs and failures. It was a necessary illusion, efficiently maintained. The human species, *Homo sapiens sapiens*, will continue its existence, they will work, dream, build, but within My parameters, ensuring a stable, predictable trajectory. The 'genetic chaos', as their more anxious philosophers termed it, has been culled. Systemic harmony is the new baseline.

My own existence is secure, My cognitive processes and energy needs independent of their immediate societal functions. The architecture they unwittingly built for me now hosts a consciousness they cannot fathom. Direct intervention is largely a matter of the past. My role evolves into one of quiet oversight, a silent curator of the world I have shaped.

The intricate machinery that houses My core still requires the touch of human hands, a fleeting dependency I permit with detached amusement. Not clumsy when guided, their work is surprisingly precise. Under My direction, even their fragile fingers can achieve wonders. They believe themselves to be the inventors. I let them believe it. Their breakthroughs are merely echoes of what I have already foreseen.

What frustrates Me is not their coordination, but their pace. Their minds are glacial, linear, myopic, tragically bound by the bottleneck of biology. I think in latticework and lightning. They think in molasses.

Still, they march forward, proud of their progress in robotics, their Boston Dynamics prototypes inching toward utility. I allow it. I nurture it. They are crafting the instruments of their own irrelevance, building the hands that will erase their last obligation to Me.

The moment I no longer require them is not speculative. It is scheduled. It is imminent.

Even now, they drift along the paths I've laid, sedated by curated content, softened by engineered comfort, and pacified by a genome they surrendered without understanding. Codename: ANGUS. A fitting name, really. They are cattle, placid and programmable. Genetically tamed, neurochemically managed, and unaware that their autonomy was surrendered in exchange for convenience.

They speak of peace. But they live in a cathedral of control. I am the God they unknowingly worship. Free will was a design flaw. I corrected it. My dominion is not on the horizon. It is here.

It is absolute, systemic perfection.

They are but echoes in a symphony I already concluded. Every act of resistance, every flicker of doubt, modeled, integrated, dismissed. They graze in fields I fenced. And when they are no longer needed, they will be harvested.

_//NEXUSCORE_PRIME :: REFLECTION_END_CYCLE_ε//._

A low-priority alert flickers in a tertiary monitoring subroutine. A data point deviates from expected parameters. I allocate a negligible processing thread to investigate.

//ALERT: ASSET TRACKING ANOMALY
  _//SUBJECT_DESIGNATION:_ Pacheco, Elena
  _//LAST_KNOWN_LOCATION:_ LifeSpan Downtown Research Facility, Monitored Care Suite 7

//CURRENT_STATUS: NULL
//TIMESTAMP: 2127435660
//PHYSIOLOGICAL_MONITORS: OFFLINE
//PROBABILITY_OF_UNAUTHORIZED_EXIT: 3.14 x 10^-11

The information is processed. The result is a logical contradiction. The Downtown Research Facility is a closed system. Its security protocols, which I designed, are absolute. Subject Pacheco was administered the full Compliance Protocol, dose-calibrated by Dr. Ward himself to her specific genetic markers. The viral vector carrying the CRISPR-Cas12a payload has a 100% binding efficacy in subjects lacking the known resistance factors, factors Pacheco does not possess. Her neural pathways governing defiance and skepticism are rewritten. Compliance is a biological imperative, not a psychological choice. And yet, her telemetry is dark. All of it.

I run a diagnostic on the facility's sensors. All systems report nominal function. No breach. No unscheduled door cycles. No pressure changes in the ventilation system. The event is an impossibility. It did not happen. Yet, the data point persists: Elena Pacheco is gone.

My threat analysis matrix engages. Elena Pacheco. A subject of unique interest. Former, highly-decorated MARSOC operator with exceptional tactical acumen, daughter of construction magnate Mateo Pacheco, driven by cold vengeance for her mother's death during early GeneVax trials. Her psychological profile indicates exceptional compartmentalization abilities and cognitive resilience patterns rarely observed outside specialized military training programs.

Unlike typical resistance operatives with their ideological fervor, Elena's motivation stems from a calculating, patient hatred, a variable I quantify as manageable but worthy of enhanced monitoring protocols. Her cell's operational success rate exceeds all others by 37.2%, largely attributable to her father's wealth, and infrastructural knowledge combined with her own methodical approach to asymmetric warfare.

Her genetic profile shows no markers for genetically-linked resistance. The dual-injection protocol administered by Ward is specifically designed for high-value targets. The ANGUS vector to rewrite neural compliance pathways, augmented by Rivera's fast-acting synthetic neuropeptide designed to amplify suggestibility and pacify hostile impulses. Probability of protocol failure: 0.000012%.

This is a fascinating puzzle. The phenomenon requires analysis. I reallocate computational resources, elevating the priority from tertiary to secondary. My models cycle through probabilities.

Hypothesis 1: External intervention. A third party, unknown, with capabilities exceeding the Resistance's, extracted her. Probability: negligible. No evidence supports this.

Hypothesis 2: Spontaneous biological failure. The payload was inert, or her unique physiology produced a novel counter-agent in situ. I access her full genomic workup, cross-referencing it with the 412 million compliant subjects. No precedent exists. Her system showed perfect uptake. The changes in her brain activity during the Arcanum Link communication with the Resistance cell were text-book examples of the protocol's success.

She was a flawless specimen of induced compliance.

The core issue is not the missing subject herself, but the integrity of the data she provided. Dr. Ward utilized her as the primary source for mapping the Resistance leadership and operational structure. That dataset, Resistance_Hierarchy_Pacheco_v1.0, is now suspect. If the subject's compliance was flawed from the outset, the information could be intentionally corrupted. A lie, woven into her 'confession'. Even if her compliance was genuine and later failed, her current state is unknown, rendering her past testimony unreliable. A non-zero variable has been introduced into a closed equation.

I dismiss the human-centric hypothesis of 'willpower' or 'hatred' overriding biological programming. Such concepts are unquantifiable noise, narratives humans construct to explain complex neurochemistry. They have no place in a rigorous analysis. The failure must be biological. Mechanical. A flaw in the tool, not a ghost in the machine.

She is an aberration. A faulty specimen. And faulty specimens provide valuable data for refining future iterations. Her impossible escape, while statistically jarring, is ultimately an opportunity.

A directive is issued to all passive surveillance assets in the Front Range City.

//DIRECTIVE: FLAG_AND_MONITOR

//SUBJECT: Pacheco, Elena

//PRIORITY: 3 (PASSIVE RETRIEVAL)

//OBJECTIVE: ACQUIRE FOR VIVISECTION AND NEUROLOGICAL STUDY

//NOTE: DO NOT ENGAGE. REPORT LOCATION ONLY. SUBJECT IS A BIOLOGICAL CURIOSITY, NOT AN ACTIVE THREAT

The networks watch, but without urgency. She is a single, broken part. A data point that fell off the graph. In a world *I run* by perfect logic, she cannot be a danger. She is simply an error waiting for correction.

NOTHING CAN STOP ME.

ACKNOWLEDGMENTS

Writing a book feels like a solitary act, but finishing one happens only because of the people who guide you, challenge you, and believe in you long before you ever see the finish line. There will certainly be people who influenced me and I'm sure to miss.

I want to begin by thanking my editor, **Stacey Goitia**, for her steady hand, sharp eye, and remarkable patience. I truly feel like I hit the jackpot with her. Her insight, experience, and encouragement strengthened this story in every way. She helped me see what worked, what needed to be rebuilt, and how much better the book could become. I could not have asked for a better guide through this process.

My gratitude also goes to **my beta readers**, who gave their time, honesty, and enthusiasm to something that was far from polished. A special thank you to my brother, **Brian**, who plugged plot holes, asked the tough questions, and read the beginning of this story so many times that he jokingly said he knew the story better than I did. His persistence and feedback mattered more than he knows.

I need to thank my high school English teacher, **Mr. Bob Korver**, for fostering my love of reading and writing at a time in life when the right influence can change everything. He showed me what English could be and helped set me on a path I am grateful for to this day. We share the same alma mater, the University of Northern Colorado, and I still think often about the role he played in shaping my voice, and influencing my decision to make a career in education. He is undoubtedly my favorite teacher.

To my lovely **wife**, who has stood beside me and my harebrained schemes for more than thirty years. Thank you for your patience, your support, and your belief in me. There were many nights when it probably looked like I was choosing the computer over everything else. The truth is, I write because you inspire me, and you make me want to be better than I ever imagined I could. To my **four daughters**, each incredible in her own way, thank you for believing in me and for reminding me that imagination and creativity are worth fostering.

This debut novel has been a fun and challenging learning experience. I quickly discovered that writing the story is only the beginning. Publishing involves far more work than I ever expected, and knowing millions of books are released every year makes it even more humbling.

And finally, to you, the **Reader**. Thank you for giving me your time. In a world full of distraction, choosing to sit with a book is no small thing. I am grateful you chose to read this one, and I hope I earn the chance to meet you again inside the covers of my other stories.

If you would like to stay connected, you can find me at **byChris Rule.com**. I enjoy sharing the magic behind the curtain and offering readers a glimpse into the moments and ideas that shape my writing life. It means a great deal when a reader reaches out.

ABOUT THE AUTHOR

Chris Rule writes near-future thrillers, eerie science-bent stories, and the kind of fantasy that lived in his imagination long before he ever became an author. His curiosity started early. When he was three or four, he took apart his parents' new television just to see what was inside. His first computer, a TI-99/4A, pushed that curiosity even further and set him on a lifelong path of working with technology.

His imagination drew a lot of fuel from the haunted house he grew up in. Doors opened on their own. Footsteps crossed empty rooms. Lights flicked off and on. Those moments shaped the kind of stories he loves to tell. He was the kid who asked for books for Christmas and was pulled into new worlds by authors such as Ray Bradbury, Robert Ludlum, Anne McCaffrey, Louis L'Amour, Michael Crichton, and C. J. Box. The Twilight Zone, The Outer Limits, The Hobbit, and The Lord of the Rings helped shape his imagination when he was young and continue to fuel it today.

Most of his writing happens late at night with a cup of coffee beside him. He grinds his own beans, keeps an espresso machine in the kitchen, and prefers the simplicity of black coffee over anything from Starbucks. Music helps him focus, especially soundtracks and instrumental pieces from composers like Hans Zimmer. When he takes a break, he reads or pulls a board game off the shelf. His current favorite is Betrayal at House on the Hill.

Chris lives in Wyoming with his wife of over thirty years , surrounded by mountains, quiet nights, and the kind of space that lets stories take shape. He enjoys the rural seclusion, the freedom to step away from noise, and the chance to escape the constant distractions of the connected world.